Lovesick in Beverly Hills

ATHENA

authorHOUSE

AuthorHouse™
1663 Liberty Drive
Bloomington, IN 47403
www.authorhouse.com
Phone: 1 (800) 839-8640

This is a work of fiction. The characters depicted in this novel exist entirely within the author's imagination. Any similarity to actual people and events is purely coincidental and is not intended.

© 2016 Athena. All rights reserved.

No part of this book may be reproduced, stored in a retrieval system, or transmitted by any means without the written permission of the author.

Published by AuthorHouse 03/08/2016

ISBN: 978-1-5049-6406-7 (sc)
ISBN: 978-1-5049-6317-6 (hc)
ISBN: 978-1-5049-6405-0 (e)

Library of Congress Control Number: 2015919532

Print information available on the last page.

Any people depicted in stock imagery provided by Thinkstock are models, and such images are being used for illustrative purposes only. Certain stock imagery © Thinkstock.

This book is printed on acid-free paper.

Because of the dynamic nature of the Internet, any web addresses or links contained in this book may have changed since publication and may no longer be valid. The views expressed in this work are solely those of the author and do not necessarily reflect the views of the publisher, and the publisher hereby disclaims any responsibility for them.

If hope has flown away

In a night, or in a day,

In a vision, or in none,

Is it therefore the less gone?

All that we see or seem

Is but a dream within a dream.

I stand amid the roar

Of a surf-tormented shore,

And I hold within my hand

Grains of the golden sand—

How few! yet how they creep

Through my fingers to the deep,

While I weep—while I weep!

—Edgar Allan Poe

Fly me to the moon

And let me play among the stars

Let me see what spring is like

On Jupiter and Mars . . . . .

—Bart Howard

This book is dedicated to the only man I ever loved.

Special thanks to David Ferrell for his guidance and encouragement with this project.

Contents

My Town 1
Homeland 24
A Taste of America 40
Millionaires, Mansions and Me 61
Rumbles from Vesuvius 84
Living on Lockdown 101
My Enchanting Attic Room 122
Eve of Battle 147
Great American Theatre 178
Mr. Wonderful..211
Lovesick in Paris 231
Another Suitor 251
Living Blissfully Together...270
Living It Up..289
A Woman Scorned 308
Breaking Up Is Hard To Do 321
Baby, It's Hollywood!..328

1

My Town

The water beyond the beach is so brilliantly turquoise that it hurts my eyes. The blinding light on the sea and the bleached white sand creates an overpowering beauty. Here on the beach in Cancun, I feel a complete sense of serenity, as if I am alone on a tropical island and nothing exists. There are people out—kids playing in the surf, couples sunbathing here and there—but they don't exist to me. They are invisible in this awesome place. I can't seem to move and feel frozen in my space. I don't want to be anywhere else. In a few hours, I'll have to think about checking out of my hotel and heading home, but for now I'm content to sit here in this huge cabana and reflect on my life again and my jewel of a town—Beverly Hills.

There always seems to be such chaos. It never ends, and yet, at this particular instant, I am completely at peace and in control. With the extra perspective that often comes from being away from home, I think about everything, my fleeting thoughts racing from the good to the bad, the difficult past to the uncertain future. I keep asking myself, where am I heading? When will life be what it is supposed to be? If I only knew what that was.

When will love conquer all? Or does it ever? The twenty-nine years that I have lived in Beverly Hills have certainly contained elements of fantasy. My spectacular little mansion above Sunset

Boulevard is two doors away from the former palace of tennis champion Pete Sampras. He listed and sold the Tudor-style estate for $20 million.

Elton John, Phil Collins, Jennifer Aniston, Courtney Cox, and Christina Aguilera also live in the neighborhood. All day long you should see all the tour busses; they go by constantly. Also I have another home—my weekend getaway—on the coast in Malibu, where I paint and take walks on a private beach, a perfect place to be when the sun is shining and the pressure of my feet on the sand feels really good.

I fly several times a year to Paris, and also regularly travel to New York and luxury resorts from Mexico to the Middle East. I have sipped the finest Grand Dame and Dom Perignon, worn Armani and Dior, and been courted by men whose wealth, if you added it up, would be enough to purchase a whole nation.

But I have suffered as much as I have enjoyed it. I have come to know the rough, sad side of me, and the city I live in, Beverly Hills, an insular little village—*my* village—filled with greed, pettiness, and cruelty. Like a Faberge egg, it's beautiful on the surface, but where is the heart? Where is the soul? I keep looking, but I'm not sure I'll ever find it. It's a dark place where most of the time no one cares about you or your pain, where your status is what counts. You're either in or you're out. If you want to be accepted by the people who matter, you'd better live in the right home, drive the right car, hang out at the right clubs and be seen with the right people. And where love is, well-sort of non-existent.

There are *right* places to live—the most famous, of course, being in the 90210 zip code. Where else does a zip code have its own television show? And there are not-so- right places to live. An address South of Olympic? Well, forget it. You're second-tier all the way. I have lived there and I know well what it does to you. Don't look for your name on A-list party invitations.

Drive a shiny new Cadillac? Move out of the way. That may signify success in Long Beach or Santa Monica, but it's almost *declasse* in my town. Roll into L'Orangerie and chances are you'll just sit there. The valet isn't going to bust his hump for any Caddie. He might get to you eventually, but he'll take that Maserati first, that Rolls Royce and so on. It's just the way it is.

I have a spare car, a Ford Expedition, that I use and enjoy most of the time for errands—quick trips to Malibu, or at four in the morning to the flower market in downtown Los Angeles. It's my four-in-the-morning car I call it. I have friends who won't ride in it. I've actually had them remind me, "Pishi, don't pick me up in the Expedition—pick me up in the Bentley."

There are unwritten rules. One of them is: Stay thin. Fat people are definitely out. If you're fat you can wait all night to be seated. Sometimes, you'll never get service. Same if you're basic and ugly. That's why this is the cosmetic surgery capital of the world—everybody knows how important it is to be one of the beautiful people. A lot of people here are absolutely miserable because they don't look like a supermodel or have bodies like you'd see on "Bay Watch." Also they look miserable after surgery.

I'm a transplanted Persian beauty queen who made my way into this world of shining stars by being me and looking as I am, since no knives will ever touch this body!

Right now square faces are in. The women are all going to particular surgeons and getting square faces. They all look alike—stupid square faces. They look like little monsters. I swear there have been times when I couldn't recognize one of my own friends after surgery. I study the eyes, I see tell-tale clues that, yes, this is the person I know, but she is completely different—and usually worse. Why do these women do it? Their lips are puffed up with silicone. They've got big, over-inflated breasts. You'd think they were call girls. The men fall for it, though. They spend fortunes on these women, showing them around town, the finest restaurants, clubs; they even marry these women, despite the disparaging term that many people apply to them—*"bimbettes du jour."*

Europeans, I think, are more real. Go to Europe and you're far more inclined to see wrinkles, normal breasts and gray hair. Men and women allow their bodies to change as they grow older, and yet they retain a certain elegance. They value what's inside a person and not how inflated and non biodegradable their chests are. They carry themselves with dignity and style. They dress to look good—*"tres chic"*—no matter what their age, as if quietly proud of the distinctive lines that the years bestow on them.

It's not like that here in my town. Face-lifts, boob jobs, hair transplants—it would be comical if it weren't so sad. Nearly every woman I know is having problems with her inflated breasts. They're bleeding somewhere inside or they're shifting inside the body. These women can hardly walk—they cannot jog, they cannot be held. Men cannot touch them.

The social ranks in Beverly Hills are very narrow and very "super" at the top. Super-rich, middle-aged men date supermodel women, trying to live a lifestyle that is one big super-fantasy. The men own corporations and vast real-estate holdings, and they set all the rules. They fool around, they cheat on their wives, who are often captives of their great wealth, have no choice but to put up with it.

Feelings don't seem to count, at least that is my experience. Love is phony or non-existent. The women want the man with money. He is the prize. That's why some of the richest men are the plastic surgeons; the wives and the secret girlfriends doll themselves up with big tits and trendy cheeks and sculpted noses to win their sugar daddies. It's much the same in the top echelons of European society; most of the older men like young babes, even though they can't get it up. They are still chasing youth.

I never felt like I needed to remodel my face, though I love remodeling houses. I'm a lucky outsider, from Iran by way of Pittstown, Pennsylvania, who in all my life has never even considered getting bigger breasts or Botox injections. But this is the reality I see, and the men seem to revel in it. It's an ego trip to be spotted in the super clubs and super bistros and with hot young super babes on their arms. They're brazen about it. They squire their girlfriends around in red Lamborghinis and yellow Ferraris. A lot of times, marriages do eventually break up—the smart women who haven't signed pre-nuptial agreements walk off with millions, and so do the lawyers—and they're another sub-set of the super-rich.

These men say good-bye to their wives and never look back. They've got their young women who look like Barbie. They've got their golf buddies and their social functions. Usually, after a break-up, most of the friends stay with the husband—he's rich, he's *somebody*—and the ex-wife, if she signed a piece of paper or not, comes away with something less than a fortune and she is a pariah. A man will then hang onto his hot young babe for a few years and ditch her for someone who's younger and more attractive.

Jewelry stores do very well, catering to the egos and demands of ever- shifting relationships. They traffic in $100,000 Rolexes and $1 million diamond necklaces. Life is quite glittery and shining in Beverly Hills. From shiny cars to shiny skin and from shiny houses to shiny glistening bodies, everyone sparkles in Beverly Hills.

I have girlfriends who refuse to go out on a date with a man if he doesn't have a lot of money. Sometimes I get so mad at them—they don't give a poor guy a chance, or even a not-so-poor guy. Most of the time, love is worthless in Beverly Hills. It's ugly and sad but these rich men have the ability to captivate beautiful women and get to set the rules and when they get tired, they ruthlessly dumped them, letting them fall into a tragic abyss of chaos and even poverty.

Looks, sex, money, power—they're everything here. It's not my own value system, which keeps me apart in some ways, but I understand it and I know how it sucks you in. It makes life harder here than it is most other places, despite all the money. It forces you to adapt. It forces you to make difficult choices. You have to play the game or you're shunted to the sidelines. I know how to play the game and when not to play the game. I'm a master at it, I have to be in order to survive, since I am not about tits and ass, nor do I look even remotely like Claudia Schiffer, although proud of what I have been blessed with.

The man I love, who's super-good looking and super grand himself, doesn't have to throw lavish gifts on me from Tiffany or Van Cleef & Arpels. That makes us a good match, because he is not that romantic, anyway. He has no time for mushy stuff. He is a rough, tough and rugged guy, a real man's man and hates materialism and can't stand to talk about money. We have our own ways of relating to each other, and our own ups and downs. Oh, my God, how glorious love is.

Our attraction to each other is far beyond physical. Yes, I'm a former finalist in the Miss Iran pageant, and yes, I'm smart enough to get by, but where I really shine is in having style. I've got great style, not to mention an attitude; when I walk in, I feel like I own the place. I think I am good and secure at just being who I am and knowing where I come from.

The fact that I have suffered over and over again, and yet made it, on my own, dozens of times, has given me the confidence to kick ass and be relentless. I can schmooze with anybody because nobody intimidates me or overly impresses me. I make people laugh and charm them with my intelligence. When I walk into my favorite places to dine with friends or clients, I'm well-read and able to converse on any subject. Love and special greetings pour out of the restaurant managers and *maitre d's*; they are invariably excited to see me, and in return I take care of all the hosts and hostesses with tips and holiday gifts. It is a part of an elegantly rite. They cheerfully escort me right to my own special table. And no, I am not a movie star! In their eyes, though, I am a super-something too. It's a kick. I love it. What's not to love? It's extraordinarily exciting—hugely expensive, but it's a high better than any drug.

On the other hand, if you can't fit in, if you decide to reject or simply can't live up to the lofty, arbitrary standards set by the "in" crowd, you're screwed. You might as well be living in Wichita—or, like me in years past, in Pittstown. What a nightmare. Nobody wants to see you. Nobody wants to do business with you. I have a friend whose husband was head of one of the biggest conglomerates in America. After he died, she was nothing—people dropped her like a hot potato. It's not a matter of personality, it's who you are and how much money you have. Lose your status, for whatever reasons, and you disappear into a black hole.

I know it sounds cynical, and maybe you'll think I'm bitter and hurt, but I have decided to pull the mask off this super-glitzy town and show it like it really is—because I've seen it from both sides, from up and down, from being in love and in with the "in" crowd, and from a much darker place.

Life has been tough and, yes, I did make my fortune by being smart and thinking without emotions. I want to tell you what it's like to be sucked into the game and try to hold onto yourself when you're in over your head.

To try to succeed in business in a cutthroat world where fortunes are at stake and you better know your stuff. To try to find your way, and be in love—to fall truly, deeply in love—in a town where love is not to be trusted, nor has any value whatsoever. Where it is viewed as only a tool for acquiring wealth and prestige. I've spent most of my years in Beverly Hills as a top real-estate broker. You do not have a clue what goes on here and what people do for money.

Over the years, I've bought and sold magnificent estates, properties costing upwards of $20 million. Once, I even held in my hand a check with eight zeroes, so many zeroes it made me dizzy: $100,000,000. One-hundred million dollars! Electricity goes through you when you're making offers involving those kinds of sums. The idea of me, a little Persian girl, sitting at a massive conference table, with two giants of the business and handling both ends of that kind of deal is absolutely mindboggling. To know you have such power makes you tingle with joy; and yet I've been stabbed in the back, screwed over, fired, and cheated out of millions of dollars over and over again. I've been set up and framed and worse—by clients, by friends, and finally by my husband, who should have done anything to look out for me, my former spouse, a man I was married to for twenty-eight years.

And then, worst of it all, by the most beautiful man in my life, my first and only love. How ruthless, callous and spiteful people can be is beyond me.

Here's one example: I had a client who was listing her place for $15 million. She said to me, "You haven't shown my house for two weeks— I'm not talking to you." She was throwing a big party—one of those extravagant events where being seen could mean a ton of business—and yet she told me to my face that I couldn't come and was no longer invited. Even though she told me that I was off the list, she admitted, I was a smart cookie and liked my enthusiasm. OK, so what!

When I say that Beverly Hills is a little village, it's amazingly small for such a famous place—only 35,000 people. Everybody knows everything about everybody, especially at the top. It's also a town that's surprisingly diverse. Almost forty percent of the people are Persian Jews, most of whom fled Iran before or during the downfall of the Shah. I came to the United States long before the revolution and helped twenty-seven other members of my family to get out. In those days it was quite easy to get a green card. After waiting three months and paying a $200 fee, I was a citizen, and consequently all the members of my family could get a green card.

My ex-husband, Dr. Boring, married me when I was eighteen years old. It was an arranged marriage—I had no choice. I had to marry him. He took me from Tehran to Philadelphia and eventually, in 1986, I bolted, packing up my two young daughters, $1000 in cash, my jewelry, and not much else, and came west. He had to follow me or lose me, so a whole year later he moved out, setting up a thriving medical practice.

Dr. Boring and I were married for twenty-eight years before it ended, in a "War of the Roses"-type implosion, though no one died, in May 19, 1999. He clung tightly to old-world customs and attitudes that grated like broken gears against the mores and ways of life we encountered in Beverly Hills.

I adapted from the day I first arrived in the United States in 1970; he never did. I just loved America, the land of freedom and opportunity. I loved meeting new people and later going to business school and talking over deals at the Polo Lounge. I loved slipping on an expensive gown and attending opening nights at the opera. I wore fabulous clothes and love the arts. In the real-estate business you have to look the part; I bought a white Conriche, with my own money too, and still Dr. Boring just about had a coronary. He said, "Move that car out of the driveway or you're not sleeping here tonight!" and he meant it; the next day, I had to take the car back, telling the debonair salesman, "My husband won't let me buy it." What a husband.

He couldn't stand it. He said I was shallow, never mind that the Rolls brought me a fortune in real-estate deals. He thought his wife should stay home, cook, and raise the children. When I wasn't working, we socialized with his friends, mostly all Persians. The families would get together all the time. Usually, the men would be in one room, the women in another. I hated that—it made me feel inferior. The guys would drink, smoke, and play backgammon. The women, never speaking any English, would discuss the most mundane things—recipes for cooking rice, how to remove spots from their sofas. I was bored out of my mind. I was outspoken and outrageous. I liked to dress up wild, to laugh and be entertaining and be treated as an equal. The women were uncomfortable with me. They resented me for the way I dressed and for constantly speaking English. Even if they spoke English, they preferred Farsi. They would say to me, in a mocking fashion, "Why do you speak English? Aren't you Persian?" I would try to be nice to them—I would always greet them by saying, "It's great to see you too! How is everything?"—but I could sense how they felt. They made it clear that I was different, that they didn't approve of my ways.

Even just walking into a party with other Persians I would create anxiety. All the men wanted to talk to me. I knew about issues, politics, the latest big-business deals and real-estate transactions, and of course the theatre. I was involved in numerous political and charitable organizations. They liked the way my mind was going all the time. They liked hearing about the market—what properties to buy, who was buying what, what they were paying. They hung on every word I said.

I had such a confidence about myself. I was a walking computer filled with information. I knew Wall Street and I had no time for bullshit. I could have cared less about the color of my sofa.

Athena

The attention I got made Dr. Boring terribly jealous and insecure. He would stand in the corner and glare. Those days he was making a huge income—$100,000 a month, an enormous amount of money even for a physician—but he couldn't handle that I was successful, too. He would always say, "I'm a doctor. You're not even very educated. What is it that *you* do to make all that money you have?" I would have to explain, "I love my job, and I am a great negotiator. I talk to people and help them and educate them to sell their homes." He didn't get it. He would say, "That's not it." He was always suspicious. "Why is it," he would demand, "that you walk into Morton's and they kiss your hand and hug you? Why are you hugging the *maitre d'*? I don't like it when you do that. Who do you think you are?" Everything was threatening. Everything was negative to him and most of all he always complained that he never had enough money. Everything I did was bad and not acceptable. He constantly criticized and judged me. This was not the way a wife should be, he would say. We fought, we fought, we fought, and finally the big explosion came. One day I walked into Director's National Bank in Beverly Hills and there was only $13,000 in my corporate account. Seeing this was a total shock. There had been nearly $1 million in that account—but it was $980,000 and some change short. He had forged my name and moved the money, hidden it in his own account without me knowing. Why? I still don't know.

I filed for divorce in May of 1997. The trial became an ordeal, a nightmare, and the talk of the town. It was a full three-ring circus with a bunch of lawyers and judges as ringmasters. The only thing missing was the lions. Oh! I forgot, I became the lion—I had to.

There were accusations that I loaded up $500,000 in cash from a bedroom armoire and smuggled it away in the dead of night in a duffel bag. True but not true. I had to transport the furniture to the courtroom in downtown Los Angeles and play out the charade in chambers. And that, I have forged his name on purpose to frame him! What? He had personally gone to bank and forged my signature. But why? Eighteen years after the divorce, I still don't know how anyone can be so cruel and dishonest.

The divorce trial was like being dunked in hot oil, whipped and tortured on a public stage, a thousand times every day, I said in an article that mentioned the proceedings on the front page of the Los Angeles Times. The suffering I endured was enough to make a woman throw herself off a tower and commit suicide. Ultimately, I proved my version of the facts and won in court, although the victory was not what it should have been. I won my house and my freedom and not much else. I got to start my life over, at age forty-five, having never lived alone, having never had a boyfriend, having never even been on a date. After twenty-eight years of being imprisoned in a marriage I had never wanted, I was free to go and live alone—my way—but without much financial support.

The alimony I got did not even cover the mortgage of the house that was awarded as my divorce settlement. Community property-my ass! But I had the freedom to pursue my own dreams in any way I wanted. That much was wonderful. It was the start of a very scary time.

What happens when the old rules are cast aside and suddenly anything goes? When you are raised in the rigid cultural traditions of an ultra-conservative Jewish family in Tehran, and then packed off to Catholic school where those ideals are zealously reinforced, and then suddenly set free of a stifling marriage in a town as fast, hard, uncaring and ruthless as Beverly Hills? Now I was entering a completely new phase of life in an entirely different environment. Boy did I find out what money does and how evil people can become.

Even the ones you always thought loved you, they can turn on you and change their minds in a heartbeat.

It was the beginning of a long, difficult rollercoaster ride—ups and down, many exciting and wonderful moments, and experiences that tore my heart out. I have never cried so many tears and for so long. I have never learned so many hard lessons. I have plunged into deep, hopeless pits of despair. I was about to be stripped of my innocence, sucked in directions I never intended to go. I could only hang on and endure it or I would fall hard. I am still hanging on, not sure where I am heading or how to get off the moving train.

Four months after I filed for divorce, my real-estate career ended up changing the course of my life. I met a man by chance who I had never met or known before in my life. He was quite handsome, and seemed very important in town. So were many other clients of mine. Nothing different. After speaking with him about selling his house, he agreed to meet with me in his office at 3 p.m. on the Thursday afternoon. I will call him Mr. Wonderful. I came in looking very professional but cute as hell, wearing a smart black Chanel suit and a pearl necklace. My hair was blonde and styled in a French twist, like a fashion model's.

Mr. Wonderful was tall and rugged-looking. He spoke with a confident, raspy voice, as he began going through my portfolio. He immediately liked my energy and professionalism. He said I was pretty amazing. "You sold all these houses? You should be working for me," he said. I smiled, and without a moment of hesitation, said,

Lovesick in Beverly Hills

"You couldn't afford me!" I still can't believe I had the nerve to say that. As usual, I was playing the big shot, secure in my knowledge and background in real-estate, not having a clue about the man sitting behind the 100-year-old desk and his financial state. Oh, was he impressed! He liked that I could take charge of the moment and recklessly insult him. He laughed. Not knowing who he was, I started to close my briefcase, preparing to leave. It was an interesting meeting, but a short one.

My policy is to keep a first visit with a client to no more than fifteen minutes. That is long enough to accomplish goals without wasting time. I left right then and immediately let him slip from my mind, not giving a second thought to what had taken place. Not knowing how that the chance meeting of that one particular afternoon was going to make and break me, over and over again.

A day later, my secretary told me that he was on the phone. Mr. Wonderful was calling to discuss the sale of his son's house. That led to a lunch meeting, and, eventually, to the discovery that his son was a drug addict. In the end, his son decided to list his property with someone else. After I relayed this news to Mr. Wonderful, he asked me for advice about his son, and I suggested that he need to talk to my good friend Jackie, a woman who had just lost her one and only daughter to a cocaine overdose.

Mr. Wonderful was amazed. He said, "We didn't give you the listing, and you're still trying to help? Why?"

I said, "Wouldn't you help me if the situation was reversed?"

Concerned about his son, he asked me to set up an appointment with Jackie. I agreed and set it up for a week later, on Thursday,

August 28, 1997, at 5 p.m., a date and time now etched in my memory. Then, he asked me where I lived. After I told him, he offered to meet her at my house on his way home, since he always used my street to go back ad forth to work every day.

Jackie agreed to meet, but she never showed. When I called her, explaining that we have been waiting for half an hour, she was distraught over her daughter. She said, "Leave me the fuck alone!"—and hung up.

He and I were left there alone. His tone with me changed. He softened and he asked about my pending divorce. He confided in me that his wife was very sick with terminal cancer. She drank heavily, and she was quite abusive. He wanted to leave her at that point. He was charming and smooth and I really believed he was telling the truth. I saw a beautiful man who was lonely and burdened by serious family problems.

For the first time, sitting across from him, I noticed his beautiful blue eyes and a very kind face. When he smiled at me, he drank me in. He looked like a little boy who had found his favorite lollipop. I was used to men hitting on me; that was no reason, nor was it in my fiber, to respond in any way, shape or form to the advances of a prospective client. I was a married woman and loyal to the end in my marriage. This was no different, except now I was to be divorced, and this tall, good-looking cowboy was about to get out of his marriage and be single, too. It made me feel great. Though was he ever going to leave her? He made me believe that he was.

I had not had sex for over a year. I had never been with any man except my husband. My girlfriends talked about having a one-night stands. It's in all the movies. Cosmopolitan always wrote about it. But was I ready for that? I could tell that Mr. Wonderful wanted me. The tension between us was smoldering. Thoughts were electrifying my brain. What about AIDS? The epidemic was raging. I was so scared and worried. Don't touch this. Don't! I backed off and went into the kitchen for some water. I tried to motion the fact that the meeting was over and it was time to leave, he did not seem to get my drift.

Talk about a scene! I was aware that my husband could walk in any minute. I was due in court in the morning on the divorce case. A one-night stand? This was it! I suddenly didn't care about anything else. I told myself, "What the heck!" I had been so sheltered. I shed the shell of that person and suddenly it happened: Mr. Wonderful grabbed my hand and pulled me toward him and said, "I thought about fixing you up with my son. You are too good for my son, but you are perfect for me."

We were entwined. Before I knew it, he was unzipping his pants. He grabbed me and kissed me. He physically overpowered me and I devoured him; I needed and wanted him. I felt like a little girl who had found her little lost toy. He was tall, with big broad shoulders, with a delicate white baby skin all over and I was a skinny suntanned youngster mad and curious about well, just "sex."

It was a super banquet with the crème de la crème of love-making, passion and just hot sweaty sex. We made love. So this was sex. Now I know why men cheat. It is wild and a fabulous drug. I'd had no idea how addictive and intoxicating it could be. It was one of the most beautiful and special days of my life. A day I will never forget.

An afternoon that shaped the next eighteen years of my life, and a day that will always haunt me. It made me who I am today—always frightened, critical and super-sensitive about the people I meet. That afternoon, I lost all concern for whether my husband would walk in and discover us. I never concerned myself with the right or wrong of it. It was just sex, one time— the raw heat of the moment. I had never done that so wildly, spontaneously and with such excitement. Boy did he show me how to make love. It wasn't going to happen again—or so I thought. The last thing on my mind was to start a new relationship. I only wanted to get through the divorce. The pressures in my life were unbearable. At times I could barely breathe. I was afraid I was going to lose everything and go to jail over the missing "million and a half," as my husband claimed.

And all the lawyers, including my own, were trying to make sure of it and were building their case on it. Including the bastard judge! What the hell were they trying to do to me? But that one illicit moment was the seed of something huge.

He called the next day, totally surprising me. In my mind, I thought he probably had casual sex all the time—he sort of looked the type—and he'd never contact me again.

But he did, persistently, and we started meeting whenever we could. I had sex like I'd never had sex before. I fell in love—fell completely in love with this married man, this strong, gravelly voiced man who seemed lonely and vulnerable and who appeared to need me. With his disdain for materialism, he liked to bring me cheap gifts, five-dollar bracelets, little stuffed mice, it didn't matter. I treasured them like Cartier treasures. I had everything I could have wanted, anyway. It was great that he showed he cared—unaware of how hurtful he could be, that his extremely frugal nature would cause me grievous hurt when I was broke and needing help and that, even eighteen years later, he would never be able or willing to commit, mentally, physically or financially, to an intimate situation with a woman. He was afraid of being loved and never could be trust a woman enough to fully immerse himself in the experience.

He promised he would be with me over and over again. He shared his misery over his wife's drunkenness, mood swings, and physical abuse. He vowed over and over to leave her— and twice, in a period of four years, he actually did, moving in with me in a house that he bought by writing a check, sight unseen. I had picked the place out for us. I cannot tell you how wonderful I felt, and how thrilled and happy I was. I pampered him. Cooked for him. Fixed his drinks. Filled the rooms of our home with his favorite flowers every day of every week. I became like a wife to him because he needed a wife, a real, loving wife—so he said.

He was my first true love. I saw our bonds grow. They were deep and unbreakable, or so I felt, not knowing he couldn't follow through. The guilt was too much for him. The guilt drew him back home to her every time. Guilt or fear or, better yet, money. *Super super*-money! How super-sad it is when money rules. He must have been aware of what the divorce would cost him: half of all his tremendous riches. He always went back to her. And yet, he could never let go of me, even when it would have been the merciful thing to do.

We broke up. I tried to move on. We saw each other. I tried to break it off. We saw each other again. And again.

As months became years, I tried harder to free myself of him and the pain I felt. There is nothing worse than being deeply in love with someone and being unable to be with him—being the second woman in his life, staying home while he is taking his wife to dinners, and on long world excursions.

During the summers he always traveled with her to France, one of my favorite places in the world. For many years I would go during the same weeks, and we would find ways to meet, never for more than an hour or two at a time.

But during the summer of 2001, I was trying to end the relationship once and for all. I needed to find some balance. And yet I also really loved and wanted him. In the end, I went to Europe—when he went. It was so very hard letting go, specially when you love someone, it is just unbearable. I did leave him and tried to live in Paris but not with him. He thought I would always be there. He called each and every hotel in Paris, checking for reservations under my name, until a friend told him where I was staying.

Mr. Wonderful wanted to see me. I tried to put him off, but it seemed as if some mystical power kept bringing us together. One night, after drinking a whole bottle of champagne and trying to sleep, and wanting desperately to forget him, I woke up and saw that a heavy rain had moved in. The next day, I slipped on my black pants and boots and decided to go out walking—sans umbrella, since I did not have one. I strolled the Champs-Elysees, crying nonstop the entire thirty-minute walk to Galeries La Fayette, the magnificent Paris department store. Just as I stepped inside, I looked up and saw him, Mr. Wonderful with his wife, coming down the escalator, and he was waving at me! I turned around and ran right out, with tears running down my cheeks.

The next morning I tried to end it in my hotel room. I decided to go back home. He showed up at my door at Plaza Athenee around seven-thirty in the morning, making sure I was in my room. "I'm never going to see you again," I told him. "I think it is best if you just leave. Get out of my life and never come back." The same day I took a flight home. I cried for eleven hours on the plane, thinking how much I loved him and how much I was going to miss him. I spent most of the next two weeks in bed, inconsolable. My heart was aching for him and to me I thought he was not telling the truth.

He did not look that miserable after all, nor did she look sick.

In July of the same year, I flew to Cannes—and the same afternoon I met a man, a tall, elegant, well-bronzed man who always wore linen shirts. His name was Giovanni. I met him in a posh seaside resort just as I was finishing a glass of wine. He was there with a young woman who turned out to be his daughter. She politely excused herself so that Giovanni and I could talk, and we fell into a long and enjoyable conversation. Before I knew it, an hour and a half had gone by—and I still hadn't eaten. He said, in his very genteel way, "Listen, I know you don't know me, but there's a place next door where we can have dinner. Would you like to join me?"

Why not? We walked over, and it seemed the maitre d' and the waiters all knew his name, so I felt safer and took a deep breath, and started to feel more relaxed. The waiters knew what wine and champagne he drank, and what food he liked. I thought to myself, *Who is this guy?* We had a great dinner together. It was eleven o'clock when we left. He followed me to my hotel, The Martinez, and was a perfect gentleman, waiting with me for my elevator. His blue eyes peered down at me. "Pishi, I know we barely met, but I would like to see you. May I invite you to lunch tomorrow?" I got scared.

"I don't think so," I said, afraid of things moving too fast. He was *tres' gentil* and insistent and assured me there was no need to worry since there are going to be a lot of people around. I ended up agreeing, and he kissed my hand good night.

I spent most of the next morning shopping. I sensed this was special, and I wanted to look just right. I went from boutique to boutique, grabbing a hat, shoes, a dress, earrings from Nina Ricci—and by the time I returned to The Martinez, around eleven, Giovanni and his driver were waiting for me in the lobby. He was an hour early. OK! I told him I have to change, with a big beautiful smile, he said fine. We rode in a black chauffeur-driven Mercedes to a small boat that ferried us to Giovanni's magnificent yacht in the Mediterranean. It was the most amazing lunch of my life.

Giovanni turned out to be one of the wealthiest men in Europe, an investor who owned more than 1,400 properties. He was also a gentleman to the core: kind, courteous, and unfailingly attentive. His staff catered to my every whim. And he fell in love with me—terribly in love.

It wasn't to be our last meal on the yacht.

We met again in Corsica. His daughters were there, and we learned more about each other's life. He told me that he had given his wife $75 million in a divorce settlement, and she had moved to Monaco for tax purposes.

After I had returned to Los Angeles, we made further plans. I ended up meeting him again in France—in Nice, where I wore a pink Channel suit. He was blown away by it. Me? I felt like I was in fairyland. Not only was I living like a princess, he was treating me like one. There was nothing else that mattered to him. There was nothing he wouldn't do for me.

There, in Cannes in one of the most beautiful settings you can imagine, he proposed to me that summer. I didn't give him an immediate answer. I knew it would be tricky deciding where we would spend our time—since my own two daughters were waiting for me in Los Angeles. But I was happy. It was the first time in my life that a man had proposed to me. And what a man! I will remember that day as one of the happiest days of my life.

It was Sept. 11, 2001. What I didn't know was that profound and tragic events were occurring half a world away. What I also didn't realize, unrelated to the terrorist attacks on New York and Washington, was that Mr. Wonderful was never going to let me go.

2

My Town

My life was forever changed, in 1967, by a practical joke. The prankster was my good friend, Miriam, a willowy, black-haired girl who was related to Iran's Royal Family. She went to school with me in Tehran. Without me knowing it, Miriam sent my picture, along with one of herself, to Zane Rouze, a mass-market magazine comparable to Vogue. It was the one and only fashion and women's interest publication in Iran, read every month by millions. Zane Rouze was conducting its annual Miss Iran contest.

Hundreds of thousands of photographs would flood in from hopeful young women and their families from all over the country. A few months later, the lucky finalists were announced—seventeen in all. They achieved instant celebrity, their smiling faces gracing the cover of Zane Rouze and appearing in prominent displays in movie theaters and other public places across Iran for the entire year. Miriam was one of those finalists. Another one was me, a shy little Jewish girl who never dreamed of being chosen, since I hadn't even bothered to enter.

Amazing? No, it was downright incredible. About a thousand people would attend the official crowning of the new Miss Iran in the main ballroom of Tehran's Hilton Hotel. A week prior to the Gala, I was selected to be the winner. The choice was made one week in advance so the proper planning could be done. My hair had to be fitted with a postige, a concealed chunk of hair to support the diamond tiara and the evening gown, in white with sequins. A red cape was specifically designed to make the cover even more attractive, bouquet of red roses in hand.

But on the night of the pageant, with the postige already in place and me radiant in my gorgeous white gown, the official hairdresser sought me out in the little room backstage where the contestants waited to appear. He needed to have the postige back. "They're saying you're Jewish," he told me. "Of course I'm Jewish," I said. "I'm sorry," he said. "But you studied in a French Catholic school." That was how they had allowed me in—a mistake, which had now been discovered. "We cannot crown someone who's Jewish in a Muslim country," the official told me, and I was eliminated before the crowning began. A Muslim winner was crowned instead. It was a cold introduction to bigotry, but at the time I didn't care.

As a finalist, I was an instant celebrity. The attention was overwhelming. Thousands of pieces of mail poured in—enough of it to fill three giant burlap bags every single day. It was flattering beyond belief. It boosted my self-esteem at a time when it desperately needed boosting, since I had already been engaged twice, and both times everything had gone to hell.

The failed engagements had shattered my confidence, leaving me extremely self-conscious about my body, especially my skinny arms and legs. To me I looked anorexic. Making matters worse, I had been raised in an environment that left me socially backward. Among the orthodox Jews of Iran, in those times, women were discouraged from looking people in the eyes. Only a whore would look a man straight in the eyes, I was taught. When I was around people, I couldn't even raise my head to say hello.

Lonely, without many friends, I wasn't allowed to visit other people's homes or have other kids come over to play with me. My father, who ran a lighting company, was very, very strict, and quite tough. He didn't want his daughter talking to strangers or going anywhere without his permission. My mother was a housewife, a kindly, beautiful woman who fought with my father to make sure I got a good education, but who, in other ways, yielded to his iron-handed rule. She never learned to drive a car. There were no toys at home. We had a bike, but I was only allowed to ride it in the yard, not anywhere else.

We lived in Tehran at a time when the city was evolving into a world-class metropolis. On the day I was born, August 17, 1952, tanks rolled through the streets. A failed attempt had been made on the life of the Shah. In the years to come, my mother would always tell me, "You're a war child—you always have to fight. You're always fighting for everything." How right she would turn out to be.

But, even with political turmoil and events moving inexorably toward revolution, Tehran was like New York City—big, vibrant, crowded, exciting, and very cosmopolitan. It wasn't quite London or Paris, but it was getting there. It was a city of culture. There were skyscrapers, expensive French and Italian boutiques, restaurants literally fit for a king, because the Shah might pop in any moment. There were street bazaars and homes as enormous as palaces.

Many of the Muslim women wore their traditional chadors—the long, black garments that covered them from head to toe. They shared the streets with women in mini-skirts. Twiggy was big then, Cacharel was hot, Mary Quant ruled, and the Beatles sizzled—and all these influences were spilling into Tehran. It was a remarkable place at a remarkable time. The wealth was fantastic, and yet every day a vendor made the rounds of the neighborhood on a donkey, selling fresh potatoes, onions, and a "vegetable of the day" while singing his favorite tune: Ha ha ha ha—a sad and depressing staccato song sung all in flat notes.

Our home, on a beautiful, tree-lined Avenue Tehran, was located in what we considered an upper-middle-class neighborhood, a block from Tehran University.

Although we were not nearly as wealthy as many of the oil-rich Muslim families near us, I remember our home for its newness and exquisite touches. It had marble floors, Persian rugs every where, and room enough in the posh living room and dining room to entertain two-hundred guests. Our maid went out for fresh food each morning—cheese, bread, milk, and caviar. There was always caviar. Caviar was like honey; every corner store carried it. I loved caviar on white toast—we never, ever mixed it with eggs or onions; we considered that very gauche. We never ate leftovers. Leftovers were for the maid.

My family then numbered four: my parents, me, and my younger brother; a second brother would arrive during my mid-teens, and my sister would come along shortly before I married. We lived on the first two floors of the house, and my uncle, his wife, and their three children shared the top story. My uncle, who was a partner in my father's lighting business, would drive me to school in the morning. I loved going to school with him. He was one of the best parts of my childhood. He was fun and happy and positive and I knew he loved me.

Education was vitally important, in my mother's view. My father thought it would be wasted on a girl, but somehow my mother was able to get him to send me to a very exclusive, private French Catholic school in Tehran.

Catholic school finished up where Judaism left off, turning me into a nice Catholic Jewish girl. The classes there were taught in French. Throughout the elementary grades and high school, I had three hours of instruction every day in Farsi and six hours in French. Not only did I become fluent in the language, but I fell in love with French history, literature, and everything French. My teachers referred to me as "The dictionary": Any time one of my classmates wouldn't know the answer to a question about history or language or the meaning of a word, the teacher would say, "Mademoiselle Dictionary, get up," pointing to me with a pretty smile, and I would stand and give them all the answers.

At a very young age, I was fascinated by the Chateaux and Cathedrals, the kings a Queens, Belles Epoque, and other luminaries. I loved reading Camus, Victor Hugo, and Comedie Francaise. I would burry myself in books about Marie Antoinette and Napoleon Bonaparte. I have read five versions of Napoleon's life story, his relationship with Josephine, and the amazing story of *Rueil Mal Maison,* the mansion she bought without his permission, finally nearly resulting in her execution. Of course he discovered what she was up to.

The Muslim teachers who taught Persian history, algebra and other basic subjects in Farsi did not like me because I was a Jew.

They were terse and unfriendly and quite stifling. But the French-speaking teachers, who came from France during the school year to live and teach, liked my passion; they appreciated my curiosity and intelligence. They encouraged me and gave me the freedom to think, to feel, and get excited about learning. Louis XIV inspired me with the gargantuan grandeur of his Versailles. Francois 1st and Henry IV excited me with their extravagant lifestyles and military campaigns. At the time, I was so highly educated about the chateaux and cathedrals that I knew every detail. I could look at a picture of a single window and immediately know not only the name of the cathedral but when it was built and the name of the architect.

While other students went crazy over Elvis Presley and American rock and roll stars, which I considered absolutely vile, I swooned over French singers Jacques Brel and Claude Francois and the French writer and philosopher Jean-Paul Sartre.

School started early and after my classes I would go to the *Biblioteque,* the library, until five or six in the afternoon, reading and browsing books with breath-taking images of France and eating and smelling every word.

From time to time, my teacher, Madame Odette, would choose books for me that they knew I would enjoy—Voltaire, Jean-Paul Sartre, and others. Twice a week, I would leave the library and go straight to the conservatory, across the street from the Shah's fabulous Kakhe Marmar (the Palace of Marble), to study the piano. During my recitals, I used to play rhapsodies and sonatas, twenty-five pages long, without ever looking at the notes.

Royalty attended my school. The Shah's nieces and their cousins sat in the seats next to me. So did the children of ambassadors and high-ranking officials from the French and American embassies. The Shah was always a presence—mainly because he would park his little red Ferrari outside of campus and watch the cute young girls. The Empress, who had attended the school, made more official visits, chatting with her old teachers. When Charles de Gaulle came to Iran, ours was the school he toured. After school let out each day, the stretch limousines would line up to pick up these privileged children of the rich and powerful.

By the time I was in ninth grade, most of the students, including me, took college courses at the Sorbonne, an extension of the famous French University in Paris that emphasized history and literature. I was already finishing the first year of Sorbonne and quite happy with me and my little pathetic world.

Jews were a minority, and I always felt different than most of those around me. I had a certain amount of pride at being set apart—I embraced my Jewish culture—and yet these differences were responsible in large part for my shyness. At home, I wore the Star of David around my neck on a gold chain, but when I was at school I had to conceal it under my clothes.

My family's considerable money seemed meager compared to the extraordinary wealth of the Muslims, French, Swiss and Belgian families around us. Many of the children of these rich industrialists and world leaders impressed me as being very sophisticated, with a great appreciation for knowledge and the finest things in life. The girls wore school uniforms with white collars and red ribbons at the neck, but when you'd see them on the street they would be wearing the most expensive Chanel and Coureges fashions. They'd fly off to London or Paris for the weekend. I wanted and wished the extravagant

life and to be like them. I developed a great awaren
classy, elegant and formal. I had a style that was hi҄
I came to the world of freedom of choice—America.

An idea took root in me that one day I would marry a Prince, just like my friends, and that I would be royalty, too. Surely, many young girls share that dream, but for me it seemed far more than a dream. In fact, when I was fourteen or fifteen, I had a crush on a blue-eyed, black-haired boy who attended a nearby French boys school. He was relative of the Shah, and I told one of my friends that he was really cute and he seemed to like me. Overhearing this, my father became angry. He did not believe that a young girl should be pursuing a man. I was grounded for a year—basically, the rest of my life at home.

In time, I grew to envy the girls my age and slightly older who were dating. They would be going out with guys and I would think, "Why can't I do that? What's it like to date?" I would never know, not while I was in Tehran. The people at school had parties, but I was never permitted to go. I wasn't allowed to go to concerts; instead, I would buy the singles, on old 45-rpm records, for less than thirty cents a piece, and read about my favorite artists in Paris Match, the French magazine.

One night, I remember, the French singer Salvatore Adamo was performing in Tehran at the request of the Empress. Tickets were impossible to get, and my father wouldn't let me go, anyway. He did, however, put me in the car and drive me past the front of the concert hall so I could see the crowds streaming in.

Every Friday, which is the equivalent of Sunday in America, I'd have lunch with my parents, and maybe once a month we'd go to a movie. I played the piano for hours on and I swam at a neighborhood pool that only women were allowed to use, but for the most part my social life was tightly controlled.

In my culture, fifteen was a ripe age for marriage. Much beyond that, it was feared that a young woman was becoming a spinster. The woman had very little say in the process. Marriages were arranged by the parents in a courtship ritual that would seem unbelievable to my own daughters, who would grow up half a world away, in a completely different society.

My family wasted no time, and I was engaged at fifteen—to a man I can now barely remember. The fact that I had just appeared on the cover of Zane Rouze as a Miss Iran finalist meant that suitors were crawling out from under every rock. It was the first time in the history of Iran that a Jewish girl had been selected as a finalist/runner up—a fact that became a phenomenal news story for years to come, after the truth got out. And despite the decision by pageant officials not to crown me the winner, I knew that my life had been irrevocably changed. There was a frenzy of interest in me among eligible Jewish bachelors. The men would ask to come over and meet me, which meant they were interested in marriage. My parents would invite them over. One would come in the morning, another at lunch, maybe another in the afternoon. At some point, while they were talking, I would be invited to come in and sit and say a few words. Then I would excuse myself and my parents would continue their discussions with the stranger about hitching me up for life.

It was sad and insane. If my parents wanted to grant their permission, they would offer the young man a bowl of hard sugar cubes, or this white little morsels called Nogle, a white hard candy made with rose water, and serve them tea. One man was granted this honor. On a separate night, soon afterward, a formal engagement party was arranged. The future husband is supposed to bring jewels—gold and diamonds. The bigger the jewels, the more impressive, the better. In a huge wooden box carted by servants, this young man offered up, on a swatch of red velvet, a diamond necklace with a center pendant the size of a walnut. To me it was no more than theater—a momentary amusement. Two hundred people were there on the night of the engagement party. I did not want jewels I wanted a Prince like the rest of my classmates. The day following the party, my parents had reached a surprising decision. "She's too good for him," they said, and the engagement was immediately called off. My father agreed. I didn't know why, and I would never find out how. It was just what they decided, and I was bound by my parents' decisions. There was no point in fighting it—and I hadn't especially liked the guy, anyway.

At sixteen I was engaged again. At that point, I didn't care who the guy was. He was okay, a special man, but not for me, and it just happened that one of my schoolmates was getting engaged to the Shah's nephew and came to class with a ten-carat diamond ring on her finger. These were the standards that imposed themselves in my mind. No one I knew or was meeting was ever going to measure up.

This time two hundred and fifty people showed up. The ritual was the same; he was chosen for me without me having any choice. A part of the process involved having a test to assure that he was able to father children. On the night of the engagement party, three-hundred people showed up. This man sent the most enormous assortment of flowers you can imagine. They had to be rolled in on a giant cart twelve feet long—all white roses, carnations, mums and hydrangeas. The man himself, however, never showed up. He had failed the lab test—his sperm count was low—and it was believed he could never bring an offspring into the world. This would prove to be untrue. Years later, I would find out that he did have children that he was married and a father and living happily in Los Angeles, but the iffy sperm count meant an end for us.

Love was never the issue. I barely knew him, but having such a grand party set up, and my would-be fiancée' failing to show, was horribly humiliating to me, too. Any woman would feel as I did—completely jilted. I cried my heart out that night. From a cabinet in the living room I took a bottle of whiskey, and I drank half of it. At two in the morning, I sat on the balcony of my bedroom, staring at the full moon, crying as if I would never stop, and fell asleep there on the bare travertine with a blanket.

During those years, a matchmaker who knew my family, and who lived in Tehran, was looking for people for a nice girl. After becoming a Miss Iran finalist, I was that nice girl. I was getting incredible attention. Everywhere I went, every function, people would follow me and try to get my number. I was constantly writing my name and number on pieces of paper—for old ladies, especially. They always had a younger brother or son or grandson who was looking for a wife, and I had massive followers and a fan club too.

Every so often I would meet someone I really liked. Some of these were Jews who were also powerful people, men with above average education and wealth, not to mention great looks. My parents disregarded my own wishes, however. My father did not consider me competent to make decisions about my future. He did not want me to marry any of the men with money. He believed that money was evil.

Here is where my friend's prank really took my life in a crazy direction, as if some great wheel of fate seized hold of me when I could not have expected it.

A copy of the magazine Zane Rouze found its way to my uncle Jami, who was living in New York. He carried the magazine with him on a trip to Philadelphia, to show it off during a Shabbat dinner at his mother-in-law's house. Evidently, at the time, the woman was trying to marry off one of her daughters, and had invited a young Persian doctor to dinner that night. This special guest, who practiced at a hospital in Philadelphia, turned out to have little interest in the daughter, but he was mesmerized by the magazine cover—so much so that, within a few months, he would return to Iran and make special arrangements to meet me through a matchmaker.

Getting sick of these guys parading in and out of the house, I was throwing a fit. I was eighteen now and I had finally spoken up and said, "No more—nobody else is coming here! I am sick of it." I wanted to continue my education and go to college, a rare thing for a Jewish girl in Iran, which immediately branded someone an old maid. So when Dr. Boring approached my parents and announced his intentions, they were obliged to schedule the meeting elsewhere. I didn't want to meet him at all, but he had come all the way from America. It was mid-August, and the date was set for late one afternoon at Café Naderi, a favorite place of mine in the plaza near our home. I got to pick the restaurant, with its fountains and gorgeous flower gardens. My mother allowed me the choice because it was the only way to get me to show up.

Dr. Boring and his mother were already at one of the long outdoor tables, waiting, when my mother and I arrived. By the way fathers never attend the first slaughter meeting. First impressions were not good. It took me no more than a minute to decide to get up and leave. These people were so unsophisticated, so dahati—country bumpkins, certainly not big-city people. The instant I stood, my mother gave me an angry pinch and ordered me to sit down.

I sat and brooded. This guy bothered me. I didn't like the way he dressed, didn't like his glasses, I didn't like much of anything about him. He had no charisma, no flash, no self-confidence, no money, and no looks—and was much older than me; he had nothing that appealed to me. He was low-key to the point of being boring. He was thirteen years older than I was. On top of that, it became clear that his bride would be unable to remain in Tehran. She would have to uproot and go live with him in that alien city that W.C. Fields hated so much—Philadelphia.

My mother and I stayed only thirty minutes. It's considered bad form to linger beyond that—it means you're really interested, and girls' mothers don't do that. You're also not supposed to eat. You order food, but you only look at it. This is part of creating a favorable first impression. As I said, it's insane.

Upon leaving, I pleaded with my mother, "Please don't answer the phone any more if they call. I totally do not like him. He's too old, and he's not my type at all." A couple of days later, to my horror, he and his entire family were in my house for tea. I had been swimming at the club, where I hurt my toe on the diving board. That was reason enough to cancel, I thought, but my parents insisted it was only tea, and all fifteen of them showed up right on time. At first, I refused to go downstairs to the living room to greet them. My mother grew upset, yelling and screaming at me, and I had to make my entry and serve the tea. I also peeled a cucumber. That's how they judge you. You're supposed to peel a cucumber or an apple to show that you will be an able wife. You're supposed to say very little, throw your eyes glued to the floor and remain silent with a little smile. I was shy, anyway, and I did well. They thought I was quite sophisticated. After a total of five minutes, I asked them to excuse me because of the pain in my toe. It wasn't really the toe that was bothering me—it was being forced to become involved with a man I didn't like.

Next was the engagement party. A week later, at least a couple of hundred people attended— yet again. It was one of the worst nights I can remember. A panic came over me, anger and sadness that I can't even describe. When the party ended, I lay awake all night, sobbing. About four in the morning my father entered my room and knocked on my bedroom door. "Who is crying in this room?" he said. It was hard for me to speak. "Please, please don't make me marry this guy," I begged him.

The next day my father called him and asked him to come by. It was a Friday, which is a holiday in Iran. Nobody was on the street. I went into my room to hide. I really never wanted to see the man again, but I left my door open to hear the conversation. My father said, "We have to cancel the engagement. She has changed her mind. She wants to go to the university and she doesn't want to get married. Beside she doesn't want to live in the United States." My father apologized for the inconvenience and gave him back his ring and gifts.

Afterward, I emerged from my room and gave my father a big hug. I was thankful and relieved. That should have been the end of it. It wasn't. Dr. Boring wouldn't go away. On his way home, he bumped into my aunt, who was living upstairs, and she encouraged him to go back and pursue me, claiming they are playing hard to get. My whole social circle, including my family, piped up with their opinions. Many of them saw me as the dumbest, most immature young women they had ever known. I didn't know what was good for me, they said. I was an old maid, anyway, and my parents should go ahead and marry me off, and get rid of me. I was a liability to them. After three failed engagements, they were going to be stuck with me. Making the marriage happen was the only solution, and I would be a prize for this young doctor.

Everyone thought my father should call Dr. Boring and invite him back—and, ultimately, my father did. I cannot describe how upset I was; a week later I was already married.

The day before the wedding, I ran away and disappeared. I ended up going back, because I knew if I didn't my father would kill me. I cried and cried. Nobody cared. The wedding was on a Thursday night. That afternoon, all alone I went to a dinky, cheap beauty shop in tears to get my hair done—swept up to accommodate the fake floral piece of disaster I was forced to wear. To me it was a crown of thorns. My father paid for the ring and the entertainment, and the Persian singer Googoosh was hired for entertainment. I showed up as radiant as they could make me look, but I was miserable, my lips full of fever blisters, my face puffy and my eyes red from tears.

In the Jewish tradition, a glass was enfolded within a handkerchief, stepped on and broken. If you can believe it, a cow was sacrificed for good luck. That was the old-world way—and the bride has to step over the cow for good luck. This all happened in front of my own house.

And I became a wife.

The wedding night was a bloody horror. There were people assigned to the door, to witness the stained sheet as evidence that I was a virgin. I was forced to submit there in the dark to this man I scarcely knew, this stranger who was now to dominate my life for twenty-eight years.

The next day, the television news announced that Jamal Abdul Nasser, the president of Egypt, had died. Wow, I wanted to die, too. Instead, I had to go and get a passport. The following week, Dr. Boring and I departed for the United States. The scene at the airport was unimaginable—leaving behind my friends, my family, a crowd of fifty people who came to see us off, to slip out of their lives for what seemed like forever. He had five-hundred dollars to his name and I was to be his wife in some strange land called Philadelphia.

It was October 14, 1970. Where the hell was Philadelphia? I didn't even speak a word of English.

3

A Taste of America

The thunderstorms, humidity and rain of Philadelphia were just unbearable. Those dark clouds in October seemed to sum up my life. No twister had come down and carried me off, but the changes were just as abrupt and dizzying as any that Dorothy ever experienced. "No Pishi," I could tell myself, "you're not in Tehran anymore." I was 6,000 miles away, no money, without my family, without my friends, lonely, miserable, isolated—no more than a depressed little girl, and sure that all my hopes and dreams were gone for good.

We lived in a tiny studio apartment barely large enough to set down my luggage on the floor and have any room left to walk. There was a twin bed that we both had to share, a tiny desk pushed against a wall, and, oy vey, a graveyard across the street.

In Tehran the cemetery was hours outside of town—it wasn't lucky to be living in the same neighborhood as a bunch of stiffs. Now, besides all the other adjustments I would have to make, I could lie in the dark and imagine all the spooks coming over to haunt us. The only nice feature that our apartment had was a window overlooking the magnificent Brownstones of Pine Street.

One of my few joys during this dismal time, was gazing out at this lovely view, and seeing the people and cars going by. Dr. Boring was busy trying to complete his residency at the local Hospital, just a block away. His shifts were unbelievable. He would work as many as three to four days in a row, and I would be at home alone, unable to drive, meet friends and unable to speak English. We had no money to live in the way I had known with my family. During our first week in the apartment, he said to me, as nicely as he could, "We have to do the dishes after we eat, you know." They had been piling up since the weekend, I expected the maid to arrive. I had never done dishes in my life; but there was no maid.

I learned to clean up for the first time. I also enrolled at the nearby public high school, since I had never finished high school or received my diploma. The campus in Philadelphia happened to specialize in international students. Fortunately, it was also within walking distance of where we lived. I had heard about the place. My goal was not just to complete my education for my diploma, but to learn English first, of course. I was good with languages, and yet I was starting almost from scratch.

At school I got a break by meeting a young black boy from Haiti who spoke French, a language I knew fluently. We hit it off, and he became my translator. Later, I would also meet a tall, skinny Italian woman named Marni, who was also married to a doctor. First time I noticed her was when I would look out of the apartment window and saw her walking out. It turned out that she lived in a midget-sized room under the staircase of a nearby apartment building. As we got to know Marni and her husband Antonio, they would often invite us over for dinner. The men, of course, would have long discussions about medicine—He spoke perfect English and very fast—and Marni, who was beautiful and built like a model, would smile and try to teach me to adapt. One time she was serving Cornish game hen. I had never seen a chicken so little before!

She had it wrapped up in aluminum foil—shocking-Imagine cooking chicken in a wrapper; I had never seen that, either. She taught me how to buy and make roast beef. On a number of occasions, she invited me over and tried to teach me how to cook—and also how to read. She was deeply saddened by my situation.

My motivation to read and speak English was very strong, partly to get out and talk to people, but also because of the challenge. I'd go out and feel like a dumb mute girl, never saying anything. I couldn't cope with any of the normal parts of American life. I'd see signs on the street—LAUNDROMAT, CAR WASH, BAKERY—and have no clue what they said. I'd stand in the grocery aisle and see shelves and shelves of canned goods, having no idea what the labels said, much less what people ate or how to prepare it. I didn't want to feel like that. I wasn't dumb. A certain amount of ego was involved, and, of course, eventually I wanted to get a job. I started using and reading the New York Times to build my English vocabulary. I would make myself memorize one-hundred new words a day, every day after school. I had a little dining room table—a used one, of course, with only four plastic-covered chairs—and I would sit there and spread open a humongous dictionary, keeping notes in a little spiral notebook. I'd divide the page, half English and half Farsi. Every afternoon after school, at three-thirty, I would sit down and look up words I found in the New York Times. I was very disciplined and began to make rapid progress. I also watched plenty of TV, absorbing what words and grammar I could from Carol Burnett, Lucille Ball, and Jackie Gleason.

The soap opera, "Another World," became one of my favorites; only I couldn't understand why they called it "soap." I also learned English from the commentary of hockey games and especially

American football. To me, football had always meant soccer, so at first the game puzzled me, and in those days I didn't know the Philadelphia Eagles from the Los Angeles Lakers, but when I saw all those big, strong men in their tight, shiny pants, I was hooked. It fascinated me to see these guys with their great butts running all over the field, jumping on each other, throwing the ball around—and it was another way to pick up new words.

My Uncle Jami was a coach for me. Jami had been in the United States for many years and was a wonderful man, even though he was responsible for my marriage, because he had shown the cover of Zane Rouze to the man who was going to be my husband. Every week, Jami would call and invite us up to Roslyn, New York, for the weekend. Roslyn was a lovely little village on the north shore of Long Island where he lived in a little row house with wood siding and a tiny green lawn in front. We would stay in a small upstairs room with a slanted ceiling—a place with wonderful memories for me. During my visits there, I first learned about Thanksgiving and learned how to cook a turkey. I just loved Jami and his family.

When he was in Iran and I was a little girl, he spent a lot of time with me. My grandfather was like a Rockefeller in Tehran, an honest banker who came to own a tremendous wealth, and a very opulent estate. He adored me, and Jami loved his niece, as if I were his child. My grandfather left much of his fortune to Jami, who lost it, got married, and moved to a new, simple life in Roslyn. Jami would often take us into Manhattan to see the sights.

Wow, what a city it was, how exciting I found it to be; seeing the fancy restaurants and soaring buildings and high-class people so finely dressed— things that reminded me of the best of Tehran.

Such a high energy city and I wanted so much to move to New York City, where people had fun, where they partied all night. My spirit was trying to break free. For my whole life I had been confined by rules, told what to do, and what not to do, prevented me from having the fun that my friends got to have—and I wanted to get out and be part of the action. And, of course, Broadway! Wow! There wasn't that sort of life in Philadelphia. People didn't dress up. The whole town seemed to close at five o'clock. I begged my husband, "Let's move to New York," but he did not care nor wouldn't hear of it.

As miserable as I was, I never, ever wanted to go back to Iran, but New York was another story. My cousins would be having bar mitzvahs, weddings and other parties at the Waldorf-Astoria, the Plaza, the Pierre and their beautiful mansions on the water in Kings Point, while I stayed home in a dinky apartment studio crying. He wasn't willing to join that idyllic world. He was tied to his residency, or so he said, but in truth there were many residencies and hospitals in New York—I had checked them out. He just chose to ignore what I wanted.

What I wanted was never what he wanted, and it was not in his nature to yield to the wishes of a wife. Certainly he would never listen to an eighteen-year-old who, in the way he viewed marriage, was like a piece of property, his woman, sworn to obey his every command. To him, I was like a child—I was immature, spoiled, I had a lot to learn, and I had no feelings. Moving was out of the question. He insisted we stay in that lonely town where our nightlife, night after night consisted of watching football, hockey, and Carol Burnett.

Uncle Jami could sense the deep depression I was in. He was a kindly, soft- spoken man who never drank but who liked to gamble.

We had a relationship that was deeper than just words. He would always ask me, "How are you, honey? Are you happy? I love you, you know. You can always talk to me." My response would be what the family wanted to hear. "Yes, of course, I'm happy. Everything is great." This was the mask I wore. I was too proud to admit otherwise. I also knew that whatever I told him would get back to my mother—the two siblings were very close. The last thing I wanted to do was to upset her. My true feelings were my own secret. Jami's face told me that he saw through the ruse, but he never pursued the subject; he chose to honor my answers. Ours became an unspoken understanding, and the truth of my misery never got back to my parents in Iran.

Stuck with a man I didn't want in a cramped apartment in a strange city, I suffered and tried to make the marriage work. He was nice, gentle, and so very, very boring and as for sex? It was awful. During the days at a time when he was attending mothers and newborns and sleeping at the hospital, I concentrated on my school work, cleaned, moped around the empty apartment, and glued fabric to the $10, second-hand sofa we owned because we couldn't afford to have it upholstered.

During this time I'd had my first exposure to real American wealth when we got invited to dinner at the home of a Dr. Zimmerman, who was head of a department at the hospital. I vividly remember his elegant young wife coming in, dressed in a gold-beaded gown, introducing herself as Mrs. Zimmerman. She happened to own a gorgeous white sofa, and I wanted mine to look like that, so I bought several yards of a lustrous white furry fabric and affixed it to our cheap couch with Elmer's Glue. It actually looked pretty great, but we could no longer open the sofa bed or it would rip!

On the nights when he would be home and we had sex, he would drift off to sleep and I would lie there and weep without him knowing it, so I would not hurt his feelings. Some honeymoon. In my letters home I never mentioned this silent agony, the fact that deep inside I was dying. I felt no love, no hope of love, and no hope of a way out. And I wanted so badly to live and love—or die, and have the ordeal be over.

There was a night, when he came home late and went to straight to bed, and I decided that I could no longer take it. That very moment I was going to leave. My suitcase was packed—I had been waiting for this instant when the pain was too much and I could summon the nerve to go. Without making a sound and with no hesitation, I slipped into the clothes I had laid out, lifted the suitcase, and got as far as breaching the front door of the apartment before realizing the futility of my plan. I stopped, thinking, "Where am I going to go?" Had I left for home, my father, as tough as he was, would have been merciless. My mother would have been equally enraged. It was beside the point, in their view of marriage, whether I needed to love my husband; love was not part of the equation. Duty, obeying your parents, being a good girl, marrying and bringing children into the world, were what mattered for a young girl—never mind her own longings, her intellect, her accolades in the Miss Iran pageant.

That night I sat outside the apartment in the cold, much as I had sat on my bedroom balcony in Iran watching the full moon after my third engagement was called off, and I cried my eyes out. For one hour, my tears streamed down my cheeks and I searched deep in my soul for some answers. In the end, I vowed to myself that I would never, ever think about going anywhere. I would stay and never leave my husband. Arranged marriage or not, this was my fate, this was the man, and this dinky apartment was my home. I swore that I would put up with those realities and make the best of them.

Slipping back inside, half-frozen, I returned to bed, waking up the next morning to a hard road that would be my course for twenty-eight years. The next morning happened to be Super Bowl Sunday, 1971. All alone, I sat on my bed, and I watched the game on our black-and-white small television set and continued to cook and do the dishes. Life went on. I explored the city and learned the American ways of living.

Race Street was the garment district. After discovering that I could see a dress in a magazine and find the pattern for it on Race Street, I became a fixture there. On lonely evenings my sewing machine would hum and I would produce the most gorgeous gowns, all hand-made of fabulous satin, linen and sequins. During later trips to visit New York, my friends would almost fight to get my clothes right off my body. They'd pay me $200 to $300 a piece for these gowns, a fortune in those days.

There were numerous aspects of American life that I enjoyed. I no longer had to hide my Star of David. My mini-skirts could be as short as I wanted them and nobody cared. It was refreshing to be in such an open-minded, tolerant nation, where Jews were embraced, where I could speak my mind in the new language I was learning. Synagogues were located up and down Broad Street and elsewhere. In Tehran, it was easier to take a flying carpet to Israel than to find a synagogue—our family knew of only one—but now we had choices.

I was also learning to enjoy American food. And Wonder Bread! Oh, my God, I loved Wonder Bread and Smucker's strawberry jelly. I could eat a whole loaf of Wonder Bread in the morning. Hot dogs were another of my passions. My mother and father would kill me for eating non-kosher hot dogs, but I would have them five or six times a day if I could. Forget about buns—I would cook them with pasta in ketchup and butter. Yes, ketchup and butter. I'd also fry them in a pan that way. Buns? I'd never heard of buns. I never imagined having them with mustard and relish.

We had very little money for food, but in Philadelphia, at that time, we could survive on $5 or $6 a week for groceries—meat, milk, canned goods. Once I learned to read a little, I bought a cookbook, "Betty Crocker for Two." The recipes were about five lines apiece and easy enough to make. Beef stroganoff, I was familiar with, since it was a French dish, except we usually couldn't afford the beef and I fixed it with hamburger. Oh, the discoveries I made: pancakes, fried chicken, chocolate shakes, brownies, and delicious barbecued spare ribs. In Iran, beef was served in little thin cuts. No steaks. I came to love a good steak!

We'd splurge once or twice a month and go out for a steak dinner—$1.50 with a baked potato—or drive to a smorgasbord an hour away and stuff ourselves. We also ate traditional Persian meals and other ethnic food. A sprawling Italian marketplace existed on South Street, where I'd sometimes stop on my walk home from school. The sights and smells of it still fill my mind because it reminded me of Tehran. Rough-hewn, dilapidated, it bordered an older black section of town where I never dared to go. Little cheese stores and indoor shops framed an expanse of outdoor tables loaded with vegetables and fruit, and where you could roam and inhale the odors of fish, chicken, and fresh strawberries and peaches—smells that reminded me of Iran. Strolling there was another new experience for me. In Tehran, girls in my neighborhood never attended the street bazaars—it just wasn't done. You had a maid to go out for groceries. Doing it yourself was a sign of poverty.

Most of the time, while living in Philadelphia, I was able to walk where I needed to go, but eventually I learned to drive and got my driver's license. That was another adjustment to American life. In Iran, all the cars are stick shift. Naturally, you would think an automatic would be much easier—and it is, except you have to keep your foot on the brake to keep from moving. I learned to drive on an old clunker, a black-and-white Ford Mustang. One of the first things I did was put it in gear and plow right into the car behind me, smashing up the rear end. Yikes! Lesson learned. Having a car meant extra freedom, of course. It's incredible to think that in those days gas was twenty cents a gallon.

One day I was at the marketplace and I stepped into a butcher shop for some cow stomach, intestines and brain. Those were Persian foods that we still ate. Brain is actually very good. It has the color and texture of tofu, and I spiced it by cooking it with salt and onions. As I glanced at the mirror behind the butcher counter, I noticed that my right eye became blurry. The following morning, my husband took me to the doctor, who referred me to a specialist. The guy took one look and immediately ordered me admitted to the hospital. The disease was loosely translated for me: This girl is in deep shit. What I had was a rare parasitic infection that can lead to blindness. It can come from cats, and I did have a cat, an alley cat named Pishi, whom I loved, and also might be genetic. But now there was inflammation inside my eye. I was seeing spots, and they were getting bigger, which meant I was losing my eyesight.

For the next two months, I was confined to a hospital bed, in the dark, while doctors and nurses came and went, jabbing me with needles dozen times a day. It took a good six months to heal, after swallowing two dozen pills, every six hours; a river of antibiotics and cortisone flowed through my system. My eyes were kept dilated for several months. No one came to see me because I had no one—no family, no friends—and I lay there in that hospital bed and cried. I was not about to call home and complain. My only visitors were the doctors who kept coming in to photograph the rare condition. If it hadn't been for Dr. Sheie who treated me, I would have been blind. Later, whenever someone would say to me, "You have beautiful eyes," I would puzzle them by saying, "They're an illusion," because to me they were flawed.

Soon after my recovery, I became pregnant. Now I was nineteen and happy at the thought of having a child. In rapid order, I would accept my high school diploma, donning my cap and gown with distended belly, and deliver my beautiful baby girl. We deliberately gave her an American name. She was an absolute delight, my tiny princess. She brightened my life. I was thrilled with her and proud of me for graduating, but our home life remained difficult.

Dr. Boring and I were never in sync. I confess, looking back, that I always looked down on him despite his medical-school education. My background and status had imbued me with a measure of snobbishness. For some reason he never could rise to my level. Never. He was just too different from me. We were always on the wrong channel—different interests, different dreams, different attitudes, and different taste in lifestyles. Though he was successful and popular at the hospital, he had no other side to him. He had no hobbies, no passions that we could share. He was like the wallpaper to me and I felt like he never really cared.

We would never buy disposable diapers, because he didn't want to spend the money, and much of my time was spent nursing and washing shitty diapers by hand. His residency had ended, and I begged him again to move to New York. He stubbornly refused. That would be the immutable pattern of the marriage—his complete unwillingness to even consider the wants and needs of a female-his wife. In New York, there was a thriving Jewish community. I had a ton of friends and relatives who lived in wonderful homes in Great Neck and Kings Point. They had parties, and lots of exiting events, were taking place. They went places and I was always at home. I was young and I wanted excitement. He was not the party type. He was shy and more of a hermit—traits I despise in a man. I wanted a Prince. I wanted to be treated like the princess I had always dreamed of being.

Where did we move when we finally did leave Philadelphia? Not New York City—oh God, no. How about a deadly dull little burg with one main street running through it, Pittstown, Pennsylvania? Talk about going from bad to worse—and all for his career, of course. A doctor had offered him a partnership there, for very good money, and he was excited. My feeling was, money wasn't everything. Let's move to New York. He was beyond happy. To me to move to a place like Pittstown was a nightmare. It was home to five-thousand small-minded, mostly anti-Semitic people, and all in all maybe hundred Jews.

Pitttstown was Podunk with a capital P, a hick town of smoke-spewing steel plants, foundries, machine shops, and textile mills, about an hour northwest of Philadelphia. It was a ghastly place, and we were right in the middle of it. Not exactly in the middle, because there were affluent neighborhoods where the corporate bosses and professionals lived, and we were beginning to sample a slightly better lifestyle. I cooked, knitted, and took care of our little girl. In the wintertime it seemed to snow day after day after day, the drifts piling up to fifteen feet sometimes, growing muddy along the roadside. The only hope and love of my life, was my beautiful daughter who actually was my reason for living.

Our first home, was a two-story townhouse that we rented for $150 a month, on a block of awful row houses. By now I was in severe depression. I would take our daughter to school and come home and go to bed. Then get up again, pick up the young princess from school, and come home, set the table, and fix dinner. Except, he would rarely be home. He would work late and dinner would be for naught. My neighbor then was an elegant, nice-looking blonde named Tamara who came from a lot of money, as did her husband. They had a little boy and the most gorgeous little apartment I had ever seen. They were the most popular couple in town, invited out every night, while I sat alone, looking out the window, watching them leave to go have fun. This went on for two years. Tamara was a doll. I got to know her and she became my best friend, many years later. I admired her and yearned for a life like she had. She and her husband not only had a housekeeper, they also had a babysitter, too. Well, we could not afford those things. Besides, where were we going to go, anyway? We had no friends.

In Philadelphia, at least I could walk from the apartment and see cars and stores and people on the streets. Not in dreary Pittstown. The stores were run down and too far away to walk to them, except for K-mart. That was it. He took the only car we had to work with him. Everyone around us had a Cadillac, it seemed, and we bought a baby-blue Buick, but it was his car and I was stranded most of the time. Even buying fruit and vegetables was difficult. Zern's farmer's market was about fifteen minutes away— and I abhorred the idea of a farmer's market. Was I to be a farmer now? Had I studied Napoleon and Henry IV to mingle with guys in overalls?

It was especially hard to find a synagogue in Pittstown. We did, but it was a small congregation. Half the time we had to bring in the gardener or someone else from outside at night to scrounge up the requisite ten men to recite the Shabbat prayer for the dead. The community liked me and also my ideas. As the chair person in charge of arranging luncheons and dinners, several times, I planned the hospital's annual banquet. Inspired by the cultures I knew, I organized a "French Night, Le Gai Paris" for the doctors, for which I hand-created one- hundred and twenty centerpieces fashioned to look like the Eiffel Tower. The next year, I was hired again and staged a "Persian Night" that everyone loved. It was adorable, with 150 centerpieces resembling peacocks, with real feathers, and oversized faux butterflies suspended from the ceiling, and a belly dancer.

Meanwhile, I had become pregnant again, an ordeal that left me bedridden for a month. On a night of the full moon, a night I instinctively knew I would have the baby, I gave birth to another gorgeous baby daughter, Princess No. 2, three years younger than our first. Two daughters would be all I would have, as both pregnancies turned out to aggravate the condition of my damaged eyes. After the new baby was born, and the eye problem hit me for the third time, a doctor in Israel told me very emphatically: no more children if I wanted to be able to see: "You want to lose your eyes, have another baby."

Over time, Dr. Boring's thriving practice enabled us to buy a little home just outside town, and a better house after that then a two-story Colonial with a huge swimming pool and gorgeous kitchen. Although we lived frugally compared to some of the upper-class families—I always shopped at Kmart—we did join the country club, where I started playing tennis, and we hired our first housekeeper to help out two days a week. He worked day and night and his patients really liked him. In that little town, where homes were so affordable, we were soon able to buy an even larger home, a real mansion, 20,000 square feet with a commanding view of a golf course. It was magnificent: hardwood floors, fabulous marble, an eighteen-foot-high ceiling in the huge living room, and a pyramid bed that I designed myself. Yet still I felt as if I lived in an emotional prison, a marital Sing Sing. My crime: Wanting a life with exitement and to be me. Wanting to live with love and passion and most of all true love. I just wanted to be happy. Wanting to live near members of my family. I missed the big city life, Broadway, the Met. Those were my escapes, and I wanted so much to be near all that. I missed living in New York City, and now I was suffocating in a tiny town of Hicksville.

Little did I realize that most of my immediate family would soon be joining me in the United States. On a snowy Sunday night in November of 1977, I watched a 20/20 program in which Barbara Walters interviewed the Shah of Iran. His answers and his mood shook me up. Oh, my God, I couldn't believe it, the Shah had gone mad; I could not believe what he was saying. I realized that the regime was about to fall. Why did I think that? I cannot explain nor do I have a clue. My gut, I guess. How did I foresee the end of the

Pahlavi Regime? I don't know, but that same night at around eleven o'clock, I phoned my family in Tehran and asked to speak to my brother, who was preparing to study at Tehran University. Get your affairs in order and get out, as soon as you can. I told him. The Shah was going mad, I said, and everything would change. I don't know what possessed me to say that, or to scare him, but how right I would turn out to be. My father opposed him leaving the country because my brother was helping with the lighting business, and they were making good money. My father got extremely angry and yelled at me the next day, saying, "Don't you ever call here again!" But my brother took my advice, and on June 21, 1978, about six months before the regime collapsed, he arrived at JFK Airport in New York, carrying a suitcase (with a big English dictionary inside), his passport, and $1,000.

I loved my brother to the point of insanity-he wa my life. He was my flesh and blood and I was so glad to see him. However, the minute U.S. Customs agents saw the dictionary, they stamped his visa for two weeks—they were going to send him back. I was shocked. But I knew, I was never going to let him go back, so I had to move fast.

We had to declare war and hire an attorney to fight it. Bright and early we drove to Philadelphia the next day and I stood in a phone booth, frantically looking through the Yellow Pages for a lawyer, while my brother hovered next to me, literally shaking with nervous fear. Luck was with us: The lawyer I picked out, because his office was walking distance from the phone booth right there on Broad Street, a block away, turned out to be a former head of the local U.S. immigration office. *Voila*! For $200, he handled the paperwork and I became a citizen, and my brother was allowed to enter America, with his green card, in my care.

The dying regime in Iran soon meant that other members of the family would later join us. As much as I craved to have a family, I knew Philadelphia was not going to work out for them. So I suggested Los Angles, and they agreed.

The twenty-seven people who got out of Iran with our help scattered on the West Coast. My mother finally came, and she and both of my brothers, along with my sister, settled in Los Angeles. My father, who so fervently believed in the Shah, was the last holdout, remaining in Tehran for another year and a half—until it was clear that the Ayatollah Khomeini was in full political control and Jews had no choice but to leave. Then, with only the clothes on his back, and not much else my father gave up hope of staying and joined my mother in Los Angeles.

Even with all the energy it took to care for two young children, I was improving my English and yearning to advance my education, so I could have my own career and make my own money. Needless to say, my husband hated the idea, but I enrolled in a college in Bryn Mawr, and after that moved on to Wharton School of Business in Philadelphia. It took all of my determination to get into Wharton. When I was trying to enroll, the highway was under construction and the drive was 3½ hours—one way. A professor who taught a class I really wanted to take, didn't want to let me in made fun of me.

"Go back to Bryn Mawr," he told me, walking away. I approached him again the next day—and was rebuffed again. The following week I tried for the third time.

"I can't do this," the professor said, wondering why I was harassing him. But he finally relented and told his aide to register me. Then I failed the mid-term, and his attitude was, "I told you so." I had to buckle down like never before. I memorized the entire textbook—300 pages. On the final, I got an A—and he accused me of cheating. "Ask me any question," I dared him. I knew the material cold. I ended up with a B for the course. It was a demanding program. In the wintertime I had to commute driving 10 m.p.h. in the snow—I couldn't see out the window.

School was my ticket out of misery—it got me away from my unhappy home—and I thrived at Wharton, struggling through difficult subjects but happy to be around such smart people and learning so much. This burgeoning pride and self-assurance ate away at my husband. After a few semesters, one of my professors advised me to think about doing something with my life. I was too sharp to stay home and take care of children, he told me. That professor helped to arrange one of my first job offers—from Xerox Canada, which would have employed me four days a week in Toronto, with flights home in between. Xerox was willing to pay me a ton of money; now I not only spoke French but English, too.

Dr. Boring was his usual understanding self. He went ballistic! It was totally out of the question. "You go," he said, "and you're going to divorce court." But other companies were interested in me. One company called IBM wanted me to move to Boston three days a week. Bloomingdales wanted to hire me in New York. A big-time advertising agency brought me in and one of the principals told me, "I bet I could give you widgets and you'd sell the hell out of them."

"Of course I would," I shot back. "Do you even know what widgets are?" he said. "No," I admitted. He laughed. It was intoxicating. The idea of staying stuck in Hick town became more and more intolerable. I wanted my parole. I pleaded with him to get his license in California so we could move there. He passed the boards, only to change his mind about going. He was really only trying to pacify me.

A year later, at a craps table in Margate, New Jersey, I met Toni, a head foreman for Donald Trump. I'd never heard of Donald Trump before, but his organization was building a major casino in Atlantic City, and I took the initiative to line up a chance for my brother to land the lighting contract. Today he has one of the largest companies in the world. My brother said, "Wait a minute, I don't even have a company here." Have you gone mad? It didn't matter to me. I pressed ahead, pretending I worked for him and setting up interviews. He had to fly out from Los Angeles and lost his luggage en route, so in desperation I bought him a sharp-looking black jacket from a waiter so my brother could make the proper impression. It must have helped—he landed the contract. The timing wasn't so great; my brother would had to live a bycoastal life.

However, there was a happy ending. Steve Wynn, the rich Las Vegas entrepreneur, was so impressed with Trump's Atlantic City casino that he gave my brother all his lighting contracts. My brother would go on to handle the lighting for major hotels and casinos around the world. This refugee was on his way to super stardom.

During those initial few weeks, when we were meeting with Trump officials in Atlantic City and New York (I billed myself as his secretary), I finally confessed to my brother my profound unhappiness. In a hotel room not far from the casino site, I broke down and cried my eyes out; leaving them so red I was embarrassed at the next day's business meeting. I had never told anyone in my family how terribly miserable I had been, for years now—to the point of being suicidal. My brother was great, completely supportive. Do what you have to do, he told me. He said, "Get the hell out." He would be there and help me any way he could.

A decision was coming. It would take time, but I began testing the waters—and testing my own resolve. In the spring of 1986, I flew out to Los Angeles and visited my family for a couple of weeks. In June, I took the kids and went West again, this time for several weeks, and Dr. Boring was extremely upset. He threatened to file for divorce if I didn't get back home. Reluctantly, as sad as hell, I obeyed. Life with this man was not getting any better. He kept pushing. Around the time of the high holidays, in the fall, I took another trip by myself, this time for a couple of days. During a service at Sinai Temple, the rabbi seemed almost as if he were speaking directly to me when he talked about following one's dreams.

"There are times in life," I remember him saying, "when we have a longing for things to change and all the things we want, somehow we are too scared to take action. The only thing is, if we don't do it now, we never will and there will come a time when we kick ourselves: Why didn't we follow our dreams?"

Sitting there, with my brothers on either side of me, I was unable to contain my enormous sadness. Tears streamed down my face like the Niagara Falls. My brothers looked at me and looked at each other, thinking, "What is the matter with her?"

Once I was back in Pittstown, in 1986, I secretly withdrew $1,000 from the bank and hid it. Then on December 17, I asked the principal to let me take the girls out of school—and then I went to Peter, my local gas station guy, and asked him for a special favor. I said someone in Los Angeles was buying my car and I offered him $500 if he could arrange to ship it there. Next I packed up my suitcases with clothes, jewelry, and the rest of my $1,000 cash, gathered my daughters, and headed to board a plane.

Dr. Boring couldn't object this time—not yet, anyway.

I didn't even bother to tell him. I was too scared he wouldn't let me go.

4

Millionaires, Mansions and Me

Was he angry? Oh, my God, there is still a hole in the roof where he went through! Over-the-top ballistic, that's what my loving husband was. "Not only am I going to file for divorce," he raged, "I'll sue you for kidnapping!" He ordered me to return to Pittstown at once. Hah! Fat chance after I'd wasted sixteen years there. It didn't help his mood that I had called him to ask for money—I had our daughters to feed—but I kept my poise and spoke as calmly as I could.

"I'm not trying to take the kids away from you," I assured him. "I'm just not going to live back there anymore and I need money; please wire me some money till I find a job; You should come out here—it's beautiful!" By the way, he never send me a dime.

For the first time, after years of living under Dr. Boring's control, I had seized the power, and no way was I going to give it back. Somehow I knew I had to make a new start and it would all work out, one way or another—I was determined to make it happen.

Despite the years we had been married, he never grasped the fact that, as his wife, my feelings and desires mattered, that I was not just a piece of property that he owned. My husband never understood my needs and he was simply incapable of creating the fun and excitement so important to me; it just was not who he was. He had no style, no sophistication, and he resented that I did. His anger made it even harder to accept his iron rule.

Finally taking action to free myself felt great. It felt like it was the right thing to do, and I knew that, whatever the future might hold, at least I would be the one in charge of it. I just did not want to die in Hickstown all alone; a lonely funeral would not have been my choice.

My family took a long time to realize I was moving. It did seem strange to them that I arrived in Los Angeles with seventeen pieces of luggage, not to mention three pairs of skis, ski poles, tennis racquets and heaven knows what else. "Why does she have so many suitcases?" they wondered. "For two weeks? She's gone mad." As December turned to January, and I still wasn't leaving, my father began asking questions: "Is she going back? What is she doing here?" There wasn't enough room in the house, he complained to my mother.

I took the hint. That same day, I went out and found an apartment—a tiny place in Beverly Hills—and registered the girls for school. We moved into a crappy apartment with no place to sit down; all I had was an outdoor wrought iron table and three chairs that I had taken from my mother's house. I had $1,000 in my pocket and figured I would quickly get a job and somehow manage to pay my bills. When I finally called my brother and told him the truth, which I wasn't going back, he was ecstatic. We were both jumping up and down hysterically. I broke the news to my parents and they were happy for me, too. The prison doors had been breached and I was able to step out into the glorious California sunshine. My father told me, "Don't ever go back, you belong here." Never go back, I won't let you.

The first job I found was working as a headhunter, finding candidates for corporate positions. It was grueling. I had to make 150 calls a day. By five o'clock, I was dead—but I was bringing home a little money. I'd take the scant income I had and divide it into a dozen envelopes to budget my expenses. I had one envelope for the electric bill, another for the gas, and so on. I kept them all in a little drawer in my tiny broken down kitchen as soon as I was paid. By claiming to be Shomer Shabbat, a small lie, I did get a break on Fridays at the end of the work week and would leave early; Jews who are Shomer Shabbat can't work past noon on Fridays, I told my supervisors and they did not object. T.G.I.F.

Dr. Boring and I remained locked in a battle of wills. He wouldn't come out and he wouldn't send money. For an entire year, he didn't send us a dime, but I refused to go back. He was pissed off at me and I was a little pissed off, too, struggling to get by in a job that took all my energy. The traffic back and forth to work took two hours and it was exhausting. But I never had second thought about moving again.

The solution was there all around me: a house that was on the market one day was sold the next. I barely blinked and a sign went up across the street from my apartment—"SOLD." The prices were incredible. In Pennsylvania, houses would sit on the market for two or three years. I figured our estate in Pennsylvania— a huge mansion on two acres—was worth around $120,000, and these teeny bungalows in Beverly Hills, with barely room enough to sleep four, were selling for close to $1 million. Not just selling, but disappearing like hotcakes! About this time, January of 1987 my brothers invested in a twelve-unit apartment complex, and their partner in the deal, a man named Dani, suggested that I try selling real-estate. "You'd be great at it," he said. Well, why not? I started a crash course, learned the laws, and breezed through the exam in no time. The test had 150 questions. It was supposed to take three hours. Twenty minutes after it started, I was done. As I went up to hand it in, I got flak from one of the proctors, an old woman in her seventies. "Sorry, you can't leave," she told me. She thought I was headed to the restroom. Be finished in twenty minutes? And pass? No way. But I did, and I think I got all of two answers wrong.

Three months after I'd arrive in this beautiful town I already was settled and now I had my real-estate license. Job hunting was a snap. At one real estate office, the broker/owner, a woman named Jan, a major player, looked me up and down and said, "You've got a license? You can work here. You'll be good for me. I'll make you a star." When I told her I'd let her know, she got huffy. "You walk out of this fucking office," she said, "and you're not getting a job in my town!" Wow! Welcome to the real world.

But she was wrong. I found the right place for me almost immediately—a narrow storefront, in the heart of Beverly Hills, where I met a graying ex-New Yorker who studied me through his reading glasses and seemed to like what he saw. Aside from an antique desk, the office was nothing special—no artwork, bare walls except for a sign, "Honesty is the best policy"—but he was a charmer, and he handled property for some of the biggest names in Los Angeles: His clients over the years would include whose who of the entertainment industry and Hollywood. Jack had happened to mention on the phone that his back was troubling him. "How's your back?" I asked him. He was impressed that I remembered. We chatted a few minutes and he said, "This is your desk, and I'm an honest man. You start here on Monday."

This realty-estate office became my piggy bank and my home, few blocks away from Rodeo Drive. It was across the street from the

Bistro Garden, an elegant courtyard restaurant where I would take clients to discuss deals and property over iced tea, poached salmon, and caviar. That was like a second office to me—a place to see and be seen. I was there at least three or four times a week, sometimes for two or three lunches a day. At Wharton, I had been taught that every encounter, every friendship, was a chance to do business, and I reversed it, too: every business dealing was a chance to meet new friends. I quickly learned to merge the two spheres into a rich and exciting life.

Thrilled at having a real career and a fabulous job, I was a whirlwind, full of energy. I'd arrived in the office every morning at seven or seven-thirty and work as long and as often as I needed to work. I was usually first to arrive and the last one to leave at night. My first deal came right away. A Persian man whom I'd met called and said, "I might have a listing for you, but first you have to appraise a house for me." The property was in Westlake Village, a community I knew nothing about, forty-five minutes north of my office, but I drove up there very early one morning, parked outside a real-estate office, and approached the first agent who showed up—because I knew that the first to arrive are the most responsible and often the sharpest. I asked the woman to look at some homes, rode around and saw ten properties, and quickly pinned down a price. I called my client and said, "It's worth $1.3 million." He said, "Exactly," and gave me the listing. I sold it in one weekend. My share of the deal: $30,000. *La dolce vita.* Wow! I did it. Now was time, to bring the husband and make him understand, making money in California is a piece of cake.

Life was never going to be the same. Immediately I made a trip to the Armani store on Rodeo Drive to buy my first Armani suit—and I still have it. In short order, I became a regular at Armani. The suits were made for me, for my business and my body. Every few months, I would be buying some new outfit, and I was always exquisitely dressed.

By the time I racked up that first commission, I was starting to realize that I was not going to become desperate and give up and go home and I was quite comfortable with me living in sunny California. This was my home and I was about to make a name for myself. And yet I felt I should try to do something for him so he could join us and keep our family together. But what could I do? I figured something will happen. The girls, especially missed their dad, and wanted their father around.

On a miserable, rainy day, I was sick with the flu, with two boxes of tissue and coughing like the dickens, I dragged out the Yellow Pages and started looking for hospitals and medical practices inquiring about offices for sale. Maybe someone needed a doctor or a partner or even wanted to sell an existing practice. Starting in the A's, I went through the alphabet, making cold calls for hours sounding like a sick rooster.

Took a little brake for lunch and again, started with the phone again, still coughing like a mad chicken. Because some facilities had more than one physician, I ended up reaching a few of the same places twice. One doctor said, "You're the same woman who called at eight o'clock this morning? God, you sound so sick and you must be desperate. How long have you been on the phone?" It was five in the evening, so he knew I'd been at it all day. We spoke a minute and he said, "I tell you what, I know of a practice. I will call them and tomorrow you can use my name and tell them I asked you to call."

The tip led to a job interview for Dr. Boring. I arranged it and called my husband to tell him to book a flight immediately and come out. He laughed and hung up on me. I called back and we had a bitter fight, but he agreed to at least go through with the interview. He came out, met the people, and they actually liked him. They offered him the job and off course he turned it down. I was incensed. Travel three-thousand miles, answer all the questions, impress the hell out of everybody, get the offer. A perfect opportunity to live in this beautiful city with gorgeous weather and reunite his family, and reject the offer? Say no? It was absurd. He was crazy. I stopped talking to him for weeks. Finally, the message started sinking in. The reality hit him that he had no other choice if he wanted to see me and his children. Pittstown was no longer an option.

Moving to follow us here was probably one of the toughest things he's ever done. He came west about a year after the kids and I arrived. We ended up practically giving away our grand house in the Pennsylvania countryside, selling it for only $100,000, a fraction of what it was worth. The house we bought, in the flats of Beverly Hills, was a tenth the size—about 1,500 square feet—and over four times the cost at $750,000! Did it really matter? Not to me. Though, when he was raking in a ton of money and I was selling property like crazy, he was still unhappy and was bitching every single day.

That first year alone we made $200,000, a fantastic income in the early 1990s, especially for a couple of Kmart shoppers who used to put furry fabric on the couch with Elmer's glue and couldn't afford disposable diapers.

I bought our house and sold it a year later, making couple of hundred thousand dollars. Now that was how to make serious money.

He was completely lost and had no idea what was going on. He was losing control and I was having the time of my life.

I won't say I was the last Persian Jew to leave Pittstown, but there couldn't have been enough left to hold a backgammon tournament. It seemed there were never more than a hundred Jews there, total.

In Beverly Hills it was a vastly different story. Persian Jews fleeing Iran during the revolution had been streaming into a number of American cities, including Great Neck, New York, where many of my relatives lived. Beverly Hills was another popular spot. Rich from oil and the wealth that surrounds oil, these uprooted souls loaded up what belongings they could and, like television's Clampett family, entered the land of swimming pools and movie stars. Not to mention Rolls Royces, Rodeo Drive, and the Polo Lounge.

The influx was tremendous. From Day One, I was being invited to Persian functions large and small. Here I was, living in the same community with men who had tried to court me during my Miss Iran days—now married, with children of their own. It was pleasant and strange to be meeting families who shared the memories I had of the boutiques and street bazaars of Tehran.

Suddenly I was spending time selling in the grand homes of my countrymen—gorgeous palaces with vaulted ceilings, Mediterranean-style courtyards, pools, and flowering bougainvillea. For one incredible dinner party I remember, I adopted a pure blonde look, my hair light and curly, and my coffee-brown eyes turned blue with cosmetic lenses. They nearly matched the turquoise top I wore as I stood talking with a friend in English. Other guests shared a joke in Farsi. The punch line came and I laughed right along with them.

Lovesick in Beverly Hills

They were stunned. "How does the American understand Farsi?" someone said. I laughed again and they got it. "Oh, she's Persian!"

It was wonderful to be in a city where it never snowed and where I could drive down Pico Boulevard and find dozen kosher markets and bakeries one after another and blocks after blocks. Every two or three weeks I'd get another listing. The Persians, of course, sought me out. I would tell them what I was going to do and how much I was going to get them for their properties, and I would end up getting it too.

My confidence was soaring. I was living my dream, dressing nice, raking in big-time commissions. I bought myself a beautiful white Rolls Royce. Boy did I get attention in the business community. I was colorful and quotable. My photo and story ran in USA Today, the Los Angeles Times, Philadelphia Inquirer, San Francisco Chronicle, and other publications. Millionaires would call me from Texas, Florida and New York to sell their properties. My husband: well, he was not a happy camper and he was having a shit fit.

Celebrities were all around us. The girls were attending Beverly Hills High School, earning straight A's. Angelina Jolie and famous stars children were in my carpool. In only a year, we had moved to a larger house, just south of Sunset—huge square feet, gorgeous location, fourteen-foot ceilings, massive living room, and a huge backyard with a pool. It was a glorious day and on top of it, I sold the Camden house for a hefty profit.

The former owners had included Edie Gourmet and George Segal. He complained about the mortgage payment—$8,000 a month—but I knew we could afford it and the neighborhood was wonderful. Steve Martin was one of our new neighbors. I used to give Martin a hard time about the way he would race down the street in his BMW sports car.

"One of these days you're going to kill me, I said laughingly" I said. "You drive so fast I cannot get out of my driveway." He was so wonderful and would smile and say, "Really?"

Tour busses and vans would rumble by all the time—as they still do. Packs of paparazzi moved about like dense flocks of birds. It was an intoxicating city to get to know, full of characters, glitzy restaurants, and social intrigue. I loved my job and worked like mad. I was on fire, and I learned fast. Nobody could keep up with me. I quickly became one of the top agents in Beverly Hills, handling some of the most expensive homes on the West side. I could appraise a place in a glance and be right on target. There wasn't a property I did not know and had not seen. At one point I had five listings in Beverly Hills of more than $5 million apiece, plus some smaller houses, and then a real whopper came my way—a place for over $7 million.

Every other month I had a $5 million, $6 million or $7 million property to sell. It was insane. Never had I slept around, or done cocaine, though I knew a ton of agents who did; my work was my high, a natural high, dealing in some of the premier properties in the world and meeting people galore, hearing all the inside gossip about who was divorcing whom, who was sleeping with whom. None of it could pass my lips, of course—an agent has to protect all of her clients' secrets—but I had some incredible experiences. It was like a game to me. There were all sorts of strategies involved.

Beverly Hills had its own culture, completely different than the Podunk town I had left behind, and I lapped it up. I discovered the opera, a passion that would always remain with me and give me a bit of peace. Every year I looked forward to attending the opening night at the Music Center in downtown Los Angeles. Greatly happy, I embraced these wonderful treasures of American life, but for the most part I worked, worked, worked, building my name and clientele in real-estate.

In those days It was perfectly legal to knock on doors to get more business. Having already sold three houses on the residential end of Rodeo Drive, north of Santa Monica Boulevard, I stopped at a place in the 700 block. A very formal guy came to the door, very gruff, and said, "Can I help you?" I asked if he wanted to sell. He said, "Call me tomorrow," and arranged for me to meet his boss—a big international businessman who spent only one month a year in Beverly Hills. He turned out to know everything about the California market. We hit it off and became very good friends.

"I'm looking for a house—a big house," he said. "If you find something, call me."

Driving around Beverly Hills, I stopped and thought, Well, this house looked interesting! Now I had a house in mind. When you have a white Rolls Royce, people always open the gate. This blonde saw me at the front gate, let me in, and met me at the front door. I said, "I've got a buyer for your house." She said, "Arabs? OK, come on in!" The insides were fabulous. The house had a bowling alley and a disco—better than Studio 54.

When I called my new businessman friend—by now he was in London—he said, "How much?" I gave him the asking price: $10 million. "How can I see it?" he said. I arranged to send him a videotape. At the time it cost $1,500 to produce such a tape, and I paid for it out of my pocket. Then came the key question: "What's the house really worth?" I was always honest. Probably between $6.5 million and $7.5 million, I told him. He made an offer for $7.5 million, and send me to pick up a check for a cool 1,000,000 for the deposit, but the owners stubbornly insisted on $10 million. It never sold. I never got a dime. The same owners still have it to this very day, but I was now very popular. Now I was selling homes with a phone call. The sale price for that house ten years later: $7.9 million.

There was a time, after I had been working a few years, and I was having trouble unloading a luxury condo in Westwood. It was priced at $1 million and nobody was selling $1 million condos in that neighborhood in those days. The place just sat on the market for month after month until finally the owner canceled the listing. He was a big-time businessman who I'd never worked with before. Three months later, I called him just to follow up. He wanted to see me. When I walked into his office there was an envelope on his desk.

"This is for you," he said. "For me?" It was a commission check. "But I didn't do anything," I told him. "Well, I did. I sold it," he said, meaning his condo. "You however worked so hard for me, you deserve it."

I was stunned. I couldn't believe it. He insisted that I take the check, and after I left I went directly to an appointment with another client—a flamboyant Italian named John, who loved to buy and sell fancy cars not to mention $100,000,000 properties. He'd buy a dozen Bentleys and a dozen Ferraris at a time. He always had thirty phone lines blinking in his office. He told his secretary, "Hold my calls Pishi's here, let me see what she has got for sale," and I sat down to present a $4 million offer on his house.

"How are you doing? What's new?" he said, making small talk.

I said, "You won't believe this," and I told him what had just happened with my previous client.

John asked who the guy was. When I told him, John said, "He's in default." John knew that the man owned a high-rise office building in the desirable commercial core of Los Angeles. "I love that building," he said, "and I want it. Get him on the phone! Now!" John demonstrated his interest by writing out a check and sliding it across the desk to me. I stared at all the zeroes—too many zeroes to count! "That's right," he said, "it's $100 million. Call him and make an appointment."

Goosebumps rippled all over my body, but I didn't let on, never even changed my expression. In my real-estate dealings, I am like Amarillo Slim—the ultimate poker player, cool as can be. Nothing ever impresses me. Nothing fazes me.

The seller told me on the phone that he didn't want to sell, but he agreed to meet us. On the day of the appointment, John and I met at the property to see the owner. The conference room was a luxurious space, done mostly in marble, high over the city. We sat down and our host again said his building was not for sale.

John, who's very sophisticated, leaned back and said, we are making an offer for $85 million—take it or leave it. We can draw up the papers later. I'll have my lawyers call you."

The owner agreed to take $100 million, but John, despite the check he had shown me, wouldn't go that high. He wouldn't budge beyond $85 million. The deal stalled. It would have meant a stupendous commission, but it wasn't goin to happen. About ten years later, I would have another occasion to make an offer on the building—this time the prospective buyer was from an Arab nation—and the numbers were even more staggering: $170 million. Still, the owner refused. His instincts were good. Today his office tower is worth over $500 million.

The same night I had presented John's offer of $85,000,000 I was flying high, feeling like a big shot. All I wanted was to share my happiness with my husband. While driving around town, I called my husband, inviting him to join me for dinner, but he said he was too busy and could not go out and had to spend the night at the hospital. I was to be alone again on a fabulous night like tonight? John called me right after I hung up the phone, asking me if I would meet him to discuss the sale of his own home. I said I will be right over.

I did not have to go home so I agreed. I met him at his house in Bel-Air. It was a magnificent piece of property, several acres. The land alone was worth $5 million. My brain kept on going, running numbers. The house was well done but was not quite of Architectural Digest caliber.

He asked me to join him in the living room. As I sat down, I said the parcel alone is worth around $5 million, and he said, "Wow, you are good," and then asked, "Would you like some Champagne?"

Well, it sounded great; except I was working and water would have been better. Half an hour later, he asked if I would like to join him for a bite to eat. All of a sudden I jumped up, and quickly walked toward the front door.

"Did I scare you?" he said. "I just thought you might be hungry." I thanked him for his kindness but told him I had to leave. As I left the front door, I noticed half a dozen red Ferraris and several black and brown Bentleys in his driveway.

Naturally I wondered to myself: Who is this guy?

I thought shopping would be a great thing to do, since I was mad as hell with myself for leaving a gorgeous guy and also mad at my husband, who never seemed to have time to be with me, even on a happy night like tonight. It was a long day and I became angry that I did not have a man who liked me for who I was. Sadness overcame me and I started crying. At a nearby mall, I grabbed a salad and sat lonely at a table. At the time there was a gorgeous store named Privileged that sold fabulous cloths and suits. Without a doubt this brown leather suit in the window was made for me. I very much wanted it. Finally, I gave the saleswoman my American Express card and bought the $1,300 suit—cheap compared to Armani. I wore the suit as I left and thought I looked fabulous, though my tears were telling me otherwise.

Life sucked but I really didn't give a shit. I had bigger things to worry about. The next day, I had to meet the Arabs for a listing that I had been working for a long time. Rushing to the computer I needed to manage my time effectively. There are so many ways of opportunities, where we can develop out talent and I was devoted to my job. I had priorities and at midnight I went back to my office, and started getting myself prepared for tomorrow; I had a presentation to make, envisioning myself rising above all obstacles.

Life was an adventure and I was going to go for a ride and try to be happy even if it killed me, remembering Machiavelli, who said, "Where the willingness is great, the difficulties cannot be great."

Over the course of some months, I'd put around $10 million in property in escrow, and yet I was very sad and very lonely. Because I spent so much time by myself, I poured myself into my job. Every deal was an adventure, every offer a gamble, and every client a trip. I learned all the tricks. Yet I never let myself be intimidated.

My philosophy was, and still is, if you play and work for the money you're finished. You have to do it for the high, and concentrate on getting the job done. Go, go, go, that was me. I'd look at thirty houses a week; get on the computer at six o'clock every morning. I'd wait for a listing to expire at midnight and show up bright and early on the owner's doorstep. I'd work fourteen hours a day, on edge all the time. I considered it my job to have a data bank in my head. If a client asks about a particular house, and you don't know anything about it, you're probably screwed. It can cost you the deal. You have to be out there on weekends, read every article you can—the L.A. Times, New York Times, Wall Street Journal. A guy would call and say, "What about this house on Shadow Hill Way?" I'd say, "Oh, my God, the kitchen is horrible." He'd say, "You've seen the house?"

Of course I'd seen it. I saw everything.

Listings are like gold to an agent. They are hard to get, but, if you have them, and you can get the deals done, they mean guaranteed income. I always got the deals done. People used to say, "If Pishi can't sell it, no body can." Selling extremely high-end homes meant having to go all out. If I had to hold an open house, I'd send embossed, personalized invitations to everyone I knew who might be interested. I would put on a show by hiring security guards and musicians. There were reasons to have security guards. Incidents had happened in which agents, or even owners, had been attacked at open houses, even stabbed, but such things rarely happened. The guards were a good safety measure but even more important as a marketing tool. Their presence gave a home status. The same for musicians: I'd have a pianist, or someone playing classical guitar or the cello. It was all about class. My open houses were one huge big party and I loved parties.

Such niceties were expensive. The agent absorbs the cost, but the expense is worth it when a commission check comes in for $100,000 or more. I remember one huge mansion that went on the market for around $12 million. I invested $25,000 just to make the brochure for it. This was before sophisticated computer graphics, and I wanted a special presentation—marbleized paper, certain artwork, the right color, a unique cover design. It took four months just to develop that brochure, but, oh, wow, was it something! Just one look at it was enough to make a buyer say, "Give me that house!" As for my husband, he said, "You are a sick girl," blowing all my money that way. I sold the house to my first client who came to see it.

My reputation grew. USA Today called to interview me, asking about my secret for selling expensive properties in a real-estate market that was stagnating nationally. The story made my life even more glamorous. After it ran, calls poured in from all over the country. One I most remember was from a guy in Miami, Florida, who was trying to sell four-hundred condos. He wanted me to handle them. I said I didn't have a license to operate in Florida.

A few weeks later, since I had refused to fly to Miami, he and his business partner showed up in Beverly Hills, just to meet me. We had dinner at Morton's, the famous steakhouse, one of my favorite places, and they made another pitch to have me work for them in Florida—which I couldn't.

My feeling always was, try to treat every client the same, whether he owned a $500,000 house or a $20 million house. Treat the customer with respect. Don't make the little person feel bad. Many, many times I ended up sacrificing a percentage of my commissions to help a deal go through. The people I met became my friends. The job was my social life. Some of the clients, who became friends thirty years ago, when I first came to Beverly Hills, are still some of my best friends today.

Needless to say, there were plenty of other people I tried to stay away from— snakes, cheaters, and unscrupulous operators. After the story ran in USA Today, I was being approached by a number of brokers who wanted me to work for them. One was a man who owned one of the biggest companies in Los Angeles—his signs were everywhere. He asked me to meet him for lunch at the Beverly-Wilshire Hotel. It was gratifying to have the attention. I wanted to at least hear what he had to say—and, boy, did he say the right things!

"I'm going to change your life," this smooth-talker told me. "You're going to be the number one agent in California. You're going to have to have a Lear jet to take you from one property to another."

Not long afterward he asked me to have dinner with him at Morton's. It began to sink in that he did not want me flying away in Lear jets. He much preferred the idea of having me in his bedroom. Not long after that, he hired a different agent to work for him—a very attractive woman with potential, and she did become one of California's top sellers. She also became his girlfriend.

Success won me attention and it also brought me resentment. Other agents disliked me. It infuriated them to see this flashy, high-powered Persian woman outselling them by a mile. I was too strong, too driven and too ambitious for them. After all I was a foreigner, and no Christy Brinkley. Some of these snakes did whatever they could to steal my clients. They were ruthless. They would go to my sellers and tell them to cancel their listings with me so these bastards could take over and make the commissions. It cost me a lot of money and of course there's no way I could ever prove it. That's how the business works in Beverly Hills.

One of my tormenters was Jan, the woman who nearly hired me before I went to work for Jack. Jan was jealous as hell of me. Once, she spotted me at a property and waited for me on the sidewalk. "Who do you think you are?" she said, complaining about the spiffy black Bentley I had bought—as if it was her business? My two assistants, and two cell phones and the music playing at my open houses had pissed her off.

"You need to come back down to earth!" she scolded. "Give someone else a chance. Haven't you made enough money?" It upset me, but it was quite a compliment.

Some years later, at a social function, I happened to bump into a man I knew who was extremely prominent in the community. He was one of my clients and then her client, but of course I said, "Hello, how are you?" and we spoke a few moments. Somehow the word got back to her and she threw a hissy fit—went straight to my manager and accused me of trying to steal her client. Is that crazy or is it crazy? What the hell is wrong with these people? They have no human feelings. What was I supposed to do, turn my back on a man I knew because he was working with her too?

That wasn't the only dark lining in my glittery world. An even darker cloud—an ugly, black nimbus—was Dr. Boring's growing resentment and anger. As bad as it was knowing that other agents hated me, it was worse to come home at night to a husband who was bitterly unhappy and completely out of place in the world. He did not like my work, the home we were living in, the town, and especially the people who lived here. We were always fighting. There was always something that bothered him. He put me down every chance he got. He nagged me about my car, my clothes, my friends, my lifestyle, and specially my American ways. God knows, till the end of the marriage I never cheated on him, and I certainly never asked him for money—I always made my own. If I wanted to buy a piece of jewelry, or whatever, I wouldn't even tell him; I'd just walk into Cartier and buy it on my own and pay for it without him knowing. It wasn't worth upsetting him, but he was always jealous and unhappy and most of all very negative. He couldn't stand that I was popular and successful, enjoying myself. He couldn't adapt. He hated me for having the guts and the will to get myself and the girls out of Pittstown and forcing him to move.

Our relationship was spiraling downward. A particular night that stands out in my mind was the night of my fortieth birthday. It was a warm summer night that I considered a major milestone in my life. The day began nicely enough, with the girls bringing me flowers and breakfast in my bed, looking out to the backyard.

As I walked into my office, one of my wealthy client from Saudi Arabia sent me a fabulous ring—an emerald and diamond thank-you for my hard work for him. A lady friend/client had the florist deliver a giant basket of pink roses to my office. The basket took over the entire desk, leaving no room for paper work. Nothing arrived from my husband, not even a phone call, though I expected it and kept waiting.

That night, when I got home, I thought he had made plans to go out for dinner, and immediately things began to go wrong. It became clear that he'd forgotten the occasion— he hadn't even made a reservation. Trying to mask his mistake, he suggested going to Bistro Garden, where the staff knew me and a reservation wouldn't have been necessary.

Then he objected to taking the Rolls. He had brainwashed the girls to hate my car, despite how vital it was for my business. I held my tongue. As I smiled, I tried to keep a positive outlook not ruin the night. I drove us to Bistro Garden and said: you know guys, I don't want to go here tonight, I am here everyday, and why again tonight? Let's go someplace else. Bistro Garden was too mundane and familiar, and I said, let's go and I started to drive.

We drove, instead, to Bistro, a place up the street operated by the same owner, but it was closed—it is never open on Mondays and I off course did not know that. Mondays was for Morton's. Next we tried another beautiful garden restaurant right up the street—jam-packed; the waiting list was enormous. On we went to a classy, expensive place not far from the girls' school. Nobody was there. The restaurant was dead. It was deader than dead, and I certainly wasn't going to mark my fortieth year in a dead, empty room. We got back into the car and I felt so unloved.

Still trying to salvage the evening, I said, "I've got a great idea— let's go to my favorite place, Stringfellow's," a beautiful jazz spot on

Via Rodeo at Wilshire Boulevard. Rich dark woods, pink lights, an ambiance like old London—it was a perfect environment. Besides, I loved jazz. But, uh-oh, when we pulled up out front there were no valets, no cars. I got out and hurried to the door. The place had gone out of business the week before.

Now it was late, we were all famished, and I was at a snapping point. "You're really pathetic," I said, getting back in the car. "You couldn't make a goddamn reservation for dinner for your wife?" That's as much as I vented, not wanting to upset the kids. But I was fuming. I picked up the car phone—which always pissed him off, since he hated me having a car phone—and I dialed Morton's. Tom, the Maitre D', who was absolutely wonderful, advised me not to come—it was crowded. "But it's my birthday," I told him. He was silent a moment. "All right, Pishi, come on, I'll take care of you."

We showed up around nine-thirty, exhausted and pretty mad. The place as always was packed and here was a Who's Who of Hollywood's elite: Julia Roberts, studio exec Barry Diller, Tom Brokaw from the television news. Tom the manager gave me a huge hug—and, oh, this really ticked off my husband. He couldn't stand it when these men would hug me.

Five minutes later we were seated at my regular table. Tom came over, got down on one knee, and said, "Happy birthday to my favorite girl!"

Now Dr. Boring was even more upset. He started flipping out, complaining and making innuendos during dinner, right in front of the girls. "Look at that," he said, "giving you hugs, getting down on their knees. What do you do that they do that for you?"

Lovesick in Beverly Hills

"You can't even make a reservation," I shot back. "You couldn't even make a goddamn reservation for your wife's fortieth birthday! After the party I threw for you!" I had gone all out for his on his fiftieth—a bash for seventy people aboard a yacht. He was unwilling to reciprocate by making sure we could get in somewhere for dinner was an absolute slap in the face. I ordered a double martini, excused myself and went to the bathroom, where I cried my eyes out. Who was sitting in the back of the room but the stunning and beautiful Claudia Schiffer, dressed to kill. One look at her and with tears running down my face, the moment and the evening was now completely ruined. I felt like a melted giant ice cream sundae. She was so awfully gorgeous and I felt so awfully sad and ugly.

Dinner was miserable. I tried to get through it. Tom sent us a chocolate soufflé' on the house, which certainly didn't improve my husband's mood. When we finally got home, around eleven o'clock, I asked him, in a sweet, loving way, "Where's my present? Or did you forget that too?" At least I would find out if he bothered to buy me anything.

The kids ran into their bedrooms and slammed their bedroom doors. We never saw them again that night. He called to our oldest, "Where's her present?" He handed me a box with real cheap wrapping paper. Inside was a little vase, about ten inches tall. "It's beautiful," I said. What else could I say? I couldn't help crying. A week later, I saw the exact same vase in a window at Pottery Barn, priced at $8.99 on sale.

I always believed class is something you cannot acquire. You either have it or you don't.

5

Rumbles from Vesuvius

My second fortieth birthday luncheon celebration was somewhat happier than the first, despite the fact that I had to throw it for myself. It took place a few days later at Bistro Garden conveniently located across the street from my office and during business hours. I chose a Parisian theme and sent out invitations half in English and half in French. Forty people attended; my husband was not among them, I guess he was too busy. "Isn't it a little ridiculous?" he said, that I would throw a birthday party for myself.

Not to me. I wanted the chance to do it right and mark the occasion with some fun. My attitude was, he didn't have a party for me actually tried to make sure it was memorable day for me. He did nothing but ruin the day. Why shouldn't I have a party for myself? Still, I was aware of the people talking behind my back, especially the Persians guests. They were making fun of me. Who does she think she is? Throwing a party for herself? Driving a Rolls Royce all over the place? Does she think she's Princess Caroline? Too good for everyone else? Never mind that I was driving the car because I was showing properties and besides I loved cars.

They didn't care. They wanted to hurt and ridicule me. They were spreading rumors, which found their way back to me, that I was not being loyal, that some lover was giving me the car. Absolutely absurd and extremely painful to a woman who had always been loyal in spite of the hell I lived in. In the Jewish faith I heard, accusing someone erroneously is a sin. To make wrong assumptions that damage someone's life is so perverse and unfair. By the way one of my biggest clients framed me too. A Fortune 500 company. Oh well! it's ok. God always has a way. It is called poetic justice.

Yet the talk was always there. My husband's Persian friends would actually show up at his office and spread these lies behind my back, implying that I had a boyfriend and that he was being played for a fool. Far, far from the truth! With my cultural upbringing, I couldn't even allow myself to look a man straight in the eyes. An affair? I wished. Yet his friends hounded him. "You let your wife have a car?" they would say. He would confront me and I would swear I needed the car for my business, swear I was faithful. It wasn't enough. "Stop showing off," he would say. "You're making me look bad."

Sometimes his friends would report that I was driving around town with a man in my car. "Yeah, I was showing him a house," I'd have to say. "Did they tell you that his wife was in the back seat?"

He was like a simple country boy who was very uncomfortable with his flashy modern wife. One thing was true: I was flashy and I liked it.

In Pennsylvania he had been a big shot; here, he was just another guy, a working stiff, while I could stroll down Rodeo Drive and ten people would know me. It freaked him out. He hated it. It was the same in Brentwood, Bel-Air, Holmby Hills—I knew the right people, because of the type of business I was in, I had connections, and he couldn't keep up. He was not my equal, but he wanted to be in control. My upbringing had ingrained me with the idea that marriage is forever. No matter what, for better or worse, you stayed together. Period. Divorce was never an option. So even as we fought and struggled and watched the relationship deteriorate, we maintained a façade to the world and tried as best we could to meet each other's needs.

He made up for the $8.99 birthday vase with a pair of expensive but small Lalique vases—one a gorgeous crystal bird, the other a lovely romantic figure of a man and woman. They were little bubbles of niceness in our ocean of misery. Later, when the marriage hit the rocks, they would mysteriously disappear. Wonder who stole them?

He was making huge money, $1 million a year, but I never took or asked for a dime from him. At any given instant, I had access to well over $100,000 in our accounts and sometimes far more than that, and I never, ever touched it. This was a key fact that he would completely overlook when we were fighting in divorce court, and he and his cutthroat lawyers were accusing me of filching nearly a million and half dollars in cash that he himself had taken. More about that later. Suffice it to say, I made my own income. I was proud of being self-sufficient and able to find my own opportunities.

Strangely enough, his chronically bad back, which had bothered him for years, soon led to another business for me in addition to real-estate: manufacturing luxurious custom multi-color cotton and silk robes. The seeds of the idea took root when I had to see a specialist in Marina del Rey for his slipped disk. The problem was so severe that he had to sleep on the floor for months at a time. During the exam, he had to wear a chintzy robe that might have come from a 5 & 10 cent store. I started thinking there should be very posh, high-quality robes for executives, just as there are in the five-star hotels in China and

Japan. Americans never seem to have such robes, even at the luxury hotels. It occurred to me that this was a niche that could be filled—and I could fill it. By education, I was a natural entrepreneur, always looking for opportunities and now I was going to take advantage of my knowledge.

Eventually, I spoke to a man named Sherman, the father of one of my daughter's classmates. Sherman had made a fortune with his own clothing company and sold it in his forties to live a life of ease. Sherman encouraged me to go forward with my idea. He showed me the vast warehouse in downtown Los Angeles where his own company had operated, and he gave me tips on setting up my own firm. Starting with my research, I made calls to China, Japan and Korea, talking to manufacturers and textile mills. I made samples in different colors and fabrics and arranged to have photographs taken for brochures. In need of a logo, and a factory, I learned that in Japan the fine robes are known as yukatas, and I dubbed my company Yukata U.S.A.

Before long, I had orders from top hotels, including the Hyatt-Regency, Ritz Carlton as well as Circus Circus, Harrah's, and Monte Carlo Hotel and Casino, in Las Vegas. At $30 a pop, the yukatas were selling like good-old American hotcakes. That first year alone I sold 10,000 robes, and I was working to the point of exhaustion, juggling orders and multi-million-dollar listings. A one-woman show, responsible for all sales, marketing, distribution and shipping.

There was a day—I'll never forget—when I got home at five in the afternoon with about 1,200 newly made robes in boxes that I had picked up myself from my factory in downtown Los Angeles. It was my job to label and ship them. I had to lift and carry them into the house by myself. One box fell apart on me, dumping about eighty robes onto the driveway. Suddenly the lawn sprinklers came on, and I scrambled to grab all the robes before they got wet. After I had picked them up, I was so beat I lay down right there on the driveway, breathing hard and thinking, "What the hell am I doing? I've got to save the robes and ship them to the client!" I didn't have an ounce of energy left. But I did save every piece and happily walked in and started to fill another purchase order. Life was just a big huge party and I was having the time of my life.

The success of my robes was another strain on the marriage, and now the robe business was too easy, so now I had decided to go back to school and study to become a lawyer. I loved political science and was very much into the "principle of things"; I thought to be in real estate plus have a law degree was something great to have. So I decided to go back to school. At the time, I thought I would make a great lawyer. He was anything but happy for me. He was stuck in a cultural mindset that frowned on women having careers, and now not only I had two careers I was going to school! We were always on totally different wavelengths. My life was a high-intensity show playing out on digital widescreen plasma, and he was tuned in to static-marred AM radio. We couldn't communicate anymore. We couldn't understand each other beside I had no time anyway; At this point I had given up and could have cared less. I was flying and he was still riding on his donkey. He was a nice guy but, he was never for me—there was no chemistry. I remember New Year's Eve, 1993, when that awful year was coming to a close. We were on vacation in Hawaii. Midnight drew near and he couldn't stand being with me. I cried. I was so miserable. Not that he beat me, or abused me, or drank too much, but he got in the way of anything that might have brought me fulfillment. My loneliness and desperation were almost too much to describe. I pleaded with God for a better 1994—"Please, God, let it get better. I feel so lonely. He is never home, and I know there is no love, but save my sanity." What I didn't know was that the tornado was only a baby; it was going to expand into a monster storm. The volcano was rumbling; there were explosions and fireworks ahead and a real tsunami.

Around this same time, the girls were graduating and going off to college. Both got accepted and chose to attend UC Berkeley, a wonderful opportunity for any student. Though I was sad, now it was clear, the house would be empty, they were going to leave me too, though he didn't see it that way.

In his skewed way of thinking, this was another example of my failings. He accused me of being a terrible mother because the girls were leaving home. The children of good Persian mothers enrolled at nearby campuses such as UCLA, Cal State Northridge and Santa Monica College, not somewhere four-hundred miles away. On the night that our youngest moved out, Dr. Boring really gave it to me, and we had an awful fight. The whole time he made me feel like I was a real loser and a bad mother.

He was certain now that the girls would never find suitable Persian husbands and it was entirely my fault—I was too Americanized. Nice girls didn't go off to some school too far away to drive home on weekends. Nobody would marry such a girl. That's actually what was going through the man's brain. A doctor no less was speaking with such utter nonsense. Naturally, he wanted a Persian son-in-law. Once again, I cried my heart out—more tears on top of tears. What's that old song, the one-hit wonder? "Man has cried a billion tears." That's me, too—the story of woman who missed her kids terribly, yet happy that they were going to attend one of the finest universities anywhere.

Four years had passed since my ruined birthday party and the fighting was worse—now it was constant. He was impossible to talk to, mad at everything. I begged him to explain to me what was wrong and what was bothering him. We started seeing a therapist—a top professor—at UCLA. The psychiatrist listened to us and, after several months, gave us his blunt assessment. "She is fine and very happy. She's OK," the therapist said, turning to my husband. "You've got learn to enjoy life and spend time together. You've got to catch up to her and share some hobbies. She is lonely and misses you. You're not going to change her."

As I sat in the huge black leather chair in his office, I started crying. I was there in my black Hermes riding boots and matching Armani cashmere jacket. My blonde hair was grown out to a nice length. I was a picture of style, and he was exactly the opposite—the square peg who had yet to face the fact that his dearest beliefs and attitudes were hopelessly out of date. He sat there and brooded. He was in turmoil, emotionally. Sheer pride was going to keep him from adapting. If he couldn't change me, I sure wasn't going to change him, either. He'd keep himself stuck in his joyless, far-away world. That meant I was stuck, too. We were like two bronzes anchored in concrete—going nowhere. But the girls came first; they were what mattered to me. During Thanksgiving, the girls came home and I tried to maintain the peace. This was 1996, a year that's burned into my memory forever.

That November, something was terribly wrong with him. The more I tried to please him, the more I tried to make the kids feel good about being home, the more antagonistic he became. If we weren't fighting, he was brooding and distant. The man was getting worse right before my eyes, picking on me at every chance and in front of the children.

Only days after experiencing the joy of the girls' arrival, I happened to open a bank statement for a dormant S Corporation account, a fund where I kept over a $1 million just for emergencies. Only there wasn't $1 million in the account. Instead, I saw a very startling balance—barely over $13,000. A nonsense figure, as far as I was concerned. A typographical error? Was it an errant deposit I hadn't known about? Impossible! But what type of number was it? It's funny how certain things can completely blindside you, catch you so off guard so you don't even have a clue. What about the million dollars?

Sure that it was a mistake, I called Director's National Bank in Beverly Hills and talked to Marla, one of the employees I had known for years. Somehow there was a mistake, I told her. She laughed and said, "The bank doesn't make mistakes Pishi." She assured me that the $13,000 was ours—there was not some erroneous deposit—but she invited me to drop by the bank when I could so we could double check and make sure the figures were right. Still thinking it was an error, I hung up and, believe it or not, I forgot all about it. I dismissed it from my mind thinking the bank had deposited the money into my account by mistake. My girls were here for a couple of weeks and I got involved in other things.

After Christmas, when the girls were home again, we took another trip to Hawaii, to the Grand Wailea Resort, to spend the holidays with some very close friends and their children. My husband fought with me from the minute we stepped onto the plane. As we reached our room, and in front of everybody, onceagain he lashed out at me. He lost control and words were coming out that I had never heard before, embarrassing me in front of the kids and our friends. Shit! This was the first and in public now. What was wrong with him? I did not say anything! All I said was, "Why two queen beds?" It would be nice to have one king size bed, a bigger bed so we can sleep together. He started fighting with me and from then on the vacation went to hell.

On New Year's Eve, we—all eight of us—agreed to have dinner and then go dancing downstairs in the discotheque to celebrate the New Year. By now he was fuddled and unhinged. One look at me and in front of all of us, he started again. Well, he hated the way I wore my hair, my tight white pants and jazzy, royal-blue top—not to mention my deep tropical tan. I just kept quiet wondering what had happened to him. He no longer was the same man. We left for dinner around eight and managed to get through it without incident. I sensed something was definitely bugging him. We arranged to meet our friends again at ten o'clock at the lobby.

Meanwhile, I went up to the room to touch up my make-up. Coming back down, I could not find anyone. Feeling strange, in my high heels I must have looked for forty-five minutes, up and down, indoors and out—they'd all disappeared, even the kids. Very puzzling, where did they all go? By 11:30 I thought maybe they are at the disco. I figured maybe I should go downstairs to look for them all. That's it, that is where they are.

Sitting all alone and trying to save eight seats I felt very stupid and angry. Midnight came and went. No sign of my family or our friends. Now I was not only worried, I was—furious. They had definitely gone someplace else and my children too. To hell with them, I thought, and I got up and started dancing by myself, trying to make the most of another botched evening while tear drops washed away my makeup. It was now one in the morning and still they were nowhere to be found. And yet I was actually started having fun. About one thirty in the morning, lo and behold, he shows up with murder in his eyes. He sees me dancing and comes charging toward me, calling me awful names and ordering me to leave.

"You leave," I told him. "You are really a sick man, I'm staying and having a great time. And how dare you spoil my New Year's Eve! Where did you all disappear to?" He left without answering.

I was pissed beyond belief. The next day, on the beach, I was not talking to anybody. The vacation was shot. The greatest yearning I'd always had was the need for respect, and he was killing that, too, being an ass. I came to believe he was having a mid-life crisis. Something was definitely wrong with him. Not having a clue, what he had done. He was not himself. At home, he reinforced this impression by trying to impose new demands. He wanted me to start getting up at six in the morning, for example, to cook him breakfast. I was to wait and not have dinner until he was home to eat with me. What? Ok fine. That was what made him happy, ok I will wait up. When he typically got home at any time from seven at night to three in the morning? I told him it wasn't fair, especially when his ridiculous hours kept me from getting any rest. "You never go and sleep in the next room," I said. "You wake me up night after night with your goddamned deliveries and I have to go to work the next day. I'm a basket case." He would get calls from patients practically every hour. My nights were so ruined that I was having to take naps on the office couch so I could get through my last appointments and have the strength to run my robe company. I tried to get him to make changes in his own life that would help to save the marriage. "Take at least half a day off every week so we can be together," I urged him. "You are never home. I never get to see you, and then you are the one constantly bitching? I can't stand you anymore, what is wrong with you lately?" "I'll tell you what, get an apartment, find a girlfriend, and in a year come back home. It's OK. You're having a mid-life crisis. I will wait for you." I said all that and I left the house—I was sick of fighting. Was it too much to ask to live in a world where I didn't have to fight with him all the time?

By this time, I was all into my political science classes at SMC in Santa Monica. I was taking all the requirements to go to law school and was now thirteen units short. I was busy and exited as ever and this man was not a very happy person. He was making my life hell.

January came and went and the bank statement again showed $13,000 balance.

Finally, in February receiving the wrong bank statement again, I decided to go see Marla. The bank was a few blocks away from my office and I had to deal with the screwy balance in the S Corporation account. The statements in hand with no thought of the missing a million dollar, I walked into the bank. That is it! Off course it was a mistake.

But now came the stunner. Now came the blindside wallop. Marla was there, so was Rich, the bank manager—I always laughed and joked around with them—and Marla brought the numbers to the screen on her computer. I pointed out the apparent mistake; this was neither my account nor my social security numbers. It was my husband's. "Do me a favor and pull up my account" I said. No, the figures were right, she said, and I started to get concerned—how could this have happened? This wasn't chump change that was missing, $980,000. Marla said: "Pishi, listen, you have to calm down. Your life is so crazy busy and you are always rushing all the time, running. Don't you remember, three or four months ago, you transferred the money out?"

"What transfer?" I said, raising my voice. "I transferred *what*? I did? Why? No one can touch this account, what are you talking about?"

Rich, from the end of the room, took one look at me and knew something was amiss. He came forward and said, "What's wrong?" I pointed to the screen and showed him the transfer dated November 26, 1996. "Show me the authorization letter," I demanded. Any such transfer requires a signed letter.

He took me upstairs to the corporate offices to show me the paperwork. My signature appeared to be on it, but I had never signed it. In fact, the so-called authorization signature did not even look remotely close to my handwriting. It was clearly a forgery. I grabbed the letter right out of the floor manager's hands, stared at it for a second, and shoved it into my bra. It was my husband's stationary and his name and address were printed on top of it.

"No, no, no, you can't take that!" scolded Susan, the executive manager. "That's the property of the bank." Rich told me to give it back or he would call security. My body was vibrating like a big Cuisinart full of nuts, and I wasn't giving letter back. It was going to go into my safe at home and nobody was going to see it until I dealt with the forgery with legal action. Not knowing, him and his lawyers had started to frame me. I begged Rich to fix the problem with the account. It was obvious to me immediately that my good old husband had somehow used his letterhead with my signature on it to fake my name on a transfer request, moving the money into an account of his own that I could not touch. Setting me up? Wow. What a piece of shit! After twenty-six years of marriage, this was how the son of a bitch was treating me. He was totally screwing me over. It froze my blood and I was suffering from a bad case of the shakes.

It made my blood boil. For four months he had kept it to himself that he had moved the funds—yelling and griping the whole time, probably out of guilt. And that's why Hawaii fell apart. I felt like such a dummy, putting up with all the hell he had been giving me while he was secretly laughing all the way to the bank. Was there another woman too? He was provoking me to file for divorce? At the time I had no way to know.

Rich escorted me back downstairs and I was still agitated. I started yelling at Marla: "How could you have let him get away with that?" She replied, "It was not me. Ask the private banking manager." There was a customer phone near Marla's desk and with trembling fingers I dialed Dr. Boring's office and got the bastard on the phone. By now I was just screaming out of my lungs. Oh, my God, I really gave it to him. "You son of a bitch, why did you do that? Why? Why? What did I ever do to you? Other than being a good mother, a wife and a decent person? How on earth could you do this to me? Why? Why?" I continued yelling. "You are a piece of shit, fuck you!"

He didn't have an answer. How could there be any answer? I hung up on him and went out and walked the streets of Beverly Hills— those beautiful streets, lined with glitzy shops and majestic mansions, the palm trees soaring to the blue sky. I remember I was wearing a size 38 Vicky Teal black-and-white polka-dot suit, trimmed with Dantel French lace, and a big black hat. *Tres chic*, camera-ready for any of the passing tour busses, but inside I was really hurting. I walked for hours, lonely, missing the girls, feeling unloved and wishing so desperately there was a man in my life who loved me. A man whom I could love in return. A man I could hug and kiss and make love to with passion. I would have given anything to be in love and experience that special sort of happiness that I knew nothing about. Maybe if I loved the man I was married to, this would have never happened. However, the pressing question in my head was really what to do about the deteriorating marriage. I needed to do something. Divorce, again was not an option. Was it finally time to get out? How much more could I take? After all I had done and gone through to keep the lousy sacred union together, it seemed to be falling apart, piece by piece. It was tragic—and terrifying.

Like any woman who has ever faced such a crossroads, I had a lot to think about. Besides the fact that divorce was against everything I believed in, it would be devastating to the girls, and I couldn't let them be products of a broken home. Divorce would thoroughly shake up my world. It would mean leaving the home I loved, maybe moving back into a smaller place, and there would be a huge fight over property and alimony. Many of my friends, and possibly family too, would disown me. I had seen it before, where the woman gets ostracized so unfairly.

No, divorce was out of the question. Beside I have never been alone. No! no way.

By the time I was done walking, I knew I was not going to leave him—despite such an awful trick. It was only money. There were many things about my life that I liked and it was all I could handle.

To sell real estate and market my robes was my high and I just could not handle life with having to go through the ordeal of a divorce and living alone. A divorce was the very last thing I wanted. I wanted to be a lawyer and that to me was much more exiting. Money had no meaning. My business was very successful and I did not need his charity.

The following day, my office assistant, Susan, announced that he was on the line. I picked up and he started yelling, "You call the bank and tell them to put the money back where I had it! "Within minutes, Director's National, fearing a lawsuit from me, had transferred the $980,000 back into my corporate account where I had expected it to be. He had a fit! I refused. I wasn't about to let him put that money out of my reach again.

Well, the stubborn SOB was not about to give up. He kept calling—every half hour, badgering me, interrupting my entire office and my work. The man was berserk. He was completely freaking out, and he wasn't going to let go of it. Finally, after a few days of his nonstop haranguing, and against the emphatic wisdom of my financial adviser, I agreed to let him transfer half of the money, while keeping the other half where it was. My half of the money would eventually go into my own account and be spent on attorneys' fees.

We were trying to negotiate a peace. I attempted to assert his power by insisting that I will be the good stay-at-home wife he had been raised to expect. He wanted me to give up my jobs—both of them—which was completely out of the question. On other matters,

I compromised. I began getting up early to make his breakfasts. By dinner time, I made sure I was home and I cooked for him, setting the table with lovely candles and flowers. Most of the time he was at the hospital, too busy to show up. In April, I got blindsided again. Our accountant called and asked me to give him a check for $30,000 for my share of the taxes. He sounded weird. Here we go again. Not sure why but for some reason, I felt (my own gut and the my power of psychic ability) he was lying and hiding something from me. Plus, the figures didn't seem right, given my enormous number of deductions. Quickly I arranged to see an independent accountant to find out why I should owe so much extra money. His name was Sam and one of my colleagues had recommended him. Sam looked over the previous returns and papers—his and mine—and raised his eyes toward me.

"This is the man you are living with? Your husband? Really?" he said. "He's cheating you. He's maximizing your taxes so you pay more and he pays less."

Right away I phoned our family accountant, and he said, "Pishi," just give me a check. I don't want to get in the middle of a family feud. I need the check now, today." Family feud? What family feud? What was he talking about? OK. Fine. Dr. Boring was screwing me over again and I had no choice but to take it. We had enough money. I had my career. I would just deal with it and go on. I came home that night furious. He was starting to truly scare me. I wrote a check for $30,000 and hand-delivered it to the accountant's office the same day in Marina Del Rey.

The month of May came. Rain was pouring down. Every Sunday, I would write the checks and pay the bills, make up all the deposits for his office and do all the household checks, a simple routine that always quieted my mind. I loved the mornings alone, particularly when it rained. To me the rainfall was magical, touching emotional chords of wonder and comfort. The rain made me glad to be indoors, enjoying the shelter of my home—the art, the flowers, and the lush garden I so dearly cared for. I put on my favorite French CD—I've always loved French music—and fixed a delicious cup of coffee. I sat down to start my book keeping work.

As I was trying to make myself comfortable in my big black leather chair behind my desk, I was shocked by what I saw. A pharmaceutical slip of paper, the kind used to write prescriptions, was lying on the desk. My adoring husband, before he left last night, had written a note and placed it in front of me, on my desk: "If you want to live in this fucking house, you pay the fucking mortgage because I am not going to anymore."

What the hell was wrong with this man? What sort of mad demons possessed him? My body froze. I was stunned. Once again, he was slapping me in the face. I picked up the note, tore it into pieces, and threw it into the trash can. I didn't know what to do. I didn't know how to react. A few awful minutes went by, I reached into the trash can and picked up the scraps of the slip of paper. Now I had enough. I had taken enough shit for twenty six years, more than any woman should tolerate. I wasn't sure yet what I would do, but I taped the note back together and hid it in my wallet. He was asking for it and now I thought it was time to stop the bullshit. He wanted a divorce and I was about to go forward and file.

It was the beginning of a 9.1 earthquake.

6

Living on Lockdown

One of the loveliest dinner parties I ever threw took place in early May of 1997 in our backyard, a fairyland of twinkling white lights—thousands of them. We had valet parking, a live band and white-gloved attendants who served a gastronomic menu of fabulous French food and fine wine. One-hundred guests showed up. The only thing that was visually missing was fireworks.

But the fireworks would happen soon enough. No one knew it, but the party was a goodbye to the home I loved—an enchanting farewell marking the end to twenty-six years of a one-sided marriage. This was my secret for this evening, a milestone marking a new direction I was taking in my life.

About a third of the guests were Persians, smiling to my face even while I knew they felt threatened by me. It wouldn't occur to me until later that I was just too Americanized for many of them, who had not yet adapted to the culture in Los Angeles–and especially in Beverly Hills. Looking back at how they mocked my English and my lifestyle, I can see the irony in it; now, most of them, are complete converts, highly intelligent and successful. They are wearing expensive designer clothes, and embracing American consumerism. Some of them have five Bentleys in their huge circular driveways in front of $20 million homes.

Athena

It was May of 1997, many changes lay ahead. Slipping on an incredible red duchess satin strapless gown and long white gloves, and wearing my stunning diamond necklace, I ignored the petty jealousies and tried to savor a poignant moment. For some reason I was so happy, celebrating my leaving behind years of pain. It was my personal celebration of the end of the lousy marriage, the end of many bad years, and a completely new start, even though my future was clouded by uncertainty. I was planning to file for divorce the first thing on Monday morning. The note that he had left me, which I had torn up and thrown away, only to rescue and tape back together, was going to be my ticket for a whole new world.

After all the conflict, all the years of fighting and trying to make the dysfunctional marriage work as hard as I could, that hostile message had been the proverbial last straw, the final act of hostility that made me realize that divorce really was the right answer, that I should summon my courage and do it. That rainy Sunday, I had tucked the note away in my wallet, left the house, and took a long drive. I needed time to sort out my conflicting thoughts. I put on one of my favorite French artists, Patricia Kaas, and ended up in Malibu, following the jagged path of Pacific Coast Highway. While driving, I drown myself in deep thoughts, gazing at the ocean I tried to figure out a plan. The powerful desire to try to salvage the marriage was crumbling beneath the weight of too much pain and too many wasted years—the endless attacks on my career, my character, my personal self, and the devastating loss of freedom from the get-go in an arranged marriage forced upon me that was so against my will.

With my girls away in college, I was lonelier than ever and there was no reason to go on enduring pain and abuse from a man who seemed to be getting worse by the minute. Divorce became the only clear solution. The dinner party would turn out to be a brief moment of joy in the middle of the swirling winds. There is no way to imagine how blusterous the storm would be, and what a humiliating and raging spectacle the trial would become, not to mention the nightmare it would be dealing with attorneys—a bunch of cold-blooded bastards who would charge enough to buy the crown jewels- not to mention the nasty and untrue garbage my wonderful husband was spread out through the entire community, about how I had ripped him off.

I don't know if I could have coped without God's intervention. Going ahead with the divorce was like stepping off a cliff—scary beyond belief and there would be no turning back once I made the leap. Dr. Boring reacted to me filing for divorce exactly as I might have expected. He took it as a personal insult. A Persian man is raised to believe he owns his wife like a piece of property—like a cow or an automobile. A wife does not file for divorce from her husband. No way.

He was angry, humiliated, horribly depressed. He was determined not to let it happen in a fair community-property state. He became rash and unpredictable.

There was $500,000 in cash locked away in the house. It was money we kept as an emergency fund inside a safe. There had never been a problem over several years with keeping such a huge amount of money, and I began to worry about it. Half of the cash was rightly mine, as community property, but I became deathly afraid he would take it, just as he had transferred the $980,000 out of my S Corporation account.

He was already trying to screw me, that much was obvious. If I were not careful, there was a real chance he would take all the financial assets and stick me with virtually nothing. I had no CDs, no bonds, no other real savings, and no way to pay the entire mortgage—$11,000 a month, including taxes and insurance—on my own, if he got everything and disappeared. I would lose it all. I knew he had already bought a condo in Israel behind my back, and maybe other properties; after the divorce, I found a receipt for the wire transfers in his desk drawer.

How could I protect the $500,000? Somehow, until the divorce was over and we were no longer living together, I had to keep his hands off it. I decided that I would move the family safe to my mother's place in Westwood because there was security in the high rise and no one could get into the elevator.

On a Saturday morning, I asked my gardener for help. Yes, the gardener. He loaded the safe onto the back of his truck and I followed him in my car. As far as he was concerned it was an empty safe. My mother had no idea what was in there either—she was clueless.

The truth is, the safe was a decoy. Knowing that he knew about the safe being moved, and he might try to recover it, I took the extra precaution of removing the half-million in cash and stuffing it into an oxblood leather duffel bag that I had bought at Galleries Lafayette in Paris. The duffel bag, in turn, went into my bedroom armoire. I hired a handyman to come in and modify the armoire, creating a secret compartment. Inside that compartment, the handyman installed a little door, with a small lock positioned where nobody could see it. I bought a tiny lock for $1.99 and secured it behind all my pocket books, records, and cassette tapes. Stashing the money there, I thought, would keep it in the house—I wasn't stealing it—but my husband would think it was elsewhere, and he would not have access to it.

Boy was I so stupidly brilliant. I am such a genius, or so I imagined. How dumb can you get? You'd better believe he was already looking for it. He was going out of his mind wondering where the safe went. He wondered where in the hell the half a million was.

Barely a month went by and I noticed that the bottom drawer of the armoire was broken—it wouldn't pull out—it didn't occur to me until much, much later that he was sniffing around too close for comfort.

My bedroom door was always locked in my absence. Later, I realized he used the master bathroom window to get in by means of a very tall ladder. Even after eight months, he still was looking and sniffing around, he had not discovered the secret compartment or the duffel bag. Beside, he and his buddies were too dumb. Dumber than I was!.

The cash would turn out to be a huge legal issue at the trial-his lawyers had set it all up.

Once I made the decision to file for divorce, I remember calling a partner at one of the biggest law firms in town. The man had class, handing me a blue-ink fountain pen so I could sign a contract and fork over his retainer—a cool $15,000. But he also said, "You have to deny that you have the half a million in cash." I said, *"What?"* I certainly wasn't going to put myself in legal jeopardy by being untruthful. I smiled and said, "You want me to lie?" I was incredulous. Sometimes you just can't listen to a lawyer. In fact, I want to emphasize that point: Don't always listen to your lawyer. Listening to a lawyer can be hazardous to your health, not to mention your financial well-being. I flat-out told this guy, "Half the cash is my husband's, and I'm not trying to steal it and I certainly am not going to lie about it. I'm just keeping it so he won't steal it."

"No, no, no, no, no!" he said, pounding his fist fiercely on his desk. "It's a Pandora's box. It will destroy you. You can't admit you have this money. Just say you don't have it. I'll take care of you. There's no record—you can deny the whole thing. Nobody's going to know. I will protect you."

This attorney, like all the others, was all about making money for himself. He asked if I owned property in Beverly Hills. If I hadn't had a $2 million home, there was no chance he would have considered representing me. As it was, he still insisted that I lie about the case. When I wouldn't promise to commit perjury, this top lawyer, who was purported to be a nice guy, venerated by the whole legal community, gave back my check and refused to take the case.

"Get out!" he said, ordering me to leave.

Next I met with another high-powered divorce specialist, a woman who was highly competent, flamboyant, and adorned in diamond and gold jewelry that failed to overcome the fact she was obese and caked in way with too much makeup. Her retainer was a whopping $20,000, I was desperate and needed representation. We met for two hours, with her writing down every detail of the conversation and the events of the past many months. I signed the contract but before I read it over, and when I skimmed the fine print I noticed that her fee for using law clerks was $190 an hour, seventy dollars more than the first guy charged. Doing my part for consumer justice, I crossed out the numbers and wrote in $120. While making the change, I asked why the cost was so high, and that turned out to be a deal killer. She got furious, I mean violently furious. "You're telling me what to charge?" No way! She yelled at me tore my check in half and returned it. "Don't ever call my office again!"

Within two hours, a messenger showed up at my office, demanding that I sign a statement saying I had never met with her or discussed my case with her in any way. It was a ludicrous piece of paper, when you stop to think about it. These people are crazy—our lawyers, seeking what they blithely refer to as justice. Hah!

Even when I finally found a lawyer, using a magazine guide to the top attorneys in the country, the man would turn out to be a wimp—no match for my husband's high- priced legal sharks—and so wrapped up in his ultra-rich corporate clients that he completely neglected my case, and I had to drop him and get someone else.

It would be almost two years before the case went to court, two years of the worst kind of stress you can imagine—personal desolation and problems galore, a diabolical kind of chaos that seemed as if it would never end.

In June of 1997, soon after the farewell dinner party, I changed my name, though not legally. I dropped my husband's surname, since I never could stand him, without the approval of the court and began using my maiden name again. Although the change wasn't yet official, it was what I wanted and it felt good to think of myself as my own person, apart from him. I was going to get rid of the cancer for good.

Neither one of us would move out of the house. Leaving it ran the risk of sending a wrong message to the court. Should I indicate a willingness to let him have the property, when my home was the one thing I figured I would miss the most?

When he was mad and tried to eliminate much of the alimony due to anger - the court did just that, cut my support. He was not about giving me a dime. Obviously the same sorts of thoughts were actually going through his mind, too. He was staying put and we both entrenched ourselves in our own halves of the home, living behind locked bedroom doors and as his attorney's advice he hired a security guard to make sure neither trespassed into the other's space. Neither one of us would yield an inch in defending our own half of the turf. The attorneys played every trick in the book to provoke me to leave my house – I hung in there and I refused to pack up and go. We split the space in the fridge. We split the space in the driveway. I would carve about my presence in the places that had to be common ground. "She gets in my way in the kitchen," he would later tell the judge.

The guard stood his post for months, planting himself in the family room from seven in the evening until seven in the morning. It was ridiculous. It cost a fortune: $80,000 in all. On top of it he was a stupid guard. I resented that someone was watching me all the time. Any time I came or went, the guard jotted it down. Was I a spy? An imprisoned terrorist? I had to park my Bentley in a covered garage at a client's home three blocks away, afraid that I would vent his anger by damaging it and I would have no car to chauffeur around my fancy clients. I could never afford the gas nor the repairs, much less a new vehicle suitable for transporting big-time buyers. I was going through hell and yet working like a maniac. If I wanted to go out to dinner—if I were meeting a seller, for example, at the Polo Lounge—I would have to walk over to my client's house, or schlep there in the little Honda I had bought, pick up the Bentley, and then return it afterward.

During the time I would be gone to go to the office, personal possessions would disappear—guard or no guard. Antiques disappeared. Several gorgeous valuable silk Persian rugs went right out the door. The housekeeper even helped to roll it up for him, and away it went!

"Roberta, where's the rug?" I said, shocked to notice it missing. "Mister took it." "Oh, my God, why didn't you tell me?" Those Lalique he bought me? The bird? The lovely crystal of the man and woman? Supposedly my birthday gifts? Vanished too! Poof! My home office had to be squeezed into my bedroom—my phone, fax machine, real-estate files, robe company files, my law books, a little round table to work on, all crowded in there with my bed, book cases, TV, the armoire, my treadmill, and my slippers and lingerie. Studying was no longer in the agenda. The round table was my desk, my kitchen table, my dining room, and my living room, because I spent a huge amount of time there, afraid to go out and leave the armoire and the cash unattended.

Since it was hard staying home all the time and beside I was a clever girl, I had invented a fabulous system of my own. A real sophisticated one. Right!

What a system. Not trusting anyone anymore, I always locked my door to my bedroom. There used to be two phone lines—one of them now broken—and a separate fax line specifically to transmit letters, listings, and copies of offers not to mention my idiot lawyers bullshit papers. Every day, and all throughout the trial preparation and the trial itself, I worked, seeing clients, scrambling for sellers and buyers even though half the community was turned against me, because of the garbage he was spreading about me. This I found out much later. He was everywhere and talking endlessly, bad-mouthing me. "She stole a million dollar and he was going to put me in jail" he would tell tales and I was getting fired right and left from my jobs." The companies I worked for, never even tried to give me a chance to explain. They would give me 20 minutes to pack and get out. My real-estate business was suffering because of it unable to make a dime. I seemed to be snake-bite for some reason. Now I had to concentrate on the robe business for extra income. Stress was killing me, and not a penny was coming in.

There is an old adage that no good deed goes unpunished and I'm inclined to believe it. I had my successful robe company stolen from me during this time period because of an act of kindness that I extended toward a woman I found on the street. One late afternoon I met her while crying and walking from my car to my office. She was sitting on the sidewalk near a gray-black Volkswagen with its hood up. She was over-weight, blue-eyed, black curly hair, and had a little baby girl with her.

"Can I ask why you're crying?" I said. "It's not so bad, is it?"

She was broke and afraid of her boyfriend who was on drugs. He also had a violent temper she told me. "This is our child," she said. "We're not married, and he beats me up." She needed to get the little girl food and diapers. Her car wouldn't start and they were both hungry.

"Here's fifty dollars," I said, giving her some cash. I also gave her my phone number, saying I might need an assistant. She got very excited. I ended up hiring her to help with the robe company. She would work for me for five or six months. I moved my computer into her apartment and put her in charge of the accounts. Still, I kept making calls, talking to clients, and getting promises from them that they would buy—and yet, nothing.

No orders came in. No money either. It turned out that my new employee was diverting all the business to herself and cashing all my checks, using my stamps for signatures. She stole all my files, all my customers, and was running her own enterprise and under-bidding me on every contract. Essentially, she stole the entire company right out from under me, while I was fighting for me life in court. And then sank it to the ground.

It was a mess. On top of that, she sued me. I counter-sued. Finally I gave her $2,500. to settle and help her out and get her out of my life once and for all. Of course she could not manage the business and she lost it all.

Then I got burned again with another fledgling business—this time a pizzeria. In trying to live as frugally as possible, I had started patronizing at a little pizza joint on Beverly Drive. For $1 a slice, I could eat for almost nothing, and I went there every night for weeks. Here I was, showing up in a $230,000 Bentley, and yet I was in desperate financial straits. The judge had cut my support to half. The chef, who doubled as head waiter, was an affable fellow named Franco, who struck up a friendship with me. Together we cooked up the idea of opening our own place, him in charge of the food, me dipping into my shrinking financial reserves to buy the equipment and lease a location.

We found a nice little spot on trendy Melrose Avenue in West Hollywood. In fact, Franco took a small apartment upstairs, giving himself an easy one-story commute. We fixed the place up. I paid for pots and pans, countertops, pizza ovens, lights, city permits—you name it. Altogether, I invested a lot of money, every penny from my commissions just went, some of it from savings, some of it borrowed from friends, and some of it gleaned from the sale of my own jewelry. The result was charming: an airy Italian dining room with a vibrant red counter and a window to watch the pizza chefs spinning their dough in the kitchen. About a dozen of my friends taped dollar-bills to the wall for luck. It must not have helped.

Almost immediately, we drew packed crowds. Celebrities hangout and they all came and loved the food. I have to say, it was about the best pizza you could find. But one morning, barely a week after we had opened, I showed up to collect the previous night's revenues. The entrance was locked and I yelled upstairs to get Franco's attention.

"You bitch, I'm going to have you killed!" he shouted back down. "Get away from here or else." Do not, I mean do not come back".

Killed? For what? Nothing, that's what. He was tied in with the Mafia- I later came to learn. He and his mob friends were forcing me out of my own place, stealing it from me even more brazenly than the ungrateful tramp who stole the robe business. I wouldn't give up easily. I tried to pressure Franco for the money. Bad idea! One day I parked and walked into my real-estate office—I was working now on Beverly Boulevard—and Franco or one of his hoodlum chums smashed the window of my Bentley and took the cash, jewelry and briefcase I had left inside. The damage to the car alone was $10,000.

While the Bentley was in the shop, I drove a used Honda. I had to leave it in the lot at LAX to fly to Las Vegas to attend to some robe customers. Someone must have followed me; when I returned the same night, I found the Honda vandalized—its window broken, the battery missing. I was stranded at the airport at 11 p.m.

Lovesick in Beverly Hills

Threats continued. "If you go near that restaurant I'm going to have you shot", Franco said. I saw a lawyer. The advice I got? "Let him go," the attorney said. "You'll be dead." Long afterward I heard that Franco was in jail—through no fault of mine. He had it coming to him. As for the business, it got boarded up. Why are people so rotten? Why did he have to rip me off and betray my trust? I'll never have an answer. I can only say that the strain on me due to these business atrocities and the impending divorce was unbelievable. It took a tremendous toll. My nerves got so bad I could no longer eat. Food wouldn't go down. I lost weight—before long, I'd be down to ninety-nine pounds—and sleep was just about impossible. I would lie there half the night. Smoking, like there was no tomorrow. I've always worked out, and I did what I could to burn off the stress, getting up at 5 a.m. every day to run on the treadmill. That gave me the energy to fight the crooked lawyers and the court system. I would blast music the whole time thinking boost of everlasting Endorphin. Gloria Gaynor was my favorite: "I Will Survive," my theme song, the message I needed to keep pounding into my brain. Listening to that defiant anthem of feminine resolve instilled me with the tough attitude I needed to deal with the lawyers and go into court to battle for the truth and also my rights.

The one miraculous change in my life during this terrible and lonely stretch was meeting the man, I had never met before, for better or worse, who would dominate the next eighteen years of my life—my tall, handsome cowboy, the broad-shouldered gazillionaire who spoke with such self-effacing kindness, the raspy voice that sounded so glad to see me: Mr. Wonderful, a precursor to everlasting love and its devastation. This man whom I had never seen before was going to love me and ruin me and scar me for life as deep as the Grand Canyon.

Our chance first encounter occurred four months after I'd made the decision to file for divorce, as if the universe were making some small effort to counter-balance all the horrible things that were happening to me. The significance of his arrival in my world took a while to grasp, because I wasn't looking for a new relationship. Relationship? Really?Far from it! Vastly more important things were on my mind, the main one being the fear of being sent to jail because of the false accusations that I had stolen the $1,500,000 that had been in the bank and the safe. A distasteful flair of an earthquake was about to erupt and the nauseating smell of hatred was permeating throughout my entire life.

Mr. Wonderful was one of the most powerful prospect/client, albeit quite a bit wealthier than most and known all over town.

After selling three houses on Beverly Drive, I contacted the owner of each house of the entire three blocks north of Santa Monica Boulevard, to hunt more listings. One day I knocked on the door, right opposite the house I had sold. A pretty and yound woman opened the door, and as I had started to say, would you like to sell your house, she banged the door shut on my face. Oh! Oh! Her reaction I sensed, psychic that I was, demonstrated she was about to sell her house. I quickly called the title company and rushed back to the office, to check out the property profile with the title company. There was a phone number attached to the title. I called. An hour later, my assistant yelled out there is man on the phone; he wants to talk to you about the house you just sold. After the usual, greetings he told me, the house, happened to belong to his son, and they were going through divorce and the house had to be sold immediately. It was his son's house and not his but he requested to meet me in his office to discuss the matter further, since he knew my boss - via high school.

After that first meeting in his office, where he was clearly so impressed with my take-charge attitude, he had decided to ask me to help his son, who was thinking about listing his home, and who was mired in his own terrible divorce. A lunch meeting was arranged at a restaurant in Beverly Hills—a meeting where the russet- haired Mr. Wonderful brought along a stocky, curly-haired man named Jerry, whom I took to be his lawyer. Jerry –his son- and not his lawyer, was young and extremely quiet, never looking up, never speaking to me throughout the meal.

Considering the lack of communication, it was no surprise that nothing came of the lunch, but the next day I got a call: "Thank you for meeting my son," and an invitation to call Jerry again to further discuss the listing. I did, and Jerry and I had dinner at the Glen Center, where he sadly felt that his divorce was killing him.

"Who's your divorce attorney?" I asked him.

He mentioned a firm—my husband's lawyers. Oh, great. What a small world. Now we had something in common: the scumbag lawyers. Afterward, he insisted on taking me to his sister Ivy's house, a completely remodeled two-story, just off Sunset Boulevard. The same house that my husband and I had considered buying right after we moved to L.A, and we were over-bided by another buyer by $10,000. What a coincidence. It was an uneventful meeting. Ivy was very pretty, sweet and nice enough to greet us not knowing she will eventually be my poison pill and responsible for changing the entire course of my life. I had a cup of tea and went home. Again, there was no commitment to list the house, and the following day Mr. Wonderful phoned to find out how the meeting had gone. I said Jerry was unsure what to do.

"Call him," again, the father urged me. He thought I'd have luck if I pursued it. It was starting to seem like a dubious situation—I sensed I was wasting my time, and the one thing you don't want to do in real-estate is waste time. But I did call, and Jerry did want to discuss the matter further. He wanted to meet again for dinner, this time at an outdoor Italian place, where the situation got weirder still. He went to the men's room and came back to table all flustered. After checking the bill, when he was about to pay, I told him there was an error of $20, and they had over charged him. Jerry badly over-reacted, throwing down the check, slamming down his drink glass and breaking it. A completely screwed-up response that made me pity him. Bolting from the restaurant in a sour mood, he stepped into my car and I tried to drop him off at his apartment. He grabbed my hand and wouldn't let go, insisting that I go upstairs, that he had something to show me. It turned out that his place was filled with gadgets and electronics from —an entire inventory of a warehouswe. He was very proud of them. His good friend Tommy was there and we all started talking. Jerry ended up playing me a cassette tape of his mother, father, and their attorney (our attorney) arguing about his divorce and his cocaine addiction. They were really going at it.

Wow, I thought, this was some Beverly Hills story! I thought I was having it bad! Why did he want me to hear this? I will never know. On the tape, Jerry's parents were talking about money— enormous amounts of money—and divorce and drugs and it was obviously upsetting Jerry. The parents were constantly fighting and yelling and how not to pay the ex-wife to be.

It was hard for me to follow exactly what was being said because Jerry started flipping out again, cursing and throwing things around the apartment. I started getting scared. At about 12:30 in the morning, I'd had enough, and I got out of there. Tommy walked me down and confided that Jerry's drug –cocaine- problem was pretty severe.

To me, I felt so sorry for Jerry and the chance of making any deal looked very unpromising. I wanted to forget it and move forward, but when I got to the office the next morning there were already several messages from Mr. Wonderful. My secretary got him on the line, and he asked how the evening went. I tried to explain that I couldn't go on with such madness.

"Look," I told him, "I have two beautiful children, who just got through Beverly Hills High School, and they don't touch drugs or alcohol. I really don't want to be around that stuff." By the way, I think, I am done here. It does not look like he wants to list the house with me.

He laughed. "Oh, so you found out?"

"It's OK," I said. "Don't worry about the listing. I don't know what to say except, 'Good luck.' I'm really not interested in this contract any more. I am going through a terrible divorce, but thank you for thinking of me." and hung up the phone.

The phone rang again, and he insisted on talking to me. I said:" hello" "oh hi again", he said, "tell me something, do you have any advice for me?"

"About the drugs?" That's what he meant, and I told him, "Well, come to think of it, a very good friend lost her daughter to cocaine last week. I really cannot help you, but maybe you need to talk to her; "do you want me to give you her number". I think she would be better for you to talk to and here is her number.

"OK, would you mind setting it up?" He must have glanced at his schedule. "Could she meet me Thursday, around five o'clock?"

"August twenty-eighth?" I agreed to try to arrange it. I promised to reach my friend and set it up, and again he said before I could hang up. "I don't understand you," he said. "I give you a hard time, my son scares you, we didn't give you the listing, and you're still trying to help. Why?"

"Wouldn't you help me?" I told him. "If the situation were reversed, I'm sure you would too." He happens to be a nice guy, He laughed. After I hung up the phone, I went ahead and set up the meeting for the following Thursday at five, despite my hectic court schedule and the chaos of a divided home. Even though I was willing to try to help this man who had appeared in my life out of the blue, now I was a beyond boiling point, working day and night, and I didn't much give a damn about anything, really.

My assistant on Wednesday tried to confirm our appointment for Thursday. He asked to talk to me to find out where I lived. He followed by saying my house was right on his way home, so he suggested meeting there. I said fine—it worked for me.

He showed up right on time, dressed very nicely in a royal blue jacket, matching his eyes, and my housekeeper brought us Perrier and fresh orange juice, not knowing that the man was a heavy whiskey drinker.

My girlfriend was late. She was having an incredibly hard time with the death of her daughter, her only child. For half an hour we waited, and I finally called to find out where she was. She was far too angry to care that this stranger was there to see her.

"I don't give a shit, Pishi," she said bitterly. "Tell him I'm still downtown in my office. I can't come." Followed by: "Leave me the fuck alone!"—and she hung up. This was my best friend, but she was severely hurting and just couldn't handle anything or anyone.

Embarrassed as hell, I had to break the news to the stranger siting in my living room: "sorry, but she couldn't make it".

"Don't worry about it," Mr. Wonderful said. "And fix me a drink. You have any scotch?"

Scotch? What was scotch? I had no idea. Was it whiskey or was it a brand name for something else? I'm not a drinker I still don't know the difference; I was baffled. There were a lot of bottles at the bar, some containing various brands with the word whiskey-scotch on it, all different color bottles, different names, and I managed to make him a drink. Chivas is what I knew.

He became less formal and we talked. He was sympathetic about my divorce and voiced the opinion that his son's attorneys—my husband's attorneys—were a bunch of nitwits. "Very dumb," he called them, his exact words.

"Don't worry, they'll lose," you are much smarter, he said with certainty, and to this day I remember that comment and how much it helped my frame of mind and gave me confidence during the two hard, unbearable years of toxic bickering and legal warfare that followed. He also told me that his wife had breast cancer, and was dying. She was an alcoholic, emotionally troubled, yelling and screaming all the time, and he was miserable in his marriage for a very long time.

The veneer of the high-powered businessman began to slip away, revealing beneath it a man burdened by problems, a vulnerable little boy who was sad and lonely. As I studied him more closely, sipping my glass of orange juice, I noticed how tall and good looking he really was, and his eyes, especially, drew my attention—the sort of cool blue eyes that I really liked. Actually, when I looked attentively, I realized that one can truly fall in love with this man. For the next eighteen years, I found it mesmerizing to gaze into his deep blue eyes.

He asked me a lot of questions about my work and my divorce. Sitting there, him with his drink and me with my orange juice, we discussed our lives and moved easily, even a bit recklessly, from a professional relationship to intimacy. I felt, it was time, and I needed him to leave, so I got up, to go to the kitchen for a glass of water, I excused myself but he suddenly grabbed my wrist. To this day, I can still hear and feel that electricity the instant when Mr. Wonderful said, "I was going to fix you up with my son. You are too good for him; but you are perfect for me," as he took my hand and pulled me toward him, his face was lighting up with happiness and my heart became a time bomb ready to explode. The thought of touch of another man on my body, gave me a thrill beyond explanation. It was the first time a man has ever touched me in this fashion aside from my husband.

It was amazing, wonderful, thrilling beyond words. Making passionate love to him on that beautiful afternoon of August 28, 1997, right there in my home, ended twenty six long, angry years in which I had not had passionate sex at all so willingly and never been hugged so hard. I was aware that my husband could walk in at any second. The security guard had not yet reported for his evening shift. The danger only heightened the intensity. What a completely amazing new experience after forty-five years, and I had missed it all. For so many years I had played the faithful wife, denying myself so many things including sex.

How can one deny such magnificent pleasure, living always in a miserable and unfulfilled life? This was pure, spontaneous sex, satisfying my own needs. Also just as so many of my American friends used to talk about, not to mention so many women who did in the movies and on TV—letting go, and saying to hell with it. To me, he was damn gorgeous and I was melting in his arms, better yet he was crushing every bone of my whole body. Strong, tall and very white, just the way I liked it and yet never imagined would happen to me. The encounter felt like nothing deep, nothing with any implied commitments or emotional bonds. I saw it only as a one-night stand, more like one afternoon stand, my first in a city where one-night stands are just another little luxury that people enjoy, like going to the day spa. "Sex In The City," Beverly Hills-style.

Only not knowing how one little thrill happened to unfold one crowded afternoon in a long, bad stretch of my life. Little did I know that this wonderful man was about to turn my life up side down, creating, a whirlwind of emotions, I never knew existed in me. Super money and super love, was about to almost totally destroy me.

7

My Enchanting Attic Room

Looking back now, I could say that the impassioned tryst with stoic Mr. Wonderful was one of the extraordinary events of my life, a memory I cherish, and yet it's amazing that it occurred at all. Certainly the part of my mind shaped by my strict parents and by years of rigid Catholic school could have thwarted Mr. Wonderful's advances. There were plenty of tough questions to consider if I had wanted to weigh them: Why go that far? Why do it with a married man? Was I going to hurt myself or open the door to unforeseen problems? Was it wrong? And why, he wanted me and why destroy me? A competing side of my brain, influenced by the easy moral ethic of where I lived, would have offered these responses: Why not a married man? I had no clue that a one night stand was anything more than one time sex. Since I had lived so many years without love and sex and being huged, really hugged, and he was living with a sick, drunken woman and hurting as much as I was we were communicating without saying a word. Boy I was so gullible and ignorant.

Maybe I was over powered by his magnetism and did not want to let go of the rush I was feeling; Feeling one time is ok never anticipating more.

Lovesick in Beverly Hills

But in truth these thoughts, if I even had them, were dismissed as quickly as they surfaced. I wasn't concerned with the right or wrong of it because I had never had a boy friend nor a relationship with a man so I had no clue what I was doing. I took action. I went for it and grabbed what enjoyment I could- and there was a lot to grab that afternoon.

It was an amazing afternoon and I was desperately in need of it. Underlying it all was the belief that the moment would come and go and never lead to anything more. Really, why should it? There was no reason for the tryst other than the passion involved and how good it felt and tasted at that moment. I was young and single now, starting life on my own, trying to find my way thirsty and starving to be hugged and made passionate love to. What used to be, the old bonds and loyalties, were finished and I had found a new bubbly. Although I did remain loyal to him for the next eighteen years; eventually he did blow it all at the end.

The real surprise was that Mr. Wonderful phoned me the next day. What? He cared enough to call? Men actually do that? Thinking it was a one time sex. At least that was all it meant to me. He was married, and I was surprised he was calling me! Married men? Why was he calling me? No, I was not interested.

My mind was focused on the fact that I had been set up, ripped-off by a ruthless and an ungrateful husband, crooked and dishonest judge and lawyers and was about to lose everything I have worked for all my life. Hearing from Mr. Wonderful was a big shocker; the possibility that he would call me hadn't even entered my head. I had forgotten all about it. This strapping guy, as big and sure of himself as John Wayne, surely spent a fair number of afternoons bedding attractive women. He once told me, every few years, he would find another girl and get rid of them after a couple of years. As for yours truly, it took him almost eighteen years- a one woman man that broke his own track record. There was no way he was new to such a thing, and yet, wow, he felt moved to call. There was something about me that he liked, and now he wanted more. Years later, I thought or I guessed I was destined to love him. Still, the answer was no. I was walking on Canon Drive when the next day, I answered his call on my flip phone. At first I didn't recognize his voice. "Who is this?" I said. He repeated his name and asked to see me again, but I said no. "You are married," I told him. "You are not supposed to be calling me. I was going through hell, with my life, and so thank you but I don't think so." As I was heading toward my office, I hung up the phone but half hour later my cell phone rang again. He wanted me to have lunch with him telling me he had a friend who was going to sell his $7,000,000 apartment. Why don't you meet us, and discuss it further. I guess he had a P.H.D from charm school.

He was persistent and called again and again. He wanted to meet at La Scala so I could meet his friends for business. He eventually showed me that his interest in me was real and sincere. He was quite a charmer not knowing that was his specialty. We began to see each other. In the beginning, it was only about sex and only one day a week. Though I was suffocating from my divorce, I craved it, and obviously so did he. He was magnificent, a tremendous lover. He gave me enormous pleasure like I had never known in my entire life. He would meet me mostly on Saturdays either in his office or sometimes in my house. Yes! No one could find us since my house would be off-limits. It made it all the more exiting. No work and no court, Superior Court was closed and so were lawyer offices. Super cool.

Eventually we would see each other even more often. Those hours of enjoyment would help to carry me through months filled with long workdays and meetings with lawyers. Not knowing, eventually he was going to be the real obstacle to my happiness. And I was fascinated by sex.

Living on lockdown in the toxic atmosphere of a divided house was more than I wanted to bear. Fortunately, I was able to find an escape. A good friend of mine, Remi owned a little attic unit, above a garage, that she was willing to rent for $900 a month. It was nine long blocks away, south of Wilshire Boulevard, with a window facing the trees and a pool in her yard. This would become my private refuge, a secret place, since it was important that I continue to appear to live in my house. Legally, I didn't want to create an impression that I was willing to give up the house, and of course I was always worried about him finding the half a million dollars stashed in my armoire. He was relentless in trying to find the money. He was desperate, as if I would ever actually cheat him. I based my life on honesty, dignity and principle and that was the secret of my success in my business. I couldn't have him in that bedroom searching for it. He had taken stolen or removed everything already. So I worked out a brilliant daily get away plan.

The lights and my radio and TV were rigged to timers so they would go on and off and he and the guard would think I was there inside my bedroom. Meanwhile, I would slip away on foot, emerging from my back bedroom sliding door and creeping past the wood bars to exit the rear of the house. In that way I bypassed the guard and was able to leave through the back gate, beyond the pool, and trudge down the alley. I had to go nine long blocks, past the rows of trash cans and the deep shadows of unlit walls and trees and dark crannies, to reach the peace and quiet of the attic room.

Many times I'd not finish work until around ten, or I'd go to a formal dinner or charity event and not get home until midnight or one in the morning. I had a routine. I continued to park the Bentley in my client's covered garage, walking those dark, palm-lined streets in my high heels and elegant gowns, out-smarting everybody to reach my bedroom in my house. Many times I was loaded with diamond jewelry. One of my priciest baubles was an all around diamond necklace with two-hundred and forty diamonds, absolutely gorgeous, worth thousands, and I never even care or feared being attacked. I could care less. I was in Beverly Hills. I would walk in the front door, go straight to my bedroom, change, putting on my black tights and black T-shirts, Keds sneakers, sneak out the back door, and disappear into the dark alley, afraid of nothing. As I would open the sliding doors to my bedroom to take off, I would close it and the metal pipe, while slanted would fall. As I closed the door, the metal bar would drop, right inside, behind the glass double door, blocking tight for anyone to reopen from outside. The next day, I would walk back blocks toward my house, and enter the house from the front door, after I see the guard leave at about seven the next morning.

Now I was fighting for my life in court; I couldn't allow myself to be scared, even when alone at night in that dark alley, passing the trash cans and inhaling garbage. The plan worked. Genius!

My mini attic room was a different story—serene, cozy, tiny and safe. It was a sanctuary with almost nothing in it. No kitchen, no closets, just a bed, an easy chair, a tiny shower, and shelves where I could store a few belongings. My music was there—my beloved

French CDs, and lots of very beautiful music to lift my spirits. I had a hot plate to cook on and a tiny bar refrigerator. I could buy a can of soup and heat it up. There was no oven, nor a microwave. It was just a hole to crawl into, a safe house where I could sleep in total peace. Having this tiny spot of my own gave me an amazing happiness and energy. Just arriving there lifted my spirits. I fixed the place up, putting up curtains and setting out comfy pillows.

Later on, when my friends saw it, they compared it to a little Bloomingdale's—but for now no one knew where I was. Angry about the divorce my kids stopped speaking to me. They loved their father, and felt more sorry for him. He was poisioning their mind with all the garbage about me and now it was sinking in their heads. Though I was the one, losing the game of life. Nobody knew about my secret room except Mr. Wonderful. When he could and wanted to see me, he would call and visit me in my tiny hole in the wall- just about every day. My only happiness was seeing him in that tiny place. We could be alone and make love two or three times a day. We could sit and talk. I would recline on the bed and he would sit in the chair and we would discuss our lives. Mine had become so very complicated and getting worst by the day. I was so afraid of going to jail over the missing $500,000 and the forgery of almost a million dollars. He was willing to listen, though he had many problems of his own. Those hours in that room were a wonderful chance to just cry, to feel, and basically to just think without interruption. The kids, the wife, the drug use, hookers and all the character of his life, including kids going in and out of rehab was all he would talk about.

Life was so difficult. I was barely hanging on. Anxiety attacks were happening once every other day. One night, when Mr. Wonderful was out of town, I was very sad, lonely and upset—about the divorce, about my daughters being away and not talking to me, and about being alone—I wanted a drink so I'd had a few vodkas. Frightful a certain panic took over me, I needed air, and wanted desperately to go out and go back to my room on top of the garage. I was drunk. It was very late, about 2:30 in the morning. I jumped into the Honda and started driving. I'd forgotten to turn on my lights and I was speeding. A cop saw me and started a pursuit. I got near my brother's house one block away from my own house, and I swung into the driveway and ducked down below the seat, pretending there was no one in the car. The cop went back and forth, looking for me. I hid there for two hours before I had the nerve to pull out again and go back to the attic.

Mr. Wonderful never helped me with money, nor did I ask him for anything. His company and affection were all that mattered to me. He didn't seem to mind that I was living in that tiny room—maybe he even liked it. The illicit thrill of having that clandestine meeting place might have been a turn-on for him. I don't know. I only know that I was afraid of expressing the feelings I was starting to have for him. If I told him I loved him, I was sure it would scare him away and I'd lose him. At least that was what I knew from my bible "Cosmopolitan Magazine. He was married and I did not want to lose him now, after nine months, so I shut up. He had talked about leaving her, but he had made no move to actually get out, and I sensed he was torn. He was my treasure and to this day, I never really pressured him to leave her. She was ill and he was loyal, in his way. He had millions of dollars tied up in the marriage. Would he allow the mess of a divorce, just because a girl loved him? I doubted it. Not knowing he was making excuses the entire relationship. Not knowing married men do just that: they never leave their wives –the reason: super money. My place and my thoughts I felt, was to keep things light and not get too emotionally involved. It took ten months before I dared to tell him that I loved him. I had thought about it for weeks. What if I said it and he got scared? What if he left me?

Finally one day he had come to see me in the attic. A beautiful moment almost all the time, and as he walked in I said it: "I love you." He was so thrilled! The way his eyes shined! "Really? You really love me?" I know you do, I love you too." He was unbelievably happy. Those few brief seconds were a turning point in our relationship. I was in love and for years to come I would lose my soul to him. He could not say I love you too all the time, for a good reason that I discovered much later. He said: promise me, you will never leave me and that sentence from him meant a whole lot. For the first time in my life, at forty-six years old, I loved a man and he actually loved me back. Oh, what an incredible feeling! I can still taste the moment. From that day on he came over every day. He called me constantly. I had taken a chance and I was right, he really did love me. And yet I was always worrying. Being in love is putting yourself at risk, especially when the person you love is married to someone else, and when you're at a vulnerable point in your life, and dealing with overwhelming problems that would end in disaster.

When he wasn't there with me, I often slipped into a deep and suffocating loneliness-more like a coma. I hurt. I longed for him. I wanted him to want to be with me, and there was no way to know whether he did. The pain and doubt would become magnified when he would tell me, usually no more than a day in advance that he was leaving on one of his many long trips out of town with his wife. He usually traveled with her five or six months a year, and the love we shared, as powerful as it was, seemed to make no dent whatsoever in his routine. Every time he left I died a little. It was a knife to my heart. I would crumple up in my room and cry my eyes out. He was and will always be the one and only love of my life and nothing was ever going to change that.

Like clockwork every summer, Mr. Wonderful went away with his wife to Europe. Watching him go, especially while I was going through such hell with Dr. Boring, was devastating. The trip they planned for June of 1998 was due to last eight weeks. How stupid and dumb can I be?

Eight tortuous long weeks—an eternity for me, and more than I felt I could endure. They were going to France, one of my favorite places in the world, where of course I spoke the language from my years at the French Catholic School in Tehran. France was more than just a beautiful city to me; it was almost home, as if I was a native there. Beyond even the language, I've always felt some strange mystical connection to the country and its culture that I cannot quite explain. My most passionate subjects in school were French history and French literature; the gardens, the churches, the flowers, the streets and cafes of Paris, they just put me over the top, into a wondrous state of bliss.

He wanted me there, I agreed and was overjoyed. Thinking I just had to go. I had to be there when Mr. Wonderful was there and try, if there was any possible way, to steal a few moments with him, sharing that exultantly romantic world with the only man I deeply loved. Somehow, I thought I did not deserve more, and never felt he was playing a big game.

There was no way I could get away from real-estate and my imploding marriage for seven weeks, but I did arrange, with Mr. Wonderful's offer and happy approval, to meet up with him for about a week in Cannes, where he and his wife booked a room at the Carlton. I stayed one floor above them, not knowing that you don't do that, not in the same hotel—it violates every rule of a secret relationship because of the risks involved. It never occurred to me-is wrong; all I cared about was being near him, seeing him whenever we could. Every hour and every minute gave me a reason to go. My legal situation was becoming unbearable so I decided to take two weeks off and go to Europe. Shopping and dancing and meeting friends, was what I needed and he agreed. Upon my return, I went on living and fighting as hard as I could to prove my innocence. Mr Wonderful took care of all my expenses for the trip. Hermes and Fendi became my buddies. I felt like Jackie Onassis shopping with no ends. From Bulgari to Cartier to Dior I was having the time of my life. Rule number one, you never carry your shopping bags yourself. You have the store deliver them to your hotel room. Every night packages were delivered to my room and were placed all over the place by my instructions including a fourteen thousand dollar Escada gown that I wore for my daughter's wedding. This was my routine every summer and I was beginning to love it.

The trip is still so alive and vivid in my memory. The morning after I arrived in Cannes, I went down to the beach alone. The weather was *tres agreable*—it was fabulous the entire week. Everyone on the beach was topless, including me. I lounged in the sun, letting it bake away my cares. It was great to be away from home, away from the fighting and hostility, just feeling the air on my skin and knowing I would soon be finding ways to see the strong, blue-eyed cowboy who had captured my heart and will remain there for ever.

After relaxing a while on the beach, I slipped on a sexy little sun outfit I'd brought along—a beautiful short skirt and top with a hat and high heels—and went to a restaurant for lunch where I sat on the veranda, gazing out to the beautiful blue sea. There, I happened to strike up a conversation with a handsome and very young guy who looked like Versace; he was dressed from head to toe in Versace and Piaget. Mr. Gorgeous took a liking to me and started speaking French and invited me to dine with him that same evening.

Why not? "Sure," I said, unaware that seated opposite location, inside of the same restaurant were Mr. Wonderful and his entire entourage. He always travels in a pack of at least twenty people—friends, friends of friends, a regular road party. He always told me having all the people around him spares him from being alone with his wife. Jerry, his son, was there too. He was the one who spotted me first.

"Oh, my God, we met last year!" Jerry said, instantly remembering me and shocked to run into me in Cannes, of all places. "Come and meet my parents—they're here too. Petrified of meeting the crowd and the wife, he dragged me by the arm and pulled me after him, resisting the whole time, trying to pull away, and Mr. Versace following close behind. Oh, shit! My head wasn't ready for this encounter. The whole group was at a huge round table, having cocktails, and Mr. Wonderful saw me and started laughing. He always laughs when he gets nervous. Jerry said, "Hey, everybody, can you believe it? She's from Beverly Hills and her name is Pishi."

"Come over and have a drink," his wife said, motioning me to join them and thinking, I guess, that I was going to be Jerry's girl. She had no idea who I was; she wasn't suspicious at all. The civilized thing to do was to sit down and enjoy the party, and we did. His wife insisted that I sit next to her. My pulse was racing. My face was blood red with anxiety, my head pounding and Mr. Wonderful kept staring at me with a big smile eating me up. Or so I imagined. I was having my own private anxiety attack, but in fact I was very slim and tanned and looked just great. Sipping a glass of champagne, sitting quietly, I tried to appear calm and behave normally while Mr. Wonderful kept watching me. Now I got a chance to observe his wife up close. She was dark-haired, witty, much older than I was, and yet not obviously not so very ill, as he had said, and she was drinking away, non stop. This was a moment that anybody in my position would dread. It was terribly uncomfortable, and yet it showed me the carefully constructed public façade of the woman who, for years, would remain my rival, the bitter, angry, hard-drinking woman who was standing between me and my love. Or was she the reason? I am not sure.

"You know what, she speaks French," Jerry said, meaning me, and then addressing me directly. "You have to help me with the scooter." He had been trying to rent a moped, but had been thwarted by not knowing the language. Thankfully, one glass of champagne was enough and I could make a graceful exit by agreeing to go with Jerry to the scooter rental store. I said goodbye, and told Mr. Gorgeous I will be back. He said he would be there for a while, and tagged along with Jerry, only to discover that the store where he had hoped to rent the moped was actually only a display set up for advertising purposes. Jerry was quite pleased when we found the right place and had arranged the rental.

"I'm picking you up in the morning," he said, promising me a ride. I kept thinking, What am I going to do now? How am I going to say no? What am I going to say?

Athena

My plan for the morning had already been secretly set: Mr. Wonderful was going to meet me at eight and we were going to take a walk along the Croisette, the lovely avenue skirting the beach. That would be our pattern whenever we could arrange it while on vacation "together"—we would meet at least once in the morning and again in the afternoon. This time it worked out perfect. Anticipating the brutal sun, I put on my parao—short skirt, cute top and clear Lucite heels with a splash of rhinestones and baubles, which I like to wear at the beach. Mr. Wonderful met me and we were out on our walk when Jerry came by and saw us.

"I'm picking you up in half an hour," he said. "Be ready." "I am ready," I said. He thought I was waiting for him. The extra thirty minutes gave Mr. Wonderful and me time to finish our stroll, and then I climbed on the back of Jerry's scooter. "Where are you going?" When are you coming back?, he yelled and I said ask Jerry. Mr. Wonderful was not amused. "I'm taking her for a ride," Jerry said. He sure was. He took off at frightening speed, barreling down the narrow roads on the twenty-minute trip to Juan Les Pains, the next town on the coast. I was hanging on for dear life, remembering that the man driving me was a drug addict though he was really a great guy. Was he sober? Was he going to get me maimed or killed? At times I wasn't sure. What the hell! Who cares, the ride was thrilling. I had never been on a motorcycle before. By the time we got there, I was exhausted, and getting off the scooter I burned my leg on the exhaust pipe.

The thrills weren't over. Jerry's next idea was that we should rent a jet ski. A jet ski? I hadn't even brought a swimsuit. That didn't seem to matter to him. Before long, Jerry had bought me bikini bottoms—that's all that was sold there in that one store—and I wore those and my white top and we went racing across the waves, out among the many dolphins. By now it was hot and the air was crystal clear. The town, the boats—everything came into perfect focus. Oh, my Lord, Jerry was flying. It was exhilarating and scary. I was bouncing, screaming, and absolutely petrified—and then, way offshore, at least a quarter mile out, the Jet Ski took a huge bounce and I went flying, right into the water. Somehow I think I hit a dolphin. I came up, treading water, and saw Jerry still aboard, circling back to get me.

Guess what, I couldn't get out of the water for the life of me. I couldn't climb onto the bobbing machine, and Jerry couldn't get off of it to help lift me up. We were stranded out there half an hour, me yelling for help, Jerry struggling to pull me up by the arms.

"Oh! Secour!" I kept screaming in French. Help me!

Finally, somehow, I got back on the Jet Ski and away we went. We made it safely back to shore and headed to Cannes to return the scooter. As we passed the hotel, I saw Mr. Wonderful at the front door impatiently waiting for me. His expression was like, "Look at those two!" or maybe, "I don't want her to go." He had been waiting for me, positioned by the front door for an hour—and he wasn't the only one. Mr. Gorgeous was also there, anticipating my arrival. Jerry and I pulled over. Mr. Wonderful mentioned that there would be a cocktail party that evening in the lobby of the Carlton. All his friends were invited and he wanted me to go.

Since I had no date, and Mr. Wonderful would be there with his wife, the only polite thing was to ask Mr. Gorgeous if he would like to escort me.

"*Bien sur*," he said. Of course. He was beaming. "I'll meet you in the lobby at seven," I told him. At seven o'clock sharp, I rode down the elevator with my hair newly styled in a French twist, wearing sky-high heels and the most gorgeous Dolce & Gabbana steel gray dress, and with my million dollar tan, I entered the spectacular, elegant lobby to find three different men waiting for me at three different corners: Mr. Wonderful, Jerry, and Mr. Gorgeous. Talk about a scene! Jerry still had no idea that I was seeing his father. Mr. Gorgeous had no clue as to what was going on. And my beautiful Mr. Wonderful was salivating over me, wanting to be alone together, wondering who in the hell was this other guy with the Versace clothes and Piaget diamond watch. As we all moved into the lobby, Mr. Wonderful's wife was already there, waiting for him. "Look and get a load of this group coming in!" she said, staring at me. It was nervous time again for me. The drinks and conversation flowed. I chit-chatted with Mr. Gorgeous and Mr. Wonderful got more and more jealous. The first moment he had a chance, after about half an hour, he said to me, "Who is that guy?"

"I met him at the beach," I said. "Get rid of him." "He's already invited me to dinner," I said. "You can't go." Mr. Wonderful was more than unhappy. He was angry. He couldn't stand to see me around someone else while he was stuck with his wife.

After the cocktails, Mr. Gorgeous and I gracefully made our exit, heading to one of the most exclusive restaurants in Cannes. The bill for the dinner must have been $1,200. He picked it up without a second thought. It was just another night, on the town for a man who obviously had money to burn. The evening lasted until one in the morning, when he left to get ready for a flight in the morning. He handed me his phone number and asked me to call him. I never did.

Lovesick in Beverly Hills

By the time my escort was boarding his plane, Mr. Wonderful was preparing to confront me. He badgered me with questions. At quarter to seven in the morning, he was pounding on my door. Open up. Who's in your room? He had gone mad and I liked it.

"Where did you go last night? How late were you out? Did you sleep with him?"

"Shame on you, are you insulting me? What the hell is wrong with you, no one is here, and I would never allow anyone in my room but you."

"I am with you, I love you, I will never betray you." I told him. "He just took me to dinner." The jealousy told me a lot about Mr. Wonderful's feelings for me, but he was able to put it aside and we enjoyed our time together. The following day, my good friend Remi arrived from Beverly Hills eager to have some fun, and I got a message from Jerry, who wanted to go back to Juan Les Pains. I had other plans—I intended to shop and spend the day with Remi—but she was fascinated to hear about the moped and the trip I'd taken with Jerry. Those two knew each other already.

"Let's go!" she said. We rented a scooter ourselves and set out to shop and see the sights. We shopped like there was no tomorrow, placing our purchases into the little basket and storage trunk of the moped. She drove and I held on to her back. We retraced the route to Juan Les Pains—no jet skiing this time—and returned in the early evening, with cars whizzing past us and twilight closing in. We were going a mile a minute and it was getting dark. She asked me to remove her sunglasses so she could see better, and immediately, as I was taking her glasses off, she lost control of the bike. Veering into the next lane, we headed straight for an oncoming truck, and as

Athena

she yanked us away from that danger we ended up careening off the pavement, crashing on the side of the road. She ended up suffering a sizable gash on her ankle. Blood was streaming out. We were on the ground, crying and yelling for help. I was begging for help in French, and nobody would help us. It was like the Jet Ski crash, only worse, because she was injured.

"I've got to call my plastic surgeon and find out what to do," she said, concerned about the chance of an ugly scar.

After a while, a man I'd met, Robert, friend of Mr. Wonderful drove by with his girlfriend in a black Mercedes, heading in our direction. At first he saw us and thought we were only waving—that we had chosen to stop there on the road—but when he realized something was wrong he turned around. He loaded the moped in his trunk and drove us back into Cannes. I entered the hotel and immediately called her plastic surgeon, even though it was five in the morning in Los Angeles. I was ready to pass out from the blood. The surgeon instructed her to have me patch up the wound with Crazy Glue—a crazy idea, but I ran downstairs and bought one, and apparently it worked. The injury would eventually heal without even a mark. And as for me, after the little surgery I performed, I walked out and just thump: passed out right on the floor. A lawyer maybe, but a surgeon I was not.

Her ankle bandaged, she and I hit the beach the next day and ended up at a party at an exclusive seaside restaurant. I was wearing my big, black hat and little white skirt with a slit up the side. Mr. Wonderful was fuming again. He knew we were there, laughing and enjoying the people, the drinks and the food, and he was unable to get away from his wife. Poor guy!

At the party I happened to run into a friend a client, and agreed to have dinner later at another wonderful place, La Concha. I was thinking that I should maybe get my hair done. Then, as I was walking, I ran into some of Mr. Wonderful's friends and joined them to go shopping. While they were inside one expensive boutique, I stood outside as a black stretch limo pulled up. Stepping out was a woman with incredible porcelain skin, her hair up, in Chignon dressed to the nines and the outfit, off course Nina Ricci. We struck up a conversation and it turned out she spoke French. She was from Jordan—a princess, or at least I imagined that she was. When I commented on her hair, she said, "I have to take you to this guy who does Pari Ghashoghi's hair." Ghashoghi was the notorious Jordanian arms dealer. The beauty shop was called D something, and she was heading there herself. "He does all the royalty," she said of the stylist.

She would not take no for an answer so I went with her. We arrived and who is the royalty she is talking about? Her husband! He is a Prince, one of the richest men I had ever met. I got my hair done and by evening there was a good group of people at La Concha, including me, Remi, Jerry, the princess and Prince, and a young lady who was with them, barely eighteen years old. But before dinner around nine the Prince had invited me and all my friends for cocktails on the Veranda at the Carlton. Two bottles of Crystal Champagne were placed at each side of the table with a fabulous bouquet of roses in a vase specifically arranged for the Prince. Then we all walked to La Concha for dinner. The place was exclusive beyond belief. It was the place to be. There were Bentleys and Ferraris parked out front. One look at the menu and Remi said, "We can't eat here. This meal is going to cost $3,000. We can't pay that, let's get out of here."

"I don't think we're going to pay," I said. "They invited us."

Athena

The Prince ordered everything on the menu—lamb, couscous, salad, champagne, the priciest red and white wine. Middle Eastern music was playing. The mood was like a celebration, a big-time event, but all of a sudden Jerry and the Prince were fighting! The Prince told him, "I'll give you $50,000. Pishi is staying with me tonight."

Jerry turned to me and said, "Do you know this guy?" "Who is he? They're bargaining over you," he said. It was funny and yet bizarre—too bizarre. "Come on, get your bag, let's go." Jerry had decided what was about to happen was not kosher.

I was ready to go. We stood to leave and the Prince grabbed my hand. "What do you think this dinner is for?" he said. "I don't know," I said. "I just came here to have dinner with you and your wife. You invited me." We left in such a hurry that Remi left her scarf behind. Just as we got outside, believe it or not, a taxi pulled up and Mr. Wonderful climbed out. What a crazy coincidence! He was coming back from dinner, hoping he would find us, so now he had seen us and stopped. He wanted to know what the hell was going on, why we were all running at midnight. I didn't tell him, but we walk with him the short walk back to the Carlton. When we arrived, his wife was there, in the lobby of the hotel waiting for him. Seeing the bunch of us out of breath, she asked the same question that he had, "What's going on?"

I wasn't planning to tell her anything, either. I disappeared. A short while later, Mr. Wonderful came to my room and I gave him the whole story. What could he do, he just laughed. That was life in Cannes. We enjoyed each other. We made love. We kept on partying. The next day was a birthday bash for one of his good friends at another exclusive place. I was invited again and shopping was on

Lovesick in Beverly Hills

the menu. I wanted to buy a new dress and ran to this adorable boutique, Leonard, where I saw one that I absolutely had to have—white, fuchsia, turquoise, green, aqua, a variegated palette of brilliant colors, exquisitely designed—price tag: $5,000. It was perfect for my body and my exquisite tan, so I called him to ask permission to buy it for the party. He said: "ok go for it, if you love it so much." It's a dress I've always kept; my memorable time with my love- is still hung in my dressing room reminding me of the delicious day. In the afternoon I had another appointment at the *coiffure*. When I got to the beauty shop, I was startled to see the Jordanian princess and her entire entourage. The young girl was there—her niece, it turned out, was engaged to be married. The blizzard of diamonds on her neck, ears and wrist and fingers were just blinding. She was a sight to see. My presence at the salon, confirmed what they had been talking about. They knew exactly who I was. "Look who's here," one of them said, "the Persian princess who wouldn't sleep with him!" They were going on and on about yours truly, and laughing, sipping Turkish coffee. I had my hair done and it was living artwork—fabulous. Later, when I had put on my amazing new dress and was standing outside the hotel, waiting for a cab, Mr. Wonderful found me as he was walking by, turning with surprise. "Is that you?" He hardly recognized me. "wow! You look beautiful!"

The smashing color of love was spread all over me and I felt like it too. What an incredible time it was. We got to the party and there were three-hundred people with Brazilian dancers, tons of food and of course Champagne and Caviar. I mingled, listened to music, and every five minutes Mr. Wonderful appeared at my side to check on me. His wife, meanwhile, was so high on marijuana that I thought she would fall over. I could smell it whenever I got near her.

It was a glorious night. The following day, my new friend Mr. Antoine, a handsome and debonair man I knew from St. Tropez, went away, so Jerry was taking care of me. He had added to the fun of Cannes, but my real interest was Mr. Wonderful. How nice it would have been if we could have stayed there forever, enjoying the good life, just the two of us without having to plan times to meet and sneak away by ourselves.

How great it would have been to become the only woman in his life— and live happily ever after. Little did I know, some men are dogs and different species of animals. No, it wasn't going to happen, at least not soon. Never? Time was pulling me toward other things. The trip to Cannes came to an end, and I was back in Beverly Hills, dealing with the thorny issues of divorce and treachery.

In October, I had to travel to Fort Lauderdale for a few days for a meeting of a Political Action Committee. Now I was serving on the executive board. Being stuck there in the hotel alone, without Mr. Wonderful, was depressing. I crashed. I fell into a deep, crushing sort of loneliness that I can't even describe. It was killing me. My husband meanwhile was still going nuts looking and searching for clues to where the money was and how to take it all. The missing money became a big piece of cheese for this dumb little hungry mouse. He wanted the house, the car, the money, all of it. I guess my life too.

In November, I was dragged into his "super" Beverly Hills lawyers' offices for a legal deposition, not realizing I was again being set-up. The two-hour meeting in the swanky conference room was a blatant violation of the law, I would discover later. It is illegal to tape such a meeting without a defendant's knowledge—and yet they did tape me, and then they edited the tape prior to giving it to the judge to

Lovesick in Beverly Hills

bolster their inaccurate claims about my actions. This was no different in my mind than the secret tape-recordings of Hollywood stars and big- wigs that landed the famous sleuth, Anthony Pellicano, a 15-year federal prison term— and it was done by high price lawyers! They had no decency and they would do anything for money, even buying the judge. Holly shit.

"Are you in possession of any cash?" was one of the questions I was asked. "Yes, I am." "So how about you putting it into escrow, and we can hold it," his attorney suggested. "After what he did?" I meant forging my name to transfer the $980,000 out of the Corporation account without my knowledge? Who could imagine what stunt he would pull next? No chance, it will never happen, I told them.

"How about if we get a safety deposit box and have the attorneys hold the key?" they said. Good God! Is this a joke,? Are you kidding me? No! Never! "So he can forge my name again and take it out?" I wouldn't budge, and I had no idea at the time that I was being taped. Later, I would learn that my own attorney knew about the taping—and he didn't object to it, nor did he bother to tell me! My edited tape recording and the answers tacitly acknowledged that I had possession of the $500,000, and would not agree to give it back, and they intended to try to send me to jail for it.

These were ruthless bastards, and my husband and my lawyer were just as bad as any of them. What my lawyer did—during this deceitful taping and throughout the bitter legal fight that I'd soon be waging—was probably worth a malpractice suit. In fact, I'm sure of it. What my husband was about to do was even beyond cruel. It was pure evil—underhanded, malevolent, despicable, and unconscionable. I could run out of words trying to describe the moral atrocity he was about to perpetrate against a woman he had sworn before God to love and protect.

In December, I left town again for a short vacation to Cabo San Lucas. I loved Cabo. When I got back, he had no clue I was gone, the cash was still in the armoire, but almost immediately there was a burglary. The alarm system was disabled and the house gate in back alley broken.

Around nine, a Saturday morning, in December I called my brother's house and asked if the kids wanted to come over and watch cartoons. His wife, in a not-so-friendly voice as always, told me they were in PJ's and to pick them up, just bring them back at noon. We were busy watching TV when suddenly the phone rang. I picked up the receiver and said, "Hello." There was silence and no one was there and then they hung up. Half an hour later the home phone rang again and still no one was there. I decided to hit *69 and find out who was calling me. The recording said, "Hello, this is the…. Hospital. If this is an emergency, dial 9-1-1…" and I said to myself, my bastard husband. I called him on his cell and told him to stop bothering me.

On Saturday around 12:00 I left the house dropped off the kids and went to pick up my girl friend and go to Neimans. I had been out shopping with a lady friend, Sonny, when all of a sudden I said to her, "Let's go! I want to go home, now. Let's go to my house." She replied, "Are you crazy? We just got here!"

For some reason, psychic or not, I insisted and then we swung by my house. I was to meet Mr. wonderful at 2:00 in his office. Struggling to unlock the door, I could not get into my room—it would not unlock. The new lock on my bedroom door had been damaged changed. I banged on it several times and called the locksmith on my cell phone while I kneeled on the floor, trying in vain to get the lock to open. "Carlos," I said, "I can't get in my room!" I think it's broken! As I was yelling at Carlos, my husband out of breath and pounding the hardwood floors almost running, approached and stood behind me with a vicious grin. He must have been waiting outside and watch me enter into the house. He probably loved finding me there on my knees struggling to unlock the door.

"Now you can have your fucking divorce," he said, throwing at me the new two keys and laughing hysterically. "Everything is all set."

Still struggling with the key, I turned and dropped my purse and the shopping bag from Neiman Marcus. "You son of a bitch!" I said. "You took the money, didn't you?"

It hit me like a ton of bricks—gold bullion bricks. He quickly left-practically ran outside and left his car behind. Someone must have dropped him off. Terror surged through me, a real outrage. Oh, my God, I went in and found slips of yellow paper all over the place—the small memo sheets where we had hand-written the amount of cash in each bundle, scattered on the floor. The oxblood duffel bag was also on the floor, completely empty. I yanked open the armoire, pulled out my books and CDs, and I found the lock on the secret compartment broken and hanging and swinging on the clasp. The little door was busted. The cash was gone, all half-million of it. The big bag of jewelry still was sitting there and staring at me. He had no time; I had walked in on him. I always did have perfect timing. How do I survive without any money? Super lawyers were now planning and writing my death sentence.

While I took in the stunning scene, he was already in a car, speeding away from the house. The rage and panic that filled me was beyond anything I could have imagined. This was my worst fear, and now it was coming true.

"OK," I said to my friend Sunny, "I have to meet Mr. Wonderful at 2:00 So let's call 9-1-1." I called the police. They never did anything, not a goddamned thing. Somebody there said, "Oh, yes your husband was just here. He told us you might be calling. We will send someone over." Prior to braking in, he had driven straight to police headquarters in Beverly Hills, a few minutes away from our home. "He reported he was missing some stuff from your house," the desk sergeant told me. "He's already filed a report." What a shame. Bastards! All of them. How do these people come up with this stuff? They should win an Oscar. After all, he had super lawyers to represent him and tell him what to do.

The lying son of a bitch had also seized the opportunity to let the cops know that his wife was "a little crazy," as I later discovered in the official police report—a document that would screw up my life for nearly two years, until the last dramatic day of the trial.

By beating me to the station house and uncorking his little slander, he was brazenly casting me as the villain and covering his own ass. It was a smokescreen so he could make off like John Dillinger with the missing loot. His status as a doctor gave instant credence to his irk about me being crazy. He knew it, too. Sophistication galore!

He must have been thrilled as could be with his dirty, ugly little trick, but it was a disaster for me. Half of that $500,000 was my entire life savings. And I knew he was not about sharing. When was it ever going to end?

8

Eve of Battle

Cheated, angry, almost certain that my so not loving husband, now would try to frame me for taking the half-million dollars; I was still many months from the start of the divorce trial and now my life was in chaos. Real-estate was awful—the vitriol directed against me continued to spread like a stain through the entire city. The huge Persian population in Beverly Hills embraced the same stiff, backward moral code as he did: You don't file divorce papers on your husband. It's unforgivable. People shunned me because he told everyone I ripped him off, bad mouthing me every where, so I was told years later by his closest friends. Nobody seemed to want to give me a listing. I was making more than one- hundred and seventy-five calls a day—twenty-seven an hour during my frantic work shifts—but most of the effort was in vain. It only wore me out. I was losing weight and smoking too much. I was desperate to find some way to get through the emotional ordeal of divorce court and protect myself from him and the high-priced sharks that he called his attorneys, his "top guns."

And now I was about to go to jail, for something I did not do. This was not the first time I was being accused of wrong doing either.

Looking for any edge I could get, I thought about a brilliant idea: I took to watching re-runs of the famed TV drama, "Perry Mason."

It came on at eleven o'clock at night, and I would already be in my night gown, in bed waiting impatiently to watch and see how Mason finds the guilty one. That taut black-and-white serial, with the dapper, studious Raymond Burr maneuvering through the thorniest legal tangles, had never particularly interested me before, but now I was hooked. Why not? I was looking for answers, and I was going to go to law school, wasn't I? Ridiculious as it was, somehow it made sense.

He was a master at finding the culprit. I had always loved some of the old black-and-white TV shows and movies—some of my favorite stars were of a certain era: Barbara Stanwyck, Audrey Hepburn, Elizabeth Taylor, Tyrone Power and of course Gary Cooper. Oh, how I adored Gary Cooper! So it became natural for me to settle in and see how Perry Mason operated in the courtroom. Watching him grill witnesses, and watching Angela Lansbury crack cases in the detective show "Murder, She Wrote," became my obsession. They were my personal instructors in my crash- course version of law school and fighting all obstacles.

My pillows would be packed around me. The TV was in the armoire—my infamous armoire. Every night as I tuned in, I was searching for my own clues— looking for a key to winning my case. In my heart, I had to believe that if I was in the right, if truth carries more weight than the lies told against me, it would come out during my trial, but I wasn't taking any chances. I wanted to be ready. No matter what dinner event I was attending, or who I was having meetings or drinks with, I rushed home every night to watch Perry Mason. The twists and turns of the plots sharpened my obsessive mind. The show taught me new ways to see things and to solve problems. The least expected person was always the bad guy. Invariably some little, crucial detail-clues that made all the difference; it demonstrated how there was always a solution to the problem. There had to be. My life was on the line. I had to find the answer somehow, somewhere.

The question was, could I? my lawyer was a loser, real life is not a TV script, and here all alone, I was faced with taking on a crooked husband and the pack of high-priced charlatans he had hired to crush me. It became a monumental psychological battle. At times I seemed to be melting away with fear. I grew suicidal. I prayed. All my life, I've believed in the power of prayers. I prayed for a solution, for help and for clarity. Somehow, as I studied the legal procedures, as I absorbed every Perry Mason episode, and voraciously read books about crime, my mood would rally, and my mind would grow more focused. I would feel with absolute certainty that I would get the son of a bitch.

I no longer cared about the money. I was determined to catch him in the lies and win the case. I've always been motivated by a challenging project, and this became my project, the biggest fight of my life. He had broken into my room and I knew I was telling the truth, and that fired me up. Always war, always fights, the real "war baby" as my mother always said.

To try to nail down what Dr. Boring had done with the missing cash, I hired two private detectives—one who was extremely competent, very professional, for $17,000, and another who took the case briefly for $5,000. Neither had any luck. Cash rarely leaves a trail, and after a few months, they came up with nothing whatsoever.

Finding an attorney had been nearly as difficult. The search went on and on and on—interviews with at least eleven different lawyers, including one bastard who took my retainer to the tune of $10,000 a criminal lawyer-cocaine addict and didn't do a damn thing. He would find excuses not to see me, after he got the money, and I never saw him again after the first meeting. Also he refused to return my calls. This could be a whole book in itself, an expose of all the ruthless, conniving cheats who practice law in Beverly Hills. They're a state-licensed bunch of blood-sucking vampires—just open a vein and they'll drain you dry. I know. I have been there. They got their fangs into me and ripped me every which way they could. But now I was bleeding all over the place and swimming in a pool of blood. Rule number one: remember lawyers are not your friends, nor always honest.

There was an attorney in Century City, a real hot shot who let me cry my eyes out for an hour and asked me for $100,000 in cash—I swear, a hundred-thousand dollars— must be in a brown paper bag, that old cliché, just to think about taking the case over the weekend. His name was Mr. Crook. All weekend I implored of God, please, please let him take the case, but on Monday the lawyer called me and said no, he was too busy. "Besides, you have no evidence, no witnesses, no alibi and I don't feel like it," he said. Talk about an arrogant bastard! For a case like mine, he told me, $100,000 wasn't enough. The retainer would have to be $150,000 just to read the depositions! Not to represent me, only to go over the material!

I spoke with a famous lawyer who had won notorious and famous cases; he was so very sympathetic, and told me point-blank, "Settle with him because you don't have a chance in hell." Once you go to trial, you will lose". So do not be stupid and do not go to trial. Now that was refreshing. Actually I don't think I cared to listen to him or anyone anymore. I did not do anything wrong, and my god knew it.

Learning to try relentlessly, I left it up to the universe to give me what I deserved, my innocence.

Life is funny sometimes, I realized, these lawyers, are stupider that I had imagined, and now I was about to put up the biggest fight of my life.

Melancholy and sadness was setting in, as I got inside my car, all of a sudden started screaming for ten minutes hitting my head to the steering wheel. Why? why? Why?

Over the next several months I experienced some real horror stories. I felt my own attorney was no longer representing me. While meeting with a lawyer who had handled a very famous billionaire's divorce case, I went so far as to pull out the pink slip of my Bentley, begging him to represent me. In his office, after he listened to my case, I placed the pink slip on his desk. "Take it, it is worth a lot of money, please represent me, I am desperate." I said. He replied, "listen I like you, but you have nothing, no alibi, no witness, what do you want me to do." he said. "You know me and you know I don't have time for this, settle with him, or you are going to lose."

"Why? I didn't do anything wrong or illegal."

As I sadly left his office around 6 p.m. I realized how desperate and lonely I was, now not only I had no one to protect me, my case now was untouchable and no lawyer would touch it. It was time! I was going to declare war and fight the biggest fight of my life.

Every time the doors closed on me, I'd find another breath and start to push even harder. I couldn't give up now.

Athena

The attorney I finally ended up with—the one I was stuck with, because I couldn't find anybody better—was a chubby, middle-aged, bespectacled, and unknown family law practitioner whose daughter had attended school with my girls. His name was Henry. He was kindly stupid looking guy who spoke in an unwavering monotone—an unflappable and consummately dull lawyer who ran a one-man show in a Century City office tower. I always felt, he stinks and never takes a shower.

He took the case immediately. Pitting this passive, well-intentioned individual against the high-powered carnivores that my husband had hired was like throwing a mouse in front of a lion. This guy was the antithesis of Perry Mason.

What I didn't realize at the time, as I agreed in my desperation to let him handle the case, was how mediocre he really was, and how, because of his lack of experience and expertise, my life was going to take a different turn.

Within three months, Henry was completely overwhelmed, as he himself admitted to me. The pre-trial legal wrangling was just too much for him. There was an absolute blizzard of paperwork—depositions, motions, issues involving the missing cash, the household expenses, my income, his income, the division of property, everything under the sun was being thrown at him. But never any forensic accounting was admitted in the court of law.

Before it was over, the case file would balloon to six thick volumes, each nearly as fat as a telephone book—for a trial that would last only three days! And all that verbiage did not even include the trial transcript; that was a whole file box on its own. The six volumes I mentioned was just the pre-trial warfare, attorneys firing missiles at one another while racking up exorbitant fees. What a circus these lawyer put on. They would provoke a fight with the other side and the next thing you knew all parties would be back in court, haggling over some pre-trial motion, a problem with a deposition, the issue du jour: Ka-ching! Another fifty grand! That's how they bleed their clients of whatever wealth they might have, inventing and creating nonsense. The legal dispute was almost beside the point. It was ludicrous. It was a crime all on its own.

Want to know how low and petty it got? Imagine a rich, workaholic doctor who is raking in $100,000 a month, and he has the security guard—the guy who is policing our divided house—give a legal declaration that I was stealing his breakfast cereal! These alleged thefts—which also included, by the way, raisins and bananas—were completely unproven; no one saw me take so much as a single Cheerio. However, I obviously thought it was more cost-effective to tie up his diamond-studded lawyers on the case than it would have been to go out and buy another box of corn flakes or Fruit Loops or whatever the hell he was eating. Unbelievable! I don't even like or eat Cheerio.

"While I have not actually seen [Pishi] throw groceries out, I have observed that the miscellaneous groceries that Dr. [Boring] has described have disappeared, leaving nothing for him to eat for breakfast," the guard said as part of the official record. And there was more! "Dr. [Boring] has pointed out to me that he has left clothes in the washing machine and dryer and when the cycle has finished, if he is not immediately present, [Pishi] has thrown his clothing on the floor," the guard stated. "Although I have not personally observed [Pishi] throwing Dr. [Boring's] clothes on the floor, I have seen Dr. [Boring's] clothes on the floor near the washer and dryer."

Athena

The guy should have folded his laundry! He wasn't the only one who needed to use the washer and dryer. So, all right, I was angry. He was angry too, and terribly abusive toward me. We weren't getting along. We were going through a divorce, and all the crap became food for the fire-breathing legal monsters.

The attacks were relentless, and docile Henry was not up to the job. He was helpless. He couldn't keep up, and as the months went on he grew less and less accessible to me and friendlier toward my ex-. Not knowing he had already given up. As the months went on, in fact, we found ourselves discussing the case one day at the round table in the corner of his office. Henry actually had the nerve to suggest that I should invite my thieving scumbag ex- back into my life.

"He is a very nice man," Henry commented. "You should get back together." Hah! Fat chance! Only a clueless imbecile would have broached such an idea, but what I didn't realize then, what I only figured out much later, was that my own lawyer had betrayed me by switching sides. He had decided, I guess, that I really did swipe the money, or found some other reason to shift his allegiance, leaving me with virtually no representation at all, except on paper. It explains why, out of every ten phone calls I made to him, Henry troubled himself to return maybe one of them—and he was charging me, anyway. To the tune of $300 an hour! There was at least one day when I didn't even see him and—ka-ching!—another bill, for an entire day's "work." I said, "I wasn't even in town!" But it didn't matter. Bill the hours! That's the barrister's creed. Meanwhile, he was blithely allowing himself to be pummeled by my husband's lawyers, who were even worse. They were double-teaming the case at $425 an hour apiece! Those two jokers were milking my husband like he was a cash cow—money that was half mine. I told him a hundred times, "You're being stupid. Let the lawyers go! Let's sell the house, you take half of everything, and I'll take half."

But no, he had to fight to the end with pride, stubborn foolishness, rage and anger so he can ruin me and have it all! Not to mention total stupidity! Complete unwillingness to let go of a wife, who was supposed to be his personal property until we were both in eternal slumber. Whatever his mindset was, it was ridiculous. Insanity is the only explanation for the pattern of incomprehensible behaviors he displayed during all those months—forging my signature to drain most of our bank accounts, and stealing the cash when I planned to divide it fifty-fifty. He was going out of his way to try to bludgeon me in every way possible.

There was one night in particular when I tried to beg him to stop the financial hemorrhaging and split everything between the two of us—just divide it up and walk away amicably, him going his way, and finally end the circus.

It was mid-March of 1998, and we were still living in separate parts of the house. He came home around 9 p.m. and immediately disappeared into his locked bedroom. I stepped to his bedroom door and knocked. He wouldn't open it, nor would he answer me. All I asked was to talk to him—nothing. Dead silence. I asked, please for the children's case, the monies are theirs, let's not waste it away, on stupid lawyers, please open the door and talk to me, begging to come out and settle this between us. As I stated my case—all I heard was silence. It was like I didn't exist for him. For half an hour, I stood at the door, crying. It was awful. Maddening!

Finally I went into the kitchen and poured myself a little drink. I needed to steady my nerves. Taking the glass into the family room,

I turned on the TV, as I sipped it and brooded over the sick state we were in, the money flying out the window, the ugly fighting, and the utter waste. I decided to try again. Walking to his door, I repeated what I had said about dividing the assets, avoiding a trial, and going on separately as friends. Why not? What would be so bad about it?

He ignored me again. I returned to the kitchen, finished my drink, and brewed a nice cup of tea. Rage was now building up inside me. The pressure gauges were moving into the red on every nerve. With my cup of tea in hand, I advanced toward his door once again and said, "I emphatically said: "You son of a bitch! Look what you're doing! You are wasting away, the children's money. Call your lawyers tomorrow!" tell them to stop this insanity." Then I slung the cup at the door as hard as I could.

Instantly, he burst out, going berserk, and with tumescent and bombastic attitude, we struggled a moment, fearing now he was going to kill me. Immediately, I spun away and ran to the living room, grabbed the fireplace poker, and went after him. The raised iron tool in my fist was more than he cared to see. In a panic, he withdrew into his room and I dialed 9-1-1.

The Beverly Hills police were there in moments—they're known for responding quickly to emergency calls-most of the times any way. They saw my scotch glass and made a note in their report that I had been drinking, but I fared much worse than he did. For blowing his cool and charging out of his room at me, and for the skirmish that followed, he earned the ignominy of being led from the home in handcuffs and booked at police headquarters on suspicion of assault and battery.

Lovesick in Beverly Hills

It was a happy moment for me, no doubt about it, but I was also extremely concerned about the chance of reprisals. Who could imagine what he might do next while we were stuck living under the same roof? The one and only night, I went to bed and peacefully slept the entire night.

That same night I phoned my lawyers. First I called my criminal lawyer—the $10,000 chief thief—one of the biggest in town. I told him what had happened and said I needed a restraining order to keep him away from me. This legal maestro, who was regarded as one of the very tops in his field, declined to help me.

"You can get it yourself," he said. Just go to Santa Monica Court House on Main Street, its very easy.

Frustrated, I called Henry, the divorce attorney, and was told exactly the same thing: I could get it myself. It's incredible to think, what do these guys do every day in a town where money—SUPER MONEY—is the only thing that matters?

The night that he was booked, my nerves were so badly frazzled that my friends worried about whether I would hold up. At ten o'clock, one of them called and said, "We're taking you out." When? Where? I was exhausted. She insisted I was going and they'd pick me up at eleven. I was wearing jeans and white Keds sneakers—black leather jacket dressed down, casual. It was raining and my world, felt the same. I had finally thrown the garbage out.

My two friends picked me up and we headed for The Viper Room, the trendy nightclub on the Sunset Strip in West Hollywood. Never mind that I was forty-six years old, the door bouncer carded me and would not let me in without my driver's license! I didn't have my wallet or identification, so I had to rush back home and get it.

Performing that night was the legendary Cuban Ensemble, Buena Vista Social Club. The rhythms of the music and the time with my friends were a tonic for me. We were there into the wee hours—a blessed escape from the bedlam I was going through. A wonderful interlude, but all too brief: At 7:30 the following morning, a Monday, I drove to Santa Monica Municipal Court to begin the onerous bureaucratic chore of trying to get a restraining order by myself. This would become its own small nightmare. I was there all day, trying to get to the right window and get the right form and fill it out properly while in a state of morbid anxiety.

One of the questions on the form was about my relationship with the person who was to be restrained— below the question were ten different boxes that I could possibly check, depending on whether we were married, legally separated, or divorced, or whether such action was pending, or whether we were living together, or whether we had dated.

It was a mishmash of information. Yes, we were married; yes, we were divorcing; yes, we were living together. I ended up checking three boxes and crossing out two boxes that I started to check before changing my mind.

When I got to the window, the clerk, a real bitch who was the epitome of unhelpfulness, interpreted my confusion as an attempt to defraud the system. She accused me of lying under oath on the application—for what exactly, I still don't know.

She refused to help me distinguish between all those options and yelled to move and let the next person in line to take my space.

Bitch! The result?

His lawyers immediately the next day asked the judge, the husband had to go back to the house. The wife has lied under oath and the restraining order is void. I had marked the wrong box. OK, so I made mistakes. It was never going to happen again.

He was back in the house the very next day! And madder than a hornet! If my life was ever in danger, that was surely the case then.

Life was not going to be easy, and every moment and every obstacle continued on and on, becoming norm in my life. Now I was getting used to disasters and I was honestly not about to give up. Talk about frustration—I couldn't even get a restraining order. Shit, Perry Mason or not, I had made a mistake. I couldn't get any kind of break no matter what I did or did not do.

Fortunately, after he returned there was no violence. But there was no talking, either, no hope of finding some compromise to avoid a trial. At that point my focus turned to trying to win, to ruthlessly pounding him in court. The attorneys were still bleeding us dry, but there was no turning back. I became ferocious in my determination to win total victory in the case. Now, I knew for sure, I was all on my own fighting the biggest fight of my life.

Destination: Victory.

Now I was going for the kill, never entering the thought that I would fail. And I am sure, he never suspected that I would eventually find the evidence I needed. I never once thought that the woman who

Athena

watched Perry Mason would trump all the lawyers and discovers the key to the whole trial and beat his irascible butt in court; Never was I going to give up, and I knew deep down, I would win.

Here's where God comes in—or fate, or luck. Call it a miracle, or call it what you want, but I trace it back to Sinai Temple. I continued to attend the synagogue, sitting quietly and thinking with terrific fervor. I loved the silence in my temple; being there was a moment of peace in a life filled with grating noise. Besides, that's when all the strategies would flow into my mind. My life being so chaotic, sitting still, quiet, calm—no phone, no distractions—just meditating and reflecting on my case, de-cluttering ideas would come, I'd think of things to do, questions to ask. Seeing Mr. Wonderful in my little attic room and going to Saturday services were the two things that restored me and preserved my sanity. I had read somewhere that if you really, really pray, if you pray to God with all your might, the spirit will move, your heart will crack and action will follow.

One Saturday morning, I remember it very clearly, and three months before the trial was to start, and the anger and anxiousness in my life had become frenetic. I was on fire, confused, disturbed and walking around with law books, papers and pencils, making notes, jotting down events—trying to find and build my case. I moved from those jarring realities into the sanctity of the synagogue, taking a seat near the back in my lovely pink Chanel suit. In that serene place I began to pray, praying so hard it felt like my heart would crack. The cantor was singing. An usher noticed me and came over.

"You look too pretty to just sit there," he said. He suggested I greet worshippers at the Torah, up on stage and of course I did.

Lovesick in Beverly Hills

It seemed like an omen. I felt there was a purpose to me being moved, that I had been summoned to be closer to God, that divine protection was being offered. A week later, the miracle itself unfolded, an inexplicable turn of events that would make all the difference in the trial so rapidly approaching. That particular morning, my sister needed to get some blue jeans hemmed and she called and asked if I would go with her to the tailor.

She offered to pick me up. I had a pair to be hemmed also, so we drove to Westwood together, coffee and cigarette in hand. She parked her car on the east side of Westwood Boulevard, North of Santa Monica Boulevard. I went in first for the hemline, and then left the shop and waiting for my sister outside, despondent again, I sat on the curve, wondering how I was going to get out of the mess I was in. Smoking and with a cup of coffee in my hand, I could feel another anxiety attack coming on. As I was crying and hyperventilating on the sidewalk, I noticed a locksmith across the street and remembered that I had promised to make copies of a house key for a new listing I had in Beverly Hills. I had scheduled an open house on Sunday. The sellers were going to be in Palm Springs, but they had given me a key and asked me to make a duplicate for myself. It would be easy enough to cross the street and do it now, so I jaywalked and entered locksmith's office, asking if he could help me with few spare keys.

"Sure," he said, he was busy—it was going to take a few minutes. He wanted to jot down the order so he said, "What's your name?"

I told him and immediately he looked up and stared. A second later, he said, "Beverly Hills, North….. Drive, right?"

Now I was surprised. "Wait a minute, how do you know where I live?"

161

He smiled and answered without thinking. "We are coming to court to testify. "Your husband is a doctor, right?" A while ago he called and said the phone was off the hook or something and asked us to break the bedroom door lock and get in. He had to get the phone back on the hook so he could use it in case of emergency."

As he was explaining, his boss walked in and said, "Shut up-you fool, are you stupid or what? "You're being subpoenaed by her husband's lawyers, not by her, so don't talk to her anymore, move, I will take care of her".

Constantly, thinking how after the brake in a year and half before, and how many times I had used the entire Yellow Pages, searching under locksmith throughout Los Angeles and the San Fernando Valley. I called the same shop several times. Every answer from every locksmith was the same: It was not them. Questioning the stores, regarding changing a bedroom key somewhere between December of 1997 and February of 1998, had become my obsession. Damn, what a difference a locksmith makes.

Mania, better yet a bipolar disorder mood and an excessive enthusiasm hit me on the forehead, and I was overwhelmed with joy. Electricity crackled through my body. It felt like lightning had hit my skull, and my brain was lit up like a filament in a jar, glowing all kinds of crazy neon colors. This was a tremendous break-through in the case, I found the "key" to the case, a vital piece of evidence. I guess god was watching over me, since for almost two years, I was telling the truth.

It was information that I had been searching for a long time. This key evidence was about to turn my life around. I had been looking, and looking everywhere for it, including his room, slipping in there

Lovesick in Beverly Hills

one day when no one was on guard, poring over receipts in hopes of locating the locksmith who had helped him to break in. Now I had found the place, as if I had been guided there—as if some higher power had led me through the door and right to a guy who remembered the name and address and had a loose enough tongue to blurt it out. It was mindboggling. I picked up the new keys and ran back across the street, jaywalking again, nearly getting myself run over, and charged into the tailor shop to tell my sister.

"I got it! I got it!" I said. "I found out what happened. Let's go. Get me home! now! I said now!" repeating senselessly over and over again: take me home. By this time, I was screaming at her from the top of my lung. She looked at me like I was crazy questioning my sanity. I was talking a mile a minute. She couldn't make any sense of what I was saying, jumping with joy, and I could not make any sense of it either. It was the key to the case.-pun intended. Out of all the locksmiths in Los Angeles—how many are there?—several hundred, I happened to walk into this shop, the right shop? I was tingling all over. Remembering how one day, in December of 1997, I put the Yellow Pages on my desk in my bedroom, and started calling every single locksmith in Los Angles and crossing with a red ink pen, the ones who did not know about a changed lock.

The psychic and spiritual side of life, plus my creative energy, went into play once again. I am no different and possess no superior intellect, but I am what I am and my gut feeling said: I was going to win-now.

Feeling revived, I had decency and a brain and that was encouragement enough to undo his concocted story for why he had needed to get into my room to search for his "missing" cell phone, but the story didn't add up, and the locksmith finding would help to explain why it didn't. Before he had clammed up on me, the locksmith, in the store, had divulged one flaw in the story—the fact that he had been paid by my-ex in the alley, behind the house, a red flag that something was wrong. On top of that, the story contained an even bigger flaw, a fatal flaw that I could exploit when I finally got to present my case in court. The second broken phone line!

Knowledge is power, and I knew enough now to gain a critical advantage. I was determined to be ready when the time came. Incidentally I never mentioned finding the locksmith to my lawyer. Not a word of it, because I knew he was a trader. No, no, he was not my friend and he was not to know what I was up to. He was no longer to be trusted. Rule number two: never trust your lawyer, first think and then listen and ten think again. I felt it for a long time that he was not going to help me. By now, I knew and was aware that he was a joke. He was useless and I didn't need him. Looking back, it occurs to me that if I'd had a really top-notch lawyer—the kind who could command $100,000 in a paper bag, or someone like him with a few more scruples—I probably would have lost the case. I'd have relied too much on my attorney, just as my ex- did with his hotshot lawyers.

What won me the victory was the fact that I had to dig in and wage the battle myself, which is one reason I constantly harp on the message: NEVER, never, never trust your lawyer! Make sure you know what he is doing at all times. By the way, originally, this was to be the title of my book.

Obstacles were dominating my life, and the trial date loomed over me life like an immense monolith—a forbidden landmark that dominated the horizon. As it drew nearer, life continued to be hard and hectic, a mad race from 7:30 a.m. when I showed up at work, until 10 at night, a cyclone when I finally began to ease up. Depositions, work, exercise, and seeing Mr. Wonderful— my Valium, filled my days. Evenings were for tears, parties, more work on the computer, and finally my time alone with Perry Mason. I was living on cigarettes and coffee, worrying, still losing weight, and trying to survive.

Sometimes I wished I wouldn't live and die so I did not have to suffer anymore. I just wanted it all to end. There was no hope. Even after finding the locksmith, I sank under waves of doubts, losing faith, drowning in despair and sorrow. Henry didn't want to talk to me—my own lawyer! He wouldn't return my calls, and meanwhile he kept charging me up the yin-yang. He wasn't representing me at all-he had given up. He thought I was lying, he thought I had the half-million dollars, he thought I would lose anyway, and so basically I was on my own, being picked apart by the wolves. Why bother to try? I rarely heard from my daughters. I spent nights alone, missing the one and only love of my life, while Mr. Wonderful was home with his wife or enjoying long-distance vacations that lasted months at a time. I remember clearly that in one span of a year, I counted he was gone for 210 days. It was awful. There was no way out, but I did not want out. Deep in my head I could hear the whisperings of a death wish.

I now drove a black Bentley, but I bought another car, an old red Fiat Spider convertible, for $1,900. It was tiny. I chose it because I had read that in a crash a little Fiat would burn in thirty seconds. If I lost the case, I was planning to go up on Mulholland Drive, the winding scenic road that traces the high ridges of the Santa Monica Mountains, and pull off a fiery crash-and-burn. Go right through a guard rail and down into a canyon. One day I actually drove the Fiat up there to look around for a likely spot. It would have been over instantly, a furious few seconds and I would have been free of my troubles. That's how serious it got. It was scary as shit, all the way, up there on the winding road. And then I said to myself: are you out of your mind?" get out of here.

During this long, bleak stretch, there was one happy moment, an engagement party for my oldest daughter, who had decided to marry a bright young law student— soon to be a criminal lawyer— she had met him at UCLA. It was November of 1998, and the trial was still months away. We rented out the Friars Club, adjacent to the old Peninsula Hotel in Beverly Hills. One-hundred and twenty guests arrive, filling the room, sitting at tables topped by magnificent floral sprays—people even fought over the centerpieces at the end of the night. There were candles and rosettes, a lovely green-and-white color scheme, and several Persian rugs that I had brought from home to dress up the place. I had designed and personally purchased every single flower and arranged the floral centerpieces by myself, fit for a princess. Working since 9:00 in the morning, I went home around 4:00 in the afternoon to take a shower and get ready for the evening. My daughter and her fiancée' were very, very happy, and everyone partied well to the wee hours. The evening cost $9,000, and Dr. Boring and I were supposed to split the bill, but more than ten years later he still hasn't coughed up a dime, the cheap son of a bitch. One of the rules for renting the club was that we had to clean up afterward, a job that fell largely on me. By the time I got home, thoroughly exhausted, it was 3:30 in the morning—and I noticed something different. His blue Mercedes wasn't there, and four of my beautiful silk Persian rugs that I had left at home were gone, too. If he wasn't there at that hour, he must have moved out, which might be critical in trying to win the house. It was a point in my favor. The difficulty was, the judge didn't like me— he had already made that clear—and my own attorney wasn't taking my calls. Four in the morning the same night, I was typing away on my word processor. The next day, I broke the lock to his room! Yes he was gone and so were all his clothes. Thank god.

Throughout all of the pre-trial haggling, the judge was a stern, tight-lipped bastard who seemed to believe the libel contained in the police report, that I was a little crazy. He had no sympathy for what I was going through. He had already said he was going to "fry" me from day one of the editing of the tape. One of his worst rulings was to cut my monthly support payments in half—from $11,000, an amount established because I was paying the entire mortgage, to $8,600, which wasn't enough to meet the bills. My husband's lawyers were still pushing me to move out, saying the house should be sold to offset the legal fees—in other words, to put money in their pockets—and I should move in with my mother, one of my brothers, or my sister. What the hell? Who died and made them boss?

Why? My main goal throughout the entire divorce was to be allowed to have the house, and no one, not even my lawyer, seemed to be behind me. Henry kept telling me it would never happen—the house had to be sold.

The judge had cut my support because he said I wasn't working hard enough. Tiny bastard!

Guessing fourteen hours a day work day, wasn't enough for him. My attorney sat there like a mute. I had kept logs and contact lists—some days I made one-hundred and seventy phone calls. Call after call after call, and I wasn't working? I had proof—the dates and phone numbers of every call—and the judge refused to look at them.

Athena

Why? I wonder why? Oh, my God, if he only knew, if there was only some way to get him down off his high throne and out to see me struggling in the pathetic little office I had, right off the rear entrance of Nibblers, the lobster restaurant on Wilshire Boulevard. In order to get to my desk I had to hold my nose passing the trash cans with their stink of rotting garbage, bad fish and decomposing meat day in and day out. It was a stench I wish the judge could have smelled. I wish I could have held his face in it. The bad parking situation meant I had to move my car every hour and park blocks away; at that point I couldn't afford the monthly rates at the lots nearby. I was working my tail off and my deadbeat lawyer wouldn't even get off his ass to say, "Here, your honor, look at her phone logs." It was a shameful disgrace. Yep! They were all in it together.

He kept taking the money, though. Ka-ching! No problem! In fact, a recurring ritual during all this madness was the lawyers appearing before Zeus to appeal for the release of more funds, all directed straight into their wallets. Bank accounts, brokerage accounts, pension funds—they were all fair game for the plundering shysters. The amounts were astronomical—$30,000, $50,000, $60,000, $100,000. They could have asked for the moon and the judge would rubber-stamp it, no questions asked. There was no choice but to pay. The wheels of justice had to keep turning and not once did the judge say no, this has to stop. He was right in there with those jackals. Although prior to November of 96, he had already bought real estate, to use up the money.

Several weeks later, pacing in the court's hall way, I remember leaving the courtroom one afternoon during a break in the pre-trial war and finding Pamela Anderson, the blonde "Baywatch" babe seated on a hallway bench. She was stunning, and wore tall stiletto heels and a black spaghetti-strap cocktail dress that exposed an elaborate tattoo on her upper arm. Her glowering expression made her a picture of torment. I asked what was wrong.

"My husband broke my nail—my lawyer is getting me a restraining order," she said.

What? A broken nail? This gorgeous woman was in court over a broken nail and my entire life was broken—twenty-eight years of marriage busted to pieces—and who was feeling sorry for me? Me and only me. Was this fair? What was wrong with this scenario?

I tried to talk with her and she freaked out.

"Get away from me!" she said. She had her security guards put a wall around her, clearing me and everyone else out of the way.

A broken nail! I still shake my head. I was on a grand tour of the bowels of hell and this magnificent woman was moaning about a broken nail. There was no justice in this world.

There seemed no end to the difficulties in my world. Everything was going wrong. I couldn't sleep. I couldn't eat. One night, when I was invited to a charity ball, I put on my gorgeous red gown and went to my client's house to pick up the Bentley from the garage where I was storing it. As I was backing up, the garage door suddenly fell by accident, causing a long, ugly scratch from the roof of my beautiful car all the way down the hood. Feeling sorry for myself I started to cry. Where would I get the money to fix it? The repairs would turn out to cost $5,000. A dark cloud seemed to be hovering over me, sending down rain and lightning bolts. The car developed other problems, too. It kept stalling for no reason. I would try to back up and it would conk out. The dealership wouldn't talk to me. I began action to file suit, looking up an attorney who specialized in automobile cases. For $5,000 promised, he would solve my woes for sure, or I would get my money back. We sat and talked, and when I stepped out into the hallways to go to the bathroom, there was a policeman looking to find the owner of a black Bentley.

"Do you know anyone who owns a Bentley?" he said. "Why? What's happened?" I asked. "The car has been hit by a truck and knocked onto the sidewalk and into the building," he said. The damage was $50,000. Meanwhile, the attorney told me later he had run into a legal technicality: I had driven the car for personal use in addition to driving it for business. The story, at least had a great ending: the insurance company paid for the entire paint and repair of the car.

"We can't represent you," he said. Case closed. And I never got my money back. He refused to return the $5,000.

I sat there and cried. Nothing was going right—absolutely nothing. I was afraid to burden Mr. Wonderful with my woes, worried that he would get turned off and leave me—and I could not lose him, not now, he was my only happiness. I would die if he left me, so I shut up. He had his own life and was very busy. Too busy, and yet I could not afford to complain. He had meetings, parties, vacations, and I suffered. There was a weekend when he was going to be out of town. It was a tough time for me, whenever he went away. I wanted to stop thinking, stop the torrent of thoughts invading my head. I wanted to empty out my brain so there was no hurt and I could recover from the tremendous fatigue and exhaustion. Meditation wasn't working. Exercise was not helping and I was not about to make any mistakes. And as for alcohol, no way I was not going to touch a drop. It would cost me my life. Sleeping pills seemed a better choice. I locked the door, pulled the curtains, shut off the phones, and took an over the counter sleeping pill. The point wasn't to kill myself—I was clinging to my own will to live—my trial now was a few moths away-but I wanted to sleep the entire weekend, escape from everything for a few days to refresh. It scared my friends. No one could reach me. Every four or five hours, when I groggily woke up, I downed another couple of pills, and out I went again. My good friend Remi showed up at my door, very upset. I wasn't up to seeing her and I sent her away. Later, my friend Sylvia came, a tough old woman who was then eighty years old, and died few years later. I let her in and we talked. My family, including my children, had no idea what was going on. I slept off the weekend and when I woke up, I was ready to jump right back into the fire. No parachute needed. I was about to leave the safety net of my lawyer and start my journey into an unknown territory. It was not going to be pleasant. I had been taught by the two biggest lawyers- and my-ex how to be a "fucking ruthless".

As I woke up, well rested and refresh, I knew I was going to get the son of a bitch!

Here and there I managed to accomplish a few things. Soon after my daughter's engagement party, I had hired a trainer to make sure I was in excellent physical shape. Eventually, I found a bank transfer slip and was able to learn that he had sent money to Israel and bought a condo there, emptying all bank accounts months before, community property that by rights was half mine. I spent hours writing a twenty-seven page chronology of my life since filing for divorce—anything and everything that came to my mind, positive thoughts to cheer myself on: I was relaxed, confident, smart, well-educated, and most of all not guilty. Things I needed to tell myself, since I was certain no one else would be a cheerleader for me. The written pep talk did rev me up; I convinced myself that I would win. Pleased with the work, I faxed couple of the pages to my lawyer, not all, which of course was like flinging them into a black hole. I'd have gotten better results by mailing them to Neptune.

Then I thought of a brilliant idea: The Law Library. No matter what, every day I started going to the law library at Superior Court in downtown Los Angeles, building on my legal education and exploring the subject of divorce. I squeezed in a break with a three-day trip to Cabo San Lucas, traveling by myself, pampering myself at the luxurious spa. The rest rekindled my spirits. I cut my hair real short—and looked the best I had ever looked. Returning home, newly invigorated, I decided to go back over the twenty-seven page memoir, giving myself a clearer perspective on what I had been through and what I could achieve in my case. The lawyers were anathema to me. All that legal mumbo-jumbo—civil code this, civil code that, rules of evidence, spousal rights, community property—it infuriated me. What the hell were they talking about? I was fed up with not being represented. I told Henry, "You're fired."

He said, "I'm un-fire able." He was right. I could not even fire him, he was a loser anyway. The bastard! But I was going to take a stronger hand in my case. Pishi was gaining momentum now, and no one had better stand in her way! Thank you Mr. Mason!

The law library in L.A. became my home. It was a huge room with high ceilings and rows and rows of towering shelves. I would stake out a table and have twenty-five books spread out around me. I yelled nervously, "Nobody sit at my table!" to anyone who dared to to come near my table and crowd me. I pushed people away. Every reference book would point me to five more. I needed space for all the references. I took notes and gobbled up the knowledge. I drove the librarian crazy asking questions. "Oh, my God," she would say, "she's here again." One day she said, "Please don't ask me any more questions, please, go away. I can't help you anymore—for God's sake get yourself a good lawyer."

"I have one—he's useless and sending me to jail," I told her. She just looked at me and ran away.

I am sure they all thought I was crazy. But, guess what, I was feeling like a lawyer, and looking like one too, in my black suit, carrying my briefcases. I was learning a lot about family law and legal procedure. I was very interested in my rights—when I could ask questions in court, for example. It turned out that I couldn't—only the attorneys could talk to the judge in open court—but there was no law against me telling my attorney what to ask. I could write notes for him and hold up questions for him that he could ask in court.

Henry was still thwarting my attempts to talk to him about the case. If he knew I was calling him, and thought I might come to the office, he would make it a point to leave. If I parked in front of his office at Century Park East, he would see me and immediately turn around and walk in the opposite direction of my car, trying to avoid me.

With the trial date drawing near, I showed up one day determined to see him. I had phoned ahead for an appointment, and I had seen his car downstairs, so I knew he was there—even when I was told he wasn't. I demanded that he speak to me. He had left, I was told. In other words, he had sneaked out. Hurrying back downstairs, I managed to spot him and got in my Honda just as he was driving away. I raced to catch up. He knew I was behind him and ran the light just to keep clear of me. I almost got killed trying to follow him—and he zoomed off like Michael Andretti, losing me in traffic. What kind of crap was that? He was getting paid! And still fleeing like a lazy-ass coward!

I collected four full boxes of faxes documenting the fact that he refused to call me back. One day I tried to call him seventeen times from my car. Another time I resorted to going to his house and waiting for him. I parked out front around 10 p.m. and sat there until 2:00 in the morning. He would drive by and see me there and keep on driving.

It absolutely enraged me. I saw his daughter one day at Neiman-Marcus. She was about my daughters' age. Here she was, shopping at this classy department store—on my money! I even told her, "That's my money you're spending in this store, you bitch!" Now I really was losing it.

"Get away from me," she said, and ran away. "Go to hell," I shot back; your father is a loser. The few times that Henry and I talked, he had no idea how to handle the case. He came up with a brilliant idea! The ass hole-wanted to put my daughters on the stand! "Over my dead body," I told him. I told him to find another way. There was no way I would drag them into it. "Put the kids on the stand or you're going to jail," he said. "There must be another way," I said. "I'm going to find another way." I did. I knew I was going to win and I was not going to listen to Henry. He was a no-good son of a bitch. But from then on, I refrain from discussing the case I had built, with him.

My patience had run out. I made a solemn promise to him in writing that once the case was over, if he lost it, I would sue him for malpractice to recover the $500,000 the case was going to cost me. I told him that if he didn't say exactly what I wanted him to say in court, and ask exactly the questions I wanted him to ask in the exact order I wanted, I would file my malpractice suit. And besides that, he could go to hell, I told him. Make no mistake: I was in charge. He had no choice but to get the message.

A printer in Korea town had given me a huge number of four-by-six-inch pieces of paper—like index cards—for free. I used those and wrote down all my questions. I ended up with 1,200 of them, a mountain of papers, all written large in red ink, so Henry, the idiot, would know what to ask when the heat was on.

The time was getting nearer. Scared as I was, I was starting to feel more in control, more confident, and very good about my chances of victory. Exited, I was a terror on the treadmill every day, pounding through the miles and nearly going deaf with the music blasting. "I will survive! I will survive!" Gloria Gaynor and me, taking on the world.

Remembering Mr. Wonderful's word: "my son's lawyers are dumb" kept coming to my head. The wave of good thoughts, and the idea of wining my freedom was beyond exhilarating. I gained strength from wresting control of the case and from my precious hours together with Mr. Wonderful. Through all of the pandemonium, he was a huge comfort with his raspy voice and broad shoulders, the gentle, loving warmth he brought me when we could be together. The incredible sex we had kept me alive. Feeling his arms around me, feeling him inside of me, were pleasures beyond what I can describe, moments of pure bliss that got me through everything else.

With all of the nervous energy I had, we had sex three four times a day. I craved his touch. His skin was snow-white and felt velvety smooth. The echoes of his voice would stay with me after he had gone. I would fill my rare quiet moments making notes in my journal, recording how special he made me feel, how much I loved him. He loved me, too, he said. This was no longer some meaningless overnight fling. Almost eighteen years later the touch of his skin still thrilled me.

The entire town and the legal community were talking about a doctor and his wife and a million and a half missing money. He had become a bit more interested in my case. He wanted to know first hand and off course I gave him bits and pieces afraid everyone would find out what I was up to. Here is a part of one of my journal entries from those days:

"His arms are like a big warm blanket . . . . I can just die in his arms and be happy. Wishing he were here and with me now, at this moment. Time goes by so slowly when I wait for him. I can almost hear his footsteps. Any minute now, he will be here. And I will have him for a little while and I would be happy . . . . He is such a sweetheart of a man. He is gentle and kind, good natured, and most of all so giving with his feelings.

And, as for sexually: "It was the most exiting sexual experience of my life. The sound of his voice gave me new promises of joy and laughter to come. What would happen if he were mine? Nights and days, all the hours and all the minutes of all the days and nights of the rest of my life?" And another: "It is heaven when I am with [him], heaven on earth. His shoulders, his neck, his beautiful hairy chest, and his arms give me strength, warmth and fulfillment. His hello lightens up my day and his goodbye saddens my soul. His eyes give me a will to live. I never want to lose him . . . . Oh, God Almighty, could it be possible that he will be mine and mine only, forever and ever? Oh, God, you know what I have gone through . . . . No, it is OK, I don't want to hurt him, let him stay with her. I have really been tormented most of my life . . . . Don't ever take him away from me. He is my life. My cowboy, my true soul mate. A man who is my tower of strength; with his smile, his charisma and the weight of his words, crushes me. He has turned my life upside down. He is my world. He is my dream."

Yes, for the first time in my life, the little Persian girl was head over heels over a man.

9

Great American Theatre

The time for trial was finally near. It was early 1999. The century was hurtling toward a close, and so was my marriage. It was a dizzying time. I didn't even know how to feel and how to process stress anymore. As much as I longed to be free, there was a deep sense of anger and sadness that twenty-eight years of my life had been utterly wasted. At times it swelled up into rage. All sorts of emotions surged through me. There were also practical concerns: How would I live? What sort of financial shape would I be in? better yet where would I live?

Depending on how events unfolded in court, I stood to lose everything and perhaps get stuck with all the legal bills. This had the potential to become its own unbearable nightmare. I thought about standing on Canon Drive in the heart of Beverly Hills and holding up one of the little cardboard signs that the homeless flash to passing cars: "Ex-doctor's wife looking for a home—will work." I felt cornered with no outlet. It seemed quite possible that I could end up homeless and $2 million in debt, and maybe it would even be worse if the judge believed I had stolen the half-million in cash.

The persistent fear was that I would end up going to jail for something I didn't do and pay him the $2,000,000. To me, the idea was like facing death, like going to the gas chamber or the electric chair. The final weeks and days before trial were filled with a flurry of last-minute legal maneuvering, much of it involving financial matters. He, who was raking in money hand over fist from his practice, was suddenly claiming in court papers to be a pauper, obviously intent on hoarding as much as he could so I wouldn't get it. Does anyone have any conscious anymore?

Despite my repeated insistence, there was never any forensic accounting to determine exactly what he was making and where he had invested it without my knowledge. It was a joke; the lawyers would not allow it and the judge never even ask for it and sided with the lawyers. How to screw the clients was the only thing that mattered to all of them. What a system. The lawyers never could give me accurate information. Wrong date, wrong office, wrong time, is what I would get every single time for the phony accounting appointments. Beware! Some lawyers are liars- ambushing you every single time.

We kept trying to schedule meetings to begin the forensic accounting work and somehow for whatever insane and dishonest reason or another it would always be a wrong address, a wrong time, or basically postponed or canceled-always blaming me for it. Not knowing his lawyers and mine too, were a master at playing games. All I got from my lawyer and from his lawyers were delays and excuses till the end. All the relevant financial papers were available. From the inception of his practice I always kept the office books and had copies since I was the one making all his deposits. Yet amazingly nothing ever got done, and I could only conclude that these shysters were in it together, making sure that no one followed the money. Not once did the ruthless judge, who sat on high like Zeus, ask the critical question: Why aren't there any forensic reports?

One of my private detectives had discovered that he had purchased a properties in the Middle East, but almost certainly there were other properties and accounts. The good doctor's entire game plan was about cutting me off from what was rightly mine. The tight-fisted bastard had even begun withholding money from my monthly support payments so he could "pay the gardener," and then stiffing the gardener, too.

This would be another issue for the zillion-dollar-an-hour legal swindlers—how much for pruning the shrubs and trees and mowing the lawn. The poor gardener and pool man were not paid for months. Henry was finally putting pressure on his attorneys, and they were fighting right back with firing ballistic missiles via fax, demanding bills, receipts, wanting me to account for practically every penny spent. Anything over $500 had to be reported to the court. The jousting was acrimonious and clearly intended to make me look bad before the eyes of the court. In one letter, his lead attorney wrote, "Dear Henry: I am in receipt of your letter and angered by the nine (9) separate letters you faxed to me on February 17, 1999 . . . some of which are so ridiculous that it is apparent the letters were sent at your client's instruction and that you have lost all control over [Pishi]."

If nothing else, we were getting to them! The same scumbag attorney sent another letter five days later, raising eight separate points of dispute, including the gardener ("Send the bills!" he suggested) and my longstanding request to have the house placed solely in my name ("Are you serious? Your proposal is preposterous").

We sent the bills—for gas, electricity, taxes, and everything else, including the bill showing that I owned the gardener and poolman $3,245 in back pay. "You have got to be kidding!" my husband's

Lovesick in Beverly Hills

lawyer replied by fax, hand grenade is a better term, taking cheap shots at me for maintaining the garden, and implying again that I had the missing half-million bucks; "[pishi''s] expenditure of thousands of dollars on flowers . . . [is] unconscionable," the idiot wrote. "I suppose, however, that if one had hundreds of thousands of dollars in cash stashed away, one would not have to be concerned with expending three thousand dollars for azaleas and the like."

No doubt the lawyers reveled in this bickering—and why not? The meter was always running. Joyfully they ran and ran the tab, piling up huge bills, with absolutely no conscience. To try to salvage what was left and trying to avoid trial, I had already paid $10,000 to an arbitrator ninety days before the trial was to start. In yet another legal motion in April, the month before trial started, the jackals again went after attorney fees: $70,000 to be paid to the lackadaisical Henry, and $45,000 to go to my husband's team. They got it through the court-ordered draining of our joint bank account. I was powerless to stop it and I was bleeding with it non stop. I had no voice whatsoever, even after seeing my name forged, the bank account emptied, the cash stolen—now I had to shut my mouth and watch the lawyers rip me off and bleed the whole estate. There never was going to be any money divided fifty -fifty. That's why these lawyers get paid for so royaly. It is their job to screw the wife or the husband for that matter.

The end was near and I kept waiting for him to wise up, but he never did. My ex- was a cash cow for the lawyers. I was getting poorer and poorer by the minute. It turned me into a desperate monster heading toward insane asylum.

Now I was on fire, and was going to set the whole world on fire. Not having a thing to lose, I was ready to kill or be killed. My decision was made: I was going to kill it. It was May of 1999, and I had decided number nine was going to be my lucky number now.

How would I ever recover? Real-estate sales were in the toilet. The divorce action had blackened my name in the community, and as for family and children, well they all disappeared too. No one wanted to give me a chance— between Mr. Wonderful and that relationship, which had become widespread public knowledge, and the notorious divorce case, not to mention the missing money, oy vey, it was a cataclysmic calamity. Still I kept getting fired, I was spending more on business and personal expenses than I was receiving in commissions, and at the time I didn't have a single sale, despite working until almost 11 o'clock every night.

Amid all the incredible waste and rancor, I continued to crave the mental and emotional support from the man I very much loved, my blue-eyed cowboy, who called me every few hours telling me how much he loved me and how we would end up together. Mr. Wonderful was just wonderful in making my life well, just wonderful.

His gruff, powerful voice always seemed to soothe me. By now he would say the word I so badly wanted to hear: I love you; promise me you never leave me. Promise me! I need you. Don't ever leave me. What is it about a voice that can have a physiological effect on the body? That can reach into your heart and make it beat faster, touch your glands and start the flow of endorphins, adrenalin, cause you to laugh, cause your skin to flush? A tone from vibrations in the throat that can produce such Pavlovian reactions in a woman in love is like a perfect sound, like a chime, a clear bell, a riff on a saxophone. Hearing his voice when he called me, and especially when twice a day he stopped by to see me, was one of the things that kept me alive.

On top of that, my confidence in winning the case had been growing. Since locating the locksmith, I had reconstructed the chain of events time and again in my mind, and I felt sure I had pieced together the puzzle. I had solved the case. I finally had found the answer.

On a Monday morning in May, two days before the trial began, I thought of a great idea. I invited my mother, my brothers and sister, and my personal friend Aron, who is an attorney, to an evening strategy session in my home so I could lay out my solution and hear their reactions- just double checking my facts.

I was practicing being a lawyer for my trial on Wednesday. Having the affirmation from the important people I knew would be a huge boost and made me feel like a winner. I wanted to double-check my theory and fill any last-second holes I could fill, but I was already excited, thinking, wow, I'm quite a lawyer for someone without a law degree! In conclusion I finally realized, you cannot always listen to the attorneys, you have to go with your own gut instincts. An attorney should be a tool, not the main part of the show.

Henry was certainly welcome to be there—I faxed him an invitation—and it would have prepared him significantly better for trial if he had deigned to show up. Who knows what chauvinist insecurities he was feeling having a client, a woman, taking charge of the fight? By now, nearly all of my plan had been written out for him on my huge stack of index cards—about 1,200 of them—with every question he needed to ask in court right there in bold red ink: Henry's road map to victory. The cards represented all the knowledge I had gained during two months in the law library, plus the insights gleaned from Perry Mason, not to mention my own suffering in living through this excruciating divorce. Henry was a no show. Thank heaven for that.

Besides faxing an invitation, I also sent Henry a blunt pre-trial warning: "I'm putting you on notice, if you ask one question out of the order, deviating from the order I've stacked the cards in, I'll sue you for malpractice; better yet, I will make sure you declare bankruptcy and I will go after you license."

In typical fashion, he didn't respond, nor did he attend the strategy session. Good! Better, I did not need the double crossing loser. Neither did Mr. Wonderful, although I knew I had his support. He was about a million times more supportive than my lawyer or anyone one else in my circle. The people who did come had no idea what the meeting was about. They showed up around eight o'clock, looking at each other like, "What does she want now?" Finally, I told them, "The reason you're here is I solved the case."

"What?" they all said.

I smiled and said, "I have solved the criminal issue." I led them all into the family room, where we sat around near the bar, overlooking the pool. They were all stealing glances at each other, concerned and puzzled. By their looks, I could see what they were thinking: She is off her rocker and has gone mad-she will lose and the judge will send her to the gas chamber. And yet I felt elated—I was flying high. "Well, I'm glad you are here," I said. "I think I've got it. I think I'm going to win, but just to make sure I want to ask you some questions. I want to go over a few things, when this so-called break-in occurred."

We started discussing the events of that horrible Saturday, December 20, 1997 when he had used the locksmith to get into my bedroom and steal the cash from the armoire. Sure enough, I was right, my family turned out to have even more information—facts I hadn't heard yet, but which were crucial. Meanwhile he, a very bad poker player, had been unable to keep from gloating and mouthing off about his dirty, filthy stunt to rip me off.

"You know," my mother said, Dr. Boring had called that same morning. "He told me that he is gladly going to give you the divorce."

Another person mentioned that the good doctor the same day, about the time I arrived home, was slipping, running more like it out of the rear alley, wondering what he was doing walking through the alley on foot at that hour.

"I already know," I said, but it was good to have confirmation, in case I had to prove it in court. Why the secrecy, doing business in the alley; if he didn't have something to hide? Some of his yakking revealed things I hadn't yet heard. My brother spoke up and said Dr. Boring had called him the day after the break-in. "He said, 'Your sister is fucked,'" my brother reported.

What an interesting thing to say if a burglar had not taken $500,000 that was half his. Of course, that wasn't the case. He felt so cocky and secure he couldn't curb his own tongue. He would regret it. I was going to knock him off his high horse. I had read, in my legal research, that in every crime approximately one-hundred and seventy-five mistakes are made. Well, I had found them all. Perry Mason at eleven every night was going to turn out to do me some good. And believe me, that Monday night, talking with my family, I completely solved the case, right down to the last detail. Evidence, alibi, witnesses and motives were what the judge wanted and now I had it all. I was going to win! What a feeling! I got back to my word processor and cleaned up and revisited all the questions and went to bed quite excited. Tomorrow, I will ask the judge to change my last name to my maiden name, legally.

The break-in scenario was now crystal clear in my head: he had asked the locksmith to help him enter my locked bedroom, but had sent the locksmith out. He hadn't realized that the small hidden compartment in the armoire, where I had stashed the red duffel bag, was also locked. And I had the key; he didn't. So he broke that lock and dumped the $500,000 in cash from the duffel bag into some other container, probably a shopping bag maybe or another bag and fled as he heard my footstep, entering the front door. At this point, I think, he heard me come home and got scared. He threw down the duffel bag—which I would find empty on the floor—and hastily fled through the sliding doors into the back yard and then through the gate bypassing the pool into the alley. He was in such a rush that he broke the gate, or maybe he damaged it on purpose to stage the burglary. He paid the locksmith in the alley since there was no time in the house better yet in my bedroom, in cash where I couldn't see him, and then came around to the front of the house, entered, and found me locked out of the bedroom, yelling on the phone to Carlos, "I can't get in!" I was still shouting when he appeared behind me, nearly throwing the two new keys in my face and saying, "Now you can have your fucking divorce!" Those words are burned in my memory, the bitter way he said fucking divorce. His righteous Persian pride couldn't handle even the thought of it.

That's when I said, "You took the money, you son of a bitch." I can still hear him like the devil laughing hysterically before he left.

Lovesick in Beverly Hills

In the depositions, he had claimed that he needed to get into the room because he had left his cell phone inside and he needed it being a doctor. Bullshit. That was a ruse. I had called him on his cell that very morning. He thought his trip to the police station, where he warned the cops that I might call and that I was a bit off, would seal his story as tight as a drum. He told them I was crazy and was going to claim items were missing from my home. He tried to orchestrate it just right, and it almost worked—but not quite.

The deputy who showed up to investigate the incident spent most of his time hitting on me. He was a tall officer who walked in, strolled around, and nearly undressed me with his eyes in the bedroom, where he inquired about any missing cash and asked about my nationality.

"I have a sister married to a Persian," this guy said, while he and his partner examined the scene and the armoire. "They hit their wives. Did he ever hit you?" he asked. I replied, "Never." He was full of sympathy and very attentive. "You are so beautiful, any man would kill for you," he said. "Don't worry." My ex's bogus assertion that I needed "psychological help" would cause me no end of problems. For two years, all through the pre-trial hearings and motions, the judge was merciless with me because of that police report. It was all based, in my opinion, on the police report. Debunking this accusation would be critically important when we got to trial. I had to prove that he did forge my name and that had planned the break-in and that events occurred in the manner I've just described. Fortunately, I had found phone records showing that he had called the house before breaking in. I got him the phone, and I had paid for it, so the bills? Well! I received them—all the copies. He wanted to make sure I wasn't home. Now, thanks to my family, I had even more of the story. My advice to whoever is reading this: Don't ever lie, or you will be caught.

My entire thesis was outlined in a huge stack of papers that, naturally, Henry as yet had not read. Following the Monday night meeting, I faxed another letter, scolding him. "Henry, you did not read these pages. Unless you read them, you don't know what to do in court, so I highly recommend that you do so and prepare yourself for trial."

This is the personal attention that $300 an hour will get you in Beverly Hills—me telling him what to do and how to do it. It didn't matter. He was no longer representing me-the man had given up a long time ago. I swore I was never going to deal with another lawyer as long as I lived, although, as I've said, having an incompetent attorney worked for my benefit. And the beauty of it was it forced me to take the case into my own hands. It was the only way I could have won.

Lying in bed the night before the opening day of the trial, I felt unbelievably ecstatic, confident in myself, intoxicated with the certainty that I would prevail. I couldn't wait to get started. I was about to royally kick ass—his ass and all the lawyers' asses not to mention the judge's, too. The jerk! Though he was small physically, I thought he had a tiny ass. It never occurred to me to worry about the incidentals of the outcome, practical concerns like what I would get and how I would live. The important thing was to prove I had been done wrong - prove it and win; I was going to destroy them all. I had a great night's sleep. Up early as usual, I jumped on the treadmill, excited my mind razor sharp. I put on my outfit—a black, stunning

Armani suit, button down off white silk shirt—and pulled my blonde hair into a taut, business-like pony tail, the ultimate professional.

Toting two briefcases, I looked like a lawyer and felt like a lawyer, too. A lawyer without a Law degree—all the way from Pittstown, PA mind you-marching into legal warfare, into superior court ready for all that ass-kicking. It was a great feeling. Harvard Law Review get ready.

Mr. wonderful called me early in the morning to say he loved me and wishing me good luck. He said: "you can do it, go get them."

I drove the black Bentley into downtown Los Angeles, parked and walked into the huge main courthouse with my thoughts buzzing. In the back of my head there was always just the faintest whispering of doubt—what if I lost, what if no one believed me, what if the judge refused to listen to the facts as I presented them? Today he was going to hang me. He had done it for two years, why would he not do it now? These were only whisperings, though, and I doubt that anyone could enter that building without at least some apprehension.

The courthouse is no place for the weak or timid. It is a nine-story house of pain, dreary and joyless. Everything about it is hard-edged and forbidding—long, drab hallways lit with fluorescent tubes, mismatched colors, white marble clashing with beige terrazzo, ceilings with stained and broken acoustical tiles, backless benches gouged with graffiti and scarred with old cigarette burns, and misery everywhere, hanging in the air like a fog. No one smiles or makes eye contact. Everyone is in a hurry, their futures at stake, nerves tight as piano wire.

All of the preliminaries had taken place here, and now after two hellish years, it was time for the real show—death sentence-the kill. I found the third-floor courtroom and almost collided with Dr. Boring's attorney, a man I'll call Mr. Colossal Shyster—that's my opinion of him anyway—an arrogant little snake so fat I always imagined he was about to have a coronary. For god sake stop eating man and get some exercise!

"Good morning," I said strongly, politely, full of self-assurance and addressing him by name as I entered the judge's courtroom. The judge had not yet arrived, and we had a moment to engage in a psychological duel.

Walking methodically toward me "By the time I'm done with you," Mr. Shyster vowed, "you will be minus $2,000,000. That American Express card? That Bentley you've got? That house in Beverly Hills?" He shook his head. "It's all going to be mine. By the end of the day, today you're going to be minus $2 million!" He pointed upward, as if to the roof of the courthouse. "Honey I will make sure you're going to go up on the roof and jump today."

I kept my smile and said, "Cool! I looked up, smiled, pointed my index finger in the direction of his tie and in full control, I said: I just love your Versace tie. It is Versace, isn't it?" as calm as I could be, in my angry voice I yelled out: "Go fuck yourself—I'm going to eat you up today, I will finish you. Just watch me you idiot, I am going to tear you and your client apart today." You will be sorry you ever touched this case, and I will teach you a lesson that you will never forget. Put that in your fucking diary.

His tie was a garish turquoise-and-yellow-orange number, outlandish and expensive—paid for by his clients. He got the drift. He saw he couldn't rattle me and it flustered him.

"Somebody get him away from me," I said churlishly, turning to his partner. "Doesn't he know it is illegal and he is not supposed to talk to me?" Fuck off, you shit, I said in a loud voice. "You talk to me again, and I am telling the judge. That's illegal, you got that?" Boy that felt great.

Steady as a rock, I was psyching him out—ahead in the game even before the proceedings started. These two hot-shot attorneys, Mr. Colossal Shyster and his trial partner, Shyster Junior, were from one of the biggest family law firms in the city, catering to all sorts of celebrities, and they had sterling reputations. A lot of people don't realize how these top-shelf law firms operate.

They're representing the deepest of deep pockets and they bill accordingly. They have a basic philosophy: Quickly bill every client at least $1 million, and go from there and then make them settle and on to the next victim. It's sick. It's legalized larceny, but that's what they do, and they get away with it. Many of these firms, like the one I hired, are very successful and very smug, but his lawyers hadn't prepared the way I had. They thought they would win because of their names. They thought they knew it all because of their reputation. Wrong! They knew nothing at all. They thought I would get into court and fold under the pressure, the little woman, and it shocked them to see me calm, poised, in total control, like a tennis champion commanding center stage at Wimbledon, psyching them out. After all I had played tennis all my life and single games were my forte. Beside they were all horse's asses anyway. They were dumb and they did not really know me. For two years, I sat there quietly and took their garbage, never saying or being aloud to say a word. Always remember honesty is the best policy no matter what.

Taking my place next to Henry at the petitioner's table, I watched the judge come in—a solemn, pint-sized man with straight black hair and a dark black beard. I always thought he must have a tiny penis that is why he is so mean and unfair. During prior motions, especially in cutting my support payments in half, he had clearly indicated his dislike for me. To him I was guilty before I even started. He resented my nice car and my high-end lifestyle; His words: bring her in, I am going to fry her.

The idea that judges are completely fair and impartial is another myth about the legal system; they are flawed human beings like everyone else, making decisions partly based on statutes and case law and partly on what they feel in their gut, on their biases and friendships with certain lawyers- and how many super ball boxes they were offered.

This particular judge had said during all the preliminary fighting that he was going to fry me. How's that for being objective? Objectivity and fairness? I happen to know that this Solomon on his high throne used to go to the Super Bowl-VIP box of course, with my opponent's high- priced attorneys—or at least that's the word I got, and I believed it. That's what I was up against. For two years I had been between a rock and a hard place, no justice at all. Well, with a loud applause to myself, in my head, I was about to change all of that- because now, I was both the hungry lion and the ring master!

Being the underdog would have been terrifying, but I knew I had the truth and the facts on my side. My briefcases, now lying on the table, contained everything I needed: photocopies of records for evidence, list of witnesses, legal pads for taking notes, post-its, blown up pictures of the scene of the crime, dozen newly sharpened pencils, erasers, red pens, black pens, green for notes, and all of my index cards with questions written out in red ink big enough for my idiot attorney to read. All Henry had to do was follow the road map and he would tear apart Dr. Boring's web of lies.

In their opening statement, his lawyers promised to "prove beyond a shadow of a doubt that this woman is in possession of half a million dollars and that I forged his name and set him up for the missing million in the bank." The good doctor then took the stand, testifying first and outlining his preposterous story, which I knew backwards and forwards. Every gesture, every movement, every facial expression he made, I knew and had already predicted his answer, and exactly what he would say before the words were out. You could have turned off the sound and put me under a cone of silence, and I could have written down a transcript. He claimed, of course, that I had taken the money, and that he had only entered my room months later because the phone was off the hook, he couldn't be reached on that line, and he needed to look around in there for his cell phone. My immediate thought was, I've got him. A total fabrication that can get you nowhere. Looking at my notes and rapidly jotting down every word, I was enthralled beyond imagination. My eyes were glued to the witness, adrenaline was rushing through my body like Vodka on an empty stomach as I attentively listened to all his answers and comments. He maintained, of course, that he had nothing to do with the cash being stolen, because he claimed that I had already taken the cash and it was never in the armoire to begin with. Lier! How did he know that? It was not true. And worst yet he swore it under oath. And that's after he forged my name and took nearly $1 million from my bank account!

Here is where my months of preparation became important. I had read the pre- trial depositions ten times over, analyzing every point and every line. I instructed Henry to ask him what phone line he had tried to call in his effort to reach me. I recited the number, but what he didn't know—because his story was a lie—that was the line that had been out of service for two years. There had been two lines in the house, and he was unaware that I had disconnected that line that he claimed was off the hook a long time ago because I could not afford a second line. I had the phone records to prove it. The other line worked perfectly—he had used it earlier, according to the phone records—which meant there was no reason to break into my space and put it back on the hook. Beside I had his cell phone records. Originally I was the one who had bought it for him so I had all the statements specially I had called him on it, the same Saturday I was watching cartoon with my niece and nephew. Liar!

Henry, discombobulated and befuddled, looking lost and confused, his eyes frozen on the witness, was acting at my direction, skewered him about the phone lines and pressed him about the phone bills for two years and the locksmith. He had no idea, where I was going with my questioning. He was so lost, but he was always lost. Why did he feel it was necessary to meet the locksmith in the alley? Why the secrecy?

The witness struggled for reasons, excuses, moving nervously but they all sounded lame. It was crystal clear to me also to the judge, that he was bullshitting. I only hoped it was as totally clear to the judge. All the while, I took notes constantly. I was really into it. Every point

Lovesick in Beverly Hills

mattered. Every night during the trial, I would go home and go over the testimony and work out my plan for the next day in court.

In one of the early motions that first day, Dr. Boring's attorneys suddenly asked that all spectators be removed from the courtroom. Fifteen of my supporters had showed up, nearly all of them family members except for my lawyer friend Aron. Mr. Wonderful didn't think it was appropriate to be there, and as for my ex-only one brother was in attendance. Dr. Boring was out-numbered and, I think, embarrassed. The judge granted the motion, and why that everyone had to leave. All I could think was, the son of a bitch is guilty and doesn't want the entire family to see it!

Now I was flying high, fearless and I was going for the jugular. In the pit of my stomach I knew this was no longer about money. Honor and false accusation, dignity and extreme anger, now had taken over my soul.

When I took the stand, with a small grin I looked everyone in the eye— especially my husband, giving him a look that said, "Wait you asshole, you ain't seen nothing yet." He couldn't stand it. His lawyer kept prodding and I would mock his questions, saying, "What do you mean by that?" and, "Can you explain exactly what you're trying to ask me?" Would you please repeat the question one more time? It infuriated them. They were like wild dogs, let lose barking away, trying to unnerve me, I've always performed well under pressure. Intelligent, articulate, in firm control, I was finally getting my day in court. For two years, these bastards had been hammering me, bashing me like a *pinata*, and now I had my chance to come after them. I was a hungry lion, with sharp fangs smelling blood and charging in for the kill.

Athena

By the end of the day, somehow I felt telling my story in words and photographs didn't seem enough. I had a couple of dozen pictures of the bedroom, but I realized the first day, they wouldn't get the story across, wouldn't really show what I needed to show about the armoire and the cash I'd concealed inside it. I just felt a certain weakness. I had to resort to something more dramatic and more real—a tactic rarely seen in any courtroom! A crazy tactic and yet a brilliant one.

Settling up with Franco, the gardener, after the trial, I prevailed on him for a favor—to bring my entire set of bedroom furniture downtown the next day. Franco adored me and truly felt sorry for me. He was happy to help, loading it all onto his truck: the armoire, the TV, the CD player, VCR, sweaters, scarves, table, fax machine, telephones, four racks of cassette tapes, and books….. One critical piece of evidence was the red leather duffel bag—an expensive item, which I had bought at Galleries Lafayette in Paris, in which I had stashed the $500,000 in cash before hiding it in the locked armoire. I considered it crucial to have the bag and the rest of the bedroom set there to demonstrate exactly what happened, and how. Not to mention: the $1.99 lock was kept in my wallet. Genious!

Unfortunately, the next day Franco got lost driving in. His tardiness upset the judge, but by mid-afternoon he finally showed up, creating quite a scene as he and other men hauled the load up to the courtroom during a recess.

The hall outside the courtroom grew crowded. People thought an estate sale was taking place. A bunch of attorneys who knew otherwise gathered to satisfy their own curiosity. The case had begun drawing a lot of attention, especially in Beverly Hills. Everyone wanted to know what was happening in the divorce trial with the missing million dollar. Like the jackals that they all are, the lawyers formed a little pack, squeezing together to peek in the little square window of the courtroom door. Huge crowd was forming outside the door-it was a wild and memorable day. The judge ordered the little window on the entry door to be taped up so no one could see what was happening inside the court room.

The next day, the judge resumed the proceedings with a surprised look at all my belongings filling one entire wall of his courtroom.

"What are we having today?" he said. "A disco night?" I laughed. So did others in the courtroom. They were shocked and wondering what I was going to do with a bedroom set. I was ecstatic, ready, and sensing my moment, I was having a great day for a change. Dr. Boring and his lawyers looked puzzled and were not very amused. He was going to have to sit there and listen to my side of the story now— the truth— and he appeared to be growing sicker by the moment.

He had already conceded meeting the locksmith in the alley. I didn't have to swear in the locksmith. The bank was at fault so I did bring in the Manager from Director's National Bank to show that he had forged my name in transferring $980,000 out of the S Corporation account, truthfully by my account, the most important part of the case. I had waited two years for this day and I needed her to show the judge the forged signature on the authorization letter.

From day one, the judge had wanted to know whether I signed and forged my own name to frame him, or whether he had actually forged my name to get the money. How can a judge be so absurd; dumb is a better word.

However, at this critical juncture in court, oops, the bank officials inexplicably "somehow forgot" to bring the one essential piece of evidence they were responsible for bringing—the signed transfer slip. She just happened to forget the only piece of paper she absolutely had to bring, and her screw-up—which was clearly intentional ordered by his lawyers—cost me a chance to make a vital point.

What the hell was she there for then? Bringing that transfer slip to court was the only conceivable reason for those bank officials to be there, and yet, they showed up claiming it had somehow slipped their minds and forgot to bring it. What idiocy! No wonder innocent people like me get cynical about how they're being shafted when they deal with the legal system. Never mind, though, I would come up with a quick solution- thinking hard I knew I would find a way.

So I pressed on, laying out my story. I testified about how I had hid the other money, the missing $500,000 that he later stole, and how I had moved the safe as a decoy while placing the cash in the red duffel bag and locking it in the hidden compartment inside the armoire. And how my darling husband had finally pulled off the ruse involving the locksmith to break in and steal it. The entire crux of the case rested on the judge seeing and understanding—and believing—that I had chosen to use the bag and the armoire as the perfect hiding place for the money. After I had explained it, and as the day's session was nearing a close, his attorney, paunchy little Mr. Shyster, made an unexpected request.

"Your Honor, we'd like to be allowed to take the bag with us tonight," he said. Frantically, I stood up. "Objection! It is against the law to take evidence home!" "Somebody tell her to sit down," the judge ordered. "Who do you think you are and what do you think you are doing? Sit down! Now!"

"What are you doing? Sit." Henry grabbed my hand and pulled me back to my seat. "Your Honor, there is no objection." Henry was harsh with me. "Shut up and sit down," he commanded. I didn't want to hear it. "Don't worry," he said. "It's fine. Let them take it."

"It's not fine," I shot back. "They cannot take it! You are such a loser." By now I was fuming.

"It's okay," he insisted. "There's nothing we can do." Why? Instead of fighting it, making an argument that I had read about at the law library, he just rolled over for them like an old persian carpet, conceding that they could take the bag that I thought was going to be an obstacle, but there are times that you just have to leave it up to god and say it's ok.

It was business as usual, exactly the way I'd been treated for two years. He was such a moron. This was one of the many times I wondered if they were all in cahoots—my lawyer, the judge, and his lawyers, all aligned against me. Henry certainly wasn't giving me the kind of vigorous defense I was paying him for.

What a night of worry this caused me, questions racing through my head: Why? What did they plan to do with that bag? Stretch it? Shrink it? Make it disappear? Not once during the three days of trial did I confer after the day's testimony with Henry, the fool. He followed my directions in court and I dispensed with him, going my own way, usually to re-read the depositions, plot the next day's strategy and squeeze in a few hours of making real-estate calls. On this night, even though I needed the rest, I couldn't sleep one second.

Athena

Knowing they had the bag scared the crap out of me, and I lay in bed picturing every possible nightmare scenario, and how they could ruin my life by some evil trick.

The fear grew even worse, if that were possible, in the morning. When court resumed, there were two men, very tall, strapping guys with guns and billy clubs— security guards/cops—standing on the sidelines, glaring at me as if they were going to shoot me.

Talk about getting psyched out! Now it was my turn. I was completely intimidated. These mean-looking characters were going to haul me off to jail, I thought. Or hurt me somehow. Each one had a huge black briefcase for reasons that were a mystery.

"What's going on?" I asked Henry.

He had no idea. Obviously the police guards had been hired by my husband's attorneys, but I wouldn't find out why until I was back on the witness stand. It was extremely a tense moment, and usually when I get tense, I often close my eyes and count to five, slow down my breathing pretending that nothing is happening. I counted and tried to get hold of myself, waiting to see what my adversaries would pull. "I can play this game," I told myself, "and I'm going to win because they are not only liars, but also so stupid."

Mr. Collosal Shyster senior, his attorney, took the red duffel bag, with the guard standing next to him, and placed it on a chair in front of the judge.

"Your Honor, can she step down and get off the stand?"

The judge said yes, and I stepped down and approached the bag. I kept thinking I was going to be arrested somehow. That crazy fear kept filling my mind. What was the plan? "You see that bag, the plastic bag?" the lawyer said. There was also a plastic bag there filled with white shredded paper.

During my testimony, he had demonstrated how I had put the cash in the leather duffel bag justlike using the shredded paper. Apparently, he wanted me to show the judge too, and prove we were using the same leather bag. He asked me to take the shredded paper that was in the clear plastic bag and stuff the leather duffel bag with it. I sat there on the floor, with the judge peering down at me, puzzled too, stuffing what seemed like boxes and boxes worth of shredded paper into the duffel bag, the small bits of paper flying everywhere. Actually, I was having fun, toying with them, and it gave me a chance to collect myself and think. After all, I had done nothing wrong and I was determined to prove my case and win.

At some point I stopped. "It's not stuffed enough yet," the attorney said. "It's stuffed," the judge said. "It's not stuffed enough yet, Your Honor," the attorney said, adding, "Your Honor, tell her to stop laughing and making fun of me." I really filled the damn thing, and finally Mr. Collasal Shyster addressed me by saying, "Okay, can you get it all out now?" I had to empty the bag, the paper flying every where again, and now I was sweating, still on my knees on the floor of the court room. I was getting mad. What in the hell was this leading to?

Now the security guard came over, slowly undoing the two bags he was holding. He turned one bags upside down and dumped it on the floor next to me—stacks of one-dollar bills bound with rubber bands and plastic, all cash three feet high. Then he dumped the other one—more cash, an enormous pile of money. High drama! My heart nearly stopped. Panic welled up in me as I tried to imagine what this was meant to show.

"Okay," Mr. Collasal Shyster said, addressing me again, "we want you to stuff the red duffle bag now with the money." He meant fill the red duffel again with the cash—but why? I had to think hard because these lawyers were crooked and who knows what they were about to do. I had to try to relax and think. "With the rubber bands or without the wrappers?" I said, jokingly laughing. "Whichever way you want, honey," the scum bag attorney said.

Now the pressure was absolutely crushing me. Fighting in court is tough enough—an ordeal for anyone who has gone through it, but being there on the floor, with guns pointed to my head was maddening.

These hostile men were putting me through an exercise I didn't understand, with my entire future at stake, and were short-circuiting all my nerves, freezing up my brain. I was acutely aware of the guard standing over me with guns as I nervously tore the wrappings off the cash and began putting fistfuls of bills into the duffel bag. The guards were certainly not there for my protection; they were guarding the cash. I was trying to calculate, how many bills will make $10,000? How many will make $100,000? How much will I have to stuff in there to make $500,000?

I couldn't even multiply ten times ten. Everything in my head was frozen, and yet I was sweating, boiling over.

"Put more in there, put more in there," the attorney said, prodding me. I was cracking like a little pop corn in a frying pan. I decided I had to get a hold of myself. I had to have a minute to think, so I had to escape; to escape and or change geographic position to think—at least for a few minutes—relax and think, relax and think, quickly.

As I raised my head, I said, "Look, I've got to go to the bathroom."

"Your Honor, she can't go to the bathroom," said Mr. Collasal Shyster.

The judge said, "Go."

I walked away to regroup, passing close to Henry, who whispered, "Don't make it so heavy." What the fuck was he talking about? The bathroom was in the rear of the judge's chambers. I ran my hands under really hot water and then under the cold—a relaxation technique that always worked for me. I let my thoughts start flowing again—positive thoughts. The truth was on my side. The truth would win out. What were they trying to do to me? They doubted my story. They didn't think I could get the money in there. Didn't think I could hide it there like I said I had.

Emerging again fresh, my thoughts in order, I was suddenly a hundred-percent relaxed, ready to handle them. I resumed the task of filling the duffel. I kept saying I was done, and they kept insisting the bag was not full. I made it heavier. It didn't matter to me; I knew I'd be able to handle it. There was no more room in the bag, and they were angrily yelling—fill it, fill it. The judge was getting annoyed with them; he climbed down from the bench and watched as I tried to squeeze in the last few stacks of bills. This was a dramatic and highly unusual moment, a judge in his robes, presiding over a trial, stepping down from his high throne to get a closer look. I was wondering if by now he was having an erection! He looked damned exited not to mention very curious.

Athena

He was truly stunned, his dark brows furrowed, intent on seeing first-hand if I was right after all, the woman whom he had considered a liar from Day One.

Suddenly it all changed in his mind. In these critical few moments, his attitude did an about-face, and he seemed to consider seriously for the first time that my version of the facts was the truth. After a moment, the judge addressed Mr. Collasal Shyster by saying, "There is no more room in the bag. Stop it."

"Now we want her to demonstrate how this huge bag fits in the armoire," the attorney said. Haughty and clueless, he now expected me to make a fool of myself trying to slip the money-stuffed bag into its hiding place. It was wonderful to have a chance to show that arrogant bastard he was clueless. "Very simple," I said. "May I get up, Your Honor?" I got to my feet, moved to the armoire, and pulled out all my CDs, lifted out the removable shelf, and removing the wood flap that locks in place across the hidden compartment. I zipped up the duffel bag and with one hand lifted it mockingly showing them you are fools. Having worked out for years, lifting weights and running, I was fit enough to lift anything. I had raised the bag four or five feet—nearly high enough to swing it into the compartment—when Mr. Collasal Shyster said: "Hold it! You picked up the bag by yourself, like that, with nobody helping you?"

Making fun of him, I said: "You want me to do it again? What do you prefer? Two hands or one hand? I can show you both" and followed it by looking into the judge's eyes and giving him a big smile. My eyes squinted with no effort while I talked through my teeth. "Make up your mind. I can do both you know." The attorney was furious, trying to order me around.

"Please allow her to do what she's doing," the judge said.

I finished the job, slipping the bag easily into the hidden compartment while I started a big smile to satisfy my ego. And I followed by: "It was built just to store that bag you know".

"Do it one more time," the judge said.

I removed it and just as easily slipped it back in again, triumphantly. A piece of cake! I was smiling like the queen of the dance, enjoying the horrified looks on those jackals' faces—my husband and his crack legal team, shot down in open court. Also I pointed out the broken lock, quickly went to my desk and grabbed the mini-key out of my wallet, and showed the judge the key. It was the right key and the right lock. They matched. I knew he believed me. The judge tried the key himself and it worked, opening the tiny $1.99 dangling lock.

The judge climbed back up to his throne. He had already seen enough to know what to do. He took a deep breath, raised his hands, and told the lawyers: "Stop everything right now. Tell your secretaries to stop, stop typing on your computers," and he turned to the court recorder and motioned her to stop recording. "I'm going to give you half an hour to settle this case with her. I think you've raped this family enough. They have children for god's sake. You've taken enough of this family's money, and it's not fair to them or their children. I am putting somebody in jail today and I promise you it's not going to be her. So get to work."

Mr. Collasa Shyster senior, showing the pure gall of a cutthroat attorney, tried one last desperate gambit.

"Your Honor, I believe the witness was not sworn in this morning, I am telling you she was not sworn in" he said. The obvious suggestion was that nothing I had said or done only moments before should count. It was a stupid tactic that only pissed off the judge more. The judge pressed his hands on his desk and stood up and said with anger, raising his voice: "Do you mean to tell me I did not legally do my job right today? Is that what you're telling me?" When Mr. Collasal Shyster hesitated, he barked, "Please answer the question!"

The judge asked the court reporter to read back the opening minutes. I had in fact, been sworn in, and Mr. Shyster reacted by childishly tossing his papers in the air, admitting defeat. He kept saying, "Fuck! Fuck!" As for my ex, now he was the one really fucked!

"Mr. Collasal Shyster," the judge said, using his actual name, "I would stop this if I were you." The judge motioned me to stand up again, and he looked straight at me and said, "Do I cuff him and put him behind bars today or not? What do you want from this court?" After thinking for a few seconds, I thought of how my children would hate me if I send him to jail so I said:

"no you Honor."

They were the nicest words I could hear. I had won and with a big smile of victory and gush of happy tears, I stood up. They affirmed my victory, that I had proved my case and defeated my ex and his lawyers—the biggest divorce attorneys in town! Though super stupid.

They were nothing but clowns, making a circus every day, really they were all a bunch of animals—cruel to the core. During my research in the law library, I had read that a judge could grant an immediate name change without the long wait necessary when going through the bureaucracy. I asked him to give me back my maiden name "Done," he said. "What else?"

I could have asked for the moon. I certainly could have asked for half of everything—which is standard in California—or even more, since I had been so ripped off. But the case was never about money for me. It was about winning my freedom, better yet about the principles involved. Counting minutes I was rushing to get out; I wanted to be home before 4:30 and make love to Mr. Wonderful. Insane! It was already two o'clock on this Friday afternoon and the ordeal of the trial had been murderous. I told the judge that my main interest was in having my house. I was willing to settle for the house and a little support money. Later, I would kick myself for being so stupid. Half of everything would have meant half of Dr. Boring's pension, half of his practice, half of the money-market accounts, half of the savings, half of the stocks. All assets that would have been hugely helpful in the bleak years ahead, when I was living in tiny apartments, going through hell, but I could not have imagined it then. I just wanted to put the marriage and twenty-eight years behind me. I had won the toughest test of my life and I only wanted to go home. Beside it just proved what a dumb lawyer I had, since he never even suggested more survival for me, his client.

My love would appear any minute. I needed to get out. It should have been my attorney's job to do the settlement; I guess he just was not a good lawyer.

"You know you are entitled to half?" the judge told me. "Yes," I said. "But I just want my house and want to get out of here, I am a bit tired." He looked at the lawyers and said all right, she needs to sign a statement acknowledging that the divorce decree is not according to California law and she is aware that she was entitled to half of the estate. He sent everyone out to start piecing together the settlement. I hurried down the hall, since cell phones wouldn't work in the courtroom, and called Mr. Wonderful with the news. Franco, the gardener, hugged me. He was relieved—he had to leave for Mexico in a couple of hours, and he was concerned about getting the furniture home.

By the time we were back in session, the settlement had been negotiated and printed out on the courtroom computer and required my signature. Not knowing what I was signing. Henry, the bastard, discouraged me from even reading it—he was in a hurry to get out of there, too. Like a dummy, I listened to him, signing my name with scarcely a glance. The support money? Are you ready? would be $6,500 a month for two years, and $5,500 a month for four years total before running out. Keep in mind this was money from a man who was making over $100,000 a month. Not a year, but every single month! Good god!

What seemed more important then was having my freedom. I walked out of that courtroom free, jubilant, and proud of myself. I was proud of who I'd become, proud of what I had done. I was proud of being smart enough to whip the lawyers ass at their own game. All my life, I had been pushed around by authority figures- forbidden to express my thoughts and feelings, and was forced to wed a man I did not want, and was told what to do and what not to do for twenty-eight years of a miserable marriage, and now, at last, I had come out on top. I was my own boss, the queen and supreme ruler of my own life. I cleared my desk area, picked up my two briefcases and exited the courthouse in my full glory. I told my gardener to clean up and handed him $4,000 in cash for his effort.

Lovesick in Beverly Hills

Words cannot express the righteous pleasure I felt. A woman crying, ran after me in the hall, saying, "Please, please, can I have your card? Can you represent me?" She knew I had won my case, and she was going through a divorce herself. I had to tell her, "I'm not a lawyer—this schmuck is my lawyer," pointing to Henry while I threw his card up in the air, letting it fall on the hallway floor. Humming the song Flying to the moon, you had to see the look in this poor woman's eyes. She was desperate, and she really thought I could help her. Remembering the days and times that I was in the same place not too long ago.

I would have made a good lawyer. I'm a tenacious fighter, and I do my homework. But the last thing I wanted was any more contact with another lawyer. I wanted to get the hell out of there. Leaving Henry behind—we could never speak again after the piss-poor job he did for me—I crossed the street, got in my Bentley and drove off alone to celebrate my victory. Gloria Gaynor's CD I will survive was playing and I ended up on Sunset Boulevard at a little sushi place called Miyagi's, where I sat outside in the gathering dusk and watched the cars go by. The sky was orange in the west, framing an impressive billboard on Sunset Boulevard. The scene was like a perfect painting. Too excited to eat, I ordered a hot Sake and just smiled and reflected on the amazing journey I had traveled—the little Persian girl, who had come to the United States in 1970 with only $500. Now, in 1999, I was half a world away from home, all grown up and in charge, living in a $2 million home with a little money—the beginning of a whole new and exciting journey. Not so bad! I'd won my case and was very proud. I'd had my vengeance, and earned my vindication. Winning had cost me two years of my life. It had been the fiercest struggle I could imagine, but it was over. From being caught in the sharks' teeth, I had wriggled free and eaten up those voracious predators. There is no denying that without Mr. Wonderful and his love and support I could not have achieved a day such as May 19, 1999.

Eventually, I would try to follow through on my threat by suing my lawyer for malpractice. The awful job he did for me was unconscionable; but I never would have won my case if I'd depended entirely on his incompetent bungling. I contacted the American Bar Association to see how a citizen like me could take action against an attorney like Henry who in my opinion, was clearly in cahoots with the other side. A woman who answered the phone informed me that the bar association did not have a president at the moment. "I don't know what to tell you," she said. In spite of that, I managed to file a grievance, but I never heard back from anyone. That shows you the sort of non-existent oversight there is within the California legal profession.

None of that clouded my mind yet; however, as I sat in the sushi place and savored my triumph my cell phone rang! It was Mr. Wonderful telling me he loved me.

Come to think of it I had won the Super bowl of all super bowls. I loved this man who loved me too.

The twilight deepened. Headlights came on. Later, at home with Mr. Wonderful, I popped open a bottle of Dom Perignon and gave Mr. Wonderful another treat in bed. He was more than eager to see me. We made our plans to get together tomorrow, the next day and the next day after that. Life was never more perfect than when I was nestled snugly in his arms.

Yes, better days were ahead. At least so I thought. Not knowing as the saying goes, "people make plans and God laughs."

10

Mr. Wonderful

Let me pause a moment to tell you more about my Mr. Wonderful, my big, broad- shouldered, god-like man with those calm, understanding blue eyes. By now, I was completely in love with him. To me, he is the sexiest man I've ever met—and hearing his distinguished voice still speeds up my pulse, even after eighteen years—but he is not a romantic. He is not a sweet- talker. He doesn't wine and dine me—not if he can help it. He doesn't like to dress up at work. At formal dinners he can command the room in a five-thousand-dollar Brioni suit, but most of the time, even at the office, he's in short-sleeve shirts, clothes that don't match, and you'd think he didn't have a dollar to his name. It's pathetic. Impress people? Show them how rich and powerful he is? What for! He couldn't give a damn. He would rather that they like him. He would rather grab a pastrami sandwich in a funky little no-name deli on Pico Boulevard than have cocktails and chateaubriand at Baoli or Mondrian.

That's not to say that he is a saint. He can be dismissive, irresponsible, indecisive and insensitive—cruel, even, in his failures to grasp a woman's needs. Little did I know what a monster he would turn out to be in my life.

The definition of a sociopath, somehow finally it seems fits the man, totally screwed up emotionally and often hides his feelings—hides from love—and yet under the gruff façade there's a very soft heart, tender and gentle, and mushy. He's genuine in so many ways. There's no bullshit about him. He drinks whiskey. He smokes cigars. He is one of the most giving human beings I've ever met. More than anything he wants to help other people—which is why he goes to more charity events than I can count. He's actively involved with synagogues and churches. He likes to listen—to hear what people are thinking, what their opinions are. When I look at that tanned, rugged face he is always smiling. He is comfortable with being the man he is. He has a quiet dignity, and a certain charisma. He never gets angry, never says anything bad about anyone, and if he hears you talking bad about anyone, he quietly tells you that you shouldn't.

Always on the phone, calling me and asking me when he is going to see me. I know he loves me. No, no he's obsessed with me. During the long, terrible ordeal of the divorce, he was always there in the background, supporting me, seeing me whenever we could make the time. My journals from those early bitter months are filled with my outpourings of love and afection for this dynamic and very special man who helped me get through some of the most difficult times of my life.

"January 14, 1999: Yesterday was a bad day. Doesn't anyone have any heart and soul left? Are there any good people left? I know of one, whom I worship." I wrote down his name and I pondered what it would be like if we were married and together forever. "My sun, moon and stars," I called him, he was the one and only love of my life. Now I've become greedy and want it forever or as long as I am alive. Without him I will be nothing. If one cannot share love and beauty with the man one loves, what good is life?"

This rhapsodizing goes on and on. Hundreds of pages of passionate poetry in ten different notebooks—my feelings and thoughts about him, my longing to love him and to be with him-not knowing he will always have commitment issues. It was amazing how my heart felt, when I read it—how lost in love I was. Even while scrambling to get Henry in line and get all the facts and evidence together to prepare for the trial, I took the time to sit down and write out in longhand: "when I am cuddling in his arm, I feel light, happy and like nothing happened this past week, although my whole life has been turned upside down." I went on and on about having him with me, "to keep on holding him in the dark, and to wake up in his arms in the mornings. To kiss him good night and fall asleep on top of him, and awake up by saying: good morning, I love you. Give him breakfast in bed and send him out and wish him a good day. To keep caressing him so I can make love to him without fearing he is going to go and leave me all alone."

What people never understood—is that I've always seen myself as a wife and not a girlfriend, and I think he did too. He had one wife North side where he lives permanently, and one south side Boulevard, where he "really lives" with a woman who truly loves him. One wife with legal papers, and the other with—well with no papers.

Our relationship in the beginning was only about sex, but that soon passed, and I gave him my heart and soul. It probably wasn't in me to become part of a cheap love affair. In my whole entire life, I had never had a relationship, never cheated, and never let myself be someone's casual fling. For twenty-eight years of a god awful marriage I was faithful to a man I hadn't loved, whom I had been forced to wed as a young teenager, and who ended up ripping me off, slandering me, accusing me in court of stealing millions of dollars that belonged to me. Now the little, sheltered Persian girl had found the man of her dreams, just like Cinderella, so I gave myself to him as much as a woman can give. I became the loving, nurturing wife that his legal wife was unable to be, or refused to be or so he would tell me. He used to say, over and over again, "Why didn't I marry you?" You have become the best companion a man could have.

He wanted that. He needed me, too. He was miserable at home with a bitchy woman who was ill and who smoke too much, drank too much, destroyed too much and hated too much and happy with a woman who truly love him. There I was, with affection, style and heart full of love- a love that I know will never escape me. He was like the sun and the moon that will go on forever and keep giving me joy. I became his one true love, the woman who kept him going and for so many years. Or so he said. Sometimes it seemed he would say or do anything to get me and keep me, and I believed all of it. In my mind, I knew he loved me and would never hurt me. It didn't matter that there was a twenty-year age difference between us—that I was forty-five and he was well into his sixties. We bonded. We had a special chemistry and the pure and authentic love made it magical. I think the book, "Soul Mate," was written for us. It was in our karma to find each other and be together. If you think about the great loves down through the ages—Marc Antony and Cleopatra, Romeo and Juliet—we fit in that category, Mr. Wonderful and I, although no one died. In my fantasies I could picture us as king and a queen, together in our wonderful Castle of Love. Though I never cheated on my man or my deep feelings for him.

With the divorce trial finally over, I longed to get beyond the painful past into the fairy-tale I imagined. But life was not so forgiving and simple. There were problems—lots of them, the main one being the wife. Why wouldn't he leave her? Was it fear? Guilt? Was he too nice a guy? Was he unwilling to see the witch ride off on her broomstick with half of his gargantuan estate? Or was it that having love twenty-four hours a day was not what he wanted? To be loved all the time seemed to somehow scare him.

And then came the conclusion that men always go back to the shit they are used to. Fish eggs will always going to be fish eggs. And Caviar? Always Caviar. You cannot speak chineese to a french who only speaks french.

It was hard to get a real sense of the answers. Maybe he wasn't sure himself. I would spend years trying in vain to sort through these questions. They were issues that would never be resolved even after many months of therapy, together and individually. Not knowing, you can never really change the animal instinct of a man. And as for a married man? Well! They almost never leave their wives.

In the meantime, I had exhausted myself physically and financially. The divorce was a torture chamber. For over two years, I'd been like a woman holding tight to a pair of high-voltage lines, my whole body in frying mode. It was like being in the electric chair. My nerves were so bad that every muscle in my body ached. Even when I was lying down, trying to rest, I hurt to a point where the pain became unbearable. Anything physically active, like walking, sitting down or lifting anything heay was out of the question. Asking around, desperate for relief, I was finally directed to an acupuncturist in Korea Town, where I endured the fifty needles three and four times a week, and only after six months of the painful therapy did I begin to feel right again.

My biggest victory in the divorce case had been winning my fabulous home in the most beautiful palm-lined street in Beverly Hills.

It was heartbreaking to realize that the settlement and the power of the court didn't seem to matter. There was no action taken to put the property in my name. Nothing happened and for two more years I sent letters and made calls to my bastard attorney Henry, without hearing back from him. When at last I got a reply, I was so shocked I fired off a note that said, "Finally, after eight months of faxes and telephone calls, I received a letter from you last week—THANK YOU!!" Again, I implored him to deal with the grant deed and get it resolved. He didn't do a damn thing for me.

Where was I going to turn for help? The fight to resolve this problem after the divorce had already cost me $25,000. I wasn't about to hire another attorney and waste more time and money on it—because I just couldn't afford it.

An interesting thought crossed my mind. Not knowing what I was doing, one day two years after the divorce settlement sham, I decided to drive downtown and see the judge. I walked into his empty courtroom—Department "Family Law"—and found him sitting there with the same court clerk who had assisted him throughout my trial. She immediately recognized me and said, "I remember you, the missing money! Right?" She remembered me alright! And she said, "How are you, what are you doing here? "You'll never believe this," I told her. "It has been two years, and I still don't have the house." The nice judge motioned to her, a gesture I could not interpret, and got up and went back to his office in the back. She was stunned. "What are you talking about? Didn't your lawyer enforce the judgment?" I said, "What judgment? No!" She replied by saying she couldn't officially help me, it was illegal, but she quickly wrote down what I needed to do to get my house back and left the instructions on her desk for me to pick up as she got up to leave. "Go on," she said, "just take the elevator up and fill out these forms."

She directed me to the main courthouse clerk's office—and to fill out a particular form, serve my ex-husband with it, get the signature and bring it back the next day, or when I had time. There was no deadline, she said, expecting that it might take a while. I cut right through the bureaucracy, ran and got the form, high-tailed it out the freeway to Santa Monica with my newly hired assistant in the car, and asked her to go to my ex-husband's office and deliver the envelope and have his secretary sign it. My assistant had just started working for me, so thankfully Dr. Boring's staff did not even know her so they signed. In no time, I got my receipt, and the bastard had no way of knowing that I now possessed the legal means to get full title to my house. By early afternoon I was racing through traffic back to the courthouse downtown Los Angeles.

The clerk raised her head and said, "I told you to go and serve him." I said, "I did. Here it is." She was incredulous that I had done it in a single day. I had to cough up a $70 fee, but it was over, the next day my house got transferred to my own name.

Meanwhile, Henry's terrible, reckless advice was costing me. He had urged me to sign the settlement without even reading it, and now I deeply regretted that decision. I hardly had any money. Basic expenses—the mortgage, taxes and insurance alone—ran $11,000 a month. The sad fact was, Dr. Boring had made off with all the loot. There was a lot of money and property that rightfully was half mine, and I had signed it all away. He ended up with sole ownership of his million-dollar pension, his medical practice (which, as I noted earlier,

I had helped him establish!), an unknown sum in CDs and money-market accounts, and all his future income.

In the crash of 2008 most of his pension and numerous other financial assets, I had heard was lost, and he was crying all the way to the poor house. What do we call it? we call it: Poetic Justice.

As I indicated earlier, there had never been any forensic accounting to determine precisely how much he held in his accounts. I'm sure that was part of his scheme. The forensic accounting was supposed to have been done before the trial, but the screw-ups on the dates and cancellations and failures to follow through make it very clear that the powers in charge, including my own attorney, did not want this vital investigative work to be done. Henry had been the one person in a legal position to demand that the critical forensic accounting work be completed, and instead he had sloughed off. Who knows how many tens or hundreds of thousands of dollars had slipped through the cracks? What was it to Henry? He had milked me for a fortune and moved on to milk someone else. He certainly didn't give a damn.

They're cold-blooded cutthroats. At some point you have to decide to take charge and look out for your own interests! When the trial ended, there was $8,000 of my money in Henry's account—cash that hadn't been spent. I was entitled to have the balance refunded to me; the shyster kept ignoring my calls. I tried to complain to the California Bar Association but that rinky-dink organization was so poorly managed and sponsored that there was no one competent or willing to deal with the matter.

At that point I really could have used the money. The support I was receiving as part of the settlement—$6,500 a month those first two years—was not even enough to pay the $8,000 mortgage on the house, never mind the taxes and insurance and my own basic necessities like food and clothing. I was going to lose the house no matter what, even before it was legally placed in my name. Nothing was coming in from my real-estate business no matter how hard I tried. My reputation had been shot. It's ok I never did live or base my life on "public opinion." I had been fired too many times. Although I was still angry and in rage, I didn't want to ask anyone for help.

The house was up for rent immediately and by now since I had a broker's license, I could list it with my own company and Ha I could fire myself, myself!

As hard as I've worked, reading the New York Times to learn English, getting myself into Business School, not to mention selling all the properties I had sold, I took tremendous pride in my self-reliance. It was humiliating to ask for help, and yet it would have been very easy for Mr. Wonderful to step in temporarily and do the right thing. As rich and giving as he was, this was the perfect chance for him to really show his love. What was couple of thousand to a man who could buy the whole city? Pocket change! A drop in the bucket! Very gently and quietly I did hint for help but he refused. Something had to be done and I had to move fast or I would lose my house. He and his wife spent months every year traveling the world, staying in the finest luxury hotels. This was my knight in shining armor; surely he would come to the rescue of his damsel in distress without waiting to be asked. I only needed a couple of thousand temporarily to brake even and rent an apartment to get back on my feet.

Now after the hellish two years I was about to lose everything. He wasn't ready for that sort of step, even after knowing each other for two years. So fine, I understood, I would have to find a way out and quickly. It was apparently too much to ask. For two weeks I did nothing but think what now? And then, in June, I had to watch him leave on another trip to Europe—with her. Not knowing it was a little sign and a tiny murmur that one day his apathetic character and cold hearted nature would turn my life into a big Tsunami.

Another week of tears after he had gone occupied my nights and days. How much more could I take? Sadness and depression took over my life. How can he do this and go away while I was hurting so bad? Not knowing that's what married men do.

The pain stabbed right through me, a cold blade running straight into my heart. This was the bitter other side of seeing a married man—the sense of abandonment, the lonely nights and mornings that would frame those moments of wonderful intimacy. Knowing he was with her, hopping from party to party in Paris and Rome, and yet stubbornly unwilling to offer the small amount of money it would have taken to save me from moving out of my home made me furious. The only thing I ended up with after twenty-eight years of marriage was six years of inadequate alimony not even half of a length of marriage. So what! I will move out and rent out my home. The house was now all mine and I will do and live with what I have.

Our lives together, our deep love for each other, have finally begun to flourish—everything could have been so beautiful—and already there was this bitter reality looming as a wall between us. I wrote about the hurt in my journal, saying, "It is a torture for me when he leaves. It is a torture when he is not here at night. It is a torture because he is married. I feel used . . . especially when he tells me that he loves me and calls me every single day telling me how much he loves me. If I ever wrote him a letter, which I don't know if

I ever will, I would say this: 'To my beloved . . . you never bought or sent me flowers, but I am always glad to see you. You never brought me a present, and yet I would die for you. And all I wanted was to dance with.

"He is great but never with me," I wrote. "I want to be with him all the time, and of course I can't. This insanity must stop. I am the Band-Aid keeping his marriage together. He is living it up. I am working twelve hours a day and every night crying myself to sleep. How stupid can I be? Why on earth am I doing this? Life is getting scary, tough and uncomfortable." I knew full well why: he was my dream come true and I would follow him to the end of the earth and wait for him till eternity". Stupid! Thinking what a loser I was.

Here I urged myself to cancel my own trip to Europe. Just as before, when he had gone to France, I had planned to travel and secretly join him, at least for a week or two. But I needed to start packing! desperately looking for a cheap and new place to live as soon as I possible could.

It made sense to stay home, and yet ultimately, after a dozen calls urging me to come out and spend money shopping, I found a tiny apartment, and I went anyway, booking myself into the same hotel, the Carlton in Cannes, where they were staying, as per his instructions, and violated every unwritten rule about keeping a relationship secret.

He wanted it this way and I said fine. This was not a completely new situation to me—and I didn't expect to run into them. In the end, it seemed to all work out. Mr. Wonderful and I saw each other mornings and afternoons, just as before, and I shopped and dined and enjoyed the cocktail parties, but in the back of my mind I was aware that he had hurt me and let me down. There were serious issues awaiting me at home but for now I was going to live it up. I was in love with the man of my dream; "So what if I have to live in a little apartment?"

My cowboy was something I had never had nor ever experienced. I couldn't give him up because simply I just loved and adored him.

I loved my house and with the way my attorney had made my settlement, I was now living poverty style. Right after I returned to Beverly Hills, I quickly had to confront the reality of living in a tiny apartment and getting rid of my belongings. It was traumatic. Leaving my home was very difficult. It was a comfortable home and there were many good memories there, despite the warfare of the marriage. It was the last place my daughters had lived before moving out on their own. The location was ideal—right in the heart of town, walking distance from Rodeo Drive. And, of course, I had fought so hard to hang on to it, but now I everything had changed and I could no longer afford it.

On the day of the move, as I rummaged through closets, I found my bridal gown—my white flag, symbolizing what I had surrendered so long ago: any chance at happiness. I had given up all my youthful hopes and dreams when I had put on that gown and tied myself to a man I didn't love, and who ended up hurting me and wanting me behind bars. It was an emblem of a life gone wrong, years lost, and so much misery stamped on that white awful gown. I grabbed it and carried it into the back yard near the pool along with every one of my ex-husband's pictures that I could find. I was so angry that I even cut the faces out of many of the photographs. I hated him. I wanted to completely forget him and forget about all the stinking hell I had been through. I lit a fire right there in the yard and immolated that wedding gown and all the pictures.

"Mrs what are you doing?" the housekeeper asked me when she saw it. "Que passó?"

"This gown has to be burned," I said.

The curling black smoke represented dark days for me—dark days behind me, and also not knowing yet of dark days ahead. My life was not going to be any better soon.

Mr. Wonderful's refusal to help me with the expenses really made me realize how I worshiped him regardless of his support. I was going to have to scale down, get rid of most of my furniture, and move into a tiny apartment. My house was five-thousand square feet and worth at least several million and I was not about to sell it. Renting it out was a better idea. Maybe someday I would return and share the space with my grandchildren. Who could know? I figured the rent would pay for the bills and my expenses—at least that was my hope.

As my luck would have it, I soon attracted interest from one of the wealthiest men in the world. This seemed like a blessing at the time. This individual owned a real-estate portfolio that was five inches thick. He needed a temporary place to stay while he was building his own huge estate nearby—a hillside mansion that would be worth upwards of $50 million, making it among the most lavish in town.

He and his wife showed up to see me in the most expensive black Convertible Bentley. She was a skinny, willowy, not so pretty girl, and he was short, fat, and stubby with dark skin and a thatch of curly hair. However, he was a hard, tight-fisted businessman, and he tried to low-ball me on the lease. Offering barely half my asking price, he promised to stay for at least a year and confidently pulled out his wallet.

"Here's a check for three months," he said. Well that did it. Now I had rent money.

What could I do? I needed the cash. I took it and signed the lease and we had a deal—a big mistake. This man and his wife would end up putting me through hell. This is a little taste of why and how people with super money piss on the less wealthy people in my town. The types of people you find even at the top rungs of society—people who will exploit you, screw you over, and not give it a second thought.

Renting my house to this couple set me up to barely break even; the money coming in was enough to pay the mortgage on the house and leave me about $1,000 a month to get an apartment. For about a year, the situation would be good. The couple took care of the house and I had no problems with them in the beginning. They even decided to renew the lease.

Then all of a sudden, I received a rent check that was $6,000 short, a deficit that threatened to destroy me. I counted on this money. There had been a plumbing problem, he explained, an emergency that he had and needed to handle immediately. He had paid for it himself, he claimed, and therefore took it out of the rent.

"Who was the plumber?" I asked him. His secretary gave me a name and I called the guy. The job had cost only a couple of hundred bucks, the plumber told me. What? I confronted my tenant and he changed the story to say there had actually been two plumbers. Total fabrication and bullshit. He was blatantly cheating me. God, does it ever end?

"Never mind about that," the lying tenant said, meaning the other plumber. "We fixed it. It's taken care of."

"I'll be glad to split it with you," I offered, wanting at least some of the money.

He balked, refusing to pay up or document the expenses. He completely stonewalled me, refusing to pay the rent any more. His in-house attorney sent a barrage of threatening letters. One day about four months later I was driving by the house and saw boxes out front. There were no cars, no signs of anybody being home. During all that time I had been unable to collect further rent and I was getting very angry about it. The boxes were a bad sign. When I investigated, I discovered that they had vacated the house without telling me months earlier. They had also wrecked it, yanking out the cabinets, allowing the refrigerator to drain on the floor and staining and destroying the entire kitchen tile with rust. Every flower in the yard was dead. The pool had become a stinking algae pond. According to the pool man, the gate had been locked for three months, so he couldn't get in.

I was able to enter the property by pulling my car up close to the gate, climbing on top of the car, and clambering over the gate. I discovered all the damage and saw that they had moved their furniture out. Incredibly, despite being 120 days behind in payments, they claimed they still had a contract and accused me of "trespassing".

What a great scenario they had concocted. They took me to court. It would end up costing me another $60,000 to deal with the legal problems and repair bills for the house. They never paid me another dime. This is the sort of rottenness you can find among people who have bartered their souls for riches. It was also another example of how low my life had sunk—one terrible disappointment after another and it was never going to end.

There would be a happy ending to this particular story, though. At least I would turn out to be very glad when this wealthy couple's karma finally caught up with them years later. They came to learn that the land beneath their magnificent new hillside mansion was unstable. The entire property—umpteen bedrooms and baths, a showcase as big as a Scottish castle—was sinking. It had dropped ten feet. Gossip about it was all over town, and one evening I happened to see them at an art-show opening.

A friend of mine, a world-renowned artist, had invited me to a cocktail party for the opening night of exhibiting his work in Beverly Hills. Wearing a gazillion-dollars worth of diamonds and a gorgeous Dolce & Gabbana suit, looking stunning—with a killer tan—I waltzed into the scene of the rich and famous.

As I noticed my ex-tenants I could no longer contain myself. Walking over, with a big smile on my face, I said, "Well, hello! It's so good to see you. How are you? How is your new house?" No response, silence. They were clearly not eager to talk to me, but she said, "Fine, why do you care? Why are you asking me that?" I said, "I heard your house is sinking some 10 feet". And as I sipped my champagne I walked away.

That comment alone was worth $1,000,000. Leaving her there standing in a state of shock and embarrassment was the best revenge, and perfect poetic justice. These people knew of my financial state, when they approached me to rent my house, and yet were so devious, ruthless. How do you take advantage of a woman who had been through so much pain and is hurting? And now they got what was coming to them. It couldn't happen to more deserving human beings.

That would be well in the future, however. At the time I agreed to sign the lease, I felt glad to have some cash flow, and I concentrated on trying to re-establish a life for myself.

The apartment I found, on Westbourne Drive, was tiny—barely nine-hundred square feet. I had to give away almost all of my furniture to charity. Looking back, I was happy in that tiny apartment till my tenants messed me up. The little money would have helped me at that point—and in the years afterward. My furniture was beautiful, but Mr. Wonderful insisted that I should help someone else with it. I ended up giving nearly all of it to an orphanage and cramming the few possessions I had left into that depressing little apartment, not even a fifth the size of the home I loved.

I couldn't stop crying. For a month I did almost nothing but cry. The sadness was overpowering. Mr. Wonderful tried to console me. He came over and looked at the place and held me in his arms.

"I can't believe that you're doing this, sell the house" he said. Yet this man with all his fabulous wealth, who was living in a veritable castle only a couple of miles away, wouldn't help. He had seen all my tears and the misery I had been through, and he was almost blind to them.

My income had completely dried up, until finally I sold a huge house in Beverly Hills to one of the biggest banking families in Los Angeles.

Athena

So many times I had moved—at least nineteen times in my life time, if I counted them all up—and to move again was just not okay. I truly gave the term "the wandering Jew a whole new meaning." By now the sight of packing boxes made me vomit.

Everything about the move was hard. I gave some of my more personal things, including much of my crystal and China, to members of my family for safe keeping. They treated it with cold indifference. I would find out later that they recklessly threw and shoved and dropped the boxes in a garage, damaging and breaking everything inside. Broken expensive Crystal and now my broken life had been shattered to pieces too except I was so happy and so very much in love.

Mr. Wonderful went on another trip with his wife while I stared at the walls of my dumpy apartment and wondered why was I having to suffer, and why I had to endure all the torture I was going through. The apartment was like a dungeon for me—a dark den where I was lashed to a rack and bleeding, where some unseen sadist kept turning a crank and my body kept stretching. I ached. I grieved. I was embarrassed to be where I was living and in such a crummy neighborhood. I kept the Bentley in a garage and still had a Honda with tinted glass so that nobody I knew would see me drive in and out of the building. It was totally demoralizing. There never seems to be any stability in my life.

At this point the fabled old spiritual bookstore, the Bodhi Tree, on Melrose Avenue, was my escape. The stacks of volumes, filled with wisdom, and the incense that was always burning there found a way into my soul. The CDs that played, with their soothing reeds and strings that evoked distant lands, helped to calm me more than any sleeping pills. Just to hear the humming and chanting made it seem, for a minute or two that I was all right.

Are there times when the Universe itself seems to turn against you? Or God? My new apartment was a disaster. The stove was broken, the refrigerator wasn't working right, and there was constant street noise. On top of that, I had a very noisy neighbor. In the midst of all my sorrow and emotional pain, I desperately needed to sleep at night and I couldn't because the bastard next door kept his TV turned up loud until 4 o'clock in the morning. His living room, where the TV was, backed up against my bedroom, and made the sounds intolerable. I banged on the wall, I tried to talk to him, I complained to the landlord, I wrote letters—nothing worked. I must have called the Los Angeles County Sheriff's Department fourteen times, and fourteen times deputies showed up at my door. Every single time, the neighbor turned down the TV to a normal level. At one point one of the deputies said, "Listen, he wants to annoy you. Move!" What was I going to do? I was going through an emotional breakdown and barely had any money and the sicko next door was insisting on keeping me up and making me miserable.

Finally, at my wit's end, I invested in $100 worth of foam and a staple gun and I covered the entire wall in sound-absorbent padding two layers thick.

One Sunday, I just climbed over my bed and started stapling away. The landlord saw it and went ballistic.

"You can't do that to my building!" he said. He threatened to sue me.

If he were angry then, he would be angrier later as my horrible luck continued. It's one thing to be single; being poor and single is something else. A particular Saturday came when I found myself forced to work. In my entire career I never worked on Saturdays, my day of rest. It's a rule, my rule and I almost never broke it, but I had sold a house—a lovely place on Marilyn Drive—to an attorney from New York. The home was in escrow, but the attorney's wife hadn't seen it yet. He called me, saying that she was in town with him and he really wanted her to have a chance to look at it. Fine!. I had no choice. I would make an exception, so I drove off to meet them. They were wonderfully happy and exited, and they loved the house, but the whole time I felt guilty for working on Shabbat. I've always felt I could work and make money every day but Saturday. While I was showing the house, I got a call on my cell phone from the manager of the building.

"Your apartment is on fire! Get over here!" he said. There had been something wrong with the stove, the very stove I'd kept complaining about in letters to the manager. One of the knobs or the pilot light—I'm not sure which—was faulty. Somehow the flame came on after I had left. The fire destroyed all that was left of my crystal and my furniture, and it ruined my computer—all of my files, my real-estate information and contacts, plus all my personal documents. The smoke and soot got to all of my clothes. My dry cleaning bill was $5,000.

The fire affected both of my neighbors, including the noisy bastard, but of all the units in the building, mine was the only one truly damaged. I would be moving again—I was sure of that. And that wasn't the end, either. If God was testing me, there were more hard questions on the way and other tragedies to follow.

There was love in my heart, and nothing was ever going to change that. I was hanging on to him, like a junkie on cocaine.

Isn't love beautiful?

11

Lovesick in Paris

My next apartment, on Palm Drive in Beverly Hills, faced north, meaning that no sun filtered in. That intensified my sadness. It was also an embarrassing place to live—small, square and boring—but I looked at it with eyes of love. Nothing a big bunch of roses and fresh flowers could not solve.

Now I was on the right side of life. It was insane how quickly I moved and adjusted to the little space I had to endure. It wasn't where I was meant to live, and yet I was stuck there, out of place, as if I were suddenly living someone else's life and I couldn't wake up from the nightmare. Money was very tight. Finally, Mr. Wonderful was helping me a little with the dry cleaning bill. I was drained and hopelessly in love. Most of the time I was also lonely and very sad. A deep depression again settled in. I thought, how much more can I take? From a beautiful life, or what should have been a beautiful life together, I had fallen to this deep, unhappy abyss, and there seemed no way to get out.

During one of my trips, while I was in Europe with Mr. Wonderful the unit above me flooded, and water poured down into my closet where the fire damaged drycleaned cloths hung. All of my clothes got soiled again—another $2,000 dry-cleaning bill. Fire and flood, I'd now had them both.

The wrath of the universe, maybe, or some cosmic joke, I was not getting it right. Whatever it was, I wanted it to end already. I often cried alone. Except for Mr. Wonderful no one came to see me.

When I had been living in my lovely home with the pool and fine furniture when I was married, people were around all the time, hanging out, visiting. Now that I was in a pitiable hole in the wall, and no one bothered. I wasn't cool any longer. Better yet I was no longer the symbol of success that matters so much in Beverly Hills. I lost all my friends and I struggled to go on working and living my life while trying to hide the sting of it.

My personality was to always look at the upside of things. Thinking I am such a dreamer, a real romantic. More and more, because of how deeply I was in love, I wanted my big, broad- shouldered cowboy to come and rescue me.

My nights were long and unbearable; I wanted him to wake me in the morning and make me feel better. By now, my memory was filled with beautiful moments we had spent together in quiet afternoons making love. When he had been able to get away from the office to see me, and times we just sat and talked, telling me about his life, while sipping his scotch. Gazing into his beautiful blue eyes, listening and thinking I am so fortunate to have found true love. We had our own vocabulary and always connected so perfectly.

One particularly sublime memory—which stirs my heart even to this day—involved a brief excursion to Mexico, where he was traveling with his wife, but where he arranged for me to meet him for a few days…Making him feel loved and special I had arranged a few hours for a picnic aboard a small rented fishing boat. I thought it was romantic and he would enjoy it.

Lovesick in Beverly Hills

Hiding what I was about to do, I told him I need you tomorrow afternoon. I asked him to meet me on the beach for lunch. He seemed to feel pressured, no doubt because of her, but he agreed to see me, and I thoroughly enjoyed arranging the mid-day plans. My hotel, the Hyatt did not prepare picnic lunches, so at around eleven that morning I ran to a little eatery next door and paid fifty peso tips—about $5—to have a couple of guys pack us something to eat. Then, I recruited one of the local fishermen to chauffeur us out beyond the waves. The final stroke was to hire a mariachi. Acting on a tip from a waiter, who recommended his guitar-playing friend, I put the last piece in place for another $50.

When I saw Mr. Wonderful crossing the gorgeous sandy beach to join me at the surf's edge, I was thrilled, of course. He looked unsure with a big smile, and nervous about the whole escapade. "What are you doing?" he yelled. "What is going on?"

"Get in the boat," I said.

At first he refused and resisted. He claimed that people were getting kidnapped all the time and he was not going to step into that dinky boat. I pushed him in. "Let's go" I said and turned to the fisherman and said: "vamonos, rapido!" It was hot, even though it was winter, and I'd brought a rain umbrella to protect his very fair skin from the intense tropical sun. Wal-Mart was across the street and the day before I ran over there thinking he might get burned so I bought a small umbrella. God knows I held it over his head the entire time so he would not feel uncomfortable with the blazing sun. I wanted him to enjoy himself. I'd also brought a bottle of the finest tequila, some quesadillas, and few bottles of Corona. He loved Corona beer. So now we had all we needed, and we were in a postcard setting—the sky a brilliant blue, the hotels and buildings standing in sharp relief on the crowded shoreline, and the short, leathery-skinned fisherman happily struggling to direct the little boat out to sea. He seemed in awe of our romantic outing, smiling as we set up our banquet far offshore. We placed our tequila glasses on the wood- plank seats; they rocked as the waves surged beneath us. The lapping of the water and the sounds of the mariachi's gentle guitar were all we heard, except when we spoke softly to each other. Once we were out where we wanted to be, the sky and the water just about swallowed us up: They both were a deep, flawless azure, joining at the horizon, surrounding us, creating a kind of extraordinary blue heaven. And Mr. Wonderful did think he was in heaven, at least for that day, but I think we both did. He just relish the thought of it all and loved it better than any hundred million dollar yatch... He would thank me for months for that wonderful sea voyage in the tiny fishing boat in Mexico. Love was what we both craved for and now this afternoon I was going to show him how much I loved him.

Neither of us had ever had this experience before. It was life unscripted, the two of us just feeling the power of the ocean below us, holding each other, feeling and touching our soft skin. A breeze moved along the swells, cooling us from time to time. There was no glamour or pretense to being there; the veneer of wealth, the polish of life far up the coast in Beverly Hills, was stripped away, and it was just him and me, man and woman, and love at its deepest glory in the company of the kindly Mexican fisherman and the mariachi. We could see nothing happening on the distant shore; the people and events there no longer mattered.

We were blissfully alone. We finished our quesadillas and drinks and took a lot of pictures. I savored every second. I loved fussing over my Mr. Wonderful and making him happy. He loved the idea that I was so spontaneous and imaginative, giving him the gift of moments like this. I filled his life with a sense of fun and romance that no one else had ever offered him. He told me he loved me, over and over again, and how no one else ever loved him the way I do. We cuddled up in each other's arms, tilting back under the shade of the umbrella. He love the idea of me, loving life.

With the waves rolling beneath us, he almost fell asleep—and the world could have ended then and there, as far as I was concerned. It was a picture perfect day. It was a dream I did not want to end.

At around four o'clock, we finally headed back, still touching, holding hands. I wanted to memorize every sensation—and I did. I wanted to keep this beautiful snapshot in time for the rest of my life—and I have. The sun, the view, his arms around me, it all burns on in my heart, a portrait I keep inside me for the rest of my life.

How wonderful is love! To be loved, to give love, and to make love! I knew then that my feelings for him will stay with me forever and my love for him would be eternal. He had to get back to attend a New Year's Eve party, and I went back to my little room to wait until the next day's sunrise, when I could see him again. I spent New Year's Eve alone, just as I was alone now, in my little apartment without him, yearning for his touch. This is the magic and the pain of loving a married man when you cannot be with the man you so very much love. I longed for him at every hour. Our love was all that mattered. I knew he was suffering, too. His wife was drinking heavily and doing drugs, he told me. After midnight he called me and said:" she is out cold on the floor, scared." She was going through $300 worth of alcohol every week. He said he would secretly mark the bottles and watch her drain them dry in a single day. The liquor sent her into drunken rages.

The whole problem with their relationship was about her screaming, fighting and throwing plates even before we had met. She was always relentlessly abusive to him, but still he refused to leave her. So many times he would say, "I am so happy when I am with you. I need a little joy in my life. That's why I am with you." We both knew that he would be so much happier if he were with me all the time—he genuinely loved me—but there was something about him that kept him with her. He wouldn't allow himself the sort of happiness that I would give him. He wouldn't trust it. He wouldn't permit himself to give in to what he really, truly wanted, maybe because he sensed how vulnerable he would be. Instead, he used me as his drug, the thing that made his life just tolerable enough to hang in there with her, surviving the abuse.

In one of my journals at the time, I made two lists:

THINGS THAT I THINK HE IS AFRAID OF REGARDING ME

He is afraid that I will betray him. He is afraid that I will leave him. He is afraid of commitment. He is afraid that I will somehow hurt him. He is afraid his wife will get sick and he will go back even if he files for divorce. He is afraid she might attempt suicide, to get to him. He is afraid she will take all his money. He is afraid I might not love him.

THINGS THAT I AM AFRAID OF BECAUSE OF HIM

I am afraid of spending the rest of my life alone. I am afraid of loving him a lot. I am afraid that he will be incapacitated or die and I will be left alone. I am afraid of sleeping alone and going to movies alone. I am afraid that if he leaves her, he will change his mind and go back to her again. I am afraid of getting old and having nobody to be with. I am afraid of him not respecting my feelings. I am afraid of him not being compassionate enough to feel my pains. I am afraid of not trusting him, and he would cheat on me and afraid to tell the truth. I am afraid, I am afraid....i am fraid..... and then I cry....

My own fears at least equaled his, but there was a fundamental difference in the nature of our fears. His tended to keep him away from me—irrationally, I thought. Mine were rooted in the need to be together.

Sometimes, however, the longing for someone can be so intense, so unbearably painful, that a woman can find herself backing off from the man she loves out of self- protection. Wounds get too deep. The hurt starts to outweigh the pleasure of the precious few moments together. It is the story of a ruthless, and obssessive relationships, and sadly enough, ours had reached that point by the early months of 2001. The apartment was shaping up and I was making money, adjusting well to my new life.

His wife was making it very difficult for him to get away to see me. She was suspicious and kept the shackles on him. In order to stop the bleeding, the thought of leaving him was now quite strong in my mind, realizing I couldn't handle it emotionally any longer. I wanted him desperately, but I finally broke up with him during a trip to France. "Enough pain and crying!" "I couldn't take it anymore" I told him. The problem was, he was not willing to let her go either. Although he loved me—and I knew it, somehow he would always manage to win me back too.

Athena

In June, as always, he was planning to leave for two months of vacation—with her, of course. They were going back to Paris and the south of France. Either I could stay home and ache or I could ease the suffering by meeting him there. I couldn't get away for six weeks, but I loved France, and I wanted to go. The idea was, I would be sad for two weeks, then I would fly there for two weeks—I would be happy because I would get to see him, even just a glimpse of him—and I would return home –like a freak-and be depressed again for another two weeks. At least the time apart would not be as long.

This particular summer, I would be going back and forth, spending two weeks there, coming home for a week, and then going back to Cannes for a couple more weeks. It meant we would be together or a couple of weeks and apart in between. Those empty stretches my days were so very hard. The streets without him seemed deserted, and my whole life would take on a dirty shade of gray. Except now, I was about to end the whole sorry and sad love story.

What a summer it would be. We did not coordinate our schedules, and I never knew his itinerary. For some reason, he would never share it with me, maybe because he would feel guilty if I knew how many different countries they were going to be in together, and where they were staying, and the parties they would be attending—always parties, parties and more parties. I had originally planned to fly to France on July 17, but instead I moved up the date, booking a flight for the first of July. That Saturday, Mr. Wonderful asked me when I was leaving. "Tomorrow," I told him; "on American Airlines."

"That's funny," he said. "I'm leaving tomorrow on American. What time is your flight?"

"Eight o'clock," I said.

Oh, my God, it turned out we were going to be on the same plane! "That's just impossible," I said, when he had told me. "You're joking!" "I know is a joke, right?." He started laughing. Perhaps it was an omen of all the strange and coincidental events that would follow. It freaked me out. That whole day Sunday, there was no air in that damn apartment. His wife was crazy and unpredictable and I was in pain, shaking and wondering how in the hell I was going to board the plane with her in it. I knew that they always flew first-class, and they would board first and be right up front, where they couldn't miss me. Late that afternoon, he called me from the airport, telling me the flight had been delayed until 9:30. It only prolonged my anxiety. I didn't let it rob me of my sense of style, however. I got there wearing my black cowboy hat and a big, black cape—and holding my business-class ticket. I dreaded the inevitable moment when I would have to walk past them. I didn't want his wife to see me. She was crazy and I had no idea what she might do.

Lingering at the gate, like a cornered cat, I watched everyone else board before me. Finally, the attendant, a large black woman, said, "Honey, are you going in? I'm going to close the door now."

"You've got to help me," I said, making up a story fast. "My ex-husband is sitting in the plane and I have to stay away from him. I hate him." I gave her the name and said, "Where is he sitting, so I can use the opposite aisle to pass him? So I don't see him?"

She checked and told me he was sitting on the right side. I hurried aboard, intent on using this information to avoid them by fixing my gaze in the other direction. Unfortunately, I screwed up. I took right side to mean my right side, when in actuality they were on the right side of the plane—on my left, as I moved from the cockpit area toward the rear of the jet. I chose the wrong aisle and my "averted" gaze fell right on them. My Mr. Wonderful was wearing a navy blazer, white shirt and gray flannel pants. He looked fantastic—distinguished and sexy. A white handkerchief in his breast pocket wrapped it all up in a beautiful package. Very European, even though he was a big, rugged, blue-eyed American.

His wife noticed me immediately, of course. Our eyes locked on each other's for a horrifying instant. By the time I got to my seat in business class, I was having an anxiety attack. My nerves were in utter confusion. On one hand, I was thrilled to be on the same plane with him, knowing we would arrive together and get to enjoy each other in Paris. It was like a shot of morphine. In a part of my mind, I began to feel that wonderful sense of optimism that we would wind up together. After all, what are the chances, that we were flying away on the same plane and looking forward to magical times together in Paris and Cannes. On the other hand, I threw myself into my seat, and passed out unconcious. Although this time, I was not so sure.

At the same time, I felt like my whole nervous system was shutting down. I couldn't cope with the anxiety, lack of oxygen in my lung and I basically passed out in my seat, scared shitless of what she might do to me, since I had heard some real horror stories. She was totally out of control ninety percent of the time, and she had basically told me once that she had been in jail, because she was going to kill someone, but he got her out.

Not sure, if he was telling the truth or not. I was afraid she might stab me. I zoned out. No dinner. No drinks. I drifted into unconsciousness and stayed there, even when he came back to check on me-he told me later. I was sound asleep and woke up only as we were descending into Paris.

Coincidences and psychic energy are forces that have always influenced my life, and they still do. I had picked my hotel essentially at random, booking it through my travel agent, completely unaware that the rear door of his hotel opened to the front entrance of mine. The streets of Paris are not exactly straight. You think you are going the right way, and minutes later you are in a totally different place. The day we arrived, he came by to see me and promised to come back for a "sexy visit" in the afternoon. It was going to be a special time, I thought. I couldn't wait to see him and I rushed back from shopping to be ready for him.

By five o'clock, I was showered, perfumed, and comfortable in my robe. The champagne, an expensive bottle of Grand Dame, was on ice. So was the caviar I had bought at the famous gourmet store Hediard. He came in and we drank and talked. He always appreciated that I listened to him. He always wanted to tell me about his day. We savored the caviar and made love. It was extraordinary—and then he quickly got dressed to leave as if there were a fire in the building. He had been with me less than half an hour and he was taking off!

"Where are you going?" I said. "I have to go," he insisted. Well that did it! Was I ever angry! Talk about insensitive! For a couple of hours I just stayed in my depressing little room—I didn't like the hotel—stewing and wondering what I should do. Finally, around eight, I got dressed to go out and have dinner alone. While I was walking, I suddenly saw them on the street. He was smashingly dressed in a gorgeous burgundy jacket and she was old and yet dolled up in a blue suit. They were headed somewhere to dine. I ducked into

Hediard, the exclusive gourmet caviar store. I watched them climb into a taxi and then my tears poured out. All I could think of now was: I need to get out of this relationship.

For a second, I didn't know where I was any more. He never saw me. I became ill. The tears were dripping onto my clothes like little baby. Such love and such sadness that really made me realize it was time to say good bye to the love triangle. Why wasn't it me going to dinner with him? Why couldn't I be there on his arm, when I knew we loved each other? Or, rather when I was so in love with him—and I was certainly younger and prettier than the wife, who brought him such misery. But tonight I was alone and sad. It was too much to endure. I couldn't take any more. Thoughts of leaving him burned in my mind.

I slowly walked over to Le Relais, my favorite restaurant, and got a table for one, and started crying again.

There I was, looking beautiful, and never felt so down and ugly in my life, with desertion and abandonment galore. I looked around and saw everyone else paired up; even the plain and homely women were with good-looking men, and I was by myself, with no one to talk to. I especially noticed an older couple who came in—a fine-looking gentleman and a brunette in a simple, elegant Valentino dress, off-white and cut low in the back. She appeared no larger than a child. They looked so romantic together. By now, I'd had the champagne and a glass of red wine and I was sinking into a bottomless funk. I'd been given the worst seat in the house. I was dressed plain and too American. The soft piano music was making me even sadder. I sobbed the entire dinner. I missed having him next to me. The whole night I would be in my room alone. I hated my life, hated the situation, and most of all I hated and resented her, the wife who didn't deserve him nor cared for him- I realized she was his wife, and either I put up with it or leave. Sad and lonely I had made up my mind: I was leaving him.

Why was I even here? I was ready to pack and go home. But what was there waiting for me; my crummy little apartment? Where no one ever came to see me? Should I go back and stare at the walls in misery while he was running around all over Europe? No, I couldn't. There was no reason to rush and leave Paris, as terrible as I felt but I had made up my mind.

Instead, I would stay and try to make the best of it. I finished eating and made my way to the Plaza Athenee to see if I could get a room until Saturday. What the hell, I was broke, anyway. I needed to get out of my hotel.

The Plaza Athenee had a door that opened to Le Relaix. A room was available, and I checked in and around midnight, I went back to my Hotel and retrieved my belongings. It was already midnight. Once I had settled into my new room, I re-opened the Grand Dame and downed it all—the whole damn bottle. By midnight I was lonely, tired, and drunk, and I cried an ocean of tears. I left a message for Mr. Wonderful on his cell that I never wanted to see him again. I needed to change my life. I just couldn't take it anymore and I begged him not to ever contact me again.

The next morning I woke up around ten with the rain pouring outside. I hoped that he would call. I wanted him to say he needed me, to make time for me. I waited until 10:30—no word from him—so I decided to get dressed and take a nice walk.

Paris was lovely, rain or shine, and just the idea of wearing my black boots, a raincoat and walking among the raindrops was enough to refresh and rejuvenate me. The rain would wash away the pain and sorrow; it was fresh and felt like new life, a new day, and new fresh air. So by 11:00 the rain had become a little drizzle. I left my room, my little umbrella in hand, and started walking on Avenue Montaigne. I took a right onto the Champs-Elysees, to Place De La Concorde and proceeding on to Boulevard Haussmann and heading on toward Galleries La Fayette, the famed department store, half an hour away by foot.

For the first time, walking this long distance, I lost track of where I was going. I walked on Champs Elysees through the little park and watch couples kiss and hold hand. I decided to cut short through the little park and sit on the bench and light a *Gauloise*. I must have been walking for an hour, crying my eyes out in the rain, feeling sorry for me, thinking how stupid I was to be wasting my life away on this man. It had been three and one-half years now and still miserable, nothing had changed but now I was done- finished. I was determined to leave him.

At last I found the department store, with its magnificent façade, an inspiring building of exquisite architecture, and I went in, browsing through the scarf department. Boarding the escalator, I glanced toward the second floor. Believe it or not, Mr. Wonderful and his wife were right in front of me, in full view, going down— and with a big smile on his face, standing one step behind her on the escalator, waiving at me! He had found me. That was it, another sign he would be in my life forever. It was too great a coincidence that I would immediately run into him in one of the biggest department stores in Paris in the middle of the day.

The store located on the 9th Arrondissement in Paris was renovate in 1912 and was for its architecure, George Chedanne, and also famous for its Art Nouveau staircases with an annual sale of a billion

Euro, was so awfully crowded. How was it possible that we would both end up there at the same instant, just as we had ended up on the same flight? It seemed as if fate was at work. It seemed pre-destined on some crazy hidden map of souls. There was no way to get away from him. My pain only got worse. Rushing to desperately look and find the exit, I flew out of there like a tornado. All I could think of was how much I loved him.

He didn't call me, not that day or the next. It was Thursday when he finally phoned and wanted to see me. The sad scene of the two of them together, made me not wanting to call him back. I must have had a dozen messages, and refused to answer them all.

We would end up in the same place again at a Fourth of July party at the American Embassy. At first, when I heard that Mr. Wonderful and his wife were going, I decided not to go. But around four o'clock, when it was time to start getting ready, I said screw it, I wanted to enjoy myself, and I put on a gorgeous emerald green dress, my cowboy hat, and long chandelier diamond earrings. I thought I looked sensational, and it must have been true, because the men started hitting on me as soon as I reached the hotel lobby. It was amazing. In the big crowd of dignitaries and VIPs at the embassy, the scene was even more incredible. Before I knew it, the Korean ambassador was attached to me like a stick-on tattoo. He wouldn't leave me alone. The guy kept trailing me, wanting to get my phone number. There were seven or eight other guys too, all from big American corporations. They all wanted my number. They were like a flock of pigeons, hoping I'd toss a little scrap of attention their way. It was fun and I loved it. I was having a great time, for a few hours forgetting my sad and pathetic life. The party was just what I needed.

It was 7 o'clock and he was nowhere to be found. Then, from the corner of my eyes, I spotted him—Mr. Wonderful, with his wife, coming down the stairs. My heart stopped. They were dressed in matching jackets that looked like American flags. So *declasse*! They looked ridiculous together in those outfits, and yet it was still wrenching to see them, ruining my mood. The men floating around me ceased to matter. I had to get away. I couldn't stay in the same room with them; it was just too tough.

Breaking away, I started upstairs, where I wouldn't see them and they wouldn't see me not knowing he had already spotted me. Another ambassador followed me, grabbing my wrist. "I want to see you again," he said. Somehow I got free of him and found a haven in the less-crowded spaces of the second floor lobby. The American ambassador's residence was up there, and I noticed an attractive young woman sitting alone on a couch and smiling. She turned out to be the ambassador's assistant, Pauline.

I asked, in French, if it was okay to sit down. By now I needed to catch my breath, I was losing it.

There was a sudden hole in my heart; I realized how much I missed my Mr. Wonderful, how terribly in love with him I was and yet, there was no way I was going back. I did not expect he would come upstairs and find me.

Pauline and I began to talk and we hit it off immediately. It seemed as if we had known each other for a hundred years. She assumed I was French, but my Stetson was screaming American. I came right out and said, "Would you like to have dinner with me tonight? It's a sad night for me; I don't want to eat alone."

Lovesick in Beverly Hills

"You don't even know me," she said. "You are so nice."

"I'm really depressed and I don't want to eat by myself," I told her. "We can go anywhere you'd like." She smiled and agreed, and a moment later who should walk in but Mr. Wonderful, carrying his camera. He had been looking all over for me, and now he had found me.

Staring at Pauline, he said, "Isn't she beautiful in her cowboy hat? Would you please take our picture together?" I was furious, his wife was right behind him. Goddamn it. What was he thinking? "Get up" I said in French "let's go." He said: "I want a picture with you." Embarrassed, I got up and we posed for the shot, but meanwhile I was dying inside—alarmed, confused, elated, and mad. This was my fix for the day, to be with him these few unexpected moments. And yet I was beside myself. His behavior was despicable. Pauline said, in French, surprised and entertained by now, "Who is this man? Do you know him?" I said, "Take the picture and let's get out of here."

We quickly left and Pauline and I went out through the drenching rain to a Chinese restaurant, where we kept talking. I told her the whole story. She told me about her own life. She and her husband, a man named Momo, were separated. He was a very unusual man; he had certain healing powers, she claimed. I felt moved to ask if I could meet him—a meeting that would soon be arranged.

I'll never forget it. Momo turned out to be a tall African man, very dark-skinned, and I sensed the spiritual power he possessed. We met late at night, at the Plaza Athenee, with the rain still pouring. I listened to him speaking and wondered if any of it could possibly be true. He told me that in fourteen days and fourteen nights my life would start to change. Things would start to happen. Those were his exact words. Only as I thought about it did it begin to make sense.

I would finish my weeks in Europe and go home, and make myself strong enough to beat Mr. Wonderful at his own game. My birthday would be coming up and I would turn forty-nine. I had been pleading with god to let me be strong enough to let him go. Not realizing it was going to be useless.

Being there, in the same space with the wife was draining me of all the oxygen in my lungs again. Not realizing I deserve better. So childish and such an immature behavior, but that is what I was feeling. I wanted to be out of there and back into my own home. Nothing had worked so far. Maybe this was the right time for change—the right time to get past him and move on.

The right time to really make it on my own and set myself free.

Momo and I talked for an hour and a half. Pauline only listened. By midnight, I was exhausted so I left to go up in my room.

That night I threw up. It was weird, because the nausea was quite pleasant. I had fallen asleep, but the storm woke me up at three in the morning, and I felt like my entire body was on fire. I was burning up, although I was not sweating and I was feeling ill. All I could think of was that the man I had met, Momo, was in my room, not physically but spiritually. His soul or spirit was all around my room, attaching itself to the ceiling, and it was on doing strange things, by telling me things. It seemed there was blood all over him—very weird stuff. In fact, it seemed that the storm itself was a thing he conjured, and somehow the thunder was affecting my body.

The hotel had old-fashioned metal shutters outside, and they were making a fearsome noises as they rattled back and forth in the wild because of the thunder storm, as if part of a horror movie. Momo's presence and the rumbling, booming storm, with its intense flashes of lightning, blood everywhere were forcing me toward an altered state of consciousness. I had not had anything to drink that night, but it was the strangest night I could remember. Suddenly I got up and found my blindfold, slipping it on and withdrawing into a deep meditation. Wild and meaningful dreams began to take over my mind. Mr. Wonderful was in them, and so was his wife. She was not nasty or mean. A voice of some kind told me that I would marry someone else. All the while, Momo's presence was still there. The thundering room was filled with lightening and spirits; I saw visions I cannot remember or describe. There was a phenomenal abundance of good feelings, the sense that my life was going to improve. The thunder seemed to be blasting away all of my pain, shaking loose the blackness that hung on my very bones. Brilliant bursts of lightning illuminated the room.

Room service woke me up, knocking on my door at 9:30. I sat up feeling light— my whole body was light—and I was free of nausea. I had no pain in me, no negative feelings, nothing but a powerful optimism. I felt refreshed for the first time in six years. I was free of hurt, anxiety, and sorrow.

Most of all I felt strong, ready to put my relationship with Mr. Wonderful behind me and start a new life.

As if reading my thoughts, he had tracked me down at my hotel and got a message to me that morning: "Don't move. I'm coming over. I love you and I want to see you, I am never going to let you get away from me." I resented him deciding when and where he would see me, and disappearing so often beyond my reach. I was angry. I ordered everything on the room-service menu—the bill must have been $400 for breakfast—and I didn't eat a bite when all of a sudden was a knock on my door. He made it alright! When he walked in, I told him that he would get the bill, and that this was our last time together. I didn't want to see him anymore.

While staring at my packed luggage, he talked for a good forty-five minutes, and I made it very clear how difficult it was to be in my position—the wants and needs that forever went unmet. I also told him about meeting Momo, the strange, interesting African man. It wasn't as long a conversation as we might have wanted, because I had a flight to catch to return to Los Angeles. He seemed sad. He did not want me to leave, begging I would not leave him. We reached a temporary state of grace, just accepting our differences, looking to the future with hope and away from each other.

At the airport, I called Pauline and Momo and told them about the incredible journey I had experienced overnight. Pauline, would turn out to be one of my very best friends. I'm sure that she and Momo both understood how strange and deep that mystical experience was for me. Ghosts and supernatural events, was quite profound for someone who had been suffering as much as I had been.

At the same time, my emotions were still at war. Sitting there in my seat on the plane, pointed back toward my children and my job and my little apartment, I had to confront the reality of the situation. I was hopelessly in love with him. Period. Did I really want new beginnings, a complete change in my life, when it might mean never seeing that rugged face and those penetrating eyes?

The entire flight home, starring into the gray and white clouds, I cried—eleven hours worth of tears. It was July 2001, and this phase of my life was coming to an end.

12

Another Suitor

Little more than a week had gone by. It was a Wednesday, and I was lying in my bed in my tiny apartment in Beverly Hills, when the phone rang—Mr. Wonderful calling.

"Are you coming back to Cannes on Sunday? Am I going to see you?" he asked me. "I know you have a ticket." I was expecting him to say, "I can't wait to see you," but I wasn't going to make it easy for him.

"It's none of your business, didn't I ask you not to call me, ever?" I said. "This is very hard for me, please leave me alone! Can't you understand that I don't ever want to see you again?"

"Suit yourself," he said. No fight. No insistence, no determination, not an ounce of the stubborn resolve you'd expect from any man who truly missed the woman he loves.

"Don't ever, ever call me again!" I said, and I hung up. I wasn't willing to take it anymore. He kept talking about loving me and yet he wouldn't leave his wife. Six times the same day he called back, hoping I would pick up. He was re-dialing my number now half a dozen times a day. He traveled with her, dined with her, went to parties with her, and I got only the leftovers, stolen moments on the sly, brief meetings in my room or secret rendezvous places when what I really wanted was him, forever, all the time, in the sort of deep, loving relationship we were meant to have, not knowing he was incapable of it all. Determined to put an end to it all, I gave up answering the phone and never called him back.

My business was still sort of suffering. The meager divorce settlement was completely inadequate to live the way I longed to in Beverly Hills. My clients were nowhere to be found.

Still, I loved Cannes in the summer. I had wanted to go back regardless of not seeing him. My bags were packed on the floor next to my bed. In my heart I hoped he would say, "Come, I miss you, I want to see you," but instead it was only, "Suit yourself." Yeah, suit myself. I would have to suit myself. Anyway I already held a first class ticket, and a confirmed reservation at the Martinez. Locking up the apartment, I decided I was going to go. I would take the trip and see what happened and try to make the most of my life. Momo, kept coming into mind; not sure why, but something pushed me to leave and get ready for Saturday's flight. Maybe my life and my world would start to change for the better. Maybe there would be the sort of profound new beginning that Momo, the mystic healer, had predicted for me. What were the chances that such a prophecy would come true?

In 2001 my first destination was actually Milan, where I did some shopping before flying on to Cannes in mid-July. My reservation was at the Hotel Martinez. In what was surely not an auspicious start to my visit, the hotel had given away my room to a Prince of one of the middle eastern countries. The desk had to put me up temporarily in the attic type room. After I settled in, I walked over to the Carlton, which was booked solid, too. The clerk offered to give me a room on

Sunday, a week later, and I said fine, I was going to be in town for the next two weeks anyway.

I wanted to relax and enjoy myself, and I put on my cute little black Gucci dress, no make-up, no jewelry, and pulled my hair into a pony tail, leaving my room around 7:00 in the evening for my favorite café on the stunning Veranda at the Carlton, overlooking the water. Despite my lack of adornments, I was a perfect size four, turning heads wherever I went. It was fun to see the stir I caused. Still, after my flight, and all the rushing around, I was very tired—exhausted, really—and wore a fabulous sad, fake smile. Sylvan, the waiter, who had become a very familiar face, brought me a glass of wine and I sat observing the view.

Wondering in which part of the world, Mr. Wonderful was. Many of the women looked plain and unattractive, and yet they were all with gorgeous men. I was painfully aware of being alone again. The former Miss Iran runner up, high-spirited, fun, charming, and yet unlucky enough to have fallen in love with a married man who couldn't, or wouldn't claim me. Trying hard to fight back the tears, I noticed a couple walking in and taking a table near me.

My terrible-tasting wine was nearly gone when I thought I don't want to be alone, He was striking—very tall and elegant, and quite well-tanned with piercing deep blue eyes. He wore a classy pink linen shirt and white linen slacks. The woman was younger than he was, a bit stout, and had curly dark hair and thick glasses. For half an hour, I watched this couple and found myself curious about them: Who were they? Where were they from? How had they met, and how had they come to be here on this night in Cannes? I called Sylvan and in French, explaining to him how I didn't want to eat alone, if he would terribly mind, ask and invite the couple to join me and I offered to pay for their dinner.

When Sylvan approached them, they looked over at me and smiled. A moment later the woman stood and left; the man wandered over with his drink, a glass of Campari. Though he spoke a little English and some French, his first language was Dutch. We introduced ourselves—he said his name was Giovanni—and I noticed his sparkling blue eyes.

"What happened to your wife?" I said. "Oh, that wasn't my wife," he corrected me. "That was my daughter, and she was very happy that I'm meeting you, because she thinks you're beautiful." We began to relax and talk. What are the chances! Before I knew it, an hour and a half had gone by—and I still hadn't eaten. He said, in his debonair way, "Listen, I know you don't know me, and I know you must also be frightened, but next door at Felix we can go and have dinner. Would you like to join me?" I thought, well, I had been there a dozen times, and that sure beats eating alone. Why not? So I agreed, and we walked to the elegant spot next door, where the Maitre D' and the waiters all knew him. They not only knew him, they knew what type of wine he preferred, what hors d'oeuvres and which entre was his favorites. I thought, to myself, how interesting. We had a great dinner together. It was eleven o'clock when we left. He followed me back to the Martinez and waited with me for my elevator. His blue eyes peered down at me. "Pishi, I know we barely met, but can I invite you to lunch tomorrow?"

"I don't think so," I said. He could see the terror in my eyes. I don't know why I'm so intimidated by men who showed a touch of romance.

Later I found out there is a medical term for it, "androphobia," the fear of men. I think my strict upbringing ingrained that in me.

He was gracious but insistent. "Don't worry, there's no need to be scared. We'll have a lot of people around. We're having lunch, and I'm coming to pick you up.

My reluctance began to ease. Lunch might be fun. Maybe I could trust this courteous, dignified gentleman. "Ten o'clock?" he said, with a note of disapproval. "I thought you said lunch? No, no, that's too early. I won't be ready until noon."

"My driver will be here," he said. Giovanni then kissed my hand and said goodnight and left. His manners impressed me. If he had been an American, I wonder if I would have accepted the offer to dine. They're in for a rush and out for an instant for an immediate gratification. Europeans are different—they're elegant, and they are gentlemen, and Giovanni truly was a gentleman.

In the morning, I had to go shopping, of course. I'd bought a lot in Milan, but this was special, and I wanted to look just right.

From boutique to boutique I went, browsing, picking things out, making sure I would look my very best, and at 11:00 I returned to the Martinez and found Giovanni waiting for me in the lobby, along with his driver. We were chauffeured in a black Mercedes to a small craft that ferried us to his magnificent yacht in the Mediterranean. It was the most amazing lunch of my life. Giovanni turned out to be one of the wealthiest men in Holland, an investor who owned a huge number of buildings and properties. He was also unfailingly gentle, kind, considerate, in every sense of the word. He and his staff catered to my every whim.

Athena

At four in the afternoon, I finally excused myself to leave. Giovanni said he was flying the next morning back to Holland, but he would return to Cannes later in the week, on Thursday, unaware that he would get tied up and be delayed until Sunday. He said he would like to have dinner with me when he got back, and I invited him to call me. His driver took me back to shore.

It had been a wonderful time—I knew I had met somebody very special—but Thursday came and went and I never heard from Giovanni. Nor did he call on the days afterward, and on Sunday I changed hotels, finally getting a room at the Carlton, where I always preferred to stay, anyway.

Although at the time I didn't know, Giovanni had been delayed in Holland and was not able to return to Cannes until Tuesday. For four days in a row he went to look for me at the Martinez, until finally someone told him—erroneously—that I had checked out and flown back to Los Angeles. He only learned the truth when he happened to be having dinner with a couple that he knew, close friends of his, and mentioned meeting this attractive woman from Beverly Hills—who, unfortunately, he said, had left to return to California.

These friends also happened to sort of know of me, another of the remarkable coincidences that seemed to be governing my life. "No, no! she hasn't left", they told him. "She had only changed hotels, and was now staying at the Carlton and she was still here!"

Not answering the phone, and living life without Mr. Wonderful, I was making the most of my time in that lovely city. Every Friday, half an hour outside Cannes, in the Italian village of Ventemiglia, there is a huge flea market. Close to three-thousand people show up; it's quite a scene, not only for shopping but also for people watching.

I went with several of my new friends, dressed in my tightest jeans, toting my Chanel bag and wearing the perfect sexy accent for it, a stylish cowboy hat with a pin that said: "You ain't shit if you ain't a cowboy." I was strolling the aisles when who should I bump into? Mr. Wonderful—and his wife! My heart was on the brink of a real coronary. Oh, shit! Oh, shit! No, no, no! How was this possible? He is here in Cannes? I cannot get away from him! Where the hell did he come from? The bumping into Mr. Wonderful and his wife was much too much for me. I was having a heart attack.

Putting on a friendly face, I said, "Oh, hi, how are you? You guys are from Beverly Hills, right?" Trying to sound upbeat, and nonchalant, I started walking away. Talk about a terrorizing moment! Seeing his wife's face, looking straight into her eyes, was like staring into the flat, menacing eyes of a shark. It was chilling—awful. And they were together. I was devastated, my only consolation being that she was old and I definitely looked hot.

Still, I hadn't seen him for three weeks; the encounter was like a shot in my gut, knocking the wind out of me. I started having a severe anxiety attack, hyperventilating nonstop. There wasn't enough oxygen in the air for me. As I moved on, out of their view, the tears welled in my eyes. Make-up was running down my face. I started walking fast toward the train station and my friends were following me, not knowing what had happened.

Around 5:30 or 6 o'clock, I entered my room completely wiped out—exhausted, sad, depressed and in a rage. He still was with her the bitchy woman who emotionally abused him, which he constantly talked about. It was such a waste of a life, such a shame that he lacked the courage to follow his heart and be with me. He would choose her and cast me aside and that was now so sad. He called me non stop. Between the hotel phone and the cell phone, they were burning fuses. I refused to answer.

I threw myself on my bed in despair. Dropping my shopping bag on the floor, I began wailing. What am I doing here? Why is he here? I had not seen him for three weeks, I wondered why today happened. I should have never come. I was glad to be leaving on Sunday. It seemed best to get far away from him. At that instant the phone in my room rang again.

Speaking of the devil I was sure, it had to be Mr. Wonderful. I grabbed the receiver and said, "What the hell do you want from me?"

"Pishi?" a sweet voice said. "Who is this?" It wasn't him. "It is Giovanni," my *genial* new Dutch friend said in his well-mannered accent. "I'm in Corsica on my boat, and I've been looking for you for a week. Several times, I went back to the hotel and they said you'd returned to the States."

"No, I moved—I went to another hotel," I said. "I've been here!" Overjoyed? I was ecstatic. What a wonderful and surprising lift. There was no way I would hesitate to see him now. "How long does it take to drive over there?" I asked. He laughed. "You can't drive," he said. "It's an island." Fly here and we will pick you up.

I immediately ran downstairs to the lobby and asked the concierge to arrange a flight for the next day. Corsica is not far by air from Cannes. However, the airlines were hopeless, totally booked, the dour little concierge told me. As I stood there, a very good-looking guy who had overheard the conversation offered to fly me there on his private jet-now isn't that nice! He was from New York. I said no

Lovesick in Beverly Hills

thanks and slipped the concierge $100 Euros to encourage him to search for an open seat. About thirty minutes later, he had arranged to book me on a flight at eight the next morning, returning the same day. The airport in Corsica was still four hours by car from the boat. Giovanni and his driver picked me up. When we finally got to his lavish yacht, I got to meet his two daughters and hear the full story of his sad and remarkable life. He had deeply loved his first wife but lost her to cancer. His second marriage had ended in divorce. He had given his ex- $75 million in the settlement, and she had moved to Monte Carlo. He'd had a girlfriend since then, but they had broken up after a paparazzo snapped a photograph of her holding hands with another man.

Successful beyond belief, he owned half of Europe, or so it seemed, including twelve houses, but all he really wanted was love. He wanted to find a woman he truly cared about, a woman who was loyal to him and who loved him back. He wanted to enjoy his wealth and enjoy being with that special person. It was hard not to be impressed. His yacht was an eloquent expression of his formidable wealth. The bathroom was done in spectacular pink marble, and in the bathroom a huge Jacuzzi was installed next to the big slap of pink marble. Even more wonderful though, was how he treated me—like royalty, like the princess I'd dreamed of since I was in High School. When I took a bath, he stood waiting outside to hand me a towel, saying, "I don't want you to catch cold." And for love?

He was completely smitten with me, infatuated, entranced, and at some point he even used that magical word, love. I was interested. Things were happening very fast, but I was willing to see where things led. Maybe Momo the psychic healer had been right: major changes were happening, good things, things that would finally make my life the way it should be.

Looking back, there were opportunities for good things to happen, unfortunately psychologically I was not used to a man, really caring and loving me for me. Now the events unfolded differently, but lost in the fog of my feelings, my overpowering and irrational love for my precious Mr. Wonderful I was still blind to a healthy relationship and wanted things move very slowly. Remember one cannot speak chineese to a french. I guess, that was my life story. Giovanni was one of those great opportunities presented to me, maybe the best one of all. He was everything a man should be, and he was prepared to give me the world.

After I returned home to Beverly Hills, Giovanni came over— he had never visited the United States—and when I met him at the airport he presented me with three dozen gorgeous roses, all nearly three feet tall that was kept refrigerated, in the plane specially for me. He booked a suite at the Bel-Air Hotel for a few night and navigated the streets in a chauffered limousine. We had a special dinner together at L'Orangerie. Money meant nothing to this man. He rejoiced in life. He ordered a bottle of the best Champagne. Whatever I wanted is whatever he wanted, telling me I am is wife.

His visit to L.A. was short, only three days. He had come mainly to accompany me to the opening of the opera and also to discuss marrying me, and take me back with him to the south of France. We traveled to Nice, where his boat was moored, and arrived to find several people waiting for us—a limo driver, the captain of the boat, and seven in help. They physically lifted me up to put me aboard, and we sailed to St. Tropez, where we spent two amazing weeks. It was the most beautiful, and incredible time of my life. By now, this man was thoroughly in love with me. My cell phone, was on fire with messages. Mr. Wonderful had gone mad, he had heard, I was a the Opera with a tall and good looking man and was calling me every hour.

The yacht sailed into Antibes and back to Cannes. Breath-taking yachts were anchored in rows. On some of the boats, we could see television screens, all showing the same images. At first I didn't know what was happening. Quickly I found out: The top of the World Trade Center was on fire. It was Tuesday September 11, 2001. That terrible event seemed too far away and too abstract to be real. Besides, I was on the yacht, talking with my friend Tamara from Miami and other people who were spending the day with us, and I was flying high in Giovanni's presence. I was the princess and he was the Prince. The horrors on TV hardly held our attention, since we really did not know what was actually going on. It seemed to us an ordinary building fire at the time, and with the sound turned low my focus was on the conversation on deck. Giovanni's thoughts were clearly on courtship.

"Tonight I'm taking you to Tetu," he told me. I had been there many times and loved it. It was and is the most exclusive restaurant in Cannes and one of the most famous lobster and seafood houses in the world. I had time to get my hair and nails done, with a personal driver to whisk me to my appointments before returning me to the boat for the ritual that was cocktail hour.

This is a special part of the yacht culture in Cannes: tourists and paparazzi crowd the shoreline just to get a glimpse of the boats going by with their famous owners and guests, all sipping their martinis and champagne. To prepare for it, the staffs aboard the yachts set out flowers and drinks and hors d'oeuvres—whatever the hosts like to serve. The sight of the lighted vessels filling the bay in the gathering dusk and the sounds of the talk and laughter make for an unforgettable evening.

Afterward, we finally made it to Tetu, with me in a gorgeous sexy baby pink beaded cocktail dress. We were escorted to Giovanni's special table and served his special bottle of wine, and he introduced me as his wife, as usual. I had no clue that he was actually about to propose to me—I'd never been proposed to by any man, including my ex-husband. The moment occurred after we had ordered dinner. He held my hands and looked into my eyes.

"I know you're my wife, when I first met you in Cannes" he told me with conviction. "Tonight I'm asking you to marry me."

Surprised and looking straight into his eyes, I couldn't help but laugh. New York was on fire, and I was in this lovely place, away from everything, feeling almost giddy. "Why are you laughing?" he said. "It's only been three months," I said. "You don't even know who I am, and at the same time, for a second deep inside I was thinking of my Mr. wonderful and what if Giovanni was my Mr. Wonderful asking for my hand in marriage." "I know you," he said, smiling. "You're the woman I've always been looking for. You are already my wife, but I want to marry you anyway." He was sincere—so sincere it wasn't funny, and he really meant it, we are going home tomorrow because, my children are having a party for us.

It was sweet, magical and terrifically touching, an unbelievably beautiful moment, even though I gave him a maybe answer. I didn't know what to think or say. This was all new territory. Deep inside, I knew I still had feelings for Mr. Wonderful, my big cowboy, the man whom I obsessively loved and yet who had hurt me so much for so long. He had phoned fifty times, leaving messages for me, and I had never responded. A large part of me felt that I should get beyond the pain of that relationship and begin something new. Yet I didn't really know what I should do, or what I wanted to do-money vs. love? Never.

We had a marvelous lobster dinner, we returned to the boat without ever directly answering his marriage proposal. We had already planned to travel the next morning to Amsterdam. He wanted to show me around and have me meet his family. They were all waiting to see this new love interest of his—me.

On September 12, almost nobody else was flying. Later, I would phone my kids and learn more about the terrorist attacks in New York and Washington, but for now we had no idea what was going on. All we saw was an airport that was a ghost town. We sat in the first row in first-class. There must have been 25 people on the entire plane. A dozen of his friends and family members showed up at the Airport, with bouquet of roses in had. He put me up at the Hotel Ancel, the most exclusive in Amsterdam, and I met all three of his children, all daughters, two of them married. They were tall and European-looking, and very beautiful. Not only they were happy for their dad, they really liked me. We hit it off, and that pleased Giovanni immensely. He was ready to make me the toast of the city. If we would marry, he told me, he would make sure that every month I would have a first-class ticket back to Los Angeles so I could see my own daughters and family as often as I liked. I asked if he would consider living four months of the year in California and the rest in Holland, but that, apparently, was the deal-breaker. Psychologically, because of his wife's death, he couldn't agree to be away from his children for a long period of time. They were a loving, close-knit family, and they loved me too. He said he would give it some thought.

Everywhere we went, meeting his friends, Giovanni introduced me as his wife.

"You can't call me your wife," I would tell him. But we enjoyed ourselves. When I left to fly home for the Jewish holidays, he held me in his arm at the airport and wouldn't let go. Total confusion- that's what I felt on the long flight back home. Was Giovanni the one? Was he to be my future? Or was it a mirage, some fanciful image that had caught my attention for only a moment, like a flashy toy? Was it too good to be true? I was captivated by this gracious, attentive Dutchman, and yet it was hard to imagine making such a radical change in my life so soon. But I decided to pack and go back to marry this wonderful man.

Two people called me almost the instant as I landed at LAX. One was Giovanni, missing me already, hoping I had arrived safely. The other was Mr. Wonderful. He had broken into my apartment, rummaged through my belongings, and found out when I was due in via my agenda that was sitting on my desk. He was obsessed at the thought of seeing me. Furthermore I no longer wanted to have anything to do with him.

My daughters rushed to my little apartment. They were so happy for me, knowing I had finally found someone. They wanted to hear all about him, and about my trip—and yet they were worried. "Are you really going to leave us?" they said. "Are you going to marry this guy and live in Europe?" Was I going to live in Amsterdam? They were afraid to lose me. I didn't want to alarm them or sound too defensive, but their concern got to me. Whatever happened, I knew

Lovesick in Beverly Hills

I had to make sure I was always there for my kids. Pink-marbled yachts were one thing, but I had to know and make sure I could spend time with my two beautiful daughters in America and a husband in Europe. And of course the big unresolved question was what to do about my crazy fixation with Mr. Wonderful, a man who was bad for me, surely but whom I loved with an unquenchable ardor—that face, those blue eyes, his sexy voice and his tall, broad stature. Those shoulders blotted out my horizon; they kept me from seeing so many other possibilities and the phone would not stop ringing.

Now I was really in a situation. Although it was never my intent, I was suddenly the center of attention of two powerful, obsessive men, both of them clamoring to have me. Giovanni called every morning; he was desperate to see me again and wanted me back in Europe and in his life. Mr. Wonderful called every day, morning, noon and night begging to see me one more time; I refused to answer his calls, he was determined to get me back. I would hang up the phone immediately, but he kept calling, even though it would be almost a month before I agreed to meet with him. Actually, my phone was ringing constantly—it's a wonder the circuits didn't fry.

Mr. Wonderful heard rumors that I was getting married, and he really freaked out. The phone calls increased. He was calling every two hours, calling my sister, calling my friends, calling my office. It was a flat-out bombardment from a guy who was single-minded and insistent on having his own way. Not yet, that was for sure. I had other things going on. My little apartment was sad and dreary. The divorce had hit me hard. I was running out of money and now I was petrified and had to make a serious decision.

Athena

He went ballistic when he found who Giovanni was and how much money he had. He went absolutely crazy. Now the calls were coming in on an hourly basis. I fought him off, but it was enough to drive me toward a nervous breakdown. This went on for a month— nearly constant calls, pestering, hammering on my defenses. It was October and fall was approaching. I hadn't seen him since July.

"You owe me at least one meeting," he begged me. "Just meet me for lunch— that's all I want from you."

Yielding to the pressure, I finally agreed to have lunch with him on October 17. Biggest mistake of my life.

"Lunch, that was it", and he had agreed. We'd talk some nonsense and go our own separate ways. His calls persisted making sure that lunch was on. He was tremendously afraid that I would cancel.

Meanwhile, Giovanni was busy planning our future together. He lined up a Dutch language class for me. Speculation hit the papers in Amsterdam about who he was going to marry. He was so high-profile and the paparazzi tracked him down. I was always delighted to hear from him. He was a true gentleman—and relentless, too but not in the rabid way that Mr. Wonderful was.

Every day there was another reminder about lunch— call after call. Invariably, I would delete the answering machine and or hang up. I changed my home number, my cell numbers, at least eight times, again. I went through twenty-four different numbers—and Mr. Wonderful never stopped! Somehow, he would always find me. He left messages: "I'm going to leave her and be with you. I'm tired of this. I want to change my life. She's abusive. She's an alcoholic. She's popping pills."

Lovesick in Beverly Hills

For quite a while I had the strength to hang up on him, to avoid him. But he wore me down. The total number of calls climbed to over 340 times—I counted them on my phone bill. My secretary threatened that she was going to quit. Slowly, though, with all that persistence, he squirmed back into my heart.

By the time the day of our lunch arrived, I was anxious to see him. Later he told me, for the month before we met, he kept asking his secretaries, if his appointment on the 17th was canceled or still on. He was obsessed and so was I.

When I arrived, oh my God, you should have seen him smile. He was so happy to see me. He took me to Four Oaks, one of the most romantic spots in L.A. It was a quaint little European eatery on Beverly Glen. He is not the type to go to romantic places and now he was *"tres romantic."* I guess one can be if deperate enough.

Cowboys never are-maybe? But he would have done anything for me at that moment, anything in the world. I was skinny, tanned, ravishing—and never looked better. We sat down and he drank me in with his eyes. I relished the attention.

He was uncomfortable, nervous, tense, scared. "What do you want?" he said. "Anything. Tell me what you want." I giggled, lifted my head, and looked at his beautiful eyes. "The menu would be good to start," I said. He flashed a child-like smile. "You know what I'm talking about." He asked me again, "What is it that you want?" I turned it around on him. "What do you want, how about buying a house and I will move in?" I asked him:" what?".

He didn't flinch. "there is nothing I cannot do, I will give you anything, I want you back and I want you not to go back to Europe."

As he was squeezing my hand he said over and over: "Don't leave me. You know I have a sad life. Let's buy a house and move in. I want to leave her and marry you and live with you. Go find a house, my gift, I will give it to you, and I'm moving in."

The words were incredible to hear and lusting with my soul. Was he serious? Was it really going to happen? The feelings crackled through me. It was precisely what I wanted too, more than anything, in spite of Giovanni, in spite of everything we had been through. Trying to keep my cool, I said:" but I am getting married".

He went crazy and started to take charge just like what I had fallen in love with to begin with. How can you leave me, you love me and this is your home, beside I love you and I am going to marry you.

Tell me where do you want to live, find a house and I am moving in. God! Life is so cruel. He was flirting and igniting my feelings deep inside of me and making me dream about how wonderful it would be to marry for love. My thoughts were having a love affair with the future thinking about the end result and how delicious and delectable finally our lives would be. My dreams come true. Heaven and earth was now moving under my feet and felt enormously fulfilling. I replied: "Funny, I already know a house that never sold and is still for sale and I know you would love it too." Months earlier I had seen a beautiful place on Alpine Meadow Drive, right there in Beverly Hills that was still on the market for sale.

When we had lunch, he asked me if I would drive him by it. We weren't able to go inside, but it didn't matter. Before I could even grasp what was happening, and while we were still sitting in his car outside the big gate, Mr. Wonderful reached into his jacket and pulled

Lovesick in Beverly Hills

out his checkbook. Forget about touring the place—he wrote out a check to the escrow company for $2.5 million, the asking price.

"Buy the house, fix it, I'm moving in," he said. "I love you. I want to spend the rest of my life with you." Those eyes were incapable of lying, never. He was going to single-handedly change the course of my life forever.

Well! He bought me back with money and love and more love. He gave me a hug and I called the listing agent and said: "I guess I will be moving again." It was incredible to imagine how sweet life would be with him. It was a fantastic neighborhood, Tom Cruise was one of our neighbors across the street and the fixer house was going to keep me busy for the next two years.

This unforgettable day resulted to moving into a house full of love that I will never forget. It was our love nest, and a great moment, not to mention the beginning of the toughest next fourteen years to follow. If anyone had suggested that I was in for a fall—that he was incapable of being honest with me, and maybe even incapable of being honest with himself—I probably would have laughed. Despite all the warning signs, I completely trusted those blue eyes and the words so gently spoken in lovely sweet voice. No question asked, I trusted this man deeply and implicitly.

Why wouldn't I? I was madly in love with him.

13

Living Blissfully Together

All I wanted was a fairy-tale love story, and to live and die happily ever after. How naive can I be, but I had high hopes. The house was beautiful, and I couldn't wait for escrow to close and this wonderful new chapter of our lives to begin. Every moment of my day, was like a blazing sunshine in heaven. And every day, a brilliant sparkle of love and joy that became a reality at the center of my consciousness. It was all I could think about.

But as for him? My Mr. Wonderful? He hired an architect and instructed him do follow my vision for the house, and do what he can to make me happy.

The second thing he did that December, five weeks after I had moved in, and despite his own promises to move in, was jet off to Mexico for a month—with his wife and his children. His wife! I couldn't believe it. I gave up Giovanni for this? I was beyond angry. I was absolutely devastated. Or was I dreaming, and this was not happening to me? It was almost too bizarre to be real. How could he do this to me? Why? What was it about pursuing me, calling me nonstop, begging me, pleading, writing a check for a house for us and now what? So he could race off on vacation with his wife? Painful moments and it was hurting, inflicting pain, a part of his way of loving? Did he enjoy seeing me suffer? He left behind an enormous amount of money to take care of all my expenses and asking me to get a ticket and meet him there in a week.

Was pain attached to love in this way? Was he saying, "I want you. I want to love you and hurt you in equal amounts"? I was confused, sad, and terrified of abandonment again. In loving him, was I hurting myself? Was pain part of the commonality of the deal? What was it that brought him back and drove him away? Why is it that when I go my own way, trying desperately to forget him and start a life of my own, it makes him want me more? And why is it that the more I became attracted to him, the more he wants to get away, ignoring me?

For a month, I ached and worried and cooled my heels, waiting, counting the days and minutes and seconds until he was back in town. He finally moved in with me on January 28, 2002—and only after a violent triggering event. They'd had an enormous fight; she was throwing dishes at him. It wasn't exactly a fairy-tale start, but by then I was too happy to hold a grudge. He was mine at last, and I was determined to be the woman of his dreams, thinking that's what he wanted. I was going to love him forever. I was going to have a life of love, this time all of the time.

To be in this special state of grace, together committed to loving each other, was transforming.

The house was no longer a house, it was a palace. Lunch is no longer lunch, it is a glorious banquet. Roses are no longer roses, they are velvety chalices of warmth and compassion—blazing expressions of the heart. And the man who takes you in his arms at night is no longer a man, he is a gallant knight, a timeless protector, a figure out of a legend who slays dragons, and you are his damsel, his princess, in a magical kingdom.

I pampered him. I cooked for him, manicured and buffed his nails, colored his hair then blow dried it making sure, he looked fabulous. The dinner table was fit for royalty. I bought fresh flowers every day—an abundance that filled our entire home with their fragrance, creating the look of a Monet painting. Every morning I would have a rose for him for his lapel; I'd make sure he was dressed impeccably. At the breakfast table, I had fresh orange juice for him, French toast, omelets, yogurt in all varieties, coffee, cappuccino, tea, and all sorts of fruit, muffins and pastry *a'la Ritz*. Everything was literally served on a silver platter. When he got home at night, his silk smoking jacket was ready for him, along with his scotch in a sparkling Baccarat crystal glass, the ice set in Christofle sterling bucket, next to his favorite chair.

I had a phone installed nearby so he could make his calls without having to move. He was a king on a throne in that chair, in our home. I used to sit in it when he was gone, studying the view out the window, imagining ways to make it more beautiful for him to enjoy. I roamed the nurseries, picking out trees and shrubs that would enhance the scene his view—in my mind, it should all look like a painting, colorful and alive, everything to please and inspire him. He loved Spanish love songs, and I collect and played those for him to sooths his soul. He enjoyed being fussed over, knowing perfectly well how crazy I was about him.

Love makes you do crazy things—from homemade peach jelly to the most expensive caviar and Dom Perignon was our evenings together. And every day he left the house with a kiss and a wish for a beautiful day. As I understood later from his secretaries, he was a changed man. There was nothing I wouldn't do to make his life better and see to his well-being.

What a big mistake and what a loser I am. All by myself and with all my heart, I shined his shoes every night just like they do at the Carlton in Cannes. Nothing mattered to me any more except this man, his wardrobe, his schedules, his diet, his vitamins, his exercise, and his company. If he planned to go to lunch, I would call ahead the restaurant and make sure they served him fresh fruit and vegetables and didn't give him too much butter or fat or fried foods. I wanted him to live forever. I purchased a huge juicer. Every day, in fact, around 10:30, I swung by his office and dropped off a bottle of fresh apple, watermelon or carrot juice.

For some reason, he wouldn't take me out to dinner, probably because he was afraid of the scandal it might cause if people saw us together. I never spoke a word, never complained. I understood. Big mistake.

The important thing was, I loved him—and he knew it. The sex was beyond amazing. Hugging him, and going to sleep with him, was the ultimate happiness. It was an experience I had never, ever had in my life—spending all night safely enfolded in the arms of the man I truly loved. And it was the same for him, I was sure. No one had ever treated him every day and every night the way that I treated him—his PJs ironed and scented, was ready every evening, and his newspaper by the bed- he would grin of happiness.

Maybe he wasn't used to that, or maybe he felt guilty, or maybe he didn't feel like he was worth all of the love I gave him all of the time.

And maybe he was a socio-path. To this day, I just cannot make any sense of it all. Or maybe it was the ugly divorce brewing—the fact that the drinking, pill-popping wife ran straight to the divorce lawyer, intent on taking him for all she could get. Whatever the case, our time together in our love nest lasted only few weeks. Happily ever after? It wasn't even a month!

The first inklings of trouble came right away, when we flew to Florida to attend the wedding of my best friend at Mare Lago, Donald Trump's fabulous private country club. Tamara's daughter was getting married there. My dream was no longer a dream, it was happening. Arm in arm, I had never been so happy in my life—never!

To travel with the man I loved, after all that I had missed during my marriage, and to sit next to him, hanging onto his arm, was sheer bliss. To rest my head on his big, broad shoulders was just heaven. There was electric current running through my entire body. And to steal a kiss or two was the purest form of ecstasy. In fact, merely being in the same space with him, sharing the air we breathed made my life worth living for. And to top it all, I was to enter the most beautiful castle in the world, Mare Lago, at his side, with our arms entwined—it could only have been a dream.

I bought the most gorgeous Monique L'heulier turquoise gown, and wore a long, stunning white fox wrap that he had given me for Christmas. Truly, I never looked better. The reception was a magical scene, and yet Mr. Wonderful did not seem to share the happy excitement. He was stern. He glowered. At one point, as I clung to him, he said, "My arm is numb. You're squeezing me too hard," followed by, "I know you love me a lot, I know."

My heart skipped a beat, but I withdrew, saying, "I love you; I never want to let you go." Did he understand that, and did it matter to him? He smiled and kissed me, but his coolness and apparent indifference made me sad.

While everyone danced, Mr. Wonderful just sat stolidly observing, as if he felt out of place. We were the best-dressed couple there—he wore a very handsome tuxedo—and somehow, in the opulence of Mare Lago, amid all of the sophistication of the fun and exciting company, the fact that he seemed uninterested in dancing with me was difficult to take. I started thinking, "He doesn't want me," and the evening began to hurt me very much.

Finally, I said, "Why aren't you asking me to dance? Everyone else is dancing?"

"You want to dance?" Almost grudgingly, he led me out to the dance floor, but the moment was already ruined because of the pain I was feeling. I cried while we danced my tears and mascara streaming down my face and onto his tuxedo jacket. I remember a terrible sadness overcoming me as we ended the night walking back to our hotel room at the Breakers.

The following day, we heard the terrible news that the space shuttle Columbia had exploded upon re-entry due to damage to its protective heat shield. All seven crew members perished.

He kept saying, "It blew up! It blew up!"—almost as if he was blaming me for the tragedy. He was extremely upset about it—far more than a normal person might have been. He seemed to be picking a fight with me. I told him it wasn't my fault.

Athena

We were due to fly back to California, and I dutifully packed his suitcase for him. He couldn't believe it. He saw what I was doing and said, "You're packing for me?" Of course I was packing for him, why?—"I love you." But no one had ever packed his suitcase for him before. No one had ever showered love and attention on him the way that I did, willingly, because it was in my heart to do so.

The gesture touched him, but more pain was yet to come—pain and humiliation that is part of going out with a married man who is weak and no woman should ever have to suffer this way.

We came back to Beverly Hills on a Sunday afternoon, and exciting things were going on. The following weekend I was due to have twenty people over for a dinner party on Friday night, followed by my nephew's Bar Mitzvah at the Ritz Carlton in Marina del Rey on Saturday. Mr. Wonderful did not quite say it, but he didn't want to be involved with my plans. I was sad about it, but I accepted his decision. Whatever made him happy was fine with me. I honored his feelings, not aware that a bomb was about to explode.

On Saturday morning he left to have breakfast with the boys and I was planning to go and get a manicure and pedicure and also to get my hair done for the bar mitzvah. It was a downer. I wanted him to go with me.

In the meantime, just before I left the house, I received two calls, one from his grandson and the other from his grand-daughter. They were all looking for him. As I left for the stylist, I decided to call him on his new cell phone and let him know that the grand kids were trying to reach him. I should note here that he had asked me to change his cell phone number on Friday the day before so that his wife would leave him alone, which of course pleased me. I had done that and no one had his new private number but me.

When I got into my car, I dialed his cell phone, he didn't seem exited to want to talk to me and tried to hang up—but he must have pushed the cell phone's ON button, thinking it was the OFF button. He was driving at the time and suddenly I could hear him talking to his wife on his other phone—the car phone. Now his wife was driving him crazy on his car phone.

He was totally unaware that I was still on the line. They talked for twenty minutes, and tragically, I just listened refusing to say a word and let him know that I was still there. As I was also driving, on my way to my appointments, my mind stopped functioning; I had no clue where I was going. No adjective can describe the shock and hurt of what I was hearing.

"She loves me," he was telling her. "You should see what she does for me, and all you do is drink."

"I love you, and I'm never going to drink again," I could hear her answer faintly. "The children are beginning to like her, but I'm their mother. They're supposed to be our kids. I am their mother. You come home. I want you at home. If you don't come home today I am going to kill myself."

"Do you promise you'll never drink again? And go to rehab?" he said.

She quickly agreed. "I want you home again this afternoon. When are you coming? We've been invited somewhere this evening for dinner. We have to go there."

Athena

"OK," he told her. "I'll pack this afternoon and come home. Let me first go and tell her."

Listening to all of this, I ended up somewhere near Hollywood, totally in the opposite direction from where I was supposed to go. It was now noon and I was crying like I never cried before. I was wetter than if I had been in a drenching downpour. This was a bad dream and I was living it. I immediately turned the car around to head back to the house, our supposed love nest. To hell with the manicure! Mr. Wonderful's cell phone was still on—I could still hear him. Somebody got into the car, it was one of his friends. His friends all knew me but now I know I was listening to the conversation between Mr. Wonderful and his friend.

"So how is life with the woman you love? You must be so happy," John said casually.

"Oh, my God, you should see how she treats me," Mr. Wonderful told him. "The clothes! The flowers! The dinners! I go home and she waits for me on the driveway. My drink is waiting for me—it's amazing. These Persians know how to treat their husbands. She loves me so much, and I don't know what to do, because I'm going to move back home this afternoon, and I don't know how to tell her."

I arrived home in a state of shock. Stupid me, having no idea, absolutely no idea how these games were played. I was soaked with sweat and tears. My hair was sticking to my face. My eyes were running like faucets. I was emotionally numb. I didn't know what do to next—whether to sit, to lie down, I was just pacing. Instead, I just stood there frozen in the middle of the room, not even moving. I was still like a statue for probably half an hour, unable to act or think

Lovesick in Beverly Hills

or cope. "He's leaving me," I kept repeating over and over. "He is leaving me."

Around one o'clock, I finally decided to call him at the Country Club, where I knew he was having lunch. "When are you going to come home?" I asked him.

"Two o'clock," he said.

"By the way, have you talked to her? Your wife?" I said.

"No. Why should I talk to her?"

I was dying. He was lying and I knew it. He showed up at 2:30. I had been sadly and impatiently waiting for him, and I repeated my question. "Have you talked to your wife recently?"

"No, why would I do that?" he replied.

"When was the last time you talked to her?" I pressed him. He stared into my eyes. He knew he couldn't elude me.

"Yeah," he admitted, "I have got to go back; we have a dinner party to go to tonight. This isn't working, and besides, my wife is going to kill herself I don't go home." He anxiously packed his suitcase and walked out, leaving behind fifteen large cartons of his belongings. It was unbelievable. It was all over, just like that! He had sucker-punched me and taken off within minutes. A short while later I got a call from his son Jerry.

"What? Is he crazy?" Jerry said. "I'm coming over."

I never made it to the manicure, nor did I feel well. I just stood for over an hour, motionless, in the same spot. My body had turned to ice, and my brain frosted over. Jerry, his son, walked in and said, "What did you do to him? Why did he leave? Don't let him go back to my mother. She will kill him."

I just cried. I remember going to the bar mitzvah, staying for half an hour, and leaving. Seven-hundred people were drinking and dancing and having the time of their lives, and then there was me, feeling like a widow who had just lost her husband. People were dancing the night way, and I was looking for the exit sign.

With bloodshot eyes, my face as red as a beet, I didn't want to be seen or to talk to anyone. As for my family: Well! They couldn't have cared less. That is a whole other book.

My eyes were puffed up, tears were dropping on my gown like tiny little sparkles of diamonds. I was there with my beautiful tan and gorgeous turquoise gown, a white fox wrap—a re-run of the Florida wedding—and wearing a fifteen-carat diamond ring, the present he gave me for my fiftieth birthday. And beneath it all was a broken heart. He had shattered all my dreams.

The next day Sunday, was a disaster. I was wasted, lovesick, angry, choked up, destroyed. I locked the door, changed the security code, and went to bed and slept for two days. He was gone and I didn't want to see him or ever hear from him again.

But he kept on calling. Why wouldn't he let me go? Just leave me alone? He couldn't. He was back at home with the wife, who of course kept on her schedule of drinking binges. I changed my phone numbers again—all three land lines and two cell phones—and still he kept on calling me for another five months.

Late in June, once again his wife went berserk, beating him this time a high-heel shoe. He called me from the street stranded in front of my gate, begging me to let him in. My heart sank at hearing his voice. I stopped dinner with my friends, and rushed back, heading home. All I could think of was him and the lack of his presence in my daily world. It was tearing me apart.

"Please open the gate," he said. "I'm bleeding." I ran like a mad woman. He was waiting out front on my driveway, carrying a suitcase, which he had hastily packed with pajamas and a toothbrush. He looked awful. He was shaking and hyperventilating. He couldn't catch his breath. His hair was standing on end. His leg was bleeding. He must have drunk half a bottle of scotch. I really thought he might have a heart attack. How could I not take pity on him? I loved every living fiber of this man. I got him cleaned up, fixed him dinner, and put him to bed in a separate room, so he could rest.

Just like that, he moved back in. Deep inside, I was ecstatic. He arranged to move a huge load of clothes—this time, twenty or thirty containers full. It was certainly more than enough for the two weeks he stayed.

The signs looked good. He agreed to go to therapy with me, to see a woman named Ana, whom his daughter had recommended. We saw her together, and we saw her one at a time, individually. But there was precious little time to get ourselves in sync. Another bomb was about to explode.

On July 2, around 9:30 in the morning, I was driving to my appointment when he called me on my cell and said, "Where are you?"

"I told you, I am going to the therapist."

"Call me when you're done, OK?" he said. I never gave it another thought. Around eleven, as I had promised, I called him. In a sad voice, he said, "I went back home. I can't do it." And he hung up. When I walked in the door, the housekeeper was in the kitchen. "Senor partir? Mister left?" I said. She replied: "Si, senora."

Yes, he had gone back, packed and left behind a drawer full of cash and all his credit cards. I couldn't cope. I went into the worst kind of downward spiral you can imagine. Every hope I had ever had, every dream, every feeling of optimism and love, was demolished. Meanwhile, what did he do? The very next day, he packed for a six-week trip to Europe—with her. *With her*!

We'd been planning to throw a Friday barbecue, a party together to celebrate the Fourth of July. Now he wasn't even going to be in the country. He left so fast, that he left behind every sign of life that we had together. I decided to throw all his credit card inside the barbecue—I could not and send them all back to his office.

They left the very next day after he moved out again. He wanted to attend a friend's birthday party in Paris. He wasn't trying to be cruel, but the cruelty of it was unbelievable. Paris. Paris was the backdrop for so many of my fondest memories, the days and evenings when we had managed to see each other there, slipping away for romantic interludes. I couldn't think of Paris without thinking that Mr. Wonderful should be with me—forever. I always recall the first time we got to spend an entire day there together, after I begged him to find a way to get free.

Lovesick in Beverly Hills

This was a couple of years ago now, during one of the early trips when I arranged to be there while he was also visiting. It took some coaxing, but he finally relented, and we set a place and time to meet, and I worked my usual magic in planning an exquisite outing. I immediately enlisted a limo and driver, then hurried to Hediard, Paris's most expensive gourmet deli, to buy champagne, strawberries, chocolate, French bread and the best Brie I've ever tasted. I loaded all of it into a picnic basket. The sky was gray and drippy, so I got an umbrella from my hotel, the Plaza Athenee, and waited for him downstairs. Around 10 a.m., Mr. Wonderful showed up, half an hour early, very nicely dressed—like John Wayne in slacks and fine black-leather jacket shoes. Mishel, the driver, held the door for him and he stepped in to join me inside the limo. The trunk of the car was already full of all of the goodies. Though happy to see me, Mr. Wonderful was full of questions. "What is this? Where are we going? What is happening?"

I had given Mishel his instructions. We proceeded toward Le Musee De Jacquemart-Andre, the fine old 1870 mansion built by the French banker and art aficionado Edouard Andre and his portraitist wife, Nelie Jacquemart, now a museum housing an exceptional collection of paintings, sculpture and antiques, mostly from that wistful era. I knew Mr. Wonderful would enjoy that. We browsed, we lingered in the airy spaces, and by the time we made our way outdoors, strolling among the forested paths and roses of the nearby Bois de Boulogne, a misty rain was falling. Mishel held the umbrella while we walked hand-in-hand, stopping occasionally to kiss and hold each other and snap pictures. We looked like quite the couple, him so handsomely dressed, me having just bought a smart pink Escada dress with the words love, romantic and sexy written all over it. I wore that with a lovely black hat and my Nina Ricci earrings. I was a vision, I have to say, and love was in the air, the gardens dripping with the rain, each rose bigger and more beautiful than the last.

After we returned to the car, and were starting to feel hungry, I took him to La Cascade, the most exclusive lunch spot in Paris. He was so happy. He said no one had ever done this for him. No one cared enough for him to show him Paris like this. We lingered and talked, and by 2:30 we finally left for our next destination: *Les Ponts des Arts,* the historic bridge that crosses the Seine near the Louvre.

As Mishel hefted the picnic basket from the trunk, Mr. Wonderful said, "What's this?" and started laughing. "Where are we going?" The look on his face was worth a million dollars. He was a portrait of delight.

"Wait and you'll see," I told him. I had also bought a beautiful Nina Ricci scarf, which I pulled over my head. The sky was lowering, and I worried that a drenching rain would descend to ruin our picnic. But I loved the gray of the sky and the moisture in the air. It was magical. Crossing the street, we moved out onto the old nine-arch foot bridge, the first metal bridge in Paris—an integral part of the city's history.

When the original incarnation opened in 1804, 65,000 Parisians paid to walk across it. Though reconstructed since then, it remains an iconic architectural statement, its elegant ironwork affording fantastic views of the river and the magnificent buildings that surround it. Every year, the bridge attracts tens of thousands of painters, photographers and lovers—people like Mr. Wonderful and me, who come to share picnics at a spot unmatched for its urban beauty. We picked a bench on the bridge to sit and opened our basket to savor our mid-afternoon repast of champagne, chocolate, strawberries and Brie taking lots of photos.

After a while Mishel thought we should leave; he thought the storm was about to unleash. Mr. Wonderful just grinned with his eyes full of love. I kept watching his face. It was lighting up with pure happiness. I drank in the moment. I craved his touch. I wanted to share everything with this man, now and forever, the Prince and the princess.

The limo eventually delivered us back to my hotel, and when Mishel dropped us off, Mr. Wonderful and I went upstairs to my room and made love. That Tuesday was a treasure I will keep until the day I die.

This was me at my best, loving him to tears. It is too bad that he could not and would not handle that love. It was too much, too strong, too intense and too real and too many tears shed for love.

So now, on this sad Fourth of July day, he was back in Paris without me, with his dreaded wife, and I was trying to maintain a brave face as I greeted the guests arriving for our party, the party that Mr. Wonderful and I were supposed to be throwing together. Most of them were shocked to discover that he was gone. He sent one of his assistants—Mr. Scumbag—over to take care of me, instructing him to telling him, "Give her what she wants. Offer her whatever she needs."

The house was to be mine. The expenses were being paid. I could have had that prime piece of property and found someone else. But I didn't want that. I didn't want his house or his things. I never took money from my ex-husband, and I wasn't about to take it from my ex-boyfriend. The man I loved? Forget it. There was nothing he could give me if he wouldn't give himself. What I wanted was to be on that plane with him on our way to Paris. The rest didn't matter. This was completely about love—and about pain.

I couldn't see living in that house without Mr. Wonderful anymore. Every furnishing, every piece of art, every window, every wall, and every door was part of a world we had created to share between the two of us. To have lost that, just hurt too much. I couldn't exist alone among the reminders. I was suffering. I was angry. I gathered up the legal papers along with a note he had given me—"I love you"—and tore them up. I found a crystal Lalique bowl and placed it on the center of the glass dining-room table. I left behind the furnishings that we had acquired specifically for the house and had Carlos, my gardener, the same man who had moved my armoire to the courthouse during the divorce trial haul my own personal belongings to a storage facility near the airport giving him back the house.

Signing the papers for the storage company felt like writing my own death sentence, obliterating the future I had imagined and hoped for, but I had no choice. The house was no longer attractive to me. It was no longer a home. I had to get out, and yet I was getting ill, plunging deep into a dangerous depression. It grew like mildew all over my body and soul.

A week after I left, they sold the house for $3.5 million, and they never offered me a dime, nor did I ever ask for anything—or any other help.

What I needed was love, not money and to be left alone. For the second time in three years, I was leaving, and forced to find a tiny apartment. So be it. I had to break free of him. Somehow I had to find space to breathe and start over. I had to get oxygen back in my lungs.

Hunting for a place was another sorry exercise, especially in the bad financial shape I was in. My income had dwindled to nearly nothing. I looked at two apartments, all in the same building complex and took the cheapest one: a one-bedroom unit on Pico Boulevard in the south part of Beverly Hills. The rent was $2,000 a month. Ordinarily, I would never be caught dead in such a grim, sunless building in that ugly part of town, which is considered a "ghetto," but there was no better option at the time. I was embarrassed to be seen that I was living there.

It was now 2003, and Mr. Wonderful and I had known each other for seven years—the time that seemed completely wasted. Bitterness invaded my spirit. I hated everything and everybody. I had never felt so rejected, abandoned, disrespected and unloved. I hated him, I hated me, most of all I hated my life. I hated him and the hatred had nowhere to go, because it kept running into my other emotion: love. And now I hated, love.

Love was a sickness with no cure, and the fact that I loved him beyond measure would hurt me even more. I was in the grip of an incurable lovesickness with no antidote, no remedy, and to top it off I was living in the pits and imagining that he just didn't give a damn about me at all.

Often, I wrote poems about him—love poems, of course. Line after line I voiced my zealous adoration of him. Now, in my misery, I reached to a higher source, writing my long, heartfelt verse, "A Letter to God." The poem was my soul crying out to the heavens. I was begging for solace, explaining myself, looking for some sense amid the destruction around me. "He gave me pleasure and so much of it, and so much pain I could no longer endure," I wrote. Remembering all his words to me, I went on to say, "I was the lover he never had . . . the kisser he never had."

It went on and on, and toward the end I digressed and spoke to Mr. Wonderful directly:

"For the first time in my life, you showed me what it is like to love a man, live with love, and enjoy and dream while loving you. And now I want you to go away, and find what life is without love, hoping someday you'll come and tell me I am the one you really love, I am the one you want, I am the one you can't live without."

Every word was another tear. Every line was another crack in my broken heart. Yes, I dearly wanted him to come back to me. But I knew if he did it would only ruin me. I wouldn't be able to take the enormous weight of his penetrating "sword," his love. And, frankly, there seemed no chance it would happen, anyway. And then I lost it and slept away my life for almost two years.

14

Living Blissfully Together

This time I was having a real nervous breakdown. For nine months—well into 2004—I simply fell into a dark ditch and couldn't function. I couldn't even get up in the morning to take a shower. I was scarcely eating. I didn't even have the energy to get up and wash my face, or to get a glass of water. Sleeping the day away, I stayed in bed and kept the place dark—and cried an ocean of tears.

Since I couldn't even make myself go to the store for food, once a week Maria my housekeeper would come in, key and shopping bag in hand, and would go across the street to the market for few basic necessities. Life without him had become unbearable.

After spending a year and half in bed mourning my loss, I thought having a dog, would be good for depression, and at some point I found a Shih Tzu puppy that I named Chin-Chin. The company of the adorable little dog would cheer me up a little—or so I thought, but I was fooling myself. In the end, I couldn't summon the energy to take care of him, and demoralized to death, I sold the dog to a more enthusiastic owner.

My kids knew there was something wrong, but they had no idea of the extent of my emotional suffering. Embedded with pain and sorrow, and overwhelmed with negative fellings, I was being dragged down to a place that was hard to come out of.

Extreme abandonment by the one person I cared for and for so long, was devastating to me.

Normally, I would invite fifty people over for Rosh Hashanah, the Jewish holiday. Not this time. Six people, that's all I had room for. I found a broad section of a large plywood from a storage room in the garage to make and improvise a table to fit six people. On Yom Kippur the Jewish High Holidays, I fasted for 24 hours, stayed home and did nothing except sit in one chair and pray while staring at the four walls. Addicted to my pain, I was reasonable comfortable in being sad with no expression of a sane person.

Nothing was going my way, no matter what I did or did not do. Nothing. Basically I was comforable being depressed.

It was no longer a nomal ups and down; I was wearing the drab color of gray most of the day, and felt a certain danger if I did not reinforce my will to live.

Realizing, I had been wrong; he did not love me, and was wrong to love a man, who was married, though later I realized that was not the reason behind his abandonment of love.

Working was all but impossible, especially in those awful first months after the break-up. The only money coming in was the rent for my home in Beverly Hills which went directly to pay for the mortgage and taxes. Emotionally devastated, I was in a desperate financial situation. Eventually, I had to sell the Bentley. There was no other choice, the Bentley had to go. An Englishman answered an ad for the car and paid cash to take it off my hands.

Amazingly, amid all this, Mr. Wonderful was still calling. One good thing about the Pico apartment was its iron security gate, twenty feet high. No one could get in without the code. Mr. Wonderful couldn't come banging on my front door. But he called—oh, my God, he kept calling non stop. Sometimes twelve times a day. For six months, eight months, a year, a year-and-a-half. I ignored the calls, trying to recover from a deep fall.

The time went by and the man just wouldn't stop. He was still completely obsessed with the relationship, even after everything we had gone through, and I was sleeping it away.

"I know you're sad, but I am miserable too," he said on my voice mail, soon after I moved out. "She's popping pills. She's drinking like never before. Just let me see you. We were meant to be together. I can't go on without you." Almost two years of calls and yet he still would not give up.

I knew better. I resisted. Although every time I heard the sound of his voice, I died a little more. I kept changing my phone numbers again. He would call at the office. I had to stay listed to retain any hope of selling homes. My secretary finally quit, telling me, "I cannot take the stress and pressure of him calling ten times a day anymore. And besides, he pulls up outside the front gate—it makes me nervous."

He literally begged to see me, absolutely begged. One day he called and said, "There's a building for sale—fifty units. They need a broker and I recommended you. Call them and here is the phone number." Never called him back but I did called the owner of the building.

Guess what, it was the same building owner where my apartment had burned. I met with the owner. He found out that I was single and suddenly *this guy* was calling me five times a day too. It was unbelievable.

The owner was asking $8.5 million for the property. I found a buyer, a buyer from India, who was willing to offer $8 million in cash with a two-weeks escrow. Now suddenly the owner wanted $9.5 million. I tore up the listing and all paperwork and decided to to get out of my funk, and live as normal as I could. I was beginning to hate my job but I needed money.

Nearly two years passed and I was finally getting stronger. Back in business, I was selling and negotiating properties, getting out, living my regular life again.

One day I was having my hair done on Canon Drive. The stylist, at Marla a well-known hair dresser who she handled such celebrities as the Governors, movie stars, and numerous prominent individuals was happy to see me again.

While Marla was teasing my hair the front door opened and in walked, who else, but Mr. Wonderful. He had seen my car parked on the street.

Lifting my head, I saw him and said, "Marla, does this guy have an appointment with you?" "No, but I know who he is," she said, smiling. "He's very famous."

My whole body was throwing a fit, a real convulsion. I was having an anxiety attack.

"Please leave," I told him. "Either you leave or I will."

"I'm not going to leave until you say you're coming back to me." He was standing in front of me with his arms crossed, his fiery blue eyes boring into me. He wore a royal-blue jacket because he knew, I loved his blue eyes, and it was the jacket we first me at my house.

Marla was eating it up. She thought it was wonderfully romantic and funny. By now I was yelling and screaming: "What do you want from me?" I said. I was dying inside. "You've changed the whole course of my life, I would have been married by now to Giovanni, you morone! You played with my life. You played with my heart. Now get out! Get out! And leave me alone."

"I'm not leaving, not until you tell me you are coming back" he said, while blocking the front door, as I was grabbing the handle to open the door and get out, my arm brushed against his hands and electricity shook my core. My heart was beating like I was going to have a seisure.

He kept on talking. "My life has never been so miserable. You go find a house, we're moving in together. I've been looking for you for two years now. We're getting married. You get a house, fix it up and I'm moving in. You know I have a lot of money and I will make sure, you are taken care of. Go find a lawyer, and set up a meeting so you are fully taken care of for the rest of your life. I have already met with a divorce lawyer, he mentioned his name (the same lawyer who would not take the pink slip of my Bentley years back) and I will marry you and move in with you.

Famous last words! As I started to walk out, trying to stay strong, he followed me into the courtyard and grabbed my wrist. He pulled me down next to him on the wrought-iron bench in front of the salon and for another half hour poured his heart out and told me how much he missed and loved me.

At that point I had lost tremendous amount of weight. The pit of my stomach was playing frizzbi with every one of his word. Being fragile and so madly in love still, I was intently listening to his talk about seeing a lawyer and seriously filing for divorce. I was melting away.

He seemed to be preying upon my confusion. But I was skeptical. I did not want to repeat any of that awful pain. He wanted me more than ever, apparently.

"You tell me when you're going to meet me," he said, "because I'm not leaving you alone. I will never let you go. Never! I promise you."

He called. He called. He called. Finally, stupidly, several months later, stupid me, I gave in again. What was I to do? I was living in a dream and incapable of letting go. I came to believe him. I loved him way too much. I was still sickly in love, like a woman addicted to cocaine, wanting more and more.

I started to see him again, and I tried to dig myself out of the funk and resurrect my career. It took a while, but slowly I began to show flashes of the old me—the go-getter, the whirling dervish, jet-setting across the globe and making deals. He insisted to find an attorney so I would be taken care of financially for life. I said: "OK." And I hired a top estate attorney in Los Angeles. Mr. Wonderful signed, notarized and we had all documents witnessed. He made an appointment with the toughest divorce lawyer in Beverly Hills. Well! OK!

During this time I took a ten-day trip to the south of France, where I happened to meet a group of Arabs who treated me—a Jewish girl to one of the most amazing experiences of my life. It started when

I was lying topless on the Riviera, the fabled *Cote d'Azur*, sipping carrot juice for my tan and listening to an Arabic-language CD that I had purchased in Madrid. Two girls came by, each in their late teens, raving about my music—they knew the singer and wanted to listen with me. We began conversing in French and in English, and I ended up treating them to lunch.

They were curious about how on earth I had such a great tan.

To my surprise, a day later, a woman found me on the same beach and said, "What's your name? Are you the one who bought my daughter lunch yesterday?"

The encounter led to a luncheon meeting with the entire family in Cannes at the posh Hotel Martinez, where I was asked to sit beside the wizened patriarch Sheikh Mohamed and his first and second wives. Yes, he had two and they always traveled together. As we were talking, I said, "Do you guys know I'm Jewish?" Naturally, I was sensitive to the possibility of Arab bias dating to my youth in the Miss Iran pageant—and being stripped of my crown. "I just want to know if I'm welcome here or not," I said. My host launched into a story about having dinner with numerous Israeli Prime Ministers. Sheikh Mohamed was a kind and a generous man. He turned out to be a big-time Egyptian player, and here I was, lunching with him and his entire family, having a great time!

That night I was invited to join the family again for dinner. We met at their vacation rental—the asking price, for six weeks, was half a million dollars!—and proceeded on to the Felix, *the* place to be in Cannes. Talk about lifting my spirits—this was the way to live. One incredible moment after another. I loved every minute. And it would get even better yet; my good friend Remi flew in the following day from Beverly Hills, and together we planned to travel on to Italy, to the isle of Capri and then to Rome.

Once he learned of our plans, Sheikh Mohamed and his family immediately threw a wonderful goodbye party for us. Wine, laughter, small-talk, and we were off to Capri. In the Villa Verde, the island's fabulous Mediterranean restaurant, my cell phone rang—and it was the Sheikh, unwilling to let me disappear from his world so quickly.

"What are you doing?" he said. He listened to the particulars of my itinerary and said, "We're picking you up in three days in Rome. We're going to see my properties, and my children like your company so get ready to leave at once." He knew I was in real-estate.

"Where am I going?" I asked him.

"Spain." He had thoughts of buying property there, and he wanted me to evaluate and appraise three houses he owned. All the details were taken care of, he told me. His plane and his driver would pick me up. I'd be staying at a hotel and I should keep my cell phone always handy.

My friend Remi was freaking out. "Who *are* these people?" she wondered. "How in the world do you find people like that?" I assured her it is all about "the suntan."

Before we left Capri, Mr. Wonderful called, saying he was having cocktails with one of our friends—a woman who always bought $1 million worth of jewelry every year from the same top-end jeweler in Capri. He asked me where I was going to be. I said Rome for a couple of nights as the guest of a Sheikh and his entire entourage, including his first and second wives. My gorgeous American cowboy was in disbelief. "What? What are doing now, a private plane?" he wanted to know.

Mr. Wonderful quickly decided to meet me in Rome. We made our connection there—and after Rome my friend Remi had to fly back to Beverly Hills. Meanwhile, I hopped aboard a Falcon 2000 private jet and zoomed off to Madrid, totally unaware that Mr. Wonderful was also heading there. For whatever reasons, he had not been willing to tell me about his next destination—as usual.

The hotel where I was to stay is one of the finest anywhere—a modern, elegant five-star oasis with lavish fountains and gorgeous patios. The Sheikh's driver, Pablo, met me at the airport and whisked me there in a black Mercedes limousine. Almost immediately as I entered my suite, my cell phone rang. To my surprise it was Mr. Wonderful.

Lovingly, feeling a surge of passion for him, I said, "Hi, I love you, and miss you. Where are you, my darling man? I am somewhere in Madrid at a gorgeous hotel, where my host has an account."

"Here in Madrid," he said.

Here? In Madrid? I was shocked; I thought he might be joking. "Tell me really, where are you really? Which hotel?" I reached into a drawer next to my bed and grabbed a pen and a pad of paper emblazoned with the hotel's name and phone number in red script. As he gave me the name of his hotel, I could not help but notice how the name I was jotting down matched the name and number already printed on my hotel note pad.

I said, "Wait a minute! Are you kidding me?"

He started laughing. I said, "What is your room number?" He said 622. Shit! It was right next door to my room! 620. Horrible!

By sheer, incredible coincidence, he and his wife had not only booked a room in the same hotel where I was staying, now they were on the same floor! Not only on the same floor, but they were in suite 622 and I was in suite 620—*the very next room*!

What the fuck?

I said, "The Sheikh has an account here—he put me up here and I have no idea where I am." Neither one of us could believe it.

What a wild life I was living—utterly unbelievable. However, a problem quickly arose: I got sick. The night I arrived I contracted food poisoning. I phoned downstairs, asking for a bowl of chicken soup, and before it arrived I was losing my cookies, vomiting nonstop.

A short while later my doorbell rang. "I can't get up," I yelled out loud, assuming it was room service. "Take the soup back! I don't want it. Go away."

The doorbell kept ringing. By this time I was totally dehydrated and physically weak, running back and forth to the toilet. Mad as hell at the damn bell, finally I got up and pulled the door open, and there stood Mr. Wonderful. "Jesus," I said, "what on earth are you doing here? Get out of here."

The fact that his wife was in the suite next door was too much to handle even if I hadn't been sick. Quickly I sent him away—and went back to vomiting. Minutes later the doorbell rang again. "I told you go away, she will kill us both," I hollered. "Get out of here! Please leave me alone!" This time, when the door opened, it was the poor woman from room service, petrified. She left the soup on the table and fled.

Around 8 p.m., as I struggled to recover, the bell rang again and Mr. Wonderful marched in, dressed like a king going to a feast, explaining that he could not come to see me tomorrow because of his wife being there.

No kidding? Had he only now figured that out?

After he left, I had a quiet meal alone—my half-frozen soup—and, exhausted, slipped into bed to watch TV.

Fortunately, my recovery was quick and I was able to go see the properties that the Sheikh was interested in. I kept a laser focus on the job, developing comparisons with the prices of other homes and condos in Madrid, trying to prepare a full evaluation.

My globe-trotting wasn't quite done; I had to deliver my report in person at the Sheikh's palace in Egypt and offer him my thoughts as per his and his wives' request. I again tore across the skies in his private jet, a jet so fast and sleek it wasn't even like flying, it was like sitting on solid ground. Thinking I might as well make my trip unforgettable, I decided I wanted to see the cockpit and give flying a shot. The crew let me sit in the cockpit in the pilot's seat, with a caveat, "Pishi," don't touch anything, or we will all go down!"

What a feeling. I could see the entire world, though everything had a tint of gray. We made a stop in Cairo to pick up more passengers—sultans and kings from other Arab countries, along with their close friends. A white limousine met me at the airport and took me to the Sheikh's lavish compound in Sharm el-Sheikh, the opulent seaside resort of the Red Sea, on the Sinai Peninsula just outside the Gulf of Suez.

This was truly another world. There were eleven castles spread across acres and acres on the coast. In their lavish private compound, I was given a suite that must have been five-thousand square feet, with a balcony that seemed the size of a tennis court, overlooking the beach and the magnificent white homes strung along stunningly blue water. Women in traditional Muslim veils and women in two-piece bikinis occupied the landscape nearly side-by-side.

Housekeepers waited on me constantly. A large antique wooden chest was filled with dates, nuts, pistachios and figs. My hosts could not have been more gracious and down-to-earth. But it was searing hot—130 degrees. Even at six in the morning it was well over 100. Servants kept bringing ice, cold water and towels. I dressed up in my business suit, had my meeting with Sheikh Abdol, the son, and dined with the family. I explored the town, which was extraordinary. Some quarters of Sharm el-Sheikh were open all night, exploiting the relative cool of temperatures that hovered around 105. I'd guess there were ten- or twenty-thousand people on the streets, crowds so dense you could hardly see your own shoes. It was scary. Many smoked their *hookahs*. Up on the terraced hillsides were caves with restaurants inside them, affording views of the hubbub below. Entire mountains were interlaced with subterranean development, like some outlandish vision from Tales of the Arabian Nights.

From this sun-broiled paradise I flew back to my tiny apartment in Beverly Hills, crashing in bed, depressed to return to my love-encumbered reality. Then, several months later, I received a call from Sheikh Abdol.

He was opening a new shopping complex in Europe, and his daughter wanted me to be there for the opening night. The appearance required a small amount of preparation, so once again I was off to the Europe, where I saw the tennis great Ilie Nastase and was interviewed by a reporter from MTV, due mainly to my elegant Monique L'Heulier turquoise gown. The same gown I had worn for the first time with Mr. Wonderful at Mare Lago in Florida.

My two grown daughters were panicked at being unable to contact me by cell phone, since U.S. service works poorly, if at all, in the Middle East. One daughter finally got through and was yelling and telling her husband, while I was holding on, that it was dangerous for me to be there. I could hear her saying, "My mother is crazy, she has not told the State Department, and we have no idea where she is, in Egypt." She was sure I was sun-bathing, probably naked, causing no end of upset among the prudish locals, who might react in any number of unwelcome ways. She thought I should leave immediately. Even my mention of the private jet sent her into hysterics. Private jet? Whose private jet? What? Where? How? She was yelling and I kept laughing while I sweated 6:00 in the morning, in the 110-degree heat, trying to cool myself with a large chunk of ice cut jaggedly, the old-fashion way, with an ice pick.

Sheikh Abdol eventually flew me back to Paris, for a couple of days of rest and on to Los Angeles, capping one of the most incredible periods of my life.

Reality awaited me again in Beverly Hills. The immediate problem was what to do about Mr. Wonderful. Break it off? See him? Love? Hurt? I could hardly endure the torment of being stuck in my miserable little apartment while his hard-drinking wife enjoyed the luxuries of royalty.

He understood and was certain he wanted me because he loved me. Now he promised to leave her and be with me. Finally, he gave me the go-ahead to find another house, and made an appointment to see a family-law attorney in his building to begin arranging the divorce proceedings.

With hope now blooming again in my heart, I looked around and discovered a wonderful house just north of Sunset in the hilly and exclusive Estates section of Beverly Hills.

He said fine, and then—how typical was this?—several days later, he changed his mind, totally blew it, and we missed out. We lost the house to someone else. Feeling badly, and changing his mind again, he directed me to keep looking. By this point the only decent estate still on the market was in the same neighborhood, one acre, with a beautiful pool and spa on secluded grounds high above the city. It was not a perfect choice for my taste, but it was light-years better than the apartment.

I moved in December of 2005. Outside the gate, in lovely Spanish tile, workmen affixed a name, "Villa De Amore," in honor of his feelings for me. Mr. Wonderful had it made for as a house-warming present.

Did he move in? No, not for over a year! I tried hard not to care. I lost interest in whether he would leave her and concentrated instead on remodeling the place—tearing out walls, erecting floor-to-ceiling glass, creating a magnificent, marble-floored dining room overlooking the pool and the lush gardens. He allowed me, to spent money like a drunken sailor, determined to make sure that he would love it, and finally he did.

He loved everything I designed and built, and promised to take care of all the expenses. Besides, we had drawn up a contract to that effect to make sure I was to be protected. He had offered to take care of me and I accepted it, knowing how obsessive his daughter and his wife were about his money. A $10 million life-insurance policy was part of the deal, a protection he purchased to offer security for my future. In the beginning, he never neglected to pay for the massive construction and living expenses, though a couple of years later he would be lagging far behind in meeting the bills, even while I slipped deeper and deeper into debt. He was breaching his contract and I was dumb to still treasure him like nothing was wrong.

Along the grassy parkway that sloped to the curving street out front, we put in a series of life-size bronze statues worth a couple of hundred thousand dollars, just like you see at many of the gazillion-dollar mansions in Beverly Hills. The villa became a showcase, and still I lived there alone. And the bills? Well! They were piling up. It was 2007 now and no matter how big or beautiful the mansion was, it was not bringing me happiness.

Turbulence continued to rock my life. While I was in Aspen in early 2006, my younger daughter, who married less than a year and was soon to be starting a career in medicine, visited her doctor for neurological tests. She had begun walking awkwardly and falling down. I won't infringe on her privacy, but this is a lovely young woman, my caring, sensitive woman, with an attentive husband who loves her. He and I accompanied her to more tests, at UCLA Medical Center, when I returned to Beverly Hills.

Athena

The diagnosis was devastating: Hereditary Inclusion Body Myopathy, a degenerative genetic illness that causes a progressive loss of muscle control. It isn't fatal, but it is incurable and tends to strike in early adulthood, eventually confining its poor victims to a wheelchair. Imagining my daughter in such a state made me realize again with utter horror that I had married the wrong man: Not even our genes were compatible. I was numb. Heartsick. Like a dead woman, tumbling through a black space in a cocoon of grief. Leaning against a wall, I thought I would throw up in the clinic's waiting room. Dealing with this horrible disease would become my impassioned crusade, as I sought to set up a fundraising board and channel money to promising research programs.

But meanwhile, I needed emotional support. I tried to be a rock of support and encouragement to my daughter and my family, and to do that I needed Mr. Wonderful's strong arms around me. It mattered now more than ever to have him in my life.

Finally, in 2007, despite the mounting debts, he moved in, but barely long enough to blink. He and his wife had another terrible fight and she threw him out. He stayed with me until hostilities subsided and he went back to her. It hurt. It always hurt. And now my baby was sick. I would shut off my phone around four in the afternoon and cry. For three months, I sailed through my nights on an ocean of tears. During the day, I was glued to the computer, reading medical reports and how to find a cure. Most of the pain centered on my daughter and the star-crossed relationship with my ex-husband. How could I have married that man? Why? Why was I condemned to be trapped for so long in a loveless marriage arranged for me against my wishes? Why? Why? Why? And now, as result of the genetic mingling of that union, my baby was ill.

Lovesick in Beverly Hills

How many tears I had cried I can't even begin to count. Mr.Wonderful's hot and cold affections only added to the torture, and yet somehow I was becoming more able to endure it all. I needed his foundation to fund my scientists. Well! He did contribute but not the way he should have. A knife was stuck in my heart and now I had started hemorrhaging. He told me to get a new car since my car was totaled when struck by a drunk driver. I said OK. Then he flip-flopped and chastised me for the purchase and never took care of the bill. Unfazed by the razzle-dazzle of the rich and powerful, I was determined to survive and keep my equilibrium. I couldn't let myself nose-dive further into a black depression and a bankruptcy.

The same night that I bought the car, I cooked and threw a party, inviting thirty people over, hoping they would contribute to my foundation.

Mr. Wonderful surprised me by showing up. He arrived around nine o'clock with a friend of his, knowing I was having company. He soaked up the laughter and frivolity, sipped his drink, enjoyed the fabulous food, and the next day hopped on a plane to fly to Europe for eight weeks—with her, of course.

Guess what, I bought a ticket and went to Europe too, all by myself, and had the time of my life. Never saw him or contacted him once. I went to see Giovani, the Dutch billionaire who had once proposed to me, to ask for money for the foundation. Bills were pilling up and I was down $500,000 and Mr. Wonderful was not lifting a finger to take care of them. Giovanni was married now. I had a lovely dinner with him and his new wife. Yes, another wonderful, upstanding man was now taken—and, in fact I had set him up with the woman, one of my girl friends.

She had called me to verify that I had rejected the Dutch magnate. Her own marriage was ending in divorce and she wanted to marry only for money; having known him before, she now wanted his phone number and I gave it to her.

The romance got off to a stumbling start because Giovanni balked at going out with her; he professed to be in love with a woman in Beverly Hills. Yep, me! She had to pursue him, moving from Switzerland to Holland just to be in his proximity, and it took two years before he finally married her. And, instead of thanking me, after the meeting she sent a nasty note saying I would not be invited to call them anymore. Somehow that possessive rancor had abated; now she wanted to gloat and show him off and show how she was living.

It was impossible not to think about what might have been, that it could have been me married to that gracious gentleman, accompanying him on thrilling nights in Paris, Cannes and Amsterdam, and tanning on his yacht in the Mediterranean. My friend was certainly enjoying the benefits of his company, living in their new 14-million-euro apartment. I felt no envy; I was too sad for my daughter and had no energy to dwell on what a bitch she was, and how now my life had become more tragic than ever.

Upon returning home, and for many months afterward, I lost myself in deep soul-searching, wondering if the time spent with Mr. Wonderful was worth the anguish of being apart when I needed him. As a custodian of my heart, the man was thoroughly unreliable—or, as I later wrote in one of my journals, "The love I have for him will never fade, but the pain of abandonment will scar me for life." That was my sorry reality—he resisted giving a chunk of money to my foundation. He seemed far more enamored of his millions than of me. And it didn't help my frame of mind to know that his wife had become insanely jealous of me and might very well harm me, if she could. She was a raging, vindictive woman. She answered Mr. Wonderful's cell phone once, when I yearned to hear his voice, and hung up on me, then called my house later that night to tell me to keep my hands off of him. I begged of her to somehow please him and make him happy because I was incapable of letting him go.

My helpful suggestion, "Keep him at home," elicited the type of sniping, sarcastic response one might expect from an alcohol-abusing, pot-smoking old tigress in a cat fight.

"I hear you give great blow jobs," she shot back.

"I do, I have a PhD" I agreed coolly. Once again I recommended that she should keep her man at home.

Exchanges of that sort never bode well. This was a woman consumed with malice, and I felt squarely in her cross-hairs.

In July of 2008, I fell and broke my knee in Malibu. It put me in bed for five months after five hours of surgery. To rehabilitate for the next five months I had to put the knee in a machine for six hours a day. In January of 2009, Mr. Wonderful came over to tell me he had canceled the $10 million life-insurance policy. Mr. Scumbag, his assistant, was making, I think, half a million a year just to be a flunky. I told Mr. Wonderful it was OK. I didn't need the policy, just pay the bills because I was going bankrupt. And he hugged me and left.

In May of 2010, without notice, he sat in my living room he informed me he was no longer paying my bills. I was on my own.

Welcome to Beverly Hills.

15

A Woman Scorned

From what Mr. Wonderful told me, his huge, stately mansion, so gorgeous on the outside, was an echo chamber of screaming and shouting due to the constant arguments between him and his wife—many of them, of course, concerning me, but these fights dated back to long before he and I met.

They were rooted in his childhood and hers, and in particular in her ever-worsening substance abuse. They were the classic co-dependent couple, clinging to each other long past the point of enjoying each other. Surely he was aware of how expensive a divorce might be; and yet they also dined out together constantly and took lengthy trips together, hop-scotching the globe bickering all the way.

Worsening conflict reached a peak one night as they tried to leave their estate for dinner out on the town. The wife insisted on driving; Mr. Wonderful sat in the passenger seat. The route along their driveway from the front door to the street was not overly long or challenging, but on this occasion she failed to accomplish it, instead mashing the gas and accelerating at great speed directly into the wall of the kitchen. While she was unharmed, Mr. Wonderful took the brunt of the accident. His right arm was broken and his head badly gashed.

He telephoned me late that night at around 11:00 from the medical center where he had been stitched up and bandaged. He was going to need surgery.

"I think she was trying to kill me," he said.

She had been drinking and smoking marijuana, which made the matter less certain, but, interestingly, an audacious act of vandalism occurred that very same night outside Villa de Amore, my house: Someone managed to cut off an arm of one of the expensive bronze statues along the parkway. Bronze is not easy to cut. The severed arm was the right arm, the same arm that Mr. Wonderful had just injured. The incident happened while I was sleeping; my gardener discovered the damage the next morning. It seemed clear that it was a deliberate, hostile gesture aimed at me, and I felt sure who was behind it. But could I prove anything? No.

Not long afterward there were two incidents that reached *inside* my home. First, someone with a gun fired several times into a sixteen-foot glass wall in my living room, leaving ominous bullet holes and lacing the glass with cracks. It happened during broad daylight. Then a burglar, or burglars, broke in through a skylight one evening while I was away. They lowered themselves directly into the walk-in closet of my master bedroom and made off with nearly all of my costume and semi-precious stone jewelry—close to $50,000 worth of earrings, necklaces, pendants and other baubles. Luckily, they never found the real stuff. A few steps away, in the marble bathroom, I had left two wallets stuffed with cash, which they never saw.

But as a personal *violation,* oh my God, it was devastating. The housekeeper claimed she never heard anything. Bullshit. I'm sure they had bribed her days before. The front wrought-iron door near the gate, I found out from my gardener, had been left open several days prior to the burglary. The next day I fired her. Anyone who's been burglarized knows what I mean—and for a woman, living alone, it's tantamount to a psychological rape. Once they're in, anything can happen, even violence. You're completely vulnerable.

And get this: The celebrated Police Department took *half an hour* to get there—from not even a mile away! Lightning-quick response times is one of the reasons people choose to live in Beverly Hills, and yet I waited, traumatized, fearing that the intruders might still be hiding in the house, scared they might kill me. Did the fact that Mr. Wonderful's wife was serving on the police board make any difference in how my 911 call was handled? I'd be naïve not to think so, especially since Mr. Wonderful's wife was giving enormous monetary donations to the department, a habit of many of the super-rich in Beverly Hills who want to be known for assuring top-notch services and public schools. In fact, after the vandalism to my statues and my discovery of the bullet holes in my glass wall, I sent a letter to the police, warning that if anything happened to me, I would hold her personally responsible. Lo and behold, when the burglars traipsed in and I needed the cops there immediately, no one came for the length of a TV sitcom! As for the police report regarding the 911 call, the officer falsified how quickly the cops got there: fourteen minutes, not thirty-four minutes.

From then on, I felt enormously frightened in my own home. I installed an elaborate security-system monitors and panic buttons everywhere. Noises and shadows made me jump. I even feared the *fear*, worrying I might have another emotional breakdown. It got so bad I even asked the cook to move into the tiny studio adjoining the garage, just to have a man on the premises.

How wonderful was my Mr. Wonderful in calming my anxieties? Sad to say, he wasn't interested in my problems. Nor did he offer to reimburse me for my losses. Though he had promised time and again that he would take care of the unpaid bills, the remodeling invoices, utility bills, property taxes, home insurance costs, and other expenses kept mounting. The debts had ballooned beyond my power to pay, and I now I was digging my own grave. When was he going to help? He was totally dismissing it. He went to Lake Arrowhead in the local mountains for three days. I didn't hear from him once. I cried every five minutes; it seemed his daughter Ivy now had a hand in my life too. In the still hours I worried about another break-in. Would I be physically beaten? Murdered? Jerry would always tell me, she is on drugs, don't get near her.

My daughter's neurological disease and her physical struggles only added to the mental strain I was under. Her illness was eroding her ability to walk and handle the most basic daily tasks. She and her husband had an adorable baby boy—my precious grandson—but she had difficulty holding him now. My heart bled for her. I was doing everything I could think of to help find a cure. The organization I set up, had fourteen board members and was already channeling funds to leading genetic research programs from Texas to Tel Aviv. Mr. Wonderful, however, showed virtually zero interest and contributed only a token fraction of what he could have to the cause every few years. Worse yet, he seemed utterly indifferent to my suffering.

What kind of life did I have? Who is this man? And why is he not serious about funding the research? He had crossed a line with me. This was my daughter and now I was beginning to see his ruthless side.

Every week, every day, every hour, I wondered if I had the strength to break off the relationship once and for all. It just wasn't working. I pleaded with him, "Let me go! Don't call me anymore!" But always he insisted on having me back, as if I were a piece of art that he owned, his own Venus de Milo. *Venus de Pishi.* "Come back, come back, I love you, I need you," he would tell me. "I will take care of you." Promises, promises, promises. It occurred to me that the debts I had run up were nothing but a big security blanket for him. He was holding me hostage.

Leave him? How could I leave when I was terribly dependent on him financially and awaiting the payment of hundreds of thousands of dollars that he owed me? What power he had! Surely he drew a perverse sense of stability and control from knowing that circumstances made it virtually impossible for me to abandon him. The awful truth was, I would not have left him for the simple reason that I was too much in love with him still. If only he really understood the depth of my feelings for him. If only he saw and trusted in the love we shared. He couldn't. He can't. He is too selfish, and too in love, maybe with himself his own brand of lovesick. He is warped and could not let me go. Lies and pain, that's all I seemed to get from him. I loved this man, but the way he hurt me, again and again, and now not helping my daughter made me think this was the effect he wanted. He must not give a damn.

These thoughts crystallized in my head throughout the long fall and winter of 2007. It couldn't go on. I was sinking, dying inside and time to quite was near. I set a deadline for April of 2008—he had to resolve the debts and change how he treated me, or I was gone.

He changed nothing. It was business as usual for him, living it up, traveling with his wife, ignoring my needs. The man was in complete control, doing exactly as he pleased, being happy. Meanwhile, I was emotionally starving, in pain beyond measure over my sick daughter.

Summer arrived and he flew off again with *her* for the usual two-month vacation in France. More torture for me. More lovesick tears. I edged closer and closer to finding the courage to get out, to bring a permanent end to the madness. "What had changed in thirteen years?" I asked myself. When I met him my life was in turmoil, savaged by the horrific divorce, and now I was half-dead, worse off than ever, beaten up by love—or what was supposed to be love. Love? How about damn rejection. Abandonment. Frustration. Anger. These feelings were all I had to show for loving this man, my Mr. Wonderful, with all my heart. He had completely wrecked my life.

He kept calling from Europe, saying we'd be together, we'd be married someday, just wait for me. The same old lines! I considered where to go if I moved out. I held an iron-clad sense of desperation and I had been bludgeoned too much to repeat the mistake; I could lease the house out and live in peace in Malibu. Another option opened up when my tenant moved out of my own house in the flats of Beverly Hills. Never mind the damage she had left—to the walls, the hardwood floors, a mess that would cost me $100,000 to repair—it was vacant and I could live there. I was fed up with lawyers and I wasn't even going after the repair costs. I was more concerned with repairing myself and living under my own roof. Best decision I ever made.

That became my escape route, leasing out Villa de Amore and re-settling into own house a few blocks from Rodeo Drive. Though

Athena

Mr. Wonderful continued to insist on seeing me, I felt at least partly beyond his reach in a house he had no role in controlling. The break was mainly symbolic and accomplished nothing in resolving my debts. Immediately I felt lighter and more self-assured. A couple of weeks passed before he discovered that I'd moved. His knees must have buckled. He had me on the phone immediately. The house on the hill stayed vacant and unoccupied for two years.

"Things are not working out," I told him. "I cannot take any more stress. I have no option but to concentrate on my daughter; now I am on my own and it would be great if you just let it go. Please, my daughter is very ill. Forget it. I love you but I think we are done here. You're never here and you don't seem to care. I need to find some peace. Do me a favor and give me some space. And honestly I want nothing from you. I will find a way to survive. I knew he was no longer that shoulder for me to cry on.

Shocked? I guess. The next thing, he showed up in my living room. The gardener was there, and the gate was left open. Mr. Wonderful barged right in. He was hovering like an aparthion when I re-entered the room and found him.

"What are you doing here?" I demanded.

"What are *you* doing here?" he countered.

"I told you I was moving out," I said. "You didn't believe me."

"Are you crazy?" he said.

Me crazy? I didn't back down. "I've had it with you," I flatly told him for probably the one-thousandth time. "I had to get out," and my

Lovesick in Beverly Hills

plan was to lease the place, which I tried to do. But the market had died and I was desperate.

For two years, while the house sat vacant, the city would send me exorbitant, impossible water bills—to the tune of $1,200 to $1,400 a month for a house that was vacant. It was a complete rip-off, but there was no way to fight City Hall.

Mr. Wonderful never did blink an eye, and kept telling me to sue him and go after what was mine under the contract we had together, knowing full well I would never do that. He knew me perfectly well and that my relationship with him about love and not money; he was just testing me, again and again. I was sick and now I realized he was sick, too. And not knowing his daughter Ivy was in charge of our lives.

I was never going to sue him for money because I loved him. No matter how unfair he was and how many millions I was entitled to, because he was my love, my gorgeous, adorable baby. A big shot attorney told me: I can make you a very wealthy woman, I said no thanks.

Mr. Wonderful didn't seem to care about the legal obligations, only in seeing me when it was convenient for him. He liked that I was no longer on the hill and instead living in the flats of Beverly Hills, because it was right on his route to work. He always took my street on his way to the office. "I like it here," he said on one visit, when I was trying to sever the relationship. "I can stop by every morning and every afternoon." "Make me breakfast."

"*What?* Who are you kidding?" I said, outraged. "I am through. You need to leave now. You are hurting me. Please leave me alone."

Athena

The same afternoon I called his wife and his daughter, begging them to keep him away from me. I was too weak and too in love to let him go and begged of his daughter Ivy to help me forget him.

His daughter replied, "I give him my blessing to marry you, though I am not sure he will leave my mother. I know he is in love with you and you love him too."

He left. But he came back. And he came back again. He just started coming over—relentless, blind to my wishes, insatiable. He demanded the remote control to the gate.

"You do *not* get the remote," I said. "This is *my* house."

"Then give me the combination."

"No. Listen to me—you can't have it."

"I'm going to tear the gate down," he said. "Just take the gate off. I'm going to smash through the gate."

"You're insane," I said.

Probably; I probably was, too, trusting his words and giving him so many chances when he hurt me so much. The situation was unacceptable in every level. I clearly remember the sunny afternoon in May of 2010, when he dropped the bombshell by telling me, point-blank, that he was no longer paying the expenses. Now, I was on my own. Sell everything and live off of it, but he was not spending any more on the property or on me and that was the way it was going to be.

Shocked beyond belief, I realized I was in an hopeless predicament. The debts had ballooned, the bank refused to refinance any of the homes, and I decided to ask for short-sale papers. A week later, I had the full packet to fill out.

Tears started down my face and the dotted lines required my signatures. Since the real-estate market had fallen off a cliff, I was facing possible foreclosure and bankruptcy.

For a year, things got so bad that I didn't once go out. I spent days and nights alone. From my romantic nights with the man I loved, I had an enormous inventory of candles. Yes, candles; I had to cut down on my electric bill, in addition to the water bill, the gas bill, and everything else.

For my birthday, in August of 2012, Mr. Wonderful gave me a $10 bracelet like you'd find in a five-and-dime store. It fell apart on me in a matter of days. I no longer placed any value in any of the gifts he had ever given me. In fact, because of the financial straits I was in, I began selling everything I possibly could. Personal belongings no longer made me happy.

My birthday was a dismal milestone, another year older, that I marked without a single party or celebration. This was love? Fuck love.

August 28 was our anniversary—sixteen full years together. He called me the night before, saying he would be coming over to see me. As angry as I was with him, I counted the minutes and waited. And I waited. And I waited. I could not believe he actually stood me up! Never came over! And the next day he had the gall to claim that we had never made definit plans. It was beyond insensitive—it was downright mean. It struck me that he had never once taken me out for dinner—not once! Lunches yes, but never dinner! He never once sent me flowers. He never once whisked me away for a romantic weekend, somewhere, anywhere just the two of us. Not even Cucamonga. I had missed a whole lifetime of love and closeness.

I was writing, keeping up my journal, which was a tremendous and valuable therapy for me. I began to fight with myself over how it would end. I anguished over how to find the strength to bring about an ending.

Meanwhile, I struggled to resurrect my real-estate business, despite the abysmal market. I prayed a lot. I watched old movies. I saw a few friends for tea. Nothing seemed important. All I wanted was to look inside and find some peace. So I sat for months quietly and kept thinking of jotting down what really makes me happy.

During the work week, I mainly stayed in Beverly Hills, poring over listings and looking at properties, trying desperately to sell my house. On Fridays, I would drive out to spend the weekend in Malibu, where I could breathe the sea air and try to heal.

Months drifted by—another year. I remember an end-of-summer afternoon, in 2011 on the beach there, when I thought I had settled on the end to this sad story. I had come to understand that the relationship was changing, that he was no longer the same man I knew. Absolutely different and yet I felt still madly in love with my cowboy!

Because of the contract he had signed, and the debts he refused to address, I had more than ample legal grounds for a lawsuit against him. Attorneys were confident that I could wring out of him millions more what he owed me, but I could not bring myself to take action. He was still very special somehow. The sound of his voice still had powerful physical effects on me, like a chime ringing in my heart.

Still, I needed to find some way to reconcile my swirling emotions and financial problems and find a way forward that was free of pain all by myself. My daughter's illness and the demands of running my foundation made the search for a solution all the more urgent. Beside, I loved him for who he was, not what he owned.

Remembering the past, and reminiscing about love, and financially secure, thanks to my friend Sean I had left for Marbella, Spain, in September, still trying to sort it all out. While vacationing alone—again—I filled up eighteen single-spaced pages with my impassioned thoughts and reflections, going through memories, evaluating where I was, where I was heading. Right before I had left, a friend advised me to place all of my problems in an imaginary box and leave them at home—and just have a good time. "It sounded so wonderful," I wrote in my journal, amid the beauty of that old Spanish city. "But what does it mean to have a good time? Good hours? Good minutes? Good dinners? Good lunches and dinners? What is *good*? Good that I eat alone every night? I was starving, but not for food; I was hungry for a bite of life with my beautiful man in it and I now I new full well he had changed, and it was never going to happen. Was it good that I was very much in love with him, and he could not give a damn anymore?" And yet Mr. Wonderful continued to call me every day, no matter where he was, the never-ending barrage. I have become numb lately to his calls, sensing that they have no meaning. No meaning at all. It is just a matter of routine. Just like going to the bathroom and shaving.

My words virtually wept as I poured out memories of places we'd been together—that boat outing in Mexico, with the lone mariachi and the cargo of Coronas and quesadillas; the picnic on the bridge in Paris. Perfect afternoons. Holding each other. Making love at the

Plaza Athenee. Like Bogie and Bacall, we'd always have Paris—and Cannes and ….. and the little attic room where we first used to meet.

"Thinking about the past is almost as depressing as thinking about the future," I wrote in the journal. "At times dying seems the easiest way out. I feel like I am a hundred years old. Life cheated me and gave me nothing but pain and is punishing me to a place I don't want to go. I don't even know why. The love I have for Mr. Wonderful . . . is killing me and destroying my life."

After a nice rest, energized and empowered, I returned home. Now I was about to change everything for good.

I was about to throw away my entire life with Mr. Wonderful and again start with ground zero.

16

Breaking Up Is Hard To Do

It was October 2012, and now there's no need to mention seeing red flags in the relationship. Red flags? There were more red flags than at a used-car lot. They were a daily fact of life, and of course I was trying desperately to escape his clutches again, in spite of the overpowering love I had for him. Still, he insisted on seeing me, and one afternoon in late 2012, I encountered another red flag. He came over, as usual, around four and sat in my living room, appearing strangely flushed.

When I asked where he had been, he told me he'd had a facial, and it was nice.

"A facial?" I was surprised; my rugged cowboy never seemed like the type to pamper himself by getting a facial. "Where? Downstairs by your office? Funny, that's where I always go! How did you ever find her?"

He said no, in Westwood, several miles west near the UCLA campus, and mentioned the woman's name, "Shamssi." It was actually an Iranian name, which I thought was very strange! For some reason her name, or the way he said her name, caused me not believe him. A Persian facialist? All the way over in Westwood? In the middle of the work week?

Why go so far out of his way?

He explained that his daughter Ivy had recommended the woman because that is where she goes, and she does great work.

It seemed so odd and unusual that I instinctively felt weak and hollow in the pit of my stomach. I felt uncomfortable for several days; the story nagged me. That evening I went to bed but could not sleep. I kept thinking, *Shamssi! Facial! Mr.Wonderful? Facial?*

He never got facials before. The next day, he called and told me he was going to have to go to a meeting and was not stopping by. Dismissing it gently, I did not show my concern nor the fact that I had become a bit suspicious. He never mentioned it again, but the thought of him taking time from his busy schedule to get a facial stuck in my mind all day and night. Without letting on that I was in any mood of investigating it any further, I asked him for Shamssi's number, which I wrote down on a little piece of paper. I kept the number for a while on my dresser but a few weeks later threw it away.

Other things were going on in my life that required my time. Now my debts no longer hovered over me as they did for four years. Despite being desperate to keep me in the latter stages of the relationship, he had canceled the $10 million life-insurance policy, failed to donate anything more than a pittance to the foundation to help my daughter, and ignored an enormous pile of bill. But I stopped caring. I was madly in love with him, with money or without. Obsessing about money was never my style. In the past I was fully capable of making my own income—I had done it time and again. To meet the unpaid bills, I ended up borrowing half a million from a girlfriend, using my home in the Flats as collateral, so all was well.

Still, my stress level was sky high. What was he thinking? How was I going to survive without him after all these years? Again, I contemplated moving so I started looking for apartments to rent. Concentrating on how to save my soul, then I decided against moving and started the process of making me happy all by myself.

Now I was fed up with the whole sorry mess and yet still could not let him go for good.

In spite of it all, I was determined to be strong and come up with ways to pay attention to parts of life that were positive and meaningful.

In all instances and in my entire life I knew there was always a way out. This time nothing was going to drag me down, like this awful and crippling love. Lovely thought started to flow into my head so I took pleasure from the simple blessings I had—spending time babysitting my beautiful grandchildren. Every day, I would find simple things or some small events that would make me happy. I had my routines, a good diet, a ton of exercise regimens, and a chance to spend time at the Beverly Hills Public Library, which looks like Bloomingdales. That became my second home. For some reason I always felt safe at a book store or a library. Sometimes I would shop at the farmer's market, picking up tomatoes and blueberries, or just listen to classical music and thank God for my life.

Eventually, I was able to lease out the Malibu house to a lovely couple, and I also found a renter for my other properties—"a tenant from hell," but that was better than the alternative. For a long time, there was no money coming in.

The real-estate market remained as dead as a doornail. With the economy a disaster, I soldiered on with no health insurance, no car insurance, and lit candles at night rather than have to pay good old Southern California Edison.

Hot showers in the morning? No thank you, not when the Beverly Hills water department was ready to rip me off at every chance they got. Instead, I bathed with a wash cloth and a splash of hot water, applying a drop of my luxurious Hermes gel. It reminded of the time I lived at Hotel Ritz for weeks at a time and I still enjoyed that happy memories of those good old days. The sink and the marble bathroom were different, but the effect on my senses was the same. I had by now dropped my gym membership and with it lost twenty seven pounds. There was no money coming and yet I knew I was going to win, because I was determine to win against all odds.

My hobby became window-shopping on Rodeo Drive. That was actually fun since I lived in the most beautiful city in the world-my little village of Beverly Hills. Once a week, I would get all decked out and walk blocks after blocks, stepping grandly into Dior and Fendi and all the gorgeous stores, and enjoy the beautiful clothes in the window, thinking: Pishi you are so gorgeous and happy, and you did not even have to buy anything. Every store manager treated me with kindness, since they all knew me from the days of living like royalty, as I would smile I would give them a hug, saying I was just looking.

Many months passed before I was able to gain control of my finances. Fortunately, I found a terrific financial advisor, Sean, and through him I stabilized my life, better than ever before.

Job offers were coming in now. I remember one day when I was approached by an attorney to become an executive producer of a

TV show he was directing. Then another attorney approached me to troubleshoot a major case he was handling. Wow! I was so popular with the lawyers all of a sudden! In addition, an Italian company asked if I would represent a product that was being newly introduced in the U.S. and Canada, a job that promised to take advantage of my English-Italian and French-speaking skills.

People were beginning to discover that I had much to offer. It was exciting and invigorating to find my life again on the upswing. The greatest evidence of that was the arrival of my fifth grand-child. Inspired, I dragged the easel from my closet and returned to painting, and of course continue to write. I got out a little more and discovered new and different things, wanting to savor and enjoy my life.

At various times I felt sure the relationship was not over yet, though I had torn myself free of his grasp. Now I was getting stronger and by providing a comfortable and happy life style for my self every day trying to ignore the past. Now I mattered to myself and I savored my own happy moments in my own place. After marathon disasters, for the first time in my life, now I was proud and free to live alone.

Basking on my beloved beach in Malibu, where the sun hung over thousands of miles of blue Ocean, I gazed at the distant boats and the people strolling along the surf, the kids playing in the waves. The beach houses—some belonging to famous Hollywood names—obscured the rush of traffic on Pacific Coast Highway. Putting past love behind, I was in a good place, and yet, with a mild salt breeze flirting with my hair, I reflected on the possibility of another birthday alone. But it was okay. An extravagant party took place for three days with my children and grand-children. A blue theme party that I will always remember!

Athena

The year 2013 was the year that I regained a sense of balance and control, and a deep plunge into understanding how to be happy. My journey toward the future had taken shape and I was pleased with where it was heading. Nothing was ugly or sad; there was nothing I could not do or accomplish. He would still call and asked me to fix him his drink. Sometimes I did and sometimes I did not, constantly testing myself to see him when I wanted to see him trying this time to wean him out slowly and gently.

Intentionally, I kept myself on guard, careful not to hurl myself into that gyrating broken washing machine. I had as much power as he did. I felt like a queen, an empress, ruling the world, fearless and a complete "Mademoiselle Pizzazz"; I had style and dressed beautifully and now I had designed a perfect and specifically beautiful life for me. Taking an active role I was mad about my life, my family and my own world of fantasy that I had the sense to create for me.

It was a small life, but a beautiful life. I was thanking that same beneficent God for my family and all my blessings. In my journal, I wrote: "This is my life and I will try to do a better job living it to the fullest. I owe that much to myself, and I will try to take better care of my soul. No one will ever treat me unkind. No husband, no boyfriend, no lawyer, and no judge will ever have the opportunity to ruin me. I have a lot to offer to a relationship—and if it never happens again, I will be glad I did what I did, having the privilege to fall in love with the man of my dream. But never again will I ever lose myself, and give up my life to another no matter who that person is especially a married man, realizing he was not worthy of a person like me.

Yes, Mr. Wonderful was extraordinary in many ways, capable of being gentle and kind, giving and generous, but also screwed up, callous, and a true *egoist*—obsessed with himself—and the evidence suggests he cannot live without me.

But something was happening to me too, and my feelings for him were still there but not as intense. He came by in August of 2013, to give me birthday wishes the day after he arrived from a two-month summer vacation. He was dressed like he had just walked out of a Kmart commercial and looked awful. The towering and powerful cowboy was no longer there. Cold and hot, was what I was feeling.

He was not the same man I knew and he was no longer giving me the vibes and the chemistry that existed all those years. He wanted to make love, but I refused, testing myself not to be at his beck and call.

Many times, he would call and tell me how much he loved me and wanted to see me. On October 3, a Friday night, while I was at my mother's house, he called me several times telling me how his wife's condition had deteriorated.

After going back home, I fell asleep and had an awful dream, which awakened me at 3 a.m. I could not fall back to sleep and was up the entire night thinking about my dream. In my dream, she had died.

The next morning, my phone rang at eight o'clock. It was Mr. Wonderful. He said hi and I immediately told him about the dream. "It was about your wife," I said. "She died in my dream."

He replied: "She died at ten o'clock last night." Cancer had spread through her entire body and she left our world and this beautiful man. He had lost someone, who had been in his life for a very long time, and I knew now that Ivy would be the one I had to face.

17

Baby, It's Hollywood!

For as long as I had known him—and we were coming up on seventeen years—the main impediment to being with my beloved man of my dreams, my rugged and gentle Mr. Wonderful, was his wife the tough, hard-drinking woman who seemed to hold him in an invisible trap.

Now, as lovely services were being planned I felt the cross-currents of all sorts of emotions: great sadness, because I could imagine and relate to the heartbreaks of his life, and also a brimming of hope. For as reluctant as I was to re-invest my emotions in a man who had hurt me time and time again, I understood that an important shift had taken place. That path between us was free now. No obstacles stood in our way except one. Superb and delicious life was all I tasted and imagined not having a clue what was about to take place.

The second day after her death, he called me early in the morning and said: "I'd like to see you."

I said: "Fine, my grand-children stayed over last night, but you can come by, I just cannot wait to give you a hug."

It was a beautiful, sunny Sunday morning and my bedroom overlooking the swimming pool was splashed with the morning sun. The children were watching their favorite movie on television in my bed, and I was impatiently pacing and anticipating his arrival. He walked in with great enthusiasm and a big smile and in front of everyone, as he entered my bedroom, I screamed and said: "I now introduce to you the love of my life!"

My middle granddaughter said, "What about me, you always told *me* I am the love of your life!" She is adorable and she knows how much I love her. It was a joy to have Mr. Wonderful in the same room as the kids. We all hugged and laughed. He joined us for lunch and we had a fabulous time, and later that day he returned for dinner.

After he arrived, we sat on the couch in my bedroom and I gently held his hands in mine. "Please sit down and listen to me very carefully," I told him. "I am going to tell you something, that I know I am going to regret later, so pay very close attention." Looking straight into his kind blue eyes, I said: "I am aware how much you love your children and I want them to be happy with us. You have an enormous estate, so tomorrow is Monday, I want you to call your lawyers and have them draw up the proper legal papers for me to sign. And since I want nothing from you, transfer all your money to your kids. We have enough and from now on we can make our own deals."

As I was looking at his beautiful face, he was kissing every one of my fingers and softly after a few minutes, he said: "I love my kids, but I am not going to do that."

"Are you crazy?"

"No I am not; they have enough money to last them two lifetimes."

The funeral took place the next day. Mr.Wonderful's daughter Ivy, who knew of our relationship and knew how much her father and I loved each other, sent a nasty message via an acquaintance, making it very clear that my presence at the funeral was not welcomed. I always thought she was weird but this was utterly crazy and uncalled for. Why would I even want to go anyway? It was not my place. She hated the thought that I might show up. Maybe that was her style, but definitely not mine.

Ivy feared one thing above all else: that I would marry her father and become entitled to half of his significant estate, never mind that I only wanted him and not his riches. The truth was, I had already made it clear that he should give all his money to his children. That idea burned in her head like a hot coal. So be it, but her message about the funeral was completely unnecessary and immature. There was zero chance that I would even conceive the thought of showing up and put any kind of cloud over the services. I loved him and would never hurt him by insisting on being a part of that delicate event.

Even though I was not present, I was constantly imagining what was going on at the funeral. On the day of the funeral I decided to get a massage and after I came home and for no reason at all I ran to the bathroom and vomited, while thinking of the scene at the burial and picturing the face of the love of my life watching the burial.

With his wife gone, it seemed understood that we would merge our lives and finally be together, although both of us were mindful about respecting his wife's memory. Now my phone would not stop ringing; every one expressing joy, for the thought of us finally ending up together, though I found the calls very inappropriate.

We did not want to appear too eager. We would let things unfold one step at a time.

Not knowing how the tapestry of my world was going to take a significant change of color and how my world of love and romance was about to collapse.

Some weeks after the funeral, I planned a family dinner at my house to celebrate "Thanksgiv-ukkah," the quirk of the calendar by which Thanksgiving and Hanukkah fell on the same night. Several days went into putting together the amazing feast. Because of various scheduling issues, I scheduled the dinner for a Sunday, just four days before Thanksgiving day, and invited Mr. Wonderful to join my family for the event.

He kept his emotional reserve and told me he had to leave at seven. "Respecting his privacy, and not asking too many questions I said fine. He showed up 5 p.m. sharp, on time and looking gorgeous, as always, happy as a bird. My children greeted him with a rapturous welcome. The exultation and joy they felt for him was amazing, they really loved this man. Beside now their mother finally was going to have a real loving relationship, a rarity they had missed. They gathered around him in the kitchen happy as one big family, giving him lots of attentions. They offered him drinks and food while I was happily tearing, looking out the kitchen window.

Promising to serve dinner at six, I started the preparation so he could leave when he needed to. It was a wonderful afternoon! Now my dream was coming true and I was in Seventh Heaven. I kept saying, "This is the love of my life. I waited seventeen years for this, and now do you believe he's here? Having dinner with us?" I had cooked enough for the cast of "West Side Story." There were vegetarian dishes and four main courses, including turkey and all its trimming, roast beef, brisket and lasagna. Also there were also lots of Persian delicacies, since I knew he loved them.

We had barely settled in our chair in the dining room, at the long marble dining table, when his cell phone rang. It was 6:05. He said hello and immediately rose and without a word left the table, walking to the far reaches of the house to hold a private conversation. When he returned he appeared to have lost his appetite and seemed very anxious and nervous.

"I have got to go, and I am going to skip dinner" he announced.

"Where are you going, you said seven, and now is only six o'clock!" I was shocked.

Again, I said: "Why are you leaving? You said you have leave at seven. That's not fair. Please stay!"

He said he was due at his daughter's for Thanksgiving dinner. He was insistent on leaving. "I have to go now. I have to go."

He was out the door like a firecracker—boom, he was gone, leaving all of us stunned. Talk about the air coming out of the balloon! The night completely changed. The excitement was gone. My heart sank to the floor. Embarrassed as hell, though always with my remarkable ability to pretend and make sure everything's OK, I carried on as though nothing had happened, and nothing was wrong, constantly making excuses for him.

Trying to serve dinner, now I was in a pretending mode—"my specialty." We tried to enjoy ourselves, but inside I was hollow and aching, as if I had just lost all of my four tires. I wanted to be unconscious, dead. I didn't want to fill the cold void caused by his absence and my sadness to ruin the family dinner, and yet at the same time I was trying hard to hold back my tears. There was no wife, but was there another woman? Or how many really were there?

Only later did it occur to me that his excuse was bogus. His daughter's Thanksgiving dinner? It was Sunday, four days before Thanksgiving. Because my children were going to be out of town, I had deliberately scheduled my holiday dinner early, also it was obvious he was not about sharing Thanksgiving dinner with me. Boy! I am so stupid!

If that was a red flag, it wasn't going to be the last one.

Days later it became clear that I was not being invited to his house for an on-the-day-of-Thanksgiving dinner. Nearly two months had gone by since his wife's death, but he kept saying it was "too early, too early. Too soon!"

Too soon for what?

Now I faced the cold fact that I would spend Thanksgiving dinner alone. Avoiding a sad day, I could make my own plans elsewhere. I decided to fly east for some fun by booking myself at a few of the best hotels in New York. A wonderful decision, or so I thought. The trip turned out to be fun and quite exiting, since I had not been in New York for a very long time. The theatre was always my passion, besides I just love New York City. Meanwhile, Mr. Wonderful called me every day to make sure I was OK. This time, I decided to thoroughly enjoy the city, reconnecting with my amazing friend Gina, one of the first women I met after arriving in America. A very pretty Russian-born immigrant, married and living with her family in New York.

Gina has always been psychic and has done readings for me from time to time, once correctly seeing that I had lost a five-carat diamond ring that had disappeared in my hotel room. Because of Gina's gifts, five months later, I was able to pinpoint where the loss had occurred and was able to recover the ring, which she also correctly predicted would happen.

Now, to my surprise she said, "I have to do a reading for you. I don't know why, but something's bothering me about you." She visited my hotel suite. Gina had me shuffle her special deck of cards and carefully laid them out on the table. She gazed into my face and said, "Oh, my God, you're so in love with him, but watch out—oh boy! Are you in trouble!"

Then came these words: "Oh, my God! There are two other women, actually several other women after him. Are you sure he's not cheating on you? Two women for sure are after him and hanging onto him, and you need to beware. They are going to destroy your relationship."

"Those must be his kids," I said, laughing.

In my heart, I felt I knew this man my Mr. Wonderful. I thought he cared for me deeply and never even conceived the thought that he had been sleeping around a year before his wife died.

Meanwhile, he was calling me every day, twice a day while I was in New York, just to talk and to hear my voice. It was easy to conclude that what Gina was seeing in her reading were not romantic interests but were instead just his daughters.

After returning from New York, in early December, I quickly left again leaving him with his kids and the dealings with the wife's estate. My friend Susan and I headed for Mexico, where I intended to lie in the sun and get a tan and give Mr. Wonderful some space to work out his loss.

Mr. Wonderful still was not taking me out to dinner, though he was partying every night, and still calling me every day while I was in Mexico. He kept asking me, "When do I get to see you and when are coming home?" He sounded demanding about it. "How is Friday night? Come home, I want to take you out."

This was going to be a momentous occasion and I wanted to look perfect. We had never gone out together as a couple, certainly not at big public events. The venue for this one was the *tres-elegant* Country Club, an old woodsy epicenter of L.A. wealth and power.

Now I was flying high. Was it a curse or a blessing I am not sure, but I was tranquilized, drunk and wired all at the same time, by the love of my man and the flow of emotions that were running through me like liquid heroine, thinking and feeling we were finally going to be together forever. Happily ever after!

Frantically that day, I had bought five dresses and six pair of shoes to match each dress. Not knowing which one to wear, finally settling on a gorgeous red cocktail dress and red satin shoes.

As he walked into my house, rushing to go out to my rose garden, I picked a gorgeous little red rose and pinned it to his lapel. Voila! "You look good enough to eat," I told him. Not only did he look divine, he also looked very festive.

As I popped open a bottle of Cristal, the flame of the fireplace was reflecting a glowing sentiment of our love for each other and was heating up the room nicely, a touch he always loved. While hugging and squeezing him hard, I could not help myself, so I started kissing him all over.

Oh, how *"La Vie est Belle."*

White Christmas bulbs lit up the entire driveway as expensive cars filed into the club's elaborate grounds. The whole place was an amazing wonderland. Mr. Wonderful, my charming date, walked in like a high school senior who had borrowed his dad's nice car, the consummate gentleman decked out in his flashiest holiday attire, topped by a red cashmere jacket.

He was excited to be with me that night—but also very tense. At moments, especially before we reached the club, he struck me as extremely happy, as if anticipating how the sight of us together would go over exquisitely among his scores of friends.

My own outlook was not nearly so conflicted. Still having my "doubts," I was simply happy, and overjoyed. My goal was to look glamorous, elegant, sexy, and to let my loving feelings shine through—and I did just that. I'm sure many of the guests imagined me a film star. I would have given Miss America a run for her money, but the real point was to be with him, in the same place together, sitting side by side. Surprisingly enough and just by chance, we were both wearing red.

My dream finally realized, I knew my life was never going to be the same. Mr. Wonderful's broad smile flashed and heads turned in every direction. With sparkles in his eyes, he was greeting everyone, shaking hands while introducing me; I can't remember when I had seen him so happy and excited. Seeing him in such a happy state was what I always dreamed of. He kept holding and squeezing my hand

and, although I felt uncomfortable, I was thrilled to death—once again he was now the center of my world.

Everything was so new and strange and he was so loving and attentive—creating a magical night, one I'll always remember. And as for his friends, they were ecstatic for us too.

That night reached a most glorious and satisfying end in bed, which is where it should have ended, except I should withdraw that statement. It should never have started in the first place. I should have never accepted his invitation so fast. It should not have started at all because the next day Saturday changed the course of our lives and blindsided me, sucker-punched and sucked the blood out of me for good.

That's my complaint about perfect and romantic evenings: Sooner or later, they are over, and new events push their way into our lives, spreading like poison ivy, spoiling everything.

The next day brought a kind of hell, a nasty twist to our long, sad, joyous, crazy self-immolating love affair from which I am still reeling.

Gina's reading should have prepared me, but nothing prepares you when a man takes your heart and slices it through with a knife. I'm being metaphorical, of course, but that's the degree of pain I felt when confronted with his betrayal. The kind of pain, if his own wife experienced it throughout the entire life of their marriage, I must admit she was one tough broad.

It was a scorching December day. The scene of the crime was Bonjourno's, a pleasant, indoor-outdoor Italian eatery in downtown Beverly Hills.

Athena

Mr. Wonderful has been a regular for many years. He likes the menu, featuring classic pizza and pasta dishes, and the location, not far from City Hall and Rodeo Drive and the hotels and banks of Wilshire Boulevard, perfect for hobnobbing with his business associates. He operates that way, conferring with his cliques, keeping his ear to the ground to hear about opportunities, informally working deals.

It's a routine, and on that day, he was having lunch at a large table with a sizable group, perhaps ten or twelve of his friends. If a woman shows up in the Saturday group, it's because she is fucking one of the guys. That's the way it is understood, and everyone understands its implication. Although I knew about his lunch plans for that Saturday, I had told him the night before I might be popping in to say hello. Not knowing his plans were for me to stop by and see her at the table, being a coward he did not know how to tell me he was seeing other women for several months. Or was it Ivy's concoction?

Meanwhile, I was so very eager to visit my Mr. Wonderful, knowing and sensing that we had turned a corner in our relationship after the fabulous night the night before. My first impulse was to meet him early for coffee since I knew a cozy little spot on Beverly Drive. Around 10:30 I called him on his cell phone. He never picked up his phone; however, I left him a message. Surprisingly, he never returned my call. It seemed strange, since I new he carries his phone with him at all times, especially on weekends. It was an exceptionally hot and beautiful day.

My dear friend Sean, who's like a smart, protective brother, was due to have lunch with me at a popular patio café two blocks away from Bonjourno's. Sean came by my house at around one, the appointed time.

Looking smoking hot, I was more than ready to step into the rarefied milieu of the weekend dining crowds, wearing my beautiful white Dior heels, white skirt and Roberto Cavalli multi color turquoise top; I jumped into my car happy and feeling fabulous. Still high from the previous delicious night, I let my favorite tune play on my lips: "Fly me to the moon, let me play among the stars . . . ." As he stepped inside my car, I said: "Oh, Sean I am so very happy, I just love him and I think God finally decided to let me live my dream with the one and only love of my life."

Refined, classy and quite *bronze,* I looked like a vision as Sean and I stepped together to the maitre d's stand, at Portofino restaurant, only to learn there was a twenty-minute wait.

No problem. We were just walking distance from Bonjourno's, and I had the bright idea that we could kill the twenty minutes by wandering over there to visit Mr. Wonderful. I was going to tell him how much I loved him and give him a big, juicy kiss. Love is so strange and makes you do such silly, romantic things.

Bright idea? Still contemplating the idea of going or not going, Sean and I decided to go and say hello anyway.

Mr. Wonderful's group is sitting inside, near the rear corner of Bonjourno's. On his right, sitting with her back to me, was a woman with thick black hair and a red coat. A red coat? Just like his wife's. In this heat? For an instant, I was thinking the impossible: It's her, alive and well. The wife never died or she's been resurrected. It was a reflex, a thought that just flashed through my brain. Then common sense took over and I realized it was someone else, a different woman.

Mr. Wonderful, meanwhile saw me as we approach the table, and his reaction spoke volumes. He never acknowledged us, never made an effort to get up, and never even tried to say hello, never mind introducing us.

"Oh, boy," he muttered. That's all he said.

It took a second for my tingling senses to feel the slap he had just delivered to my face. A bit confused, dumb me, I still wasn't sure what was happening.

The reality of this moment unfolding ran completely contrary to what I knew in my heart, since the man was obsessed with me. For God's sake, we just made love the night before. Like a lost soul, I experienced a horrible, sinking sensation, like plunging into a dark and frozen black well. Constantly thinking, no it can't be!

The catatonic look of his face and the faces of the men at the table were enough greeting, and as for their smiles? Well! They were frozen and chalky like a dead man's body in a morgue. Eyes round, mouths open, they looked like scared children in the monster movie when the Creature bursts through the rickety door. Nobody made a peep and silence like death took over the table. This is what happens, when you love too much? Not having a clue what to do, the moment was agonizing. Suddenly it was like I was locked in an electric chair struggling and trying hard to cut off all straps to get out and fly away. The charge was sizzling through me and, confused as hell, I was about to lose my equilibrium.

Something was definitely not right here and helplessly I was searching for words to carry on. Trying to seem normal, better yet choosing to ignore the sad scene, not to mention protecting myself against embarrassing and uncomfortable moments, I tried to bounce back and be my own happy self. As I waved my arms and greeted his friends in a rush of enthusiasm: "*Helllll*-lo! Hello, everybody! How are you? Happy Holidays. Hi, John. Oh, and hi, George"—madly trying to be noble and save his ass, too.

Nobody spoke. Nobody moved. What the fuck? They had all been in my house for lunch just a few weeks earlier and they all knew me very well for years. What was happening?

Mr. Wonderful was still sitting there cold as a stone, showing amazing body language, by not bothering to get up. Now I focused on the woman beside him. Her face was in full view now, a chubby, sweaty face with heavy thick black pencil-drawn eyebrows, too much blood-red rouge and a very severe red lipstick the type you see on Sunset Boulevard in Hollywood. As respectfully as I could, and with enormous dignity, I turned toward her and smiled. "Oh, hello, and how are you? Who are you?" I said. "I don't think I've ever met you before, what's your name?"

Mr. Wonderful uneasily blurted her name out, "Shamssi." At this point I ignored his words and walked over to Mr. Wonderful's good friend, Jimmy, who was sitting across from the Shamssi. I gave him a hug as I fixed my gaze into the woman's eyes. She was shocked to find me staring and I could feel the anger and a sense of madness that radiated from her homely face while devouring a $1.99 slice of pizza.

Her round, beady eyes never left me, and she looked like an angry owl, crumpled, and plump, sitting motionless and mute, not even breathing. She never responded to my hello. Her expression was intensely sour, as if she had just swallowed a live frog. I realized I had hurt the woman's eyes. Remembering how a year ago I had heard her name before. Mr. Wonderful had mentioned her once as someone who had started giving him facials.

Facials? On both cheeks and both ends I am sure. Little by little, my knees were collapsing from under me, and I was only beginning to sense the real story.

My friend Sean was much quicker to grasp the truth. "Come on, let's go," he said. "Let's go, I am telling you, lets go," is what he nervously kept repeating. He grabbed my arms and pulled me away from the table.

Around 1:45, bothered but still trying to deny my findings, I called Mr. Wonderful, thinking the woman could have been someone else's date. He still ignored my calls so I left him another message to stop by my house after lunch. He never called back.

As I drove Sean back to my house so he can pick up his car, I called Mr. Wonderful again. This time he picked up and quickly said he would call me back and, no, he was not meeting me at my house. Abruptly the phone went dead.

He hung up on me? Why? With a certain instinctive panic beginning to set in, I nearly drove to his house, but I refrained and quickly changed my mind, turning the car around and returning home.

Finally, at mid-afternoon, he phoned. I asked him, "Why did you hang up on me?"

"Friends came over after lunch to discuss business," he explained. And I replied: "The facial girl too?" I had expected he would deny it and tell me he would come over that afternoon or evening to visit me. But no. "I'm tired," he said. "I want to take a nap."

In my heart I was sure the woman had just left. Now it was around three o'clock. Remembering that his favorite nap time was always right after sex, I realized he was lying.

Were we through, he and I? That should have been the end. I should have sworn him off for good, but being so crazy about him, I decided and chose to ignore the whole thing. Again, I let this man dance into my heart even when all the signs said no.

He was off that Sunday on another trip, this time again to Panama, where he always spends most of December and part of January. Rather than be stuck in Beverly Hills by myself, I left for Las Vegas. Anger festered inside me and kept thinking he is going through a phase and off-course his most recent tragedy, the loss of his wife. Why is it that as women, we always make excuses for our men? Why?

Tossing and turning all night, I called my psychic friend Gina, asking her to better explain what she had seen in the cards. She promised to fly out and meet me in Vegas. We sat in my suite at the Wynn and one more time she read the cards.

After shuffling and meditating and making all kind of facial gestures: "Look," she said, pointing out the figures. "There are two women; I didn't want to tell you, back in November, but he's sleeping around. He's not loyal to you and yes one of his kids has declared war on you."

The woman at Bonjourno's was one, but who was the other? I've never seen her, but later, from Mr. Wonderful's malicious daughter Ivy at my doctor's office I would hear the whole story.

The news was devastating. After my return from Vegas, I was due to leave again for some serious shopping in Paris, my favorite city and a sheer heaven during times of crisis. Strangely, though, the weather intervened.

A massive atmospheric event that forecasters were calling a polar vortex plunged much of the United States into sub-freezing temperatures, grounding thousands of flights. My flight to Paris was one of those canceled.

Mr. Wonderful, of course, kept calling me, finding out that I would not be going away. Was it love or obsession, I am not sure, but his feelings with me always trumps everything else; craving for my affections, he called and asked me if I would make him dinner. Sad but yet, kind and understanding, I said to myself: OK, so be it!

Now what I needed was honesty, so I said fine and hung up. Figuring now he will come clean, and tell me the truth and making me promise I would never mentioning his betrayal again I ran to the market for groceries.

"I get it! I get it!" he said, fending me off. That night he never did come clean.

On Tuesday, he called me to say he was on his way. A feast naturally was awaiting him. He was coming over for love because deep down we had a long history together and we both knew we are crazy about each other.

Lovesick in Beverly Hills

The house I was living in, my own, was just full of love and affection and he knew I always made him feel good.

It was a cold rainy night so I turned on the fireplace and got dressed up in a very elegant evening gown, looking my best, right down to my red panties, sexier than a Playboy bunny's.

We had a memorable evening, but around midnight he wanted to go home, refusing to spend the night. As I begged he got up and got dressed, insisting he had to go. Fearful of how he might drive because he'd had a couple of drinks, I followed him with my car, just to make sure he got home safely and said good-bye on his driveway.

To be so in love with a man who does not possess a single normal, human emotion toward a woman is the sick sign of a sociopath.

The next day he called, asking me to pick him up and drive him to my doctor friend, who had operated on my knee back in 2008.

Mr. Wonderful's knee was bothering him and he needed medical care. Dressed in my gorgeous, royal-blue Escada dress with my beautiful Renee Covilla brown alligator heels I was ready to pick him up, when the phone range again. He said, "Do not, I repeat do *not*, pick me up at the office." He would drive to my house, and then we would leave together. I said: "Why?" He got upset and said, "Just do what I say." "OK, fine," I replied, and hung up the phone.

He was nervous, flushed and upset when he arrived and started nervously stepped into my car.

"What is the matter?" I asked, giving him a bottle of fresh carrot juice that I had made earlier. He said his daughter Ivy was mad and screaming at him all day, wanting to know why he had asked me to take him to the doctor. I said she could come with us. "Let's go and pick her up," I suggested. He said, "No, stay away from her. She is crazy. She will hurt you."

As we both walked into to the doctor's office, someone seemed quite familiar. Yes, his daughter Ivy was already there and she had the nerve to light into me. Yelling, screaming, losing all her senses, she closed her eyes and opened her filthy mouth.

Like a mental patient who had neglected to take her medication, she caused a scene that embarrassed everyone in the waiting room as well as the doctors and the nursing staff. She would not stop, and Mr. Wonderful never troubled himself to tell her to shut up and be quiet.

While fixated on a magazine, he just sat there motionless and did not make a move nor say a single word.

She quickly referenced her father's debauchery with Shamssi and several other women. "He's been cheating on you. I am the one who found all these women for him and Shamsi too. I even paid her to sleep with my dad." And then she kept going with even crazier rants, saying I was performing voodoo, some kind of magic, and God knows what else, to make sure he wasn't leaving me, that he kept going back to me.

True or not, Ivy's message was clear: She had lined up several women and hookers for him, knowing her mother was about to die, making sure her father and I did not end up together.

The money, in the form of her future inheritance, was far more important to her than Mr. Wonderful's happiness—the twist being that maybe I was dead wrong. Maybe he was as much as fault as the rest of the cast.

Her tremulous behavior was shaking the chair beneath her and I was wondering how to leave the doctor's with dignity. As I pulled myself together, feeling so beautifully sane and quite normal, I knew the time had come. Now I was going to end this madness and leave him for good. Life is so strange! But I always felt that things happen for a good reason. Finally I had given up and I was not going to fight to get him back. Boy! I was to be in Paris and look what happened.

After twenty minutes of listening to her parched mouth and gutter-style garbage, I kept wondering how I was going to dump him in a very classy way.

All of a sudden something hit me: Clearly, he was no good for me anymore and did not deserve a woman like me. Trailer park girls, hookers and a bunch of losers is what he wanted. It was over and now I knew I no longer wanted him and this afternoon was going to be the last time I ever saw him again. This man cost me eighteen precious years of my life, time utterly wasted for a sick and a hollow love.

Somehow he was no longer the beautiful, sexy man I used to knew. Thinking I used to be proud to stand next him and now I was so very embarrassed to be in the same room with him. Why was he not saying a word? He just sat there embarrassed and motionless.

Ivy's attack went on amplifying her anger in her own unhappy and love less life. Her face by now was like the color of a cadaver, white with a faint hint of yellow and green. She was constantly moving like she was sitting on a chair full of spikes and nervously rubbing her arms and her face, totally out of control. She said she was happy and delighted that he was cheating on me. My suspicions had now been confirmed.

Then, in a low and loving voice, I told her: "You must have had a terrible childhood, and really must hate your father to actually go so far as to hire women for him. You are such a beautiful girl and yet so angry and bitter at life. It looks to me like you have never been in love. I feel sorry for you."

The whole time I was trying to be calm and collected and in full control of my every word that came out of my mouth. She claimed responsibility for all his women, just like a terrorist organization claiming credit for a deadly bombing.

As I sat quietly watching Mr. Wonderful and his stoic reaction to Ivy's garbage, I felt only pity for him.

Dressed impeccably, I took a look at Mr. Wonderful, thinking he had everything and yet he had nothing at all, a lonely old man with a bunch of spoiled and crazy kids and raunchy women running after him for his money.

He sat like a statue, a red bust done by Dali, his face crimson with embarrassment. It was time for me to leave—for good. *En fin.*

As I stood up I gave Mr. Wonderful a hug and I said, "Get yourself a therapist. I think you all need it. I am pretty sure you can get a great family rate. Oh! And good luck." Before I walked toward the exit sign, I walked back toward him, smiled, held his hands for the last time and after a moment of silence said: "I am so ashamed of you; not once did I ever bed- or bar- hopped in my whole life, no matter how tough my life got because I loved you and now you spoiled it all.

The daughter had been right and it was going to be a face-off one last time. True or not, her comments about hiring hookers was the malicious talk of a sick and a troubled woman; a woman who would rather see her father in the filthy beds of tramps than allow him to be with a woman so in love and for so long.

The money was a problem to her, even beyond the usual level of the duty of a daughter and she was going to grab it all. She was her father's keeper and love had no place in her heart. What was she doing; a quest for the world dominance? Not in my world! The fight was over and I had given up trying over and over again to have him in my life.

Mr. Wonderful called me half a dozen times that evening after the doctor's visit, and so did several member of his family, apologizing for Ivy's behavior, leaving me several messages. My life was beautiful and I was letting go of this toxic and sick love.

My ex-husband, coming from a Jewish Orthodox family, only told his children of his marriage after he married the woman, because he did not want anyone to object to his new wife being a Muslim or was a Muslim. The children never really objected either because that's what made their father happy. But this man, whom I had loved for seventeen years, was afraid of his kid? What a loser.

Finally I was done with Mr. Wonderful and the "variety pack" of his lies. As I left the doctor's office, I felt like a dope addict who had triumphantly battled and overcame an addiction- to a sick and miserable love that almost destroyed my whole life.

Later that day, feeling more sentimental, I left on his car a photograph of us from the wonderful night we'd had at the Country Club wearing the beautiful red cocktail dress. On it, I wrote: "I forgive you, I will always love you, though I never want to see you again—I tried to give you some class and a beautiful life but you sabotaged it all by yourself."

A month later, he told me he loved me and will always love me forever. Ivy called me to tell me that she had hired a detective to keep an eye on me, to make sure her dad never comes over.

Knowing full well there must be so much chaos in his life, I was happy not to have to deal with it all.

His daughter was involved and engaged in his life and a permanent fixture, like his hundred-year-old desk, rippled by time and money and weathered by lack of love.

Her insanity, and their destructive behavior, are the background noises of my life, and after many years with my Mr. Wonderful I can only say that I am not a victim of anyone's boorish behavior, nor am I seeking sympathy or feeling bad about how things worked out, despite all the heartbreaks. Although terribly tough, and with all its ups and downs, I had a magnificent life and did experience this thing called: true love.

For sure I am assuming the full responsibility of being so dead wrong for not knowing what I was doing and who I was dealing with. Recognizing how super money rules and now I did not want any part of him.

Yes, this was not the type of fairy-tale story where in the end love conquers all. Still, I have grown so much and lived a life so full that cannot be matched.

In this phase of my life, feeling unleashed, I have full power to run my life any which way I see fit, trying to enjoy every moment with loving me. A self-reliant girl that time and time again has gone into the dragon's mouth and succeeded in coming out all in one piece.

Looking back, my feelings are intact now, and I had learned a lesson or two about life.

Thinking I had lived only for love, a temple I had worshiped at for so long, perfecting the art of love. I was excited to be alive. People don't change really—do they?

A married man is a kiss of death, and no matter what, they are miserable and unhappy all the time, vain enough that they need for you to be miserable too, creating a never-ending, vicious cycle.

Reflecting on the word love—glorious love, I wondered, what does love mean? What has love done to me? There must be two dozen books in my library shelves, books I've collected over the years in my pain and loneliness, dissecting love from every conceivable angle.

I thought about a dozen novels, where he says, "I love you," and she says, "I love you," right back. It's mutual, and uplifting. I keep thinking: *Why can't I have that?* The honesty that existed in those words: I love you.

How did I let myself waste eighteen years on a man incapable of those emotions? A man who was unable to leave a poisonously bad marriage? A man who was unable to be with a woman who truly loves him?

This was not supposed to be how this book would end—a hostile takeover of my life by the man I have loved. The right ending to me should have been: *And they lived happily ever after.*

Many other scenarios always played in the cinema screen of my life but not this poison ivy, spreading and destroying the plain basis of living with the man I thought was to be mine. Super money finally destroyed a beautiful love story.

In retrospect, maybe I was dreaming of a perfect love and was lost in an illusion of being in love. Maybe this was my "happily ever after" because, although I did not want him anymore, he will remain my "happily ever after." For whatever reason, we made each other very happy because we were the male and female version of each other, the two halves of a complete organism.

Mr. Wonderful will probably always be in turmoil but will remain a very beautiful part of my life.

Love conquers all? I certainly have doubts. My Prince Charming became an ugly frog and for a very long time my loving eyes refused to recognize it.

Since I met him, and every day of my life, I always loved him and yet love conquered nothing. Love doesn't make sense and a married man will make you sick because they will never leave their sadness to welcome happiness.

At the end, I was intending to wrap up this book with some dour and meaningful conclusion about love.

Is love only chemical, a stew of adrenalin, oxytocin and endorphin? Maybe it is a hard-wired circuit that we activate by certain means, a primitive track of neurons way down deep in our brains called chemistry.

Lovesick in Beverly Hills

But I will go on thinking I am a very lucky girl, falling in love with the man I always dreamed of. An invaluable commodity, that not too many of us can have the capacity to afford.

As I drove my new shiny white Rolls Royce west into Santa Monica, veering north onto Pacific Coast Highway toward my beloved Malibu, I could not help but remember how he had brought me so much joy in spite of it all.

Now to see myself relieved of pain, teardrops of happiness started to fall, washing away all my sorrows. A Dinah Washington song kept playing in my head: "What a difference a day makes, just twenty four hours . . . ." On this day I felt light and free, like a beautiful Grand Marnier soufflé, totally irresistible.

Oh God, how beautiful the late afternoon sun looks shimmering on the blue water of the Pacific Ocean; millions of tiny little sparkling pieces of diamond floating all over the universe, spreading a feeling of joy.

Rolling past fabulous hillside homes and stretches of lovely golden sand—the playgrounds of the rich and famous—it was Hollywood all right! Then I reflected on the momentous past eighteen years and tried to imagine the years to come, how I was going to shape my life my own way, free of heartaches or interferences.

It was sure to be exciting, different, fun, and of course tragic and challenging at times—but it would be a voyage into the deep and beautiful blue waters of the future. My nerves tingled at the thought of leaving behind a sad and obsessive love.

As I was deeply in thoughts of the past, and happily murmuring my favorite song lyrics, "Fly me to the moon," when my cell phone rang. A gorgeous little voice said, "Hi!" It was my granddaughter, asking me to stop by to see her.

After I spoke with her, I smiled as I put my phone aside, gazing out toward the spectacular horizon, so blue, and now I was free and feeling fabulous. This was the story of love and how an illicit afternoon love affair, in an August month, was coming to an end. An arduous journey but worth every minute of it. Now in full living color my entire past flashed like the speed of sound. Proud of who I was, I knew I will be OK, because I knew I deserved better.

Was it all a big mistake? That's not easy to say, since some people live and die and will never get a chance to taste this amazing and extravagant potion called love.

Now my life was a whole new song with a whole new meaning. I was proclaiming my sovereignty and would dominate my own world passionately, the way it pleased me. Turbulent life? Yes! But with a smooth landing. Yes and yes! I did live a life of a dreamer.

Love is forever, will never fade and will always be the only way to live. Living happily ever after? With him or without him, it was all a wonderful dream and will remain just that: "A dream—my dream."

I think, Elizabeth Barrett Browning, the great poet, said it best:

How do I love thee? Let me count the ways

I love thee to the depth and breadth and height

My soul can reach, when feeling out off sight

For the ends of being and ideal grace.

Lovesick in Beverly Hills

I love thee to the level of every day's

Most quiet need, by sun and candle-light

I love thee freely, as me strive for right

I love thee purely, as they turn from praise

I love thee with the passion put to use

In my old grief, and with my childhood's faith.

I love thee with a love I seemed to lose

With my lost saint. I love thee with the breadth

Smiles, tears, all my life; and, if god choose,

I shall but love thee after death.

END

K
Po
Er
Te
K
I
U
O
Mo
V
I xx.
N
S
Os
In
Se
H
D
K

Steve + Vic.

(Debbie + Mark)

Nd.
Ni
Li
F
C
Al

(Spencer
 Ch.
 = P+C

✓ Charlie +
   Fr. Ho
   =
   Av +
   Ho

Gabe = ✓
Ga
+ Y.